THE SOLID MANDALA

THE
SOLID
MANDALA

PATRICK
WHITE

The
Viking Press
New York

For Gwen and David Moore

CONTENTS

There is another world, but it is in this one.
—Paul Eluard

It is not outside, it is inside: wholly within.
—Meister Eckhart

. . . yet still I long
for my twin in the sun . . .
—Patrick Anderson

It was an old and rather poor church; many of the ikons were without settings; but such churches are the best for praying in.
—Dostoevski

ONE

IN THE BUS

"THERE'S MORE life up this end," Mrs. Poulter said.

"Yairs," said Mrs. Dun. Then, because never let it be hinted that she did not make her contribution, she added, "Yairs."

"It's the shops that gives it life," Mrs. Poulter said. "There's nothing like shops."

"It's the shops all right."

"These days a woman could do the whole of 'er shoppin' in Sarsaparilla. But it isn't the same."

"It isn't the same."

"Not like you catch the bus to Barranugli and spend the mornin' muckin' around. Mind you, it isn't the ha'penny. There's some women will spend a shillun to save the odd ha'penny."

Mrs. Dun sucked her teeth.

"But it makes a change in a person's life, muckin' around the big shops," said Mrs. Poulter. "With a friend," she said.

"Yairs," agreed Mrs. Dun. "Yairs."

She was looking straight ahead, past the mounds of hair. A young lady couldn't squeeze a hat on nowadays even if she wanted to. Mrs. Dun was fascinated by the ha'penny. If what Mrs. Poulter said was true, some women lost one-and-eleven on the round trip!

"You can muck around on your own, of course," Mrs. Poulter was saying, "but a friend is what makes the difference."

"A friend," said Mrs. Dun. "Yairs."

Each of the ladies sat rather careful, because they had not known each other all that long, and the situation had not been proved unbreakable.

"If I hadn't of spoke to you in the bus that morning," Mrs. Poulter said, "we mightn't of got to know each other."

Mrs. Dun smiled, and blushed as far as her complexion allowed. Mrs. Dun was the sallow sort.

"Though living in Terminus Road," said Mrs. Poulter.

"Both down the same road."

The bus became a comfort. Even when it jumped, which it did fairly frequently, all the young girls frowning, or giggling, the bolder of them knocking the ash off their cigarettes with their mother-o'-pearl fingernails, the two ladies were not unpleasantly thrown against each other. Mrs. Dun perhaps benefited from it more, though Mrs. Poulter, it could not be denied, enjoyed the involuntary contact with her small, dry, decent friend.

Mrs. Poulter sighed. It was so important to be decent.

"What, I wonder," she asked, "made you"—she coughed— "come to live down Terminus Road?"

"Mr. Dun took a fancy to the veranda."

"You've got a nice veranda all right. I like a veranda. A good old-fashioned veranda."

"I'll say!" said Mrs. Dun.

"Nowadays it's all payshows. You can't sit on a payshow."

"Exposin' themselves!" said Mrs. Dun quite vehemently.

"In all weathers."

Everyone was too obsessed by the start of another day—no hope this side of the tea break—to notice the in no way exposed ladies in the eight-thirteen from Sarsaparilla, though it was perhaps doubtful whether anyone would ever notice Mrs. Poulter or Mrs. Dun unless life took its cleaver to them. For the present, however, they had the protection of their hats.

"Why did *you*?" asked Mrs. Dun.

"Did I what?"

"Come to live down Terminus Road."

"Well," said Mrs. Poulter, peeping inside her plump glove to see if the ticket was still there, "when we first come from up north— both my hubby and me was country people—we wanted it quiet like. We was young and shy. Oh, it was Bill's nerves, too. Bill said, 'It'll give us time to find our feet. It'll always open up in time. Land is always an investment.'"

"Oh, yairs. Land is an investment."

But a sadness was moistening Mrs. Poulter.

"In those days," she said from out of the distance, "all the roads at Sarsaparilla were dead ends. Not only Terminus. You couldn't go anywhere as the crow."

"Eh?" Mrs. Dun asked.

"As the crow flies," Mrs. Poulter explained.

"Oh, the crow," her friend murmured, seeming uneasy at the idea. "There was a Chinese woman lived on a hill up at the back. I never ever knew her. I seen her once. They were people of means, so people said. Growin' vegetables and things. They'd planted one of those what-they-call wheel-trees. Well, I seen her standing under it when it was in flower."

Mrs. Dun sucked her teeth.

"You wouldn't of said she was without refinement," Mrs. Poulter remembered. "But a Chinese is never the same."

It was something Mrs. Dun had not even contemplated.

"And anyway, the Chinese person isn't the point."

Just then the bus nearly shook apart, and one of the young lady typists lost her balance. It was those stiletto heels.

"These old buses!" Mrs. Poulter heaved, and laughed.

Mrs. Dun went a deeper yellow as she grasped the rail.

"They're a downright disgrace!" Mrs. Poulter laughed.

The sadness had been shaken out of her. She was happy again.

Presently she couldn't resist: "That veranda of yours must be a real luxury, dryin' laundries in the rain."

"I'll say it is!" said Mrs. Dun.

She had a certain relentlessness of conviction. If it hadn't been for her gloves her knuckles would have shown up white on the chrome rail.

The bus was making slow progress, on account of the pay-as-you-enter, and queues at the shelters, and kiddies who had missed the special. Mrs. Poulter looked out. She was proud of the glossier side of Sarsaparilla, of the picture windows and the textured brick. She brightened with the leaves of the evergreens which the sun was touching up. Then she saw Bill, and waved. But he did not respond. He went on sweeping the gutters for the Council. It was against Bill Poulter's principles to acknowledge his wife in public. Sometimes on her appearing he went so far as to take time off to roll himself a cigarette. But never wave. She accepted it. She was content enough to realize he was wearing the old fawn sweater, no longer presentable except for work, because the loose stitch she had been trying out had begun to stretch and sag.

"Mind you," she said to Mrs. Dun, "I wouldn't want to live up here, though it's nice and bright. You can live your own life down there."

"It's snug down Terminus Road." Mrs. Dun wriggled on the lumpy seat.

The eyes of the two women followed the tunnel which led inward, through the ragged greenery and sudden stench of crushed weeds. You could hide behind a bush if necessary.

"It must of been a comfort, though, when Mr. Dun retired from the railways."

"Yairs," Mrs. Dun admitted, and would have made it higher if some phlegm had allowed. When she was again free, she blurted, "It took getting used to at the start. Then it was a comfort. Hearin' 'is boots. Before that I used to think: They could come and murder you in broad daylight. Often do, too."

It was long-winded for Mrs. Dun. Mrs. Poulter was surprised. She was surprised at the substance of it. But she did not comment. Her lips were slightly open, as when she listened to the dahlias and heard nothing except the thick green silence.

When the bus jolted her back to the surface of her normally bright nature—you could always rely on the bus—she said, "With us, there's the neighbours. There's the Mr. Browns opposite."

"Who?"

"The two brothers. Two twins."

"Oh," said Mrs. Dun, suspicious.

"Two retired gentlemen. Like Mr. Dun."

"Never 'eard of 'em," said Mrs. Dun, as though she were cranky, or a man.

"But I told you. Or didn't I?" said Mrs. Poulter.

Mrs. Dun might have got crankier if the easement of confidences had not stretched before them through the flannelly atmosphere of the bus. The private lives of other parties act as the cement of friendship. The Brothers Brown could be about to set the friendship of the friends.

"You'll see," said Mrs. Poulter, "when you come down to my place. Though their hedge has grown thick by now. That's for privacy like."

"A 'edge is all very well," said Mrs. Dun. "You can't be seen. But praps there are times when you'll wanter be. When someone's got you by the throat."

Mrs. Poulter decided not to bother.

"The Mr. Browns have got a veranda," she said, and sighed. "Only it's sort of different."

"How?"

"It sort of comes up to a peak."

"Oh?"

Mrs. Dun could not believe.

"Mr. Brown senior—that was the father, they was there before we come—Mr. Brown told me the front was in the classical style."

"Waddayaknow!" said Mrs. Dun.

Words made her that nervous.

"Of course I don't know," Mrs. Poulter said, "but that's what the father told me. He had their weatherboard home built with a veranda sort of rising to a peak. He was an educated man, they say. One of the white-collar workers," Mrs. Poulter added, not without sucking in her lips.

"A what collar?"

"He was at one of the banks, and read books in 'is spare time."

Mrs. Dun shrivelled somewhat.

"They come out from Home," Mrs. Poulter said, "when the boys were only bits of kids."

Mrs. Dun was partly pacified.

"All these foreigners," she said, "we are letting in nowadays. I admit the English is different."

"Oh, Mr. Brown senior was a gentleman," Mrs. Poulter said. "But not any better than us."

She came as close as she would ever come to tossing her head.

"Once Mrs. Brown give me an old raincoat for Bill. Mr. Brown was sick, and you couldn't refuse, but Bill took the coat and threw it down the gully."

Mrs. Poulter could feel that Mrs. Dun was vibrating approval.

"But Mr. Brown was a good man. Now *Mrs.* Brown—that was

the mother of the two boys—she was always doing a favour. Even to her own husband. She was good too, mind you, but she never stopped letting you see she had thrown herself away."

"How?"

"I can't tell you exactly how. She was the lady. You never saw such beautiful lace insertion. Some of it she dipped in tea, for variety like."

"You don't say!" Mrs. Dun was entranced.

The bus was jolting only softly now, bowling along like your own thoughts. Because Mrs. Poulter was growing misty with the past her friend felt it at last her duty to direct her.

"What became of them?" she asked. "The parents of those two boys?"

"Passed on," said Mrs. Poulter, mastering something. "Mr. Brown was the first. His wife took her time. The boys looked after her and saw their mother was comfortable."

"Appreciate a mother," Mrs. Dun murmured.

And Mrs. Poulter lightly touched the white chrysanths she was protecting on her lap.

"What did they die of?" Mrs. Dun asked, suddenly, feverish.

Mrs. Poulter had hoped to avoid it.

"Mrs. Brown died of something incurable," she said, looking out the window at the solid homes. "Mr. Brown, so they say, was disappointed in his sons. Anyways, Arthur. Arthur had been his favourite."

Mrs. Dun sucked the warm air, past her plastic gums, down the extended webbing of her throat. She waited, though.

"Arthur is not all that bright," Mrs. Poulter confessed; she could have been protecting Arthur.

"But must of done somethink. To retire from."

"Yes," said Mrs. Poulter. "They put Arthur with Mr. Allwright. He was there all 'is working life. He was clever with figures—in spite of all. He knew where everything was on the shelves. He knew what people wanted, sometimes even better than the customers themselves. Arthur mightn't of retired if Allwright hadn't died and 'is widow sold the business. Though she carried on for a bit with 'er sister, Mrs. Mutton."

Mrs. Dun waited, but could not wait long enough.

"What's the other one called?" she asked at last.

"Waldo," said Mrs. Poulter.

Mrs. Dun's teeth snapped. Shut. She made a slight worrying sound.

Then she said, "What sort of a name is that?"

"I dunno!" Mrs. Poulter sighed before laughing. "One of the names people think of. The father was only George, but I expect Mrs. Brown wanted to go one better, at least for one of the twins. It was all those books. Mrs. Brown used to read too. Like 'er husband. You'd see 'er with 'er crochet, or a bowl of peas. They put Waldo to the books. Waldo was at the Library."

Mrs. Dun hissed. She was terrified. In the circumstances it did not occur to her to ask whichever library. Then she remembered, and announced rather primly, "Mr. Dun was in the Information. He was good at the timetables."

"Well now, you see," said Mrs. Poulter, impressed by the logic of it, "he would have something in common with the Browns!"

She turned to investigate her friend's seamed and yellow cheek, but Mrs. Dun was too discreet to cash in on anyone's approval.

Mrs. Poulter was a pigeon-coloured woman, whose swelling forms, of a softish stuff, seemed to invite the experimental pin. Often got it, too. Mrs. Poulter was sometimes moved to smile at strangers, until they started frowning back. She professed to Love All Flowers, and grew a few as a sideline, lugging them to Barranugli to a florist, though usually only when there was a glut.

"They're taking you *down!*" Bill used to shout.

"But what can a person do?" she answered. "When they need them for the wreaths."

Her husband would have spat if it didn't normally happen in doors.

"You're simple," he said instead.

"That is how I was born," she replied.

"You ought to move in with that pair of poofteroos across the road."

"There's more in the Brothers Brown than meets the eye," she would defend them.

"I bet there is!" her husband said, doing things with his tongue to the tooth which was always with him.

He would sit with his back to her most evenings, or that was how life seemed to have arranged it, and when he had finished his glass of beer—he was very moderate; she was fortunate in that—she would slip the plate of food in front of him, somehow from round the side.

"A couple of no-hopers with ideas about 'emselves," he would grumble, and then regurgitate: "The Brothers Bloody Brown!"

When the sight of his hands hardened by the shovel would rend her, and she would say, "You've gone and tore yourself again. The sleeve."

"What?" he used to say, throwing off her concern with his shoulder. "What's this old thing for but tearing?"

Attempts on herself seldom hurt Mrs. Poulter; it was the attacks on other people. The Mr. Browns, for instance. Unable to decide how they might be protected, she would take them a baked custard. And return the better for it.

Seated in the flumping bus, her own charity made her smile with faint pleasure. When suddenly she seized her companion quite roughly by the arm.

"Look!" Mrs. Poulter almost shouted.

Mrs. Dun was so shaken her upper plate was prised from her jaw and lay for a moment with its mate.

"What?" she protested.

Looking stricken for the accident. Twice at least she had dreamt of being rammed by a removal van.

"What we was talking about!" cried Mrs. Poulter. "The two men! The retired brothers!"

Then Mrs. Dun did resentfully notice the two old men, stumping, trudging, you couldn't have said tottering—or if so, it was only caused by their age and infirmities—along what passed for pavement between Barranugli and Sarsaparilla. The strange part was the old gentlemen rose up, if only momentarily, blotting out the suburban landscape, filling the box of Mrs. Dun's shuddering mind. She was still shocked, of course, by Mrs. Poulter's thoughtless alarm. It could have been that. But she almost smelled those old men. The one in the stiff oilskin, the other in yellowed herringbone, in each case almost to the ankle. And, as they trudged, or tottered, they were holding each other by the hand. It was difficult to decide which was leading and which was led. But one was the leader, she could sense. She sensed the scabs, the cracks which wet towels had opened in their old men's skin.

Several of the young typists in the ladies' vicinity had been roused by Mrs. Poulter's outcry. But barely giggled. It was as though they had seen it all before.

"There!" exclaimed Mrs. Poulter, turning in triumph to her friend. "It might have been laid on!"

She was so pleased she laughed. But she did not succeed in making it a joke. Mrs. Dun had screwed up her mouth.

"Looks funny to me," she said, and with added disapproval: "I thought you was warning of an accident."

"Mr. Waldo Brown was hit with a car," Mrs. Poulter conceded. "Once."

It was the best she could offer.

"I never saw two grown men walkin' hand in hand," Mrs. Dun murmured.

"They are old." Mrs. Poulter sighed. "I expect it helps them. Twins too."

"But two men!"

"For that matter I never saw two grown women going hand in hand."

The breath was snoring between Mrs. Dun's corrected teeth.

"Which was the big one? The one that was leading? The one in the oilskin?"

"That was Mr. Waldo. But I never thought of 'im as big. He's thin."

"Seemed big to me."

"Arthur Brown is big-built. The thick-set one."

Although the gentlemen had been left far behind by now, Mrs. Poulter glanced over her shoulder. As if hoping to confirm something.

The old men rose up again in Mrs. Dun's mind, and she hated what she saw.

"You come on down sometime to my place," Mrs. Poulter coaxed, "and they're bound to be around. Somewhere. Potterin' about behind the hedge."

Don't catch *me!* Mrs. Dun decided.

"And those blue dogs?" she asked. "Do they belong to the gentlemen?"

"That's their dogs. They're attached to their dogs," Mrs. Poulter said firmly.

"Scruffy old things," said Mrs. Dun. "I hate dogs. They might bite yer."

"One of them does," Mrs. Poulter had to admit. "Runt does. But they've had them so many years. Nearly as old as themselves. As dogs go."

The bus faltered.

"Between you and me"—Mrs. Poulter hesitated—"I don't like dogs eether. But what can you do?"

Mrs. Dun did not answer, and it seemed to give her the upper hand.

"Do you have any family, Mrs. Dun?" Mrs. Poulter asked with a formality which made it unobjectionable.

"Got a niece," Mrs. Dun said.

"Ah," said Mrs. Poulter, "a niece is nice."

She was attempting to repair some of the bent petals of the white chrysanths. Excitement had not been good for them.

"Bill and I are alone now. There was no kiddies," Mrs. Poulter said. "One or two relatives up north. But I think they're gone by this. It's Bill that writes the letters. If ever any of the relatives come—and some of them did, once or twice—Bill stayed up the end of the paddock."

The petals of the white chrysanths were, it seemed, beyond repair.

"You drift apart, don't you?" Mrs. Poulter said.

"Yairs," said Mrs. Dun, and: "Yairs."

In High Street the overstuffed bus began to spew out its coloured gobbets.

"Wonder what those two old fellers were doin' so far from Terminus Road." Mrs. Poulter nursed her curiosity as they waited to be carried by the common stream.

"You wonder what goes on in some people's minds," said Mrs. Dun.

"I beg yours?"

"What goes on in people's minds. Because it does go on. You've only got to read the papers."

"But two respectable old gentlemen like the Mr. Browns? They was probably only taking a walk to get their circulation going." Mrs. Poulter had turned mauve. "Anyway," she said, "what goes on in other people's minds is private. I wouldn't want to know what goes on inside of my own husband's mind."

Although Mrs. Dun might have wanted, she suggested she didn't by drawing in her chin.

"I was never one," she said, "not to keep to meself, and mind me own business."

"Aren't I right then?" Mrs. Poulter continued, still too loud, and still too mauve.

Creating in the bus. Mrs. Dun wondered whether she had been wise in the first place to accept Mrs. Poulter's friendship.

"As for those old men," said Mrs. Dun, "they're nothing to me."

"They're nothing to me," Mrs. Poulter agreed.

But the situation made her want to cry. And Mrs. Dun could feel it. She could feel her own gooseflesh rise. As they waited to escape from the suffocating bus the features of their familiar town began fluctuating strangely through the glass. Like that blood-pressure thing was on your arm. Nor did it help either lady to know the other could be involved.

"Only those old men of yours had a look—had a look of—" Mrs. Dun stumbled over what was too much for her.

"Yes?" Mrs. Poulter's voice reached out.

The lips were parted in her mauve cheeks. The eyes were so liquid. It was as though she were waiting to swallow down some longed-for communication, while half expecting it to choke her if she did.

But Mrs. Dun could not oblige. Her neck jerked, the wrinkles closed, and Mrs. Poulter, ruffling up her chrysanthemums, remarked in a neutral tone of voice, "After I've left the flowers, I usually make for the cafeteria and have a coffee. It warms you up on cold mornings."

"Yairs," said Mrs. Dun. "Or a malted. The malted's what I go for."

TWO

WALDO

"PUT ON your coat, and we'll go for a walk," he decided at last. "Otherwise you'll sit here brooding."

"Yes," Arthur said. "Brooding."

But he sat, and might have continued sitting, in that old leather chair with the burst seat where mice had nested the other winter, the woodwork scratched by dogs reaching up to claim right of affection. Arthur sat in their father's chair.

Waldo brought the two coats. He helped Arthur into his. Waldo treated the old herringbone rather roughly, to show that what he was doing had been dictated by duty and common sense. He set the matching cap very straight on Arthur's head. It was, in any case, the angle at which Arthur wore his cap. Waldo was relieved the performance of duty had at last set him free. But duty was honest, whereas he mistrusted the snares of sentiment set by inexhaustible tweed. (It was that good English stuff, from amongst the things discarded by Uncle Charlie, some of which were lasting forever.)

"When it comes to illness there's too much giving in to it, not to mention imagination," Waldo warned.

As he put his own coat on he glanced at his brother's head, at the shagginess of hair falling from under the tweed cap. Very white. Waldo might have contemplated the word "silvery," but rejected it out of respect for literature and truth. Arthur's hair was, in fact, of that doubtful white, with the tobacco stains left by the red which had drained out of it. Unlike Waldo's own. Waldo on top was a thinned-out dirty-looking grey.

Arthur continued sitting.

And the two old dogs, turning on their cat-feet, forgetful of their withered muscle, watched out of milky eyes. One of them—it was

Scruffy—clawed once at Arthur's knee. The dogs made little whinging noises in anticipation. They were easily delighted.

"You do feel better, though?" Waldo asked, so suddenly and so quietly that Arthur looked up and smiled.

"Yes, Waldo," Arthur said, and: "Thank you."

"Pains in the chest are more often than not indigestion. We swallow too quickly in cold weather."

"Yes, Waldo. Indigestion."

Then the older of the two dogs, of whiter muzzle, and milkier marble-eyes, threw up his head and gave two ageless sexless barks. The second of the two dogs began to scutter across the boards on widespread legs.

Waldo was leading his brother Arthur, as how many times, out of the brown gloom of the kitchen. The cold light, the kitchen smells, had set almost solid in it. Yet here they were, the two human creatures, depending on habit for substance as they drifted through. If habit lent them substance, it was more than habit, Waldo considered bitterly, which made them one.

Some had made a virtue out of similar situations: naked-looking identical boys; laughing girls, he had noticed, exchanging the colours which distinguished them, to mystify their friends; neat elderly ladies, in polka dots and similar hats, appeared to have survived what was more a harness than a relationship.

But the Browns.

Waldo could feel his brother's larger, fleshy hand in his thinner, colder one as they stumbled in and out of the grass down what remained of the brick path. The wind drove reasons inward, into flesh. They were reduced, as always, to habit. But stumbled, even so.

Only the old potbellied dogs appeared convinced of the mild pleasures they enjoyed, frolicking and farting, though somewhat cranky with each other. One of them—Runt—lifted his leg on a seedy cabbage and almost overbalanced.

His brother was breathing deeply, Waldo saw.

"Which direction are we going to take?" Arthur asked.

"There's only one."

"Yes," said Arthur, "but after Terminus Road?"

"Why, the main road, in the direction of Barranugli."

Sometimes Waldo would look at his brother and try to remember when he had first been saddled with him. But could not.

"Why the main road?" Arthur asked, fretful today.

He blew out his red, fleshy, but to no extent sensual lips.

"Because I want to see life," Waldo answered brutally. "You don't want to deny me that?"

Arthur said, "No."

Waldo was punctured then. He continued on, a thin man in a turned-down stiff grey felt hat. What he should have answered, of course, was: Because, on the main road, if anything happens on any of those hills, there will always be plenty of cars to stop. It depressed him he hadn't been able to say it.

"I like the side roads best," said Arthur. "You can look at the fennel."

He had difficulty with his words, chewing them to eject, but when he did, there they stood, solid and forever.

There was the sound of Waldo's stiff oilskin nothing would free from the weathers which had got into it. Waldo's oilskin used to catch on things, and he always expected to hear it tear. On that gooseberry bush, for instance. Which had not succeeded. Arthur had advised against it—Sarsaparilla was too warm—but Waldo had planted the bush. To demonstrate something or other.

On the broken path Waldo's oilskin went slithering past the gooseberry thorns. The wind might have cut the skins of the Brothers Brown if they had not been protected by their thoughts.

"We could ring the doctor if you felt you wanted," Waldo said carefully. "We could go across to Poulters', though I don't like to ask favours, be beholden to anybody."

"No. No."

Arthur spoke quite briskly. Time, it appeared, removed him quickly from the sources of pain. Sometimes Waldo envied the brother who did not seem to have experienced—though he should have—the ugly and abrasive roughcast of which life was composed.

My brother, Waldo would breathe, at times indulgently enough, and at once he became the elder by years instead of the younger by several hours. Waldo could modulate his voice, more to impress than to please. The rather fine tenor voice, of which the parents had been proud, and Dulcie Feinstein had accompanied in the first excitement of discovery. Men, the insensitive ones, sometimes recoiled from the silken disclosures of Waldo's voice.

Waldo's voice and Arthur's hair. So Mother used to say. (It should have been Waldo's *mind*, Waldo knew.)

Sidling brittlely down the path, to negotiate the irregular bricks, now pushing Arthur, who liked to be humoured at times into believing he was the leader, Waldo could not avoid staring into his brother's hair, fascinated, when the wind blew, by the glimpses of pink skin beyond. This head might have flaunted an ostentation of cleanliness, if it had not been for its innocence, and the fact that he knew Arthur was in many ways not exactly clean. Every third Sunday Waldo made him sit on a stool on the back veranda, behind the glass, behind the scratching of the roses, to hack at the excessive hair, and as it first lay against, then flowed away through his fingers, the barber always wondered why he got the shivers, why he hated the smell of his own mucus as he breathed down his thin nose, while the hair lay on the boards, in dead snippets and livelier love-knots, quite old-girlishly, if not obscenely, soft. It had seemed much coarser when Arthur was a boy.

And Arthur had grown into a big strong man. Was still, for that matter. It was Arthur who lifted the weights. His muscles had remained youthful, perhaps because his wits had been easy to carry.

"This gate, Waldo," Arthur was saying gently, "will fall to bits any day now."

Sighing.

He was right. Waldo dreaded it. Averted his mind from any signs of rusty iron or rotted timber. Unsuccessfully, however. His life was mapped in green mould; the most deeply personal details were the most corroded.

He touched the gate with a free finger. And the gate opened. Once again.

None of the men in the family had been handy. Nor was Mother. But Mother had struggled with the taps, while the boys looked on, hoping that too much water wouldn't squirt up into her face. Shall I fetch Dad? Arthur would ask. But she did not think it worth an answer.

The wind was frittering with Arthur's hair, tinkering with the fragile gate.

Suddenly the smell of rotting wood, of cold fungus, shot up through Waldo's nose. He could hardly bear, while exquisitely needing, the rusty creaking of his memory. If Arthur had been, say, a dog, he might have touched the back of his head. That hair.

But Waldo Brown, although he kept them, did not believe in touching dogs. It gave them, he said, a wrong sense of their own importance. But why, Waldo? Arthur would persist, I like to touch dogs, I'd like to have Scruffy at least in the bed, if you'd allow it. Half the time it was useless to explain to Arthur.

"This gate," Waldo said, "will outlast us both."

"I hope so." Arthur laughed. "It would be dreadful if it didn't. No one would put up another. Remember when I cut my hand on the saw? I'd try, though. Again. I'd have a go."

It was too feeble, too foolish. Waldo Brown took his brother by the hand as they entered Terminus Road.

"Mrs. Poulter is probably bunching the flowers. I saw her picking them," Arthur said. "White chrysanths for Mother's Day."

Waldo did not comment. Already he was too tired.

"Perhaps if we hang around she'll come out," said Arthur, "and then we can walk together to the bus."

"No," said Waldo.

His thin, male steps crunched. He walked primly, in the sound of his oilskin, planning in advance where to put his feet.

Whereas Arthur was not exactly running, but lumbering and squelching, while some distress, of feminine origin, was fluttering in his big old-man's body.

"Oh, but why, Waldo? She's such a good neighbour."

I am very fond of Mrs. Poulter, she is a thoroughly good-hearted, reliable young woman, Mother used to say. Doors closing. Waldo remembered sitting alone with his mother, in the dining room, at the centre of the house, while Mrs. Poulter roamed calling round: I don't want to intrude Mrs. Brown on you or anyone but Mr. Brown could have the use of the mower if he likes any time any time provided Bill is at the Council. As he and his mother continued hidden, in collusion, as it were, though this was never discussed. Waldo was officially her favourite, Arthur her duty.

Arthur had been Dad's favourite, in the beginning. Who's coming for the ice-cream horn? Not Waldo, George, it only brings the pimples out.

"I wonder why Mrs. Poulter is so awful?"

Arthur, puffing, threatened to topple, but saved himself on Waldo's oilskin.

"I don't say she's *awful*!"

"If you don't say, it's likely to fester," said Arthur, and sniggered.

Some of his remarks were of the kind which should have crumbled along with the cornflour cakes in the mouths of elderly women.

"It's splinters that fester," Waldo answered facetiously.

"Perhaps," said Arthur and sniggered again.

Because they were brothers, twins moreover, they shared secrets warmer than appeared.

The two old dogs were having a whale of a time amongst the fresh cowturds and paspalum tussocks. They growled on and off to proclaim their pleasure and virility.

Arthur was thoughtful.

"You ought to write something about Mr. Saporta."

"Whatever made you think of Saporta?"

"I saw them."

"When?"

Arthur was silent, stumbling.

"When? When, Arthur?"

Arthur had begun to pout.

"Some time ago, I think."

Waldo averted his face from something. Then he said very distinctly, enunciating from between his original teeth, in his cold, clear, articulate voice, "I don't want to think about the Saportas."

The sun caught the gold of his spectacles with a brilliance which turned the skin beneath the eyes to washed-out violet.

"What made you think about Leonard Saporta?" he asked more gently.

"I don't know," Arthur grumbled.

But not bad-tempered. Arthur was never what you could have

called bad-tempered; it was just that sometimes the more difficult thoughts grated on the way out of him.

"I expect it was Dulcie," he said at last.

Waldo went on crunching over the bush soil of the neglected surface of Terminus Road. Soon at least they'd come out on tar.

"But Leonard Saporta was such a very *ordinary* man. I have nothing against him. But why I should *write* about him!"

Lady callers had inquired about Waldo's Writing as though it had been an illness, or some more frightening, more esoteric extension of cat's-cradle.

"There is nothing in Leonard Saporta," said Waldo, "that anyone could possibly *write* about."

Arthur walked looking at the stones.

"Well," he said carefully, "if you ask my opinion"—and sometimes Mrs. Poulter did—"simple people are somehow more"—he formed his lips into a trumpet—"more transparent." He didn't shout.

But Waldo was deafened by it.

"More transparent?"

He hated it. He could have thrown away the fat parcel of his imbecile brother's hand.

"Yes," said Arthur. "I mean, you can see right into them, right into the part that matters. Then you can write about them, if you can write, Waldo—can't you? I mean, it doesn't matter what you write about, provided you tell the truth about it."

Scruffy and Runt had started a rabbit.

"What do *you* know?"

Waldo was worrying it with his teeth.

"No," said Arthur.

"You were always good at figures," Waldo had to admit.

He was yanking at his twin's blue-veined hand.

"Yes. That was useful, wasn't it?" said Arthur. "Even Mrs. Allwright, who didn't like me, admitted it was useful."

Waldo was striding now. The great gates of his creaking oilskin had opened on his narrow chest and the long legs stuffed inside the gumboots. His flies were spattered with fat from a remote occasion at the stove.

"Oh," cried Waldo Brown in anguish, "but I have not expressed half of what is in me to express!"

The heavy Arthur had to run to keep up with his brother. He was whimpering, too.

"Don't worry," he blubbered. "There's time, Waldo, isn't there? There's still time. You can write about Mr. Saporta and the carpets, and all the fennel down the side roads."

Just then that Mr. Dun straightened amongst the stakes up which he had been coaxing his peas. He looked away quickly, though, from what he saw.

Waldo Brown saw a small mean face recognizing.

"One of the carpets had," Arthur whimpered, "right in the centre, what I would say was a mandala."

Waldo could not walk too fast. He had hoped originally for intellectual companions with whom to exchange the Everyman classics and play Schubert after tea.

"Come on!" he mumbled.

He hated his brother.

Mr. Dun, who had finished looking, erected a behind.

"He didn't look at us. Or not properly," Arthur said.

"He hasn't been here long enough to know us."

"But I know him."

"That is different."

The Brothers Brown had almost emerged from the subfusc vegetation, the clotted paddocks of Terminus Road, into the world in which people lived, not the Poulters or the Duns or themselves, but families in advertised clothes, who belonged to Fellowships and attended Lodges and were not afraid of electrical gadgets. Waldo yearned secretly for the brick boxes to an extent where his love had become hatred. He would have to control, as he had always known how to control, himself, his parents, his colleagues—and his brother.

Now when he heard his own breathing united with Arthur's, and realized how it might startle a stranger, he thought it better to advise, "It won't do not to remember that your heart may be starting to give trouble. When I said not to brood, I meant *not to brood*. To *take care* is only reasonable."

Arthur trotted a little, the white hair flopping at his neck. He was obviously giving thought to what his brother was trying to impress. But it could have been that Arthur was not impressed by reason, or that reason did not concern himself.

"Reasonably reasonable," he said, and frowned. "If he isn't careful the lorry will overturn and all his cauliflowers get bashed."

In spite of his equable nature he sometimes suffered from anxiety. But would immediately cheer up.

"After they pulled the store down, if I hadn't retired, I might have gone and worked at the petrol station. I like cars when they don't swerve. When they're stationary. And the money's so good I could have kept you. If I'd started early enough I might have kept everybody. In an overall."

So they were sitting down to dinner in one of the brick boxes. A hot dinner in the middle of the day, except that everyone is at work, has its advantages, Dad used to say; you can put your feet up at night and read.

Waldo held himself so rigid Arthur must have felt it in his spongier hand. But made no sign. In some ways you were so close you did not always notice.

Waldo freed his hand for a moment. The wind, getting in behind his spectacles, had stung his rather pale eyes. It was so many years, he realized, since he had looked at himself without his glasses, he could barely see his youth's, not to say his boy's, face. Only sense it. And that, though less concrete, was more painful. In more normal circumstances there were only the scars where the acne had been on the back of his neck.

"These are our twins." Mother touched their hair to explain. "Yes, Waldo is the smaller. He had his setback. But is better. Aren't you, Waldo, better? You're strong now."

He had heard it so often he didn't always answer.

"No, there aren't any others."

Mother might have been grunting it if she hadn't been taught how to behave. She was what people called vague, or English. She didn't Come Out of Herself, which was a Bad Thing in a new country.

"Well, two is plenty, I think," she said and laughed. "Especially when they grow out of their clothes. And fall ill." She turned her cheek to their questions as she answered in her high, embarrassingly educated voice, "Who knows? I didn't *expect* to have *twins*."

Waldo knew, from what he knew, that there wouldn't be any more, of any combination.

Dad was usually more specific, especially about illnesses.

"He was born with his innards twisted. We had to have the doctor sort them out. That's why Arthur got a start on him."

So Waldo grew delicately in the beginning. It was expected of him. When he had a cold he stayed at home and learned the names of plants from Mother. There was a certain pale green sickly light which made him feel sad: the light of delicate plants and waiting for Arthur to return from school. Because much as he loved to drift about the house, touching the furniture and discovering books he only partly understood, he was lost without his twin. He could not have explained it, least of all to Arthur, who certainly knew.

"Arthur's the fair one, the copper-knob," Dad used to say, mashing Arthur's hair with his hand as though the hair had been something else.

People said Arthur was a fine-looking kid.

Even if the word had not been used, Waldo would not have admitted beauty in Arthur, but enjoyed studying his twin. Arthur's skin, ruddy where it ought to be, dwindled where protected to a mysterious bluish white. Almost edible. Sometimes Waldo buried his face in the crook of Arthur's neck, just to smell, and then Arthur would punch, they would start to punch each other, to ward off any shame, as well as for the pleasure of it.

There were many such games and pretences. Sometimes on evenings of sickly light, before Arthur had returned, Waldo approached the looking-glass, his face growing bigger and bigger, his mouth flattening on the throbbing glass, swallowing, or swallowed by, his mouth. Until he would hear Arthur, books falling on the kitchen floor; Arthur had not cared for books. And Waldo would drag himself out of the mirror's embrace and run to meet his brother. He never kissed his twin, even when they tried to make him, or at least he couldn't remember. Instead they wrestled to-

gether, and laughed, and even their breathing was inextricably in-
tertwined.

Dad used to say in the beginning, "Arthur's so strong he'll make
a wrestler. Or some kind of athlete."

As if he already saw his boy throwing a javelin or putting the
weight. Like somebody in the paper. Because Dad never went to
sports. If you take the trouble to invent gods, he said, you don't
turn them into sweating lumps of human beings. He read to them
sometimes about the Greeks, after he got home from the bank. He
sat there ruffling Arthur's hair, and Waldo would only half listen.
Whether Arthur understood, or had listened at all, Waldo
doubted. Nor did he inquire, because it was better not to be sure
how much, or how little, his brother understood.

All this reading from the Greek myths was really for Arthur,
whom Dad loved best in the beginning. There was a point where
he seemed to go off him. Not that Arthur hadn't continued receiving what was due to him in affection, but more like some dog you
had around the place. You had your duty towards him, because
you'd got him, and he couldn't help himself.

And Waldo. There was never any question of Dad's ignoring or
not being fond of Waldo. He was just in his dealings with everyone. But Waldo was born with that small head, with what you
might have called that withered-looking face, if you had been inclined to unkindness. The heads of father and son were both, in
fact, carved in rather minute detail, and where they gained in simi-
larity was in the eyelids, not the eyes, the hair-coloured hair, the
thin lips which tended to disappear in bitterness or suffering. Physical suffering, certainly, was something Waldo hardly experienced
after early childhood. But Dad probably suffered without telling, or
giving expression only indirectly to his pain. There was his leg. His
foot. Often strangers, and always children, were fascinated by
George Brown's boot, which was something members of the family
hardly noticed. It fell into the same category as inherited furniture.

One evening Waldo was hanging over the gate, watching their
father limp down Terminus Road after his journey back from the
bank. It was one of the steamy months of summer. How very yellow and horrid you are looking, Waldo thought.

As Dad walked, his thin lips were slightly parted. His shoulder was moving inside his coat, fighting for greater ease. When he caught sight of Waldo it was something he obviously hadn't been bargaining for. But had to speak, and at once, otherwise it would have seemed peculiar.

So Dad wet his lips and said what jumped into his head.

"Where is Arthur?" he asked.

Waldo did not know. Or rather, he did. Arthur was in the kitchen with Mother, who was allowing him to knead the dough.

Dad began spluttering, reaching out with his lips for something he was being denied. Then he realized. He bent and kissed Waldo. Waldo kissed him. Or touched with his lips his father's cheek, which, in spite of the clammy summer evening, was colder than he remembered of any other person's skin. It was a shock to discover, through the smell of sweat and crushed weed. While Dad and Waldo stood looking at each other.

So Waldo was in the position of a stranger, but one who knew too much.

He wanted to make amends, however, both at the moment and afterwards. At the time, to correct himself partially, he said, "Arthur is in the kitchen, doing things for Mother," as they walked up the brick path. And Dad, too, perhaps wanted to soothe some possible hurt. He put his hand on Waldo's shoulder, through which the limp transferred itself. They were limping and struggling, as if in one body, all the way to the front veranda.

Presently, when Dad was sitting on the corner of that old day-bed—"*pausing*," which is how he used to describe his flopping heavily down—Arthur came out. But Dad's need was less by then. It would have been different if Arthur had been hanging over the gate as he came limping down the road. And now, Waldo was watching.

Mother and Dad used to watch Arthur, or at least up to a certain stage. At first, it seemed, they could not see far enough into him, when Waldo, who could, and who had grown used to what he found, might have told them. Mother's hair began very early turning grey. She used to sit on the front veranda, twisting the wedding ring on her finger. It was pleasant for all of them to be together there, particularly after the southerly had come. Once when the southerly was blowing, Dad jerked his head in the direction of the wind and said, "Just about the cheapest fulfilment of anybody's expectations." It was the kind of remark which appealed to Mother. For touches like that she had Married Beneath Her.

So the boys were taught to wait for the southerly, and after Dad had grown disappointed in Arthur the southerly even helped improve the situation. Mother never grew disappointed to the same extent, because, if she wanted to, she could dare the truth to be the truth. For a long time after everyone realized, she persuaded herself Arthur was some kind of genius waiting to disclose himself. But Dad was not deceived, Waldo even less. Waldo didn't believe it possible to have more than one genius around.

Arthur was certainly born with his gift for figures. He did not need coaxing to help out with weights and measures. He liked also to fiddle with the butter and the bread, finally even to make them himself. Dad was disgusted. He said it was nothing for a boy, but Mother approved, as though Arthur's head for figures were not enough; she seemed to be trying to turn the butter-making and bread-baking into some sort of solemn rites.

On occasions when he asked whether he too might squeeze the butter or knead the dough, Waldo was told, "No. That's something for Arthur. He has a particular gift for it."

Once Arthur, who was watching the buttermilk gush out from between his fingers, laughed and said, "It's my vocation, isn't it, Mother?"

Waldo was more jealous of that word than he was of Arthur's privilege. He wondered where he had got it from. Because words were not in Arthur's line. It was Waldo who collected them, like stamps or coins. He made lists of them. He rolled them in his mouth like polished stones. Then Arthur went and sprang this vocation thing of his.

One evening Dad, after he had stumped down to the old butter-coloured, barrel-bellied cow they kept tethered round the place, said between pulling out the milk, "Now this is a job for a boy like you, Waldo. It's time I taught you to milk Jewel. What would you think of that?"

"I think that's part of Arthur's vocation," Waldo said.

Then he took out the bull's-eye he was sucking, and found it had run interestingly, and went away.

As it happened, Arthur, who was bigger and stronger, learned quite naturally to milk Jewel, and was proud to struggle back through the tussocks with the awkward slopping pail. All the jobs peculiarly Arthur's became in the end a mystery which other members of the family accepted. Waldo even realized he was going out of his way to protect his brother's rites from desecration. Supposing, for instance, other boys found out that Arthur Brown patted butter and baked bread. Waldo would have suffered agonies.

As the dedicated Arthur practised his vocation Waldo used to watch him, half guilty, half loving. The evenings of lamplight, with the smell of bread and the white sweat of butter, were not less mystical than some golden age of which Dad read them from a book.

When they were building the house—not they, the Browns, because the boys were too small, and Dad's affliction prevented him, and none of them could have, anyway, ever—but the men who had been coaxed to do it, cheaply and strictly under direction, Dad announced, "I know it's no more than a bloomin' weatherboard, but I want to suggest, above the front veranda, something of the shape of a Greek pediment."

Mother was standing by, in support, though nervous with her beads.

"Don't you see? Don't you understand?" Dad asked the men.

Fear that they might be as stupid as he more than expected shrank his lips, turned his skin to porous lemon.

Even after he produced the illustrated book everyone else remained paralysed by doubt.

"You must see, Mr. Allwright," he appealed, "what I want— what I *mean*—a pediment in the classical style?"

Because the storekeeper, whose wife had owned the land, encouraged them from the beginning and used to drive them down to the site.

"Ye-ehs," Mr. Allwright said, and smiled.

He was a tall man in thick glasses. Waldo and Arthur loved the little soiled calico bag in which he carried his change.

But you could see that nobody would ever really understand about the classical pediment. And Dad's hands, thin and yellow, trembled as they offered the open book.

"Good-o, Mr. Brown!" Mr. Haynes said helpfully at last, after it had grown embarrassing. "We'll make yer happy! We're gunna see you get what you've set yer heart on."

So the classical pediment rose by degrees above the normal weatherboard, giving it the appearance of a little, apologetic, not quite proportionate temple, standing in the trampled grass.

"That what you had in mind?" asked Mr. Haynes, stepping back with his hands in the pockets of his leather apron the evening they were officially finished.

"More or less," Dad replied low and indistinct.

It had been auditing week at the bank.

Later on, when the twins got to refer to their father as "George Brown," Arthur affectionately, Waldo with irony and understanding, they would look back and see him seated on the front veranda under the classical pediment, the branches of increasing quince trees hemming him in, the long trailers of the rambler drenching his taut skin with crimson. The boards at the edge of the veranda were eaten by the weather already in his lifetime, but the daybed held out till well after, only giving in to the borer the year the boys retired.

But in the beginning, when the house stood square, smelling of timber, and still wholly visible, they used to sit on the veranda in a fairly compact family group—Arthur a little to one side, picking his nose till Mother slapped him. (Waldo, who picked his in private, would watch to see his brother caught out.)

"We haven't thought what colour to paint our house," it suddenly occurred to Dad.

Mother was stringing beans because they were in.

"What do you fancy, Annie?" he asked.

"Oh, I!"

Mother held up her long throat.

"Haven't you any ideas?"

"Ideas?" she said. "Yes!" she said. "That is what they accused me of."

"But we must have *some* sort of colour. Red white green."

Arthur began to snigger and shake.

It was about this time that Waldo decided every member of his family was hopeless but inevitable.

"Or brown," said Dad. "Brown is a practical colour. And, by George, appropriate, isn't it?"

He too was amused at last because he had made an appropriate joke.

"Brown, yes, is a practical colour," said Mother softly, looking at her fingers and the pared beans.

There was black by then in the cracks of her fingers, to say nothing of the rough patch the needle had pricked on one, which was possibly the most interesting finger of all.

Anyway, when the money was saved, they had the house painted brown, and it was accepted by the landscape, because at that time all the other houses were brown. As the hot brown box settled into the steaming grass the classical pediment was no longer so painfully noticeable.

It was Waldo who disturbed the peace.

"I'm thinking of writing a play," he announced. "It's going to be a Greek tragedy."

Dad raised his head as though scenting an approach.

"How?" he asked. "You never ever saw one. Haven't even read one."

"I read part of a play," said Waldo. "The one about the man on the rock."

It was difficult to tell whether Dad was annoyed or pleased.

"You'd better learn to live first."

"Don't discourage him, George," said Mother, enjoying the possibilities.

Waldo began to sidle. He was never easily carried away.

"I'll write it," he said. "Afterwards I'll act it. Here on the veranda."

Then Arthur, who had come up carrying the full pail, on the way from the tether to the scullery, halted, and started gulping for words.

"Waldo," he said, "I can act in your play, can't I? Can't I?" he repeated.

It was suddenly too much for everybody else. They fell silent, in the light through the young quince trees. The western horizon was thin, strangling copper wire.

Arthur had put down his pail. They heard the clank when the handle fell.

"Can't I?" he gulped.

"No," said Waldo.

Because he knew this was something he could not bear to share with his brother, whose breathing he used to listen to whenever he woke in the night, the brother who looked almost right inside him when they opened their eyes on twin pillows in the morning.

Arthur was not put off. He was as usual so good-tempered. Leaving the pail, he began to clamber up on the veranda.

"Oh well," he said, "I'll have to write a Greek tragedy myself. Then I can act all the parts."

Dad was prepared to humour him, and Mother said, "Yes, dear. Certainly," in one of her softer voices, and touched him.

A gentle attention prevailed, because from certain angles and at certain moments Arthur was a strong and handsome boy. Now he was standing astride the veranda, raising his flushed throat, so that the words rising were clearly visible inside.

"And what will your play be about, Arthur?" Mother asked.

"A cow," Arthur blurted out.

"But a Greek tragedy!"

"A cow's as Greek, I suppose," said Dad, "as anything else." Then he added, in the voice of somebody whose opinion is sometimes asked, "Whether she's a figure of tragedy is a matter for consideration."

Arthur was grappling with his problem.

"This is a big *yellow* cow," he told them. "She's all blown out, see, with her calf. Then she has this calf. It's dead. See?"

There was Arthur pawing at the boards of the veranda. At the shiny parcel of dead calf.

Everyone else was looking at the ground by now, from shame, or, Waldo began to feel, terror.

"You can see she's upset, can't you?" Arthur lowed. "Couldn't help feeling upset."

It was suddenly so grotesquely awful in the dwindling light and evening silence.

"Couldn't help it," Arthur bellowed.

Thundering up and down the veranda he raised his curved yellow horns, his thick, fleshy, awful muzzle. The whole framework of their stage shook.

"That's enough, I think," said Dad.

"Oh, Arthur"—Mother was daring herself to speak—"we understand enough without your telling us any more."

Arthur stopped at once, as though he had been going to in any case.

"But it isn't all tragedy," he reassured. "Because she can have other calves, can't she? And does. She has eighteen before she dies."

"Yes," sighed Mother. "Cows often last for years, and lead very useful lives."

"So you see?" Arthur laughed.

Dad got up and limped inside. You could hear him lifting the porcelain shade off the big lamp.

Mother continued sitting on the daybed, which she used to say had an elegance, a character of its own, even though vicissitude had battered it a bit. In time, in the dusk, she might have forgotten about her family.

At least Waldo was the only one who had remained standing by. He could not help wondering how Arthur of all people had thought about that play. Ridiculous, when not frightening. Waldo would write a play, something quite different, when he had thought of one.

Then Dad, who had brought the dining room to light, called from inside, "What about tea, Mother?"

He sounded tired again, and patient.

Mother said, "Yes," and went in as if nothing had happened, to get the meal she had stopped trying to call "dinner."

Only Waldo lingered on the stage, which no longer contained their wooden play.

These were the flickering, barely experienced, obsessive moments with which the mind dealt more fully after they had been stored up. At the time, the rambling structure of days impressed its greater importance on the eye by sheer mass of repetitive detail. The Brown boys never stopped, it seemed, marching up the hill to

school. There was the endless, suffocating, chalkdust fear of wondering how little you could get away with. There was the rather
exhilarating traffic of the yard: taws for liquorice, or liquorice for
taws. Brutality left its victories and its bruises. Once Arthur got a
ferret from a boy called Eb Honeysett. I'm going to love it dearly,
Waldo, Arthur confessed privately, I'm going to call it call it
Scratch. Scratch looked over his shoulder and never came up out
of the burrow. They were marching up the hill to school. Waldo
could not bear to listen to Arthur breathing the way he breathed,
and would look round to see whether anyone behind might be
hearing, though of course if they were, he never let on there was
anything unusual. He could not bear what he had to bear, his responsibility for Arthur.

Occasionally they went up the hill earlier with Dad—Mother
said he would appreciate it—when their father left to catch the
train. Dad had to leave pretty early. At times it was barely milky
light. The stationmaster's lamp grated on the morning. But everyone, wider awake than normal, was exchanging conversation about
the weather and other matters which had suddenly assumed importance. Dad, who had spent the night clearing his throat and
turning, the other side of the wall, was perhaps the widest awake of
any of them. As they walked with him past the loaded thistles
and rusty docks, or crunched around the little painted-up siding,
Dad's head, in spite of the hair, the eyebrows, and moustache, had
the naked look of cherrystones. At that hour, but only then, he
seemed to see through anyone. His eyes, Mother said, were black,
though Waldo knew that that was imagination; they were brown.
They were terribly brown as Dad stood shuddering in the dewy
morning under the billycock hat he continued to wear, and which
gave him away as a Pom.

Waldo was always glad when the little train steamed off with
Dad in the direction of Barranugli, and they need not expect him
back till evening. He had an idea Arthur was glad too. But Arthur
would grow sleepy again, and catch hold of Waldo's hand, which
even then Waldo hated.

He would say, "You're a big fat helpless female," as they
mucked around the sideroads in the blazing dew. In the empty
classroom, waiting for the time to pass, he would say, "We're not

propping each other up, are we?" Then, of all times, perhaps he loved Arthur most. It was good not to have to think, but sit.

"I'm that tired," Arthur used to say, laying his head on the desk, and making the noise as though he had constipation and was straining on the dunny.

"It isn't 'that.' It's just 'tired,'" Waldo used to say, ever so prim.

It made Arthur giggle. Then Waldo might giggle too, motion rubbing their skins together. In the empty classroom hatred had never broken itself against the blackboard.

Johnny Haynes sometimes arrived early, looking for Arthur's help with a sum, and they went down under the pepper trees. Waldo no longer counted, but tagged along. Everything had that varnished look.

"But can't you see?" Arthur used to say, sternly, officiously. "It's that easy."

All the time his lips would be moving through some mysterious maze of numbers, until, at the end, he produced the miraculous, always the correct answer.

Waldo and Johnny had to make an effort not to show they were impressed. It was all too uncanny. In Arthur. Waldo kicked the ground as though he were a little brother waiting. Johnny Haynes, in many, though not in all ways, the brightest boy in the school, grew shiny-lipped and deferential, because for the moment Arthur Brown was necessary.

Poor Arthur, Waldo thought, and might have been loving himself, it was so genuine, in the early sunlight, under the pepper trees.

While numbers, or something, continued to strengthen Arthur against greater evils than Johnny Haynes.

Waldo hated Johnny. Johnny was good at history, geography, English. And, by arrangement, maths. When Waldo wrote the essay "What I See on the Way to School," and it had to be read aloud to the class, he could not get his breath because of Johnny Haynes sitting in the fourth row. Whenever he could control himself Waldo read in a prim imitation of Dad's voice, of Dad reading from an intellectual book, say, *Urn Burial* in the Everyman, which Waldo had suspected might be of interest until he found out.

"'Many curious and interesting weeds grow in the dust beside the road I take to school,'" Waldo read aloud.

Then he added a catalogue of names which went slightly to his head, like the stench of crushed weeds at certain expectant or exhausted moments.

" 'Boggabri or red-leg, cobbler's pegs, which some call cow-itch or devil's pitchforks, the cotton- or woody-pear, and frizzy fennel.' "

Arthur heard that, because he was interested in fennel.

"*Frizzy* fennel!" Arthur laughed low, loving it.

Mr. Hetherington pointed at him, which was what he did when he wanted to frighten boys.

Coming to the bits he knew to be the best, Waldo could feel his heart choking up his throat, till he almost couldn't bring out the words.

" 'There is the old stone tumbledown house amongst the pear trees where nobody lives any longer, the roof has gone, which looks like a house in which somebody might have committed a few murders. . . .' "

He almost could not bring himself further, in front of all those others. And Mr. Hetherington. And Johnny Haynes. Some things were too private, except perhaps in front of Arthur. As if Johnny Haynes cared. He was chewing a supply of paper pellets, to soak in ink, to flip at Norm Croucher's neck.

" 'Sometimes when it is early or late,' " Waldo's voice came bursting, gurgling, wavering like water escaping from the bath, " 'I have thought I saw the form of a man hurrying off with a basin of blood.' "

Here Mr. Hetherington grunted in that fat way.

" 'Of course it is only the imagination. But I think this person, if he had existed, would have murdered the many children he lured in through the black trees.' "

Some of the class were laughing and hooting, but Arthur clapped, and Mr. Hetherington called for order.

Afterwards, in commenting on the essays, Mr. Hetherington remarked that Waldo Brown displayed keen interest in botanical detail, but relied too heavily on imagination of a highly coloured order.

Waldo was not so much listening as watching Johnny Haynes's back, wondering how much Johnny had heard.

Next day Johnny showed how much he had. He called to Norm Croucher, who was Johnny's permanent offsider, and said, "Come on, Normie, we'll show Waldo what we got in our bloody basin."

They walked all three down to the pepper trees. If Waldo accompanied them voluntarily it was because he knew it to be his fate.

There he stood, a little apart, on the white, windswept grass. With Johnny saying, "That bloke hadn't reckoned on one more murder. Amongst the pear trees," he added.

Waldo heard the knife click. Though he couldn't see Norm Croucher's face, he could feel him holding his wrists from behind, he could feel Norm's breath in the nape of his neck.

Then Johnny came with the knife, and went prick prick prick with the point right away round under what Dad called the gills.

"Just as a preliminary, like," said Johnny. "He doesn't fancy the prick, eh?"

Norm sniggered, who on one occasion had been caught at it.

Waldo shivered, and his gooseflesh must have been visible as the blood shot out in little jets of scarlet fountains. Because although he knew none of it was real, it was. Not even his mother's hand could soothe the fear out of him, his mother's hand dappled and dripping with his lost blood.

His vision made Waldo whimper.

"Arrhhh let me don't Johnny Norm I'll give I can't," he whimpered past slippery lips.

"What'll you give?" Johnny asked. "You dunno what it's worth. Not yet, you don't, by half."

And he drew the knife in a loop round Waldo's wincing flesh. Waldo could feel the point bumping against the lumps of gooseflesh.

When they all had to turn suddenly round. Even Waldo.

It was as if the flaming angel, though Dad said there was no such thing, stood above them, or didn't stand, flailed and flickered.

"You let my brother alone!" Arthur Brown was bellowing.

Johnny and Norm would not have known what to answer in much easier circumstances. Now they were frightened. Waldo was frightened.

Because Arthur seemed to have swelled. The pale lights were

flashing from the whiter edges of his skin, from under the normally hateful hair.

The fire was shooting in tongues from every bristle of Arthur Brown's flaming hair.

"I'll kill," Arthur continued to bellow, "the pair of you bloody buggers if you touch"—he choked—"my brother."

His fist had split, it seemed, Johnny Haynes's lower lip. Now the blood was really running.

The bell tolling.

They were all four as suddenly still. Even Arthur. Except for his panting.

They went in to geography.

Afterwards, as they walked down the road called Terminus, where nobody else had begun to live, or some perhaps, in the past, and given up, the Brown brothers were alone as usual, at last, and Arthur tried to get Waldo's hand, to keep level with him.

"Leave me!" Waldo shouted. "How many times have I told you not to hang on to my hand?"

"But when you walk fast!"

Arthur was shuffling and running, bigger than Waldo, a big shameful lump.

"You only want to make a fool of me," Waldo said; he could not, he hoped, have made it sound colder. "And splitting Johnny Haynes's lip. You've always got to show us up."

"But you was the one they were making a fool of." Arthur snivelled.

" 'Were,' " said Waldo. "Only I wasn't."

He could not explain a ritual to Arthur, who could not even remember always how to lace up his own boots.

They walked on, between the red-leg, the cotton-pear, and cobbler's pegs, which some call cow-itch. Waldo Brown shuddered to remember his deliverance by what had appeared to be the flaming angel. It has been proved, Dad had already told them, that everything of such description, everything ignorant people refer to as the supernatural, is nonexistent. Waldo was proud to know. He would have liked to go permanently proud and immaculate, but his twin brother dragged him back repeatedly behind the line where knowledge didn't protect.

"It was all because of the old essay," Arthur was keeping on, "that Johnny Haynes thought was silly. Because the bloke couldn't have collected the blood. See? Not in the basin. The kids he was murdering would have been kicking too hard. But I liked it, Waldo —the idea. Waldo? Those black old trees—they're black all right, and perhaps there was a possum scratching in the chimney."

Waldo decided not to listen to any further dill's drivel.

And soon other things had begun to happen.

That evening after tea he slipped round quietly, hearing Mr. Haynes had come. Arthur was down with Jewel for something, taking a cabbage leaf, or filling the water-bucket. While Mr. Haynes was standing on the front veranda, under the classical pediment he had built.

"I warn yer, Mr. Brown," Mr. Haynes was saying, and his usually jolly chins were compressed, "you'll have to restrain 'im. Yer don't realize a big lump of a boy like that can turn violent. In his condition. It's hard, I know, for the parents to see."

"I'll see when there's anything to see," said Dad.

"But Arthur is the gentlest creature," Mother was trying to persuade.

"I didn't bring along my boy's lip to show." Mr. Haynes was turning nasty now. "His mother is too upset. But I warn yer."

"Thank you, Mr. Haynes," said Dad. "You already have."

Mother was protesting with her tongue. She had fastened her long hands together like people did in church.

"Next thing he'll be peering in at windows. Frightening women. Jumping on girls. That's what happens before parents'll admit they've got a loopy boy at home."

Dad was sitting on the old daybed. He could have been hit over the head.

"Mr. Haynes," said Mother finally, "parents realize more than you, apparently, believe."

So Mr. Haynes was ashamed and turned grumbling down the path.

"What is it?" asked Arthur, who had come up suddenly through the grass.

His thick white nostrils scented something.

"Nothing, darling," Mother said. "There's that bowl of cream waiting to be churned."

While Waldo, who was the cause of it all, had shrivelled up. If it came to that, in moments of exposure, his common state was one of runtish misery. He longed for Mother's hand to reach out and touch some part of him which perhaps could never be touched.

So he went away into what they called the Side Garden, which the grass had already reclaimed. While Dad continued sitting, as though considering the problem Arthur was becoming. As though Arthur was only Dad's problem. When Arthur was Waldo's club foot. As Waldo limped, over the uneven ground, through the sea of grass and submerged roses.

That night Arthur tried to drag him back behind the almost visible line beyond which knowledge could not help.

"What is it, Waldo?" Arthur golloped. "What were they talking about?"

Arthur was taking, had taken him in his arms, was overwhelming him with some need.

"Nothing," said Waldo.

He should have struggled, but couldn't any more. The most he could do was pinch the wick, squeeze out the flickery candle flame.

"We don't mind, do we, Waldo?"

The stench of pinched-out candle was cauterizing Waldo's nostrils. But he did not mind all that much. He was dragged back into what he knew for best and certain. Their flesh was flickering, quivering together in that other darkness, which resisted all demands and judgments.

Waldo suspected early on they could not expect more of their father. He was too pathetic. Dad had not recovered from the evening of Mr. Haynes's accusation, though he went about trying to show he had, Waldo realized later. "George Brown," as he referred to their father when he had learnt to tolerate him, clung to his principles, or illusions, but did not succeed in impressing himself.

Once Waldo had come across the parents sitting at that deal table they had dragged out into the shade of the plum tree. (Waldo was of the age where his pants would no longer button at the knees—"the leggy stage," Mother called it.) The light falling on his mother and father through the branches had jaundiced them. They cringed slightly, for they were not, in fact, protected, as they had really been hoping and expecting.

"Well," said Dad, "we have each other."

Waldo at first resented what he heard. It was as though he, and less immediately Arthur, had been cast off.

"Oh, yes," answered Mother. "We have each other. We needn't regret."

"And our conscience is intact. We got out. No one can say it wasn't for the best."

"Oh, yes," said Mother. "They were intolerable. Beastly! What else could one expect from people so warped by tradition? My family!"

Although he was standing outside the blast, Waldo shivered.

"Sitting in their pews," she said, "Sunday after Sunday. Keeping in with God and society. Then going home to sharpen their knives for the week."

She laughed one of those laughs, and looked down to see what it was, and crushed the little green plums which were grating under her feet.

"We are free, at least," said Dad, "here."

"Oh, yes," said Mother.

"Give the children a chance."

"The children."

She put her hand over her husband's. She was so preoccupied, it seemed there would be nobody but Arthur left for Waldo.

Then George Brown their father, a wizened man with a limp, got up and went in to stoke the stove for Mother as he usually did before tea. There were times when Waldo loved their father, he really did. He would have liked to, anyway, and often the intention is acceptable.

About the same period those Miss Dallimores called.

First Mother received the letter, so small, so that you didn't have to write too much, and scented, ever so slightly scented. Waldo realized later that the Dallimores were specialists in what is done.

Mother said she would bake some scones, and perhaps a few of her rock-cakes.

"Ooh, yeees!" said Arthur. "The rock-cakes, Mum!"

He liked the sugar crystals on them.

When the boys returned from school the Dallimores were already seated. Their hats were almost more important than themselves. Like their letter, the Dallimores were slightly scented.

"Have you got a cestrum?" Arthur asked.

"I beg your pardon?" Miss Dallimore replied.

"A cestrum. A kind of bush that smells at night. We've got one outside our bedroom window."

Waldo could have kicked Arthur, but Miss Dallimore only thought it a quaint remark.

"Old-fashioned," her sister improved on it, but faintly.

For the most part Miss Dorothy Dallimore wiggled her ankle instead of speaking, and helped underline what her sister had to say. It was Miss Dallimore—Miss Lilian—who did the talking. Her dress had little holes in it, which bees began to investigate, till she brushed them away. Angrily, Waldo suspected.

"It is a most curious coincidence," Miss Dallimore said, and her sister Dorothy supported her in muffled tone, "that we should be paying this visit to Sarsaparilla just when we receive the letter from your cousin."

"Most," said Mother, "considering Mollie is not the best of correspondents."

"But sends the drafts at Christmas. Doesn't she, Mum? Eh? She never forgets that," said Arthur.

"Oh, we adored Mrs. Thourault!"

Miss Dallimore almost gargled with the name, and Miss Dorothy agreed in undertone, watching her own ankle, which she wiggled worse than ever.

"Even as a little girl," said Mother, "Mollie was the soul of kindness."

"I bought the penknife, didn't I, Mum?" Arthur said. "Last time. With my share of the draft."

"Oh dear, Arthur, you're tilting the table!"

It was the little rickety wicker-and-bamboo one they had brought out from the living room.

"Won't you," she said, "fetch us another plate of cakes?" Then

Mother looked shy, for her. "That is, if Miss Dallimore or her sister would care for another cake."

The Miss Dallimores agreed they adored rock-cakes. They also found Arthur so amusing.

Waldo did not believe it for a moment. He himself was disgusted. If it had been possible he would have taken the two Miss Dallimores, leading them away from the house in which his family lived, while telling them something of interest, preferably about himself, he would have to decide what.

"I am sure Mrs. Thourault will be quite excited to have us report on you all," said Miss Dallimore, who, unlike Cousin Mollie, might have been taught her kindness.

"She speaks so *warmly* of you," Miss Dorothy added, and seemed surprised at herself for having got it in.

"I do wonder whether Mrs. Musto will see her way to visiting Tallboys. We did give her the address. We should so love her to meet Mrs. Thourault. That would forge yet another link."

Miss Dallimore's sister giggled her pleasure. For Mrs. Musto was the lady in whose house at Sarsaparilla the Dallimores were spending the few months of her trip to Europe. Waldo knew all about it, and was bored at last, he realized, by people.

"I can't tell you what it did to us," Miss Dallimore continued, "our visit to such a"—here she was searching—"to such a *historic* English home."

Miss Dorothy, to show she was sharing the experience, gave what sounded like a moan.

"Our only disappointment," Miss Dallimore confessed, "was that Lord Tolfree himself didn't put in an appearance. Was indisposed."

Mother blushed, and Waldo on hearing the name again felt the little twinge, of anxiety as much as pleasure. He returned to Miss Dallimore with greater interest. She was the colour of marmalade under her sugar hat.

"A chill, I believe—wasn't it, Dolly?—on his liver."

"Uncle Charlie's liver," said Mother, "was always playing up."

The Miss Dallimores appeared distressed, though the elder one quickly found a reason for brightening up.

"In any case," she said, "it has been so delightful to make the acquaintance of the Honourable Mrs. Thourault's cousin. In Sarsaparilla."

"The *Hon*-our-able Mrs. *Thou*-rault!" Arthur repeated, or almost sang, pronouncing the H dreamily.

"The only pity is," said the persevering Miss Dallimore, "that Mr. Brown should still be at his bank."

"It's a long journey from Barranugli."

The skin between Mother's eyes grew pinched as it did when she thought about Dad and the bank.

"Oh yes, *tiring!*" Miss Dallimore agreed emphatically. "Australia *is* tiring. The distances are tiring."

"The Hon Mrs. Thou-ou-rault!" Arthur sang, dreamier.

Miss Dorothy giggled, but turned it nervously into a sigh, and sat waggling her ankle some more.

"But perhaps"—Miss Dallimore revived again—"perhaps in time"—she was at her marmalady brightest—"they will give him Sydney, and then you will come to live among us!"

It was obviously the only place to live. But Mother looked down. Just as Waldo, and at last Arthur, were looking up, at Miss Dallimore's idea. That Dad should be given Head Office.

Mother did not speak. Arthur could have been about to start the hiccups. Never before, Waldo saw, had he been closer to his mother, to his brother. They were close enough to suffocate.

Then Arthur hiccupped. "When are we going to the bank, Mum? It's time we visited the bank again. Mr. Mackenzie gives us humbugs. Mr. Mackenzie has a stuffed fox."

"Why," said Miss Dallimore, "what a very interesting and thoughtful person Mr. Mackenzie must be."

She had got up. The two Miss Dallimores were on their feet. They were doing things to their clean-smelling gloves.

"Why has your dress got holes in it?" Arthur hiccupped, looking rather too closely into the elder Miss Dallimore's material.

"That is part of the design, I expect!"

Miss Dallimore laughed to make it sound braver as, followed by her sister, she tried to walk slowly down the path.

Mother seemed to have forgotten the rickety bamboo table,

from which Arthur finished the rock-cakes, and from which only much later she began to sweep the crumbs. As Dad was coming through the gate.

"Two women," Mother told him. "Two ladies."

She showered the grass with sugary crumbs.

"Ladies? What ladies?"

"I mentioned them," said Mother, "only this morning. The ones who have come to Mrs. Musto's."

"Tenants?"

"They are doing a little caretaking—oh, but very genteel—while Mrs. Musto is away."

The Miss Dallimores did not call again, and there was no reason to remember them—except when Arthur asked, "When will they give you Head Office, Dad?"

"On their day of judgment," their father answered.

The bank.

It was a squat building, solid, the brown paint of which had blistered in the Barranugli sun. In the brownish-yellow glare Arthur always stood to burst a few of the paint blisters, and once had said, only for himself, in little higher than a whisper, "Diarrhoea." Outside the bank it was so hot, so brown, everybody, as Mother would call it, "visibly perspiring." Cool inside the building, though, and solemn. Several times when they were smaller Mother had taken them to Barranugli, shopping, and visiting at the bank. But had stopped, Waldo realized, because Dad no longer wanted it.

"But it's their only little outing," Mother had protested.

"He's big now, Anne. What if he got out of hand?" Waldo heard. "What if you couldn't control him?"

Waldo regretted they no longer visited the bank. His sense of importance suffered from the lapse. The bank itself was so reliable, permanent, with its smell of fresh paper money, and the neat young ladies in patent-leather sleeves, and Mr. Mackenzie, who came out from behind the frosted glass.

"So these are the boys," said Mr. Mackenzie the first time.

"The twin boys," Arthur corrected.

Because people did not always realize, though in the case of Mr. Mackenzie, naturally he must have known.

Even if he hadn't he would not have shown any surprise. He was, it seemed, all right, in spite of the dandruff, and smelling like the bowl of an old treacly pipe.

Mr. Mackenzie took them up into the residence to show them to Mrs. Mackenzie, who was an invalid, they said. She was in every other way uninteresting. But Mr. Mackenzie produced the humbugs, slightly melted in their paper bag, and pointed out the fox in its place on the window-ledge of a landing. Teeth bared. Arthur got so excited on first acquaintance with the fox he almost embraced it, board and all—the red fox, not quite so red as Arthur, and softer. Arthur's hair was what you could only call coarse until length and age softened it.

Afterwards, sucking humbugs, they went back into the public bank, and stood in front of the cage in which Dad was counting money. Mother would smile to encourage him. But not the boys. It was too solemn a moment for the boys, the way Dad flicked the stiff notes, as though to tear the corners off, and writing down figures in pencil. Sometimes a group of young ladies would gather, to ask questions, and laugh, and flatter. Once a Miss Simpson had touched Arthur's hair and exclaimed, "Oh, but it's such *harsh* stuff!" She had done it, though. Possibly she had won a dare.

But Dad very seldom looked up, even when there weren't any clients; he was so busy.

It was, he thought, the occasion of their last visit to the bank as children, that Waldo noticed their father looking out from the cage in which he stood: the citron-coloured face, its seams nicked by the cutthroat with flecks of black, morning blood, the moustache, interesting to touch before it had grown raggedy. Their father's eyes were brown, which Arthur had inherited. Their father's stare was at that moment directed outward, and not. He had not yet developed his asthma, though might have that morning in the tearing silence of the brown bank. Suddenly his shoulders hunched, to resist, it seemed, compression by the narrow cage, his eyes were more deeply concentrated on some invisible point. More distinctly even than the morning he found their father dead, Waldo would remember the morning of their last visit to the bank.

Afterwards in the rackety train which was taking them back to

Sarsaparilla, Mother asked, "What is it, Waldo? What is it, dearest?"

Unusual for her; she was by no means *soft*.

But how could he tell her? And he knew, what was more, she was only asking to be told something she already knew. (In his crueller moments as a man, Waldo suspected their mother was not always able to resist a desire to probe their common wounds.)

So he sat in the spidery local train and willed it to dislocate the vision of those normally liquid eyes set like glass inside the cage. Forever, it seemed, and ever.

But the train did not cooperate, and it was only on walking up their garden path, when he trod on one of those brown slugs which had come out too soon in search of evening moisture, that Waldo was able to relieve his feelings. As he crushed the slug, his own despair writhed and shrivelled up.

The old men weaving along the main street, the one stalking, the other stumping, had known their surroundings so long they could have taken them to bits, brick by brick, tile by tile, the new concrete curbing, and Council-approved parapets. They would even have known how the bits should be put together again. The old men were still fascinated by what they knew, while often overwhelmed by it. For it was overwhelming, really. Take Woolworth's. Though Arthur Brown loved Woolworth's.

"Can't we go into Woolie's, Waldo?"

"It isn't open yet."

Arthur liked to spend mornings in Woolworth's, costing the goods. Because of course things were marked up higher than should have been allowed. Often they told him not to be a nuisance, and sent him out. Once the manager had searched his pockets, and found the bus tickets, the rather grey handkerchief—Arthur's laundry always came out grey—and the glass taws he carried around.

"Those are my solid mandalas," Arthur explained to the manager.

Today the manager was parking early.

"Shan't be coming in this morning," Arthur called. "I'm with my brother. We're going for a walk."

The manager screwed up one of his cheeks in a freshly shaven synthetic smile.

Gathered by the wind, the two old men flitted across the plate glass, each examining himself, separately, secretly. On the whole each was pleased, for reflections are translatable symbols of the past, Chinese to the mind which happens to be unfamiliar with them. Some of those who noticed the old blokes might have seen them as frail or putrid, but the Brothers Brown were not entirely unconscious of their own stubbornness of spirit. Arthur, for instance, whose mechanism had in some way threatened his continuity earlier that morning, was still able to enjoy the gusty light of boyhood in the main street of Sarsaparilla, his lips half open to release an expression he had not yet succeeded in perfecting. His body might topple, but only his body. The drier, the more cautious Waldo walked taking greater care in spite of the strength of his moral convictions.

Everybody to his own. The Presbyterians had their red brick. The convicts had built the Church of England. Over his shoulder the Methoes had hung out their business sign. Waldo Brown, so thin, was filled out considerably by knowing that nothing can only be nothing. It was almost the only gratitude he felt he owed his parents—not love, which is too demanding in the end, affection perhaps, which is more often than not love watered down with pity, but gratitude he could allow himself to offer, a cooler, a more detached emotion when not allied to servility. So Waldo stalked through the main street, in the wind from his oilskin, on only physically brittle bones, knowing in which direction enlightenment lay. Waldo stiffened his neck and skirted round the Church of England parson with a smile, not of acknowledgment, but of identification. As for priests, jokes about them made him giggle. He would look for the vertical row of little black buttons, for the skins of priests which flourished like mushrooms behind leather-padded doors. Waldo believed his parents had just tolerated clergymen as guardians of morality, priests never. Myths, evil enough in themselves, threatened one's sanity when further abstracted by incense and Latin, and become downright obscene if allowed to take shape in oleograph or plaster.

On this hitherto evil morning, of a cold wind and disturbances, of decisions and blotting-paper clouds, Waldo Brown's convictions helped him to breathe less obstructedly. He failed for the moment to notice the smell of mucus in his nostrils. Putting his mind in order had eased the oilskin at his armpits. Intellectual honesty glittered on his glasses, blinding his rather pale eyes. How dreadful if Dulcie. But she hadn't. It was the kind of near-slip which made him hate Dulcie's judgment rather than deplore his own temporary lack of it. Suppose his exercise in loving Dulcie had been forced to harden into a permanent imitation of love! The intermittent drizzle of resentment is far easier to bear, may even dry right up. It had, in fact, until Arthur.

Why had Arthur? Where was Arthur?

"Look, Waldo, it's turned to clay!" Arthur called, dawdling, fascinated by the crumbling turd of Mr. Hepple's overstuffed cocker spaniel.

"Come along," Waldo ordered. "It's only old."

The old man and two old dogs gathered round the whitened stool shocked the youth inside Waldo Brown.

Each of the blue dogs, pointing a swivel nose, sniffed with a delicacy of attention, lifted a leg in turn, aimed sturdily enough, then came on, chests broad to the wind, not so good in the pasterns. It was the old man who lingered, as though unable to decide on the next attitude to adopt.

Then Arthur Brown spat, or dribbled. It faltered on his chin, hung and swung silverly against the knife-edged light.

"That sort of smell," he said, "could give a person diphtheria."

It choked Waldo. What had Dulcie seen in Arthur?

"Didn't I tell you come along?"

Arthur came.

He took his brother by the hand, who would have resisted if he had remembered how to resist. But twin brothers, brothers of a certain age, at times remember only what has been laid down in the beginning.

They were walking on in the direction Waldo knew now he had not chosen; it had chosen him.

"Did you ever have diphtheria, Waldo?"

"You know perfectly well I didn't."

"Yes," said Arthur.

The habit of motion, the warmth of skin, were so very comforting, he put out his tongue and licked the air. It might have been barley-sugar.

Arthur said, "You know when you are ill, really ill, not diphtheria, which we haven't had, but anything, pneumonia—you can't say we haven't had pneumonia—you can get, you can get much farther in."

"Into what?"

It tired Waldo.

"Into anything."

The wind coming round the corner, out of Plant Street and heading for Ada Avenue, gave Waldo Brown the staggers. Arthur, on the other hand, seemed to have been steadied by thoughtfulness.

He said, "One day perhaps I'll be able to explain—not explain, because it's difficult for me, isn't it, to put into words, but to make you *see*. Words are not what make you see."

"I was taught they were," Waldo answered in hot words.

"I dunno," Arthur said. "I forget what I was taught. I only remember what I've learnt."

If he stumbled at that point it was because he had turned his right toe in. Although she tried, Mother had not broken him of it.

"Mrs. Poulter said—" said Arthur.

"Mrs. Poulter!"

Waldo yanked at the oblivious hand. Mrs. Poulter was one of the fifty-seven things and persons Waldo hated.

"She said not to bother and I would understand in my own way. But I don't, not always, to be honest. Not some things. I don't understand cruelty."

The little flat sounds which accompanied dangerous approaches were issuing from Waldo's mouth.

"I don't understand how they can nail a person through the hands."

Waldo would not listen any more, though Arthur might be tired of telling. He did tire very quickly, and, if you were lucky, might not revive for half an hour. He seemed to withdraw, to recline on the hugger-mugger cushions of an unhealthily crammed imagination.

In any case, there were the shops, there were the houses of the street you knew, providing signs that man is a rational animal. Waldo liked to look into the houses he passed, obliquely though, for on some of those occasions when he had stared full in he had been faced with displays of perversity to damage temporarily his faith in reason. From a reasonable angle the houses remained the labelled boxes which contain, not passions, but furniture: *Green Slopes, Tree Tops, Gibber Gunya, Cootamundra, Tree Tops, The Ridge, Tree Tops*, less advisedly, *Ma Rêve*.

"Not mine!" he said aloud.

Waldo knew he was bad-tempered. Long ago, in the days when he was taking up Yoga, Pelmanism, Profitable Short Story Writing, and making lists of what must be achieved or corrected, he had decided to do something about his temper, but had failed, as, he consoled himself, many important people had.

Watching him walk controlled along the street, leading his backward brother by the hand, no one probably would have guessed he had failed, in that, at least. How convincing an impression he made Waldo knew from observing himself obliquely in the plate-glass windows of shops, and anyway, he had decided early to be his mother's rather than his father's son. Anne Brown, born a Quantrell, had created an impression even in one of her old blue dresses with tea-stained lace insertion, or until her last days and illness, which were beyond human control. Waldo understood that those who lowered their eyes in passing were paying homage to someone of his mother's stock.

Many were perceptive. Others, who turned deliberately away, only wished to disguise their inferiority. Or were disgusted by Arthur. There were, on the other hand, some who hid their embarrassment in a display of exaggerated bonhommie. Like the men in overalls at the Speedex Service Station.

"Hi, mate! Hi, Arthur!" they called, raising their muscular throats. "How's the Brown Bomb?"

Arthur loved it. He loved the service station. He loved to stare at people, and into houses, which was all very well for Arthur, Waldo allowed, because he could not have interpreted half of what he saw.

All that was steel and concrete—service stations, for example—appalled Waldo, though he would never have admitted in public, he would never have rejected any usable evidence of human progress.

Arthur loved the Speedex Service Station because Ron Salter sometimes had the lollies for him, and Barry Grimshaw on one occasion let him take the gun and grease the nipples of a truck.

"One day I'm gunna come and work with you boys. Permanent," Arthur called, tagging back on Waldo's hand. "Then we'll have a ball! And improve my savings account!"

Of course the men were laughing at Arthur, Waldo knew.

The Speedex Service Station, safely past, thank God—Waldo would allow himself a lapsus linguae if the error had grown into the language—had risen out of what had been Allwrights' General Store. Exhaust fumes and the metallic idiom of mechanics had routed the indolent mornings which used to weigh so heavy on Allwrights' buckled veranda, bulging with bags of potatoes and mash, stacked with the boxes of runty tomatoes the growers brought out from under the seats of their sulkies. To protect the goods on Allwrights' veranda from the visits of dogs had been one of the extra duties of Arthur Brown. Arthur seemed to enjoy that, as a relaxation, while regretting he could not coax the dogs into a permanent relationship.

Nobody seeing the Browns now connected them except in theory with the past, because the past was scarcely worth knowing about. It was remarkable how many of those walking along the Barranugli Road on present errands had only just been born.

"Mr. Allwright died lacing up his boots." Arthur Brown clumped and mumbled, his thick white hair flumping at his collar. Then he had to laugh. "Mrs. Allwright thought I'd stuck to the change from Mustos' order. She'd put it behind the candles. Put it herself. Couldn't add up, either, except with a pencil and paper."

After that the road opened out into one of those stretches, a replica of itself at many other points. On the road to Barranugli it was usual for Waldo Brown to forget which bits they had passed, even going quickly in the bus. In the end the bush roads of childhood were no slower than those made by men in the illusions of speed and arrival. The same truck, the same sedan, would stick screeching, roaring, smoking, on its spinning, stationary tires, no longer in the same rut, but in the same concrete channel, the same stretch of infinity. If Waldo Brown had not been a superior man, of intellectual tastes, it might have become intolerable, or perhaps had, because of that.

He yawned till remembering why he had chosen to commit a deliberate assault on distance on that morning. He stopped the yawn. They seemed to be making very little progress. Pedestrians were overtaking them, not to mention the 8:13.

The dust-coloured bus plunged, elastic-sounding, not too rigidly riveted, down the road to Barranugli. Look into a passing bus, and more often than not you will see something you would rather not. Smeared mauve against the window, Mrs. Poulter's face was too stupid exactly to accuse Waldo.

Waldo snorted, even laughed.

It was unusual.

"What's the joke?" asked Arthur.

"Ain't no joke!" said Waldo in the comic voice he put on for jokes.

It was most unusual.

And obviously he did not want to tell. So Arthur kept quiet.

Mrs. Brown admitted from the beginning that Mrs. Poulter had her good points. A cheerful young woman with a high colour and the surly husband. Almost too deliberately on the opposite side of the road, directly opposite—two houses, you were tempted to conclude, eying each other for what they could see. Not that the Browns would have been so indiscreet. Excepting Arthur, who loved to talk to Mrs. Poulter. He loved to ask her questions, and Mrs. Poulter, curiously enough, although an inalterably stupid creature, usually seemed to find an answer. That was one of the reasons Waldo found her so difficult to put up with.

Once Waldo Brown, in one of his less oblique moments—he was quite a bit younger, cruder of course—was tempted to cross the road. *How* tempted, he had never been sure. It was so dark. It was by that time night, eloquent with leaves and crackling sticks.

Waldo heard himself crunch a flowerpot. But he felt he had to walk around a while. He could hear his heart. He could hear the bandicoots, their *thrrt thrrt*. It was so dark, it was understandable he should have been drawn to the square of light. He couldn't resist it. And there stood Mrs. Poulter, normally so high of colour, turned waxen by the yellow light inside the room. Her breasts two golden puddings stirred to gentle activity. For Mrs. Poulter was washing her armpits at the white porcelain washstand basin. As she returned it again and again the flannel dribbled the water sleepily back, over the porcelain rim, of white, frozen cabbage leaves. Mrs. Poulter dipped, and the tendrils of black hair which had strayed from the yawning armpits were plastered to the yellow, waxy flesh, Waldo observed. He saw the draggle of jet in the secret part of her thighs.

He had never felt guiltier, but guilt will sometimes solidify; he could not have moved for a shotgun. There was no question of that, however, for the door was opening, and Bill Poulter was entering their room. *Ohhhh*, his wife seemed to be saying, dropping the flannel into the white porcelain cabbage. Mrs. Poulter, too, it seemed, was overcome by guilt for her offence against modesty. Her fingers were almost sprouting webs in their efforts to uphold decency, which was exactly what, in fact, they did, for her surprised nipples were perking up over her honestly-intentioned hands. While Bill Poulter advanced, into the room, into the lamplight. Waldo had never seen Mr. Poulter look less scraggy, less glum. Because he was wanting something apparently unexpected, a straggly smile had begun to fit itself to the face so unaccustomed to it.

Then the room was consumed by darkness—and was it mirth? was it Mrs. Poulter's? In that direction at least, the darkness seemed intensified in a concentrated fuzziness. Then there was the sound of what was probably Bill Poulter's belt slapping the end of the iron bedstead, followed by the jingle of brass balls and dislocated iron.

Waldo went home, not without crunching two more flowerpots.

Trudging along the Barranugli Road, Waldo Brown was tempted to glance, if only obliquely, at Arthur.

Arthur's lips were slightly open, if anything slightly purpler than before.

He said, "Those chrysanths will get crushed in a full bus. They'll have had it by the time she arrives."

"Who?" said Waldo.

"Mrs. Poulter."

Then they were walking somewhat quicker, because Waldo had to defend himself from the kind of conversation he had been making with his brother ever since speech had come to them. Or rather he must withdraw his mind from his mind's mirror.

Altogether they were rocking a bit, in an effort to gather speed, or avoid reflections. The blue dogs, who had settled down to a steady trot just ahead, barrels rolling, tails at work like handles, pinned back their ears on sensing a threat to their heels. One of the dogs looked back over his shoulder to see what the men could be getting up to. His splather of tongue hung, palpitating suspiciously, against the yellow stumps and bleeding gums.

When Arthur, as though in sympathy with the dog, held up his thick white muzzle and began to howl.

"Aohhhhh!"—actually it was a man—"I never went on such a walk! What's it leading to?"

The two dogs were terrified. Their tongues thinned, till exhaustion forced them to spread them again. They would have liked to continue looking straight ahead, but their slitted eyes were drawn perpetually towards the corners of the slits. Their ears had become the ears of crouching hares. Their necks wore staring ruffs.

Waldo Brown simply jerked at his brother.

"It's nothing," he said, "but exercise."

And jerked again, so that Arthur was trotting like a dog, while Waldo strode on longer legs, the loosened sheets of his iron oilskin chattering in the surrounding wind, his shod heels gashing the stones. The cryptomerias the retinosperas the golden cypresses were running together by now. At times the brothers reeled.

When the flap of Waldo's oilskin struck the driver's door of the semi-trailer lurching past, it brought a man rushing out of the garden of one of the homes.

"Steady on!" cried their protector. "You'll get hit, if that's what you're after, and I'll have to call the ambulance."

"The ambulance? Oh, no!" Arthur began to shout.

Waldo was forced to stop.

"Thank you," he said. "We're in full control of ourselves."

It was his glasses made him look colder. The rimless glass might have been an emanation of the rather pale eyes.

"Okay," replied the man, and laughed—he was bald, the big pursy type, with a joggle of belly. "I don't wanter interfere. Only thought," he dwindled.

Waldo continued dragging his brother in his course, though he had already decided they would turn when the helpful man was out of sight.

Arthur was lagging.

"But the ambulance," he blubbered. "And you were hit, Waldo! That other time. Remember?"

Yes, Waldo Brown had been hit somewhere in the middle stretch of Pitt Street, it must have been 1934. He did not like to think about it now, not only because it was connected with complete loss of dignity, his broken pince-nez, the herd of human beasts halted in their trampling surge only by the skin of his body, then Arthur at the hospital, but because the accident had taken place soon after, you might have said *because of*, the Encounter. Waldo had been too angry, too upset after running into the last people he wanted to see, their children too, a memorial to all those who had contributed towards their embodiment. Waldo recognized for instance in her granddaughter Mrs. Feinstein's ridiculous nose, in Mr. Saporta's son the promise of the father's manly shoulders, and in both her children Dulcie's eyes, Dulcie's eyes, in less commanding, more supplicatory mood. More nostalgic still was the absence of those qualities with which Waldo might have endowed the children he had not got with Dulcie.

Dulcie herself was quick to destroy nostalgia.

"If I met a ghost in Pitt Street I'd be more inclined to believe! But it's you, Waldo—or isn't it?"

She did not touch him, but looked as though she would have liked to, as she started to break up into laughter. Dulcie fizzed. It came spluttering unconvincingly out of her middle-aged body, dressed in what he remembered afterwards as affluent black, in no way remarkable except that it made her look hotter. Out of the dress her neck, thicker than before, rose reddening and congesting. She was embarrassed no doubt by the presence of the ox her husband.

Saporta stood smiling in the manner of those men who will never have anything of importance to say and in its absence hopefully allow goodwill to ooze out of the pores of their faces. He had despised Saporta from the beginning, but what Waldo was now ashamed to realize was that he, too, had nothing to say. He was smiling more widely than any boy inescapably face to face with kind friends of his parents.

Then he said, "Oh, I'm real enough—Dulcie." It made him cough, his smile teetered, and it was most fortunate he saved himself, in his arrested state, from adding: Touch me and see.

In any case the Saportas would have been too stupid to grasp the full extent of any such banality. He was glad. Because everything about him was temporarily so unlike him.

"Are you well, Waldo? I hope you are well. At least you *look* well," Dulcie babbled with the greatest ease. She had become, evidently, one of those women.

Waldo could have told her one or two things about mental anguish, but did not wish to involve himself. It was significant, he thought, looking at her, at her heavy moustache—he had been right—and the glistening buckle of her strong teeth, that she did not inquire after *Arthur*'s health.

Saporta began rocking on his heels, in his waisted, too blue pinstripe, too much shirt-cuff showing, too obviously check—in fact what you would have expected.

Saporta said, "Why don't you come out and see us? We're still out at Centennial Park—the old people's house. Come out and have a bite of tea."

It would have stuck in Waldo's throat. Saporta did not add: Come out, *both of you*—though the eyes, half sharp, half dreamy, wholly Jewish, and *brown*, seemed to express it.

Waldo said, "Thank you. It would be very nice."

He could feel his awful smile returning. At least the sun was on his side. The sun was a battering-ram.

And what about the children? They stood looking too neat, too well behaved, for the moment docile, whatever springs might be waiting coiled inside them.

"These are the children," Waldo said, because one had to.

The little girl, dangling a miniature handbag, tinkled with tiny golden earrings. The boy, older, stood looking up. The beige flannel circles round his eyes, Dulcie's eyes, would have turned them into targets if Waldo hadn't been the target.

"The children." Waldo did not exactly gasp.

"Yes," said Dulcie Saporta.

And at once she began throbbing and vibrating, her black dress trickling and flashing with the steel beads he seemed to remember on her mother. Dulcie put a hand on the girl's head, and the three of them, the four even, because you could not separate Saporta from his flesh, the four then, transcended their own vulgarity.

"Looks as though we've got an intelligent boy," Saporta said. "This other one, this monster, is a woman. She only thinks about running around."

Jokey. At this juncture Waldo would not have trusted himself to retaliate.

"What are they called?" he asked instead.

"The girl is Lynette," Dulcie said, as though nobody would ever question it. "The boy," she continued, and stopped.

Waldo, who was tingling with certainty, could feel the tears starting not even ridiculously behind his pince-nez. All moisture was delicious, voluptuous, redeeming, as he waited for his certainty to be confirmed by the cello notes of Dulcie's voice. In the blazing sun a green shade of white hydrangeas had begun to dissolve the mounting beauty of Dulcie's face.

"Yes. The boy," Waldo blared; it was more confident than a question.

Still Dulcie hesitated, either from excessive sensibility, or because she was one of those wives who finally expect their husbands to deal with the difficult matters. So Saporta, an ox, but a benign one, heaved and said, "The boy we called Arthur."

The sun taking aim fulfilled its function of battery—in reverse. Waldo was staggered. Perhaps after all the children were not the coiled springs he had feared, rather the innocent objects of a discussion, for they were looking frightened.

Dulcie too, though not innocent, was visibly, was deservedly frightened.

"Are you well, Waldo?" she had returned to asking. "You are not *looking* well. The sun. Let us go into Bergers' for a little—they'll give us a chair—till it passes."

Saporta put a meaty hand.

"Thank you," Waldo said, only then, and only to Dulcie. "I can't spare the time for illness."

Then he made his dash. He had to escape to somewhere, away from all those who had possessed while ignoring him over the years. Nothing would have stopped him, though Dulcie did run after him half a block, to use the advantage of her eyes at the point of their overflowing.

His voice flew fatuously into a higher register.

"No, Dulcie!" he was fluting over his shoulder. "What need is there to argue, to explain, when we all understand the situation? Arthur perhaps, *my* Arthur, is the only one who won't. Or does he?"

After all that had happened, he couldn't have dragged Arthur in, if Arthur wasn't the chief of those who had possessed him, and also perhaps to hurt Dulcie, to force some secret unhappiness into the open, to push it over the brink.

Only he had not dared wait long enough to see, but raced off down Pitt Street, catching his toe in a grating, recovering, sticking out his jaw, a pronounced one in its delicate way. All down Pitt Street he raced, past the stationers' shops, through a smell of pies. The stiff collar he still made a point of wearing to the Library, his butterfly collar, was melting. Although not of the latest, there is a period at which anybody's style is inclined to set, Waldo Brown liked to think, in timelessness.

Then, every one of his bones was breaking. He was lying on the melting tar, immovable amongst the timeless faces, trying to remember what his intentions could have been. But he was unable. Intentions exist only in time.

"Give me my spect—my glasses," he was able to order.

Perhaps if he saw better he would see.

They handed him his pince-nez. It was broken.

Just how bloody an accident he was he could not tell, because blood and tar are similarly sticky, nor could he see whether the blur of sympathy was hardening into contempt or that fleshy slab of hostility.

He was feeling around, then allowing himself to be felt. He was lifted drifting in the extra-corporeal situation in which he found himself placed.

When he could experience distaste again he knew that Arthur was approaching. Somebody, a sister, from the volume of starch, the stir of authority, was leading his brother down the ward. He could tell from the way enamel was clattering, hangings twitching.

"Mr. Brown," said the sister, "your twin brother."

It sounded spaced out in a smile.

"Only for a couple of minutes. And you," she said to Arthur, "mustn't be upset, because Mr. Brown isn't really hurt."

If she only knew.

Who had inflicted Arthur on him? Somebody well-meaning, or sadistic, from the Library, he could only suppose.

"You must pull yourself together," the sister was saying. "I can see you know how to."

Because at first Arthur was so upset. Waldo could feel rather than hear his brother gibbering and blubbing. Waldo did not want to hear.

Finally, from behind his eyelids, he could sense Arthur subsiding.

Arthur asked, "Did they give you oxygen, Waldo, on the way?"

"There was no need," Waldo replied.

At least that was the answer it was decided he should give, always from behind those merciful walls, his eyelids.

"If you were to die," Arthur was saying, "I know how to fry myself eggs. There's always the bread. I could live on bread-and-milk. I have my job, haven't I? Haven't I, Waldo?"

"Yes," said Waldo.

"I might get a dog or two for company."

Arthur's anxiety began, it seemed, to heave again.

"But who'll put the notice in the paper?" he gasped. "The *death* notice!"

"Nobody to read it," Waldo suggested.

"But you gotta put it," Arthur said. "I know! I'll ask Dulcie! Dulcie'll do it!"

So relieved to find himself saved.

When the sister came and led Arthur away, Waldo knew from the passage of air and the gap which was left. His eyelids no longer protected him. He was crying for Dulcie, he would have liked to think, only it would not have been true. He was crying for Arthur, for Arthur or himself.

"That time you almost died," said Arthur.

They were struggling against the Barranugli Road.

"When you might have, but didn't," Arthur gulped.

"No! The point is: I didn't, I didn't!"

Waldo had perhaps shrieked. The two blue dogs sank their heads between their shoulders.

Waldo had shrunk inside his oilskin, which was so stiff it could have continued standing on its own.

"People die," he said, "usually in one of two ways. They are either removed against their will, or their will removes them."

"What about our father?"

Waldo did not want to think about that.

"That was certainly different," he admitted. "In the p-past," he stammered, "I think some people simply died."

"Oh dear, this walk is pointless!" Arthur began to mutter. "Can't you see? What are we doing? Can't we turn?"

"Yes," said Waldo. "It is pointless."

So they turned, and the two old dogs were at once joyful. They tossed their sterns in the air, and cavorted a little. Their tongues lolled on their grinning teeth. One of the dogs farted, and turned to smell whether it was he.

The two brothers walking hand in hand back back up along the Barranugli Road did not pause to consider who was who. They took it for granted it had been decided for them at birth, and at least Waldo had begun to suspect it might not be possible for one of them to die without the other.

His father's was the first death Waldo literally had to face—for that matter, the only one, as Mother was taken to the home and at the end he was able to avoid her death-mask. So the first remained the only occasion, which was probably why he had always been disinclined to remember. He was the first to discover, though not the first to announce, for the obvious reason that Waldo had always recoiled from explosions, and what is the announcement of death but the unpleasantest of all explosions?

It was early morning too, which made it worse, the light that gentler dandelion before the metal starts to clang. Arthur was down milking the cow. He had to milk, separate, and grab his breakfast before leaving for the store. Waldo by then was working at Sydney Municipal Library, and had decided on his type. He was the neat, the conscientious type, tie knotted rather small, the expanding armbands restraining the sleeves of his poplin shirt (white). Mostly, as on *the* morning, he would go outside, walk round the house neither fast nor slow once or twice, or into what they called the orchard, before putting on his coat. His usually nondescript hair glittered with sunlight, and the brilliantine, of which the normally too synthetic scent was oddly convincing amongst the real smells of early morning. Reality is so often less convincing, unless involvement such as Waldo was at that moment experiencing translates it into a work of art. There were many sensations, many sights he felt he might transfer to a notebook if only they would grow more distinct. (Waldo by this period had written several articles, there was the fragment of a novel, and he had joined the Fellowship of Australian Writers.) He had already written in his notebook: "Death is the last of the chemical actions," and although, like all great truths, it sounded familiar, he had no reason to believe it was the fruit of someone else's mind.

Then, on that morning of dew and light, Waldo Brown found himself looking through the window, into the room in which their father kept his nights, dark still, with the reek of saltpetre from the papers the old man used to burn on account of the asthma he developed in the years preceding his retirement. George Brown, as the boys referred to him in fun, was stuck at the table where usually he sat out the darkness. His knees were most irregularly, not to say uglily, placed. He had laid his head on the table, where, it seemed, he had not been able to get it lower. So his outstretched hand was protesting, if not his other dangling one.

It would not at first trickle through Waldo Brown's mind that their father was dead. It was too much an outrage against habit. But facts are facts. And Waldo Brown respected facts as much as he respected habit. Suddenly, that which would not trickle, gushed.

Immediately Waldo went away—he had to—deeper into the garden, where the prairie-grass pierced the serge trousers he had pressed that night under the mattress. He stood picking off a leaf or two, waiting for somebody else to handle an intolerable situation.

In the circumstances, as he stood picking at the quince leaves, it was a minor shock to notice the hairs on his man's wrist, when he had shrunk up inside his man's body. Without the reminder of his wrist the boy inside him might have remained in possession. And Miss Huxtable, of intellectual doubts, had asked him only that Tuesday his opinion of Sheila Kaye-Smith. He had given it, too, in sternest terms.

It made him look over his shoulder, wondering whether he would ever be accepted again, at the Library where he was a man strutting, or by his family, who must by now have known the worst. Or had realized and forgotten. That was the virtue of families, their willingness or determination to forget.

When the morning, that golden vacuum, was filled even quicker than he had expected.

Arthur, apparently, had come up from the milking, gone through the house to ask or tell something, then run through the hall in a slither of linoleum, and erupted onto the veranda. There he stood, in front of the still quivering fly-screen door, under the classical pediment which their father had demanded, and where Arthur himself, years ago, had conceived his first tragedy. Now this one was actual. The greasy old rag with which he washed the cow's tits twitched where his fingers ended.

He was bellowing.

"Our father," he bellowed, "our father is *dead*!" His eyes were swivelling, his crop of orange hair stared. "Waldo?" he cried, looking at his brother coming up the path, quickly, wirily, to share their grief.

Arthur's annunciation, blared out in brass despair, had freed Waldo. They were wringing the grief out of each other on the wormy old veranda. If he knew of his defection Waldo believed his brother would never refer to it—Arthur was too dependent on him —but could he be sure of their mother? With Arthur supporting him, physically at least, Waldo wondered.

He heard her fumbling through the house, breaking it open, flinging back the frail doors, to arrive at the disaster of her life, forgetting that her marriage had been just this. He dreaded that she might burst too precipitately into that dark room and call for him to confirm that what had happened had truly happened.

But when she came, pushing against the rusty gauze, she was in possession of something they might not be able to grasp, and he resented that too. What had happened had no connection, finally, with her children. What had happened had happened already many times, and concerned only her.

So their mother appeared to ignore them. Although she wore the rather frowzy dressing-gown, which bacon fat had spotted, and spilt porridge hardened on, she was clothed essentially in grief. She could still have been soothing his withered leg. Which she had accepted in the beginning out of pity. Which had now been taken from her by force. So her arms hung. So she went on down the steps, her red-roughened chest ending where the secrecy of white breast began.

Waldo followed her because she was technically their mother. Whereas their mother crossed Terminus Road because she was their father's widow.

Mrs. Poulter could have been expecting Mrs. Brown. She came down quickly out of her house. Mrs. Poulter was already a woman filling out, and prepared to pounce heavily on possible disaster.

Mrs. Poulter said, "Oh dear, don't tell me! If there is anything I can do!"

She had begun to whimper. If she did not embrace Mrs. Brown it was because she was afraid to. Mrs. Brown was too erect and cold.

"It's my husband, Mrs. Poulter. I should like to ring for the doctor. If you will allow me. Though we must realize nothing can be done."

Her pure, inherited voice erected a barrier between herself and not only Mrs. Poulter, but those she had conceived in an adulterated tradition. Though Waldo could imitate voices, even adapt himself to situations, if they didn't threaten to extinguish his individuality.

So he said now, "Wait, Mother. Let me see to it."

It appeared to convince, because she stopped where she was with Mrs. Poulter. Nobody but Waldo, and he only in passing, was surprised at his sung command, his *Rigoletto*-tenor tones. After briefly rehearsing the part, he was running springily in, ignoring Bill Poulter in his own house.

"George Brown, Terminus Road." He was telling the receiver of a man who had died.

The carefully phrased words forced his lips into a smile. He was seducing himself, not the telephone. Just as Dulcie, for a moment in the beginning, in the living room at *Mount Pleasant*, had been seduced by the same silky tenor voice.

When he turned he was not surprised to find Bill Poulter looking frightened. While Waldo himself was loving his own moustache with the tip of his tongue.

He went outside, if not muscular, slim and supple, to where his mother was waiting with that woman. Mother and son crossed the road naturally enough, though in silence, because words were unnecessary, and without his touching her, because they seemed years ago to have come to an agreement not to touch.

He could hear her slippers in the dust, her old blue woollen dressing-gown dragging through the damp grass on the verge of the road.

Arthur's blurry face, which strangers often found disturbing, was waiting for them on the veranda where they had left him, his skin still smeared, though drying. And Mother went up the steps to Arthur, suddenly quicker than Waldo could account for. In the present unsettling circumstances of course she would feel she must comfort somebody afflicted like Arthur, who in many ways had remained her little boy. But Arthur, he saw, was holding their mother. She was looking not so much at him, as to him, into his blurry face, which perhaps was less confused than it should have been.

Waldo was trembling for unsuspected possibilities. Standing above him, his brother appeared huge.

If only he could have focussed on Arthur's face to see what Mother was looking for. Because whatever it was she might find would soon be buried in words. The little boy on the step below stood craning up, wriggling his nervous white worm of a neck, to see. But could not. The sun was shining on his glasses.

"We'll have to have our breakfast, anyway. Won't we?" Arthur was gobbling.

"Yes, darling," Mother agreed.

Waldo had never heard her sound so natural.

"You shall get it for me." She sighed. "Wouldn't you like that?"

Because in a crisis, Waldo admitted, Arthur had to be humoured.

"Shall we have milk for a change? Warm milk?" Arthur suggested. "That would be good and soothing, wouldn't it?"

It was quite an idea.

Soon they were holding in their hands the chipped, while still elegant, porcelain bowls with the pattern of little camomile sprigs, which they had brought out with them from Home.

"When the doctor gets here I'd better be making tracks," Arthur mentioned anxiously, looking at his watch, at Mother. "Allwrights'll be wondering what's come over me."

"I'd hoped you would stay with us," Mother said, "today." She added quickly, without looking round, "I'm sure Waldo would appreciate it."

As though her little boy Waldo would take for granted anything she might arrange for him with his big brother. Naturally Waldo was grateful. Somebody would ring the Library.

So he continued watching Mother as she smoothed back Arthur's moist hair, looking into Arthur's face, into the avenue she hoped to open up. Finally Waldo saw them only indistinctly, because he had deliberately taken his glasses off.

Their father, then, was dead. Encouraged by his death, Waldo was often tempted to re-enter his own boyhood. He was only beginning to learn about it, and even where there were flaws in the past, they fascinated, like splinters in the flesh.

There was no reason why visitors should have guessed at the flaws in Waldo Brown. His confidence appeared firm without being aggressive. His hair was so *candid*. He would take water to it, and brush it carefully down; it was only later on that he felt the need for brilliantine. During his boyhood strangers were moved by the streaks of water in his innocently plastered boy's hair.

He was growing up taller and straighter than had been expected. His long, bony, usually ink-stained wrist was exposed by the retreating sleeve. Because he was growing too fast. His shirt-cuffs would not button and frayed at the edges. Naturally they couldn't afford to buy him so many clothes so often.

He developed into a Promising Lad. Although weak in mathematics, his gift for composition persisted as vocabulary increased to decorate it. There was some mystery of literary ambitions, which his parents scarcely mentioned, through shame or fear, or simply because they didn't believe. (Waldo began to suspect parents remain unconscious of a talent in their child unless you rub their noses in it.)

They were proud of him, though, especially when he jumped up, in his just buttonable knickerbockers, to offer a plate of scones without being prodded. Strangers compared him with potty Arthur, who would have scoffed the lot. Big lump of a thing sitting on a creaking stool, knees under his chin, crumbs tumbling down his chin onto his knees. Munching. Beside the promising Waldo, Arthur tended to fade out. Began to work for Allwright, both behind the counter and in the sulky, delivering the orders, after Allwright taught him to drive. Arthur was good with animals; it was perhaps natural for them to accept someone who was only half a human being. It was sad for Browns, not to say a real handicap to a fine boy like Waldo, who, they said, was the twin of the other, you wouldn't believe it. You'd see them sometimes walking down the road together of an evening, Waldo in the Barranugli High hatband, carrying his school case, Arthur shambling in the old pair of pants and shirt he wore to work at the store, because you couldn't expect the parents to spend good money on an outfit just for that.

Anyway, there they were. Two twins. You wondered what they talked about.

Waldo knew it all by heart from listening—even when he couldn't hear.

So they moved through the landscape of boyhood, two figures seen at a distance, or too close up, so close you could look into the pores of their skin, you could see the blackheads and the pimples. Waldo hated that. He hated his interminable pimply face. He preferred to listen to the voices of strangers murmuring what they had decided were the truths. How they would have jumped if they had seen him pop a pimple at the face of the glass. People did not go for pus. So he learned to give them what they wanted. Occasionally, in passing, after returning the scones to the table, he would very carefully brush the crumbs which had fallen on Arthur's knees, with a candid though unostentatious charity which moved the observer—as well as the performer. Quite genuinely, once he had performed the act. Funny old Arthur was no more funny than your own flesh suffering an unjust and unnecessary torment.

Because Arthur was part of his own parcel of flesh it was easy with Arthur. Less so with Dad. With Dad it was downright difficult, not to say painful at times, particularly during those years when Waldo was going in to the High. There was no escaping his father. They travelled together in the train, one way at least.

Seeing them off in the early light that first morning, Mother said, "You will have each other for company."

They had. Each used to walk carefully. Going up the road, Waldo remembered how their father, to amuse, had told them about the bank messengers in London, in their top hats, the bag chained to a wrist. Later on, when the custom of the walk to the station had been established, and it was not always possible to shorten it by visiting the dunny or remembering books, Waldo felt in his bitterest moments he would have died willingly while performing his regular act of duty. With Arthur it was different. There was no escaping Arthur. At best he became the sound of your own breathing, his silences sometimes consoled. But you might have thought of an escape from Dad, if you had been cleverer, or brutal. Fathers are no more than the price you have to pay for life, the tickets of admission. Life, as he began in time to see it, is the twin consciousness, jostling you, hindering you, but with which, at unexpected moments, it is possible to communicate in ways both animal and delicate. So Waldo resented his twin's absence and freedom as he walked with their father between the throng of weeds up Terminus Road, George Brown lashing out with his gammy leg to keep up with the son holding back for him.

On one occasion Dad said, "You run on ahead, old man. I'll take my time."

And Waldo had. Literally. Spurted up the road on twisting ankles, arms jerking, books thundering in his half-empty case.

Afterwards when they were seated whiter together in the train, they hadn't spoken, but probably wouldn't have anyway.

Dad, who had been good for stories for little boys, myths of ancient Greece and Rome, to say nothing of recitations from Shakespeare, grew silenter in the face of silence. He had taken up Norwegian, to "read Ibsen in the original," or to protect himself in the train. Waldo used to watch the words forming visibly under the raggeder moustache. Dad leaned his head against the leather and closed his eyes. The eyelids looked their nakedest. For many years Waldo could not come at Ibsen, out of respect for the private language in which he had written.

Dad, though, was not unaware, so it seemed, painfully, of some of the responsibilities he shirked. Laying down *Teach Yourself Norwegian* on the seat of the Barranugli train, he opened his eyes one morning and said, "Waldo, I've been meaning to have a talk. For some time. About certain things. About, well, life. And so forth."

The spidery train was clutching at the rails. The smuts flew in, to sizzle on Waldo's frozen skin.

"Because," continued George Brown, "I expect there are things that puzzle you."

Nhoooh! Waldo might have hooted if the engine hadn't beaten him to it.

It wasn't the prospect of his father's self-exposure which was shaking him. It was the train, shaking out every swollen image he had ever worked on.

"The main thing," said Dad, sucking his sparrow-coloured moustache, "is to lead a decent—a life you—well, needn't feel ashamed of."

O Lord. Waldo had not been taught to pray, because, said Mother, everything depends on your own will, it would be foolishness to expect anything else, we can achieve what we want if we are determined, if we are confident that we are strong.

And here was George Brown knotting together the fingers which had learnt to handle the pound notes so skilfully. Who had nothing to feel ashamed of. Except perhaps his own will.

O Lord. The Barranugli train bellowed like a cow in pastures not her own.

"For instance, all these diseases." George Brown found himself looking at his own flies. He looked away.

Waldo, though he did not want to, could not help looking at his father, at the sweat shining on the yellow edge of his celluloid collar.

"There's a bit of advice, Waldo," he was saying, "I'd like to give any boy. You can't be too careful of these lavatory seats. I mean, the public lavatories. You can develop, well, a technique of balance. And avoid a lot of trouble. That way."

When he had sweated it out George Brown turned again to *Teach Yourself Norwegian.* Waldo could recognize by then the shapes of the repeated phrases: *Hun hoppet i sjøen.*[1] . . . *Han merket det og reddet henne.*[2] . . . *Jeg har spart penger for a kjøpe en gave til min søster.*[3] . . . Because Dad had frightened, then embarrassed him, which was worse, he grew angry. He began to relate the solemn idiocy of the recited words to the unrelenting motion of the train. He would have liked to shout: A pox on old lavatory seats! Or worse—the scribbled words he had seen on walls. He sat looking sideways at his father. *Min* bloody *søster!* He sat there, muttering, "I fucked my auntie Friday night."

In the varnished box in which they were sitting, George Brown shifted on the parched leather, while holding down the pages of the book the draught was agitating. *Hun hoppet i sjøen. . . . Han*

[1] She jumped into the sea.
[2] He noticed it and saved her.
[3] I have saved money to buy a present for my sister.

merket det . . . It looked as though the only way was to memorize.

While Waldo, it seemed, was all memory and brutal knowledge. Tell me, Dad—he was tempted to make a challenge of it—tell me something I don't *know!*

The raucous train gave to the unuttered words the cracked accents of insolence. The more scornfully Waldo rocked, the more the obscene upholstery swelled, in contours of bulbous women and opulent crutches of purple men. One serge gorilla, tufted with orange hair, passed his gold-and-ruby ring under a corseted bum in Shadbolt Lane. No man is all that attractive, she said, that there isn't a copy or two of him about. The man called her his copy-cat, and both laughed to bust their guts, to split the narrow stairs up which they were feeling their way.

Night thoughts, struggling from under the cestrum, floated on the surface, bloated and gloating. The cestrum was at its scentiest at night, filling, and swelling, and throbbing, and spilling, while all the time rooted at a distance in its bed. Its branches creaked, though, enough for Arthur to breathe your dreams.

Sitting in the train, Waldo suddenly looked straight into his father's face. The train sniggered smuttily. Waldo might have leant back to continue enjoying the escape he had made, if his clothes' tightening hadn't constrained him, together with the fear that freedom might be the equivalent of isolation. So that in the end he would have liked to touch his father's goodness, but could only be touched by it. His narrow body began not exactly to shiver, it was the train, running them over the outskirts of Barranugli, past the seeding docks and rusty tins, the tethered goats, and, in their back yards, women whose pale skins still showed traces of night and mutton fat.

Dad was stuffing his book into his pocket—Dad alone must have kept the pocket editions going—and they were getting out at Barranugli. Amongst the other arrivals at the station Waldo usually saw to it that they drew apart gradually, to avoid what, for both of them, would have been the embarrassment of saving goodbye.

If George Brown threw away *Teach Yourself Norwegian* it was

not because he no longer needed it. He could never rely on himself
to sit in the train without a book. He began *Thus Spake Zarathu-
stra* and, shortly after, went over to *The Autocrat of the Breakfast
Table*, which he had picked up, he was proud to tell, the one for
ninepence, the other for sixpence, second-hand.

As far as Waldo was concerned the journey to Barranugli repeated itself for more than years. Towards the end, not by choice,
he was growing his first moustache. The truth was, they wouldn't
give him the money for a razor to shave it off.

"Arr, why?" he shouted at them angrily, in the house which had
grown too small for him.

His father put on his gravest expression, and said in his most
prudent voice, "Men who start shaving too early always regret it.
Besides," he said, "at your age most young fellows get a lot of en-
joyment out of cultivating a moustache. Moustaches are in fashion, I would have thought."

Waldo looked at his father. It was bad enough to be a twin
without having to identify himself in other ways.

Mother, who was mending, had to try to smoothe things over.

"You wouldn't want to turn into one of those *blue* men," she
said, "who are all shadow by five o'clock."

"I'm not that colour," Waldo said. "I'm not a dago."

"That is not a word," said Dad, "I ever want to hear in my
house."

And Mother's fingers started trembling. Later on, when she was
ill, and fanciful, and old, Anne Brown, born a Quantrell, said to
her sons absently, "It was for his principles, I suppose. And kindness. Poor George, he was too kind. It left him too often open to
attack. And I, yes, I grew tough, I think. It often happens that the
wives of kind men grow tough and stringy protecting them."

For the present, a victim of their unconcern, Waldo could do
nothing about himself. He could not afford a razor, so he cherished
his resentment in unfrequented corners, his pulses raging, nursing
his threadbare elbows. (His school things had to "do.")

Arthur said, "Don't worry, Waldo. Lots of people like a moustache. Let me feel."

He might have done it, if Waldo hadn't shouldered him off.

The great lump. Arthur's fingers smelled of aniseed and honey.

Waldo shouted, "You stink!"

Nothing was said by anyone else because so much had been said already.

"I think Dulcie," said Arthur, "will probably grow a moustache. I like Dulcie."

"Who?" Waldo shouted worse.

"That girl."

"You know nothing about *any* girl!"

Nor did Waldo. Nor did he want to. He hated almost everyone, but, above all, his family. They knew too much and not enough about one another.

But they were proud of Waldo. While remaining weak at maths, he carried off prizes for other subjects. He had *Idylls of the King*, and *Travels with a Donkey*, and Tacitus in two volumes. He even read them. He was always reading books, but because Dad was the reader in the family he did most of it furtively.

Most of what he did he did secretly, as though making a secret of his acts gave them a special importance. It was only too bad that more people were not in the secret, for in the circumstances he could only appear important to himself. And Arthur. Arthur hardly commented when Waldo read beside a shielded lamp half the night, or in the dunny, or copied extracts into notebooks, but it was natural for Arthur to accept a twin brother's secret life. Perhaps Arthur even had a secret life of his own, but necessarily of such simplicity you did not stop to think about, let alone enter, it.

On one occasion Arthur paused in some involved, though unimportant, activity as Waldo was sitting with a sheet of paper, his hand held to protect it, like a wall.

Arthur felt the need to ask, "What are you doing, Waldo?"

When he had considered long enough, Waldo answered, "I am writing."

"What about?" Arthur asked.

"I don't know," Waldo answered, truthfully.

But Arthur was never deterred by vagueness of any description, or absence of trust.

"I hope it will be good," he said, and smiled.

To satisfy his curiosity, the expression implied, was less important than his brother's self-fulfilment.

Waldo's throat could have wobbled for some repeated hurt he had to suffer. If he had not been so importantly occupied he might have felt mortified as well. As it was, he accepted the wounds inflicted on him by circumstances—or his own nature. He accepted Arthur his twin brother, who was, as they put it, a shingle short.

So the lives of the brothers fused by consent at some points. Arthur's harsh blaze of hair would soften in certain lights, drenching his expression in that secrecy of innocence. Partly his white skin helped, though more than partly, his simplicity. It explained why Arthur would suddenly take leave of his face.

Whenever it happened Waldo could only allow himself to feel irritated as opposed to annoyed.

"Get along, then!" he used to say. "I've got to concentrate."

As Arthur continued hanging round.

"All right"—he could be so reasonable—"I *am* rather clumsy, aren't I? I do barge around and knock things over. But sometimes those things are standing in my way."

Waldo frowned, and stared at the paper. When Arthur went out of the room he wouldn't have any excuse left.

"I'll go, then," Arthur promised sweetly. "I hope you think of something interesting."

Other people continued to reduce Waldo's intentions and make them appear foolishly capricious, if not downright idiotic. They did not grasp the extent of his need to express some *thing*. Otherwise how could he truly say: I exist. The prospect of remaining a nonentity like the schoolteachers or his parents made him sweat behind the knees.

Perhaps it was through his, you could not say *wilfully* abnormal, behavior that other people in the end got wind of his secret intentions. His mother, for instance. She herself would put on a kind of milky smile and walk softly, as though he were sick or something. Then in his presence she began to make mention of "Waldo's writing," but so discreetly that for a long time no caller dared infringe on her discretion.

Finally Mother foolishly said, "One day, Waldo, you must tell me about your Writing."

It was too much.

If no comment was made by Dad, the reader in the family, who sat there in painful attitudes, pushing his bad leg in yet some other direction, rereading *Religio Medici, Sesame and Lilies,* and then *Essays in the Study of Folk-Songs* by the Countess Martinengo-Cesaresco, which the other day he had picked up cheap—if Dad seemed unaware behind his eyebrows and his sucked moustache that anything unusual was going on, it was because their father, Waldo was suddenly convinced, had failed to be a writer.

To the end of his life Waldo cultivated his gift for distinguishing failures. With the exception of Johnny Haynes, about whom he couldn't make up his mind, he was particularly sensitive to those failures who had been dumped in the long grass at what was called Sarsaparilla. Sars-per-illa! Had a history in the early days, they told you. Then, apparently, history drew in her horns. There was Allwrights' store, and the post office stuck in the side of Mrs. Purves's house. There were the cow cockies and market gardeners. There were the homes of the aged, the eccentric, the labourers, the rich, though the last hardly counted, existing only spasmodically on kept lawns, amongst their shrubs, in varnished dog-carts, or, in Mrs. Musto's case, behind the windscreen of a motor car. It was really the grass that had control at Sarsaparilla, deep and steaming masses of it, lolling yellow and enervated by the end of summer. As for the roads, with the exception of the highway, they almost all petered out, first in dust, then in paddock, with dollops of brown cow manure—or grey spinners—and the brittle spires of seeded thistles.

When his thoughts grew too much for him, too blurred, or too entangled, his mind a choked labyrinth without a saving thread, Waldo Brown would stalk along the county roads, exchanging his own blurred world for that other, dusty, external, but no more actual one, in which he continued hoping to discover a distinct form, some object he hadn't noticed before, while Arthur kicking up the dust behind—it was impossible to escape Arthur unless Arthur himself chose to escape—conducted his monologue, if not dialogue with dust or sun, peewee or green-sprouted cow turd. Like injustice, the dust always recurred to daze, unless, from a sudden mushroom of it, Mrs. Musto's chariot unwound, honking by her orders to warn pedestrians of her coming.

Stubbens, her chauffeur, did not like honking.

"But if you've got one," she used to insist.

Everything was geared to Mrs. Musto's orders.

"You boys care for a lift?" she would call when she had pulled Stubbens up. "By ghost, isn't it hot, eh? Hot enough to burn the parson's nose!"

Because she was so rich—Fairy Flour—it was accepted that Mrs. Musto should speak so authentically. Her chauffeur Stubbens never turned a hair.

When you had wrenched the door open—Stubbens didn't open doors for boys—and climbed, pulling Arthur, somehow, up, it was coolly awful to sit beside Mrs. Musto in her motor overwhelmed by her appurtenances: the green veil, which did not prevent her adding to her freckles, the too collapsible parasol, the alpaca cape, prayer book; and smelling-salts; on longer journeys, it was said—though Waldo had never travelled far enough in Mrs. Musto's company—cold plum pudding and a bottle of port wine.

When they were seated Mrs. Musto would give her usual command: "Wind 'er up, Stubbens"—and to the objects of her kindness, as Stubbens wound and wound: "Hold yer ribs, boys, or he'll crack a couple for yer!"

She loved perpetual motion, and clergymen, and presents—to give rather than receive, though one so rich as Mrs. Musto naturally received a lot. She loved to eat rich food, surrounded by those who condescended to call her their friend, after which she would drop off in the middle of a sentence, to revive, burping, in the middle of another. Music was her grandest passion, which did not prevent her snoring through it, but she could always be relied upon to applaud generously at the end. And sometimes she would organize tennis parties for those she referred to as the "youngsters." Youngsters, Mrs. Musto used to say, are my investment against old age.

Mrs. Brown once remarked she hoped the market would not let Mrs. Musto down.

But somehow Mother did not altogether care for Mrs. Musto, who had "known about the Browns" in the beginning. She could not bear Mrs. Musto's kindness.

"Oh, but she *is* so kind!" Mother used to sigh. "One can't deny it. I will not hear a word against the poor thing, though she is—one must face it—what I call a soloist."

Certainly Mrs. Musto loved to talk. In fact, talk was another of her grand passions.

"What are mouths given us for? Yairs, I know—food. Lovely, too. Within everybody's reach in a country like Australia. Give me a good lump of corned beef, with a nice slice of yellow fat, and a boiled onion. Ooh, scrumptious! There are, of course, other things besides. But never forget one in remembering the other. As I said to the Archbishop, it doesn't pay, never ever, not even an evangelical, to neglect the flesh altogether. The Archbishop was of my opinion. But She—*She*—She's not only a poor doer, she's clearly starving 'erself to make sure of a comfy passage to the other side. As I didn't hesitate to tell 'er. But as I was saying—what was I saying? Conversation is the prime purpose this little slit was given us for—to communicate in *words*. We are told: 'In the beginning was the Word.' Which sort of proves, don't it?"

She had a snub nose you could look right up.

"In the beginning was what word?" Arthur asked, seated on that beaded stool, looking up Mrs. Musto's nose.

"Why," she said, "the Word of God!"

"Oh," said Arthur. "God."

He might have started to argue, or at least to wonder aloud, but fortunately stopped short, lowering his thick eyelids as if to prevent others from calculating the distance to which he had withdrawn.

Mother was holding her head on one side, smiling at something, not necessarily Mrs. Musto. She had also turned slightly red. Waldo knew he was the only one of those present who understood the reason why, which made him contemptuous of other people's stupidity and proud of his alliance with Mother. He might even have admitted his father to their circle of enlightenment if Dad had walked in.

As it was too early, Waldo continued looking at Mother. He hadn't quite the courage to laugh but, even so, felt delightfully unencumbered and superior.

All told, Ma Musto wasn't such a bad stick. The timid protested that she bullied them. Certainly she bullied her men of God into

preaching what she wished to hear. Nobody remembered her husband, or knew whether she had ordered him out of existence so that
she might enjoy a breezy widowhood. On the other hand Mrs.
Musto was bullied by her maids and the chauffeur Stubbens who
wouldn't honk.

Stubbens had been a coachman, or groom, and the leggings
moulded to his thick calves suggested horses still. He was an invariably surly man who refused to hear visitors' requests, and those of
his mistress only on their becoming commands. He had trouble in
breathing through one of his nostrils, which forced him to dilate it
from time to time, which gave the impression that Stubbens was
smelling a permanently bad smell. In spite of his shortcomings,
ladies, the more forward ones, complimented Mrs. Musto on her
personable chauffeur. He was, too, in some way. His broad hands,
resting on the wheel, had thickish fingers, the skin of which ended
surprisingly cleanly round the nails.

"He was too long running with the horses to adapt himself to
progress," his mistress would explain, not always out of earshot,
sometimes adding, "Though Stubbens will tell yer the trouble is
he's been too long runnin' *me*."

That the chauffeur did run Mrs. Musto, Waldo discovered by
witnessing.

Mrs. Musto had just dismissed that boy—the brighter of the two
Browns—who had come with a note of thanks from his mother.
Waldo was winding crunching round the gravel drive, when Stubbens came out of the house to where Mrs. Musto had continued
standing, under a cedar, on her perfect lawn. Stubbens was carrying a cardigan. He was wearing the leggings of his office, but for
the first time, Waldo saw him without his cap, in his own crisp,
startlingly silver, hair. He was certainly improved by hair.

But Mrs. Musto had grown used to it, or seemed in no mood to
be startled.

"Southerly's come," Stubbens announced.

"Oh," she said, keeping her heavy back turned, tossing her head
peevishly, more like a girl. "It isn't *cold*," she complained.

"Well, I brought yer woolly," said Stubbens. "So put it on!"

And Mrs. Musto did. She shrugged herself into the sleeves,
without letting him touch her, though.

Mrs. Musto would come out shrugging off the advice or accusations of her servants on the occasions when she entertained. There were the big shivoos with celebrities from Sydney, many of whom had forgotten they had met the hostess; there were the afternoons for local talent; and there were what she herself particularly enjoyed, her parties for "youngsters," to one of which Waldo Brown was asked, only one and not another, not that Mrs. Musto was fickle, she just had to press on. In any case, what was done was done, whether Mrs. Musto realized or not, or Waldo himself, except later and in his sleep. (Awake, he only used to wonder whether Mrs. M. would leave him a hundred pounds in her will.)

Anyway, Waldo was grateful she had issued the invitation with what appeared like thought and care. That was to say: in the holidays, on an afternoon during the week. Though on the morning of the day he didn't know exactly what attitude to take.

"Oh, I shan't *worry*," said Arthur. "I've got my job, haven't I? Mr. Allwright depends on me."

"Yes," said Waldo.

"We have stock-taking," Arthur added ostentatiously.

Then, just before leaving for the store, he came up with something which was on his mind and spat it out, wet: "Tell Mrs. Musto I'm concentrating on words. *The* Word. But also words that are just words. There's so many kinds. You could make necklaces. Big chunks of words, for instance, and the shiny, polished ones. *God*," he said, and the spit spattered on Waldo's face, "is a kind of sort of *rock* crystal."

Waldo was disgusted by his brother's convulsed face and extravagant, not to say idiotic, ideas.

Although this started him off badly, as he approached down Mrs. Musto's winding drive of raked gravel he realized worse was in store for him. He could hear quite plainly the felted sound of tennis balls as they were struck thudding back and forth. The gathering of "youngsters," judging by its numbers, was fully assembled on Mrs. Musto's lawns. There was positively a smell of tennis. The four elect performers, each older than himself, it seemed to Waldo, were also far more adept, more graceful, if not better born, at least wealthier. Young men reaching overhead with their rackets revealed their glorious ribs through transparent shirts. Delicious girls, in pearls of perspiration, appeared to have been at it all their lives as they controlled their skirts in running to dish up a ball.

Waldo was appalled.

He plodded farther, over the rocks of gravel, in the pants he had pressed under the mattress the night before, and the Barranugli High hatband, from which Mother had tried to sponge the sweat mark. He knew that he was poor, pimply, stupid, and if not ragged, definitely frayed.

Mrs. Musto came. She was all in white. She smelled of white.

She said, "Waldo, I'm glad you came. I was beginning to be afraid yer'd found something better. This is Waldo," she announced, "Waldo Brown."

It sounded dreadful.

Several of the initiated youths and maidens compressed their faces in little set expressions of acceptance, as they had been taught.

Then Mrs. Musto took him aside and said, "Look, Waldo, we're all only having fun. I've got a racket for yer inside. It's pretty good, but mightn't be good enough. You'll have to think it over. You look nice. Oh, dear," she complained, stepping back, "we're upsetting the eatables! Whatever will Louie say!"

For during her diplomacy she had knocked a meringue off a trestle table, and had just crushed it with her blancoed toe.

Waldo hoped to withdraw, and did finally, to a less obvious position, behind a grazier of at least twenty, discussing rams with two young ladies worthy of his attention.

"But wool is so important," said one.

"Yes, I realize. But I'd be terrified," the other said, "of rams. I mean, they're sort of curlier, they're less direct than bulls."

Then all three exploded into fruit cup and understanding.

Waldo hated their aggressive white. He envied them the language they spoke. Their eyes grew filmy observing over their shoulders somebody they had not known from childhood.

He went away.

Under the cedars a peacock, perhaps enamelled for the occasion, appeared more approachable, putting up its tail as though to oblige. The thrilling, quivering tail had eyes for Waldo alone. He tried to touch the bird, but it too slipped expertly out of reach.

He had nothing then.

He went and scorched himself with a glass of iced lemonade.

Mrs. Musto was marshalling her pawns.

"Ronald and Dulcie versus Dickie and Enid. There! I call that a match!"

Whether they liked it or not, they were going out for Mrs. Musto's satisfaction.

Dulcie, it appeared, was expected to serve. Her arms were too thin, too pointed at the elbows. Too dark. She was wearing a pink pink dress.

"Who is that?" one of the young ladies asked.

Nobody exactly knew.

Anyway, Dulcie managed to get the ball over the net. Back and forth, forth and back went the felted fated ball.

It was Dulcie's in the end.

Dulcie scooped it.

How it soared its slow white rocket above the black cedars into taut sky returning into ball as it plummeted past the black cedars down. It hit the hard grass. And bounced. It hit Dulcie in her burnt face.

"Who is it?" they asked one another. "In the pink dress?"

No one knew, exactly.

"Coconut ice," suggested a future barrister of whom answers and jokes were expected.

Everybody laughed.

The game finished eventually.

The girl Dulcie came off the court, rubbing, washing her perspiring hands with a screwed-up handkerchief. She felt the need to detach herself from the others. Threw down the racket. Which probably only Waldo guessed was one of the instruments of torture Mrs. Musto kept in the house. Dulcie's fate confirmed his intention not to be made an exhibition of. By Mrs. Musto or anyone else.

Now that he had stopped being afraid he had begun to despise their hostess, along with her kindness, her riches, and her choice of politely insulting guests. Poverty was the only virtue. The girl Dulcie was probably poor. In her pink, as opposed to white, dress. Not that he didn't despise Dulcie as well. In his crusade of bitterness there was room for only one ardent pauper. The girl in pink, besides, was about his own age and might handle too clumsily some of the truths he was anxious to establish.

So he avoided Dulcie. Even when he was looking at her you couldn't have told. Or only Dulcie could have.

She appeared overheated. The uncontrolled tennis ball had plainly branded the side of her face. She was also plain. If not downright ugly. Waldo would have hated to touch her, for fear that she might stick to him, literally, not deliberately but in spite of herself.

Then why was Mrs. Musto bringing Dulcie through the cool ranks of immaculate white initiates who stood about her lawn sipping fruit cup and giggling through the fragments of meringue?

Dulcie was equally mystified but made some attempt at disguising it. Though she looked away, she was smiling and breathing deep. Waldo noticed that her strong teeth formed a prow, as it were, in profile.

"You two, Dulcie and Waldo, ought to find something in common. You are about the same age," Mrs. Musto said—she was as stupid as that. "Aren't yer stoking up?" she asked, looking sideways at the trestles, believing, and in this she was wiser, that food would fill silences.

So Mrs. Musto went away.

Dulcie took and dropped a meringue, which she picked up, dusting off the lawn-clippings. Waldo chose a sandwich, of very thin wet cucumber, because it was nearest to him. He put it in his mouth whole, it was so dainty, and did not notice it after that.

They had nothing to say. Even if he had, he would not have allowed himself, not to this ugly dark girl. If Arthur had been there he would have let Arthur bear the brunt of Dulcie. But they circulated a little, from necessity, and, if nothing else, mere motion lubricated their stiffened minds.

"Do you live here?" she asked at last.

"Yes," he said.

And blushed because he thought perhaps she despised him for something, his clothes, for instance, which he had forgotten about, or his high-school look.

"Do *you* live here?" he asked.

"Yes," she said, and quickly: "No."

She came rasping out with what was intended as punctuating laughter.

"That is," she said, "we have a house here. And come here on and off. When Daddy feels he wants a change of air."

"Funny not having to live at Sarsaparilla," he said, "and wanting to come here."

"I don't see what's funny about it."

He wasn't going to tell her if she didn't realize. It was too long, anyway. He couldn't take an interest in her.

She did not seem in any way put out. She began swinging her thin dark arms. She began humming a tune, leading a life of her own. It irritated him not to recognize the tune, but admittedly he had not yet fully decided whether to develop a talent for music, or whether it might queer his pitch in literature. In the meantime they paid for him to take a lesson once a week from Miss Olive Fischer of Barranugli. He used to stay on after school, gnawing at a trotter on the journey home. Between lessons, if he remembered, he aspired to Schubert on the terrible upright in the living room.

"What does your old man do?" It was time he condescended.

Deliberately he used an expression he had always found repulsive. Now it had the right *coarse* sound, to show what he thought of this Dulcie, and Mrs. Musto and her overcultivated garden.

"He has a music house," she said.

"What," he said, afraid to show his ignorance, "he doesn't print it, does he?"

Now he would have liked to look at her. He had always longed to acquire an intimate intellectual friend, with whom to exchange books, and letters written in the kind of literary style which went with such relationships. If ever it began, he would write two, or perhaps three, letters a day, to express his deepest thoughts. Then would come a pause of several days. That was the way, according to collections of correspondence, he knew it to be done.

"I mean, he isn't a publisher of music, is he?" Waldo asked, inhaling the moistening air of the garden.

"No," she said. "He sells it."

"What? Just music?"

"Instruments as well," she replied with a candid reserve.

She might have been bored, or did not care fully to reveal her father's unimportance and poverty.

"Do you like him?" he asked suddenly.

He really wanted to know.

"Yes," she said, rather high, breathy with what sounded like sincerity.

At the same time she turned towards him and he noticed a dark shadow on her upper lip. It made him bite his own and contract his nostrils.

"Of course I do," she insisted, though in a questioning tone of voice.

"I just wondered," he mumbled.

He wished she would not continue looking at him. She had the eyes, he saw, of certain dogs, and he had never cared for dogs. They were something to be feared, for their treachery, or else despised for stupidity.

"I'd hate not to love my father," Dulcie said. "I can't imagine what it would feel like."

"I don't love mine. I'm fond of him, I suppose, because he's there. And you feel sorry for them."

He was getting some satisfaction out of telling, yes, he had never put much of it into words before, but it was—the truth. He looked at her to see whether she admired him for it.

"You're a queer sort of boy," she said.

At least that was better than being somebody nobody ever noticed. Dulcie was noticing him all right. Those silly, brown, watery eyes.

(Later on when Waldo got to know Dulcie he realized that her brimming eyes were not necessarily a prelude to tears.)

Now she said, "I don't think I'd like to be you."

Quickly, and surprising to himself, he jerked a branch off one of Mrs. Musto's shrubs. And threw it away.

"I wouldn't want you to be," he said, again surprisingly. "I don't like myself all that much."

But gave up because he was stranding himself somewhere he had never been before. And anyway, he was not saying it for this girl; it was only that she was there, and provoked him. He didn't believe all he said, ever.

"You needn't believe it if you don't want to."

"I like to believe what I'm told."

"You'll be caught, then. Sooner or later."

It was the first time he had thought about that too. She had begun to exhilarate him.

"Don't you think we ought to go back?" Dulcie suggested.

He turned, to please her, only taking an oblique path.

"Sometimes I think I'd like to become a great actor." He had never thought it in his life. He had never seen a play, other than the one Arthur had acted on the front veranda. "Wouldn't you like to act out great tragic parts?"

"I'd never be able to. I'd get stage-fright," Dulcie said.

Either she was losing interest or she didn't believe in him.

He would have to try another direction.

"What I really want to do," he said, "is write."

He heard himself make it sound like a natural function. Perhaps it was because, until now, he had shied away from expressing anything so personal and complicated. It would not be possible even to try with Mother or Dad. But in this girl he might be addressing the kind of complicated human being his reading told him did exist.

"Oh," she said, "I like to read. I've just finished *The Mill on the Floss*."

She was looking at him again.

"Maggie Tulliver," he said, to show.

"Yes!" she said, her eyes brimming once more, so it couldn't be with tears.

"A very passionate girl, Maggie," said Waldo Brown, making it sound particularly precise.

Dulcie blushed and withdrew the expression which had been growing on her face.

"What you are going to write," she said, "do you think it will be novels?"

"I haven't decided yet," he said, "what," he said, "what form it'll take. Sometimes I think novels, sometimes plays. It might even be some kind of philosophical work."

He was leading Dulcie back now towards the other members of the party. With things becoming so difficult, he had had to abandon a plan for luring her deeper into the garden by carefully chosen, oblique ways. The prospect of listening to a dialogue between the young grazier and would-be barrister seemed momentarily preferable to his own efforts at invention. It would have been so much easier if he had been able to tell her: I want to, and am going to, write about *myself*.

Some of those dressed in white were looking absently, though not all that absently, Waldo could see, in their direction. He suspected they were really wondering what he had been up to with a girl in pink alone in the garden.

Somehow they involved him with Dulcie more deeply than before.

"Don't they make you want to vomit?"

"Oh!" She made a little unhappy sound. "Some of them are probably quite nice. If you get to know them."

"I wouldn't trust them."

Dulcie was silent, and he would have liked to think he had won her over, but was afraid he had simply fallen flat.

"What's your other name?" he asked.

"Feinstein."

She pronounced it frankly, and in the foreign way, which made Dulcie Feinstein sound suddenly darker, exotic, though superficially there was nothing foreign about her. He put the tip of his tongue between his lips to stop the smile of pleasure coming to them. Not that his trend of thought wouldn't have stopped it in due course.

"My name's Brown," he said.

"I know. I heard Mrs. Musto when you came."

That made it sound worse.

He said, "It's the most horrible name anyone could ever have. Brown!" He drew it out as though blaming the person responsible.

"Probably most people hate the name they've got," she said. "Take Dulcie."

"It's not *bad*," he said slowly. "It's sort of exotic."

That was a word he had decided to adopt.

"No, it isn't. It's awful, really. It means 'sweet.' And Dulcie's a plump girl with fair hair and blue eyes. A complexion."

She was so anxious to reveal the true state of affairs, get it over quickly, that she was licking the dark shadow on her upper lip between the rushed phrases.

Arthur had been right, Waldo realized. Dulcie would probably grow a moustache.

Although they had almost reached the group of guests, there was one more question he wanted her to answer before he could feel satisfied.

"Do you know my brother?" he asked.

"No," said Dulcie.

Surprise had turned her reply into a query. But of course you could never tell. A spasm of malice made him want to shout: I bet you don't, he's only that ginger dill who serves you with the sugar down at Allwrights'!

He was safe, though. You could always control your own impulses, if it was important enough to control them, and perhaps Dulcie Feinstein would continue in ignorance of his uncontrollable twin.

Mrs. Musto's tennis party was going limp by now. She herself had the air of wanting to put up her feet and enjoy a boiled egg on a tray. So she was giving her last commands.

"Stubbens will run down to the station with those of yer who aren't motorin'."

Of course most of them were motoring. They were of the very best, though none could compete with Fairy Plain and Self-Raising Flour.

While the motorists were disguising themselves their hostess approached Waldo as though to conspire with him.

"You," she said, clearing her throat, because, he was sure, she had forgotten his name, "wouldn't mind, I know, walking across with the Feinstein girl. It's not very far out of yer way."

Since their return from the garden Dulcie had disappeared, and he rather hoped he had lost her. He had had enough of a good thing. Nor did he feel he might impress her more on that occasion. But here she was, coming out of the house, smoother than before, and, in the lesser light, her dress a deepening coconut ice. Carefully she looked away, to show she did not understand what was being arranged.

"That will be nice!" she said at once, however, and so brightly it could have meant more.

Her hitherto moony brown eyes could also flash, he observed.

Yet as soon as Mrs. Musto had dismissed them, he and Dulcie began to behave mechanically. While the charge of the motor brigade suggested that the others were exercising their own free will, the two on foot could only accept their portion of dust. They looked at their fellow guests as though they had never seen them before, nor did the motorists attempt to wave, the acquaintanceship was so obviously closed.

Dulcie walked without giving much thought to grace.

"Aren't you hungry?" she asked. "I am! I'm looking forward to a good tuck-in. All that stuff at Mrs. Musto's, I hardly dared touch a thing!"

"Food isn't so important," said Waldo.

"Mmmmm," she answered on a high note.

He was afraid his remark hadn't sounded too effective, so he had to try to improve on it.

"We could exist on a handful of dried dates if we were Arabs."

"But we're not. And aren't you a gloomy old thing!" Dulcie replied.

Was she laughing *at* him?

"You needn't tell me we're not Arabs," he said, even surlier. "But we might be before we're finished."

"I shan't. I shall work. You can always live simply, but well, if you want to."

It sounded so plain and sane his throat contracted as it did sometimes on his going into the kitchen and smelling an ovenful of Arthur's bread. He was glad he didn't have to answer Dulcie.

Objects were growing fuzzy in the fading light, a dark green to greenish black. Dust was whiter for the shadows. The silence might have lain heavy, but Dulcie didn't give it a chance.

She almost burst.

"You know what—oh, I shouldn't!" She giggled.

"What?" he asked.

"Just before we left," she said, quieter, looking behind her, "I went up to the bathroom. Beautiful bathroom—all blue and white, a big bowl of powder . . ."

"Go on!" he said. "Sure it wasn't flour?"

She nearly split.

"Aren't you awful!" she giggled. "No, though. This is what tickled me." She could hardly say what she had to. "There was a big bottle of scent, and you know what it was called—*L'Amour de Paris!*"

Dulcie Feinstein was enjoying her good giggle, and his rather tinny laughter was genuine enough, except that it disguised a certain envy and admiration. She prounounced the French words in a way which sounded real French.

"There was a Pierrot"—Dulcie was busting herself—"sitting on the *moon!*"

She dabbed and mopped.

"On the *bottle* of *scent!*" She shrieked.

It was strange, when he had decided she should be a serious-minded girl, that she should show this other frivolous side.

"Oh dear!" Dulcie moaned.

But she could not quite destroy his vision, to which the dusky trees pandered with broken hints.

"Do you learn foreign languages?" he asked, with a casualness to hide his interest.

"We have to," she said. "One of the grandmothers was—well, not exactly French, but lived for some years in France."

He might have caught her off her guard.

"And German?"

"Daddy," she said soberly, "is fluent in German."

Sobriety descended quite. And very soon they were approaching what could be the lit house. It was less impressive than Mrs. Musto's, far less, but neat and solid, a villa more suited to a town, trimly finished, painted up. There was a pepper-pot tower at one side.

"Is that your room?" he asked. "You could write up there."

"But I couldn't."

"Letters?"

"I'm a terrible correspondent. The girls at school are always complaining."

An elderly gentleman of bald head was putting back his watch and looking out from a lower room, trailing a newspaper after him. Those outside felt safe, knowing the darkness favoured them.

A lady was bringing in a huge tureen.

"Anyway, there's soup," Waldo said.

"Yes," replied Dulcie in her most practical voice. "Mummy lives to make us eat."

He wished she would go inside because departures always embarrassed him.

"Thank you," she said.

Oh, Lord.

"And don't remember the worst things about me." Again she was giggling, splitting, bursting. "That *Pierrot* on the *moon!*"

She just wouldn't go. And he stood rooted in the dust.

Suddenly she stopped. "Your brother," she said, calm and serious, "is he anything like you? Is he older?"

"No," he said.

After that she was saying good night and running up some steps set in a grass bank.

He went away quickly, and decided before reaching home he would think no more about Dulcie Feinstein, whom he didn't understand in any case. On the whole, though he would have confessed it only to himself, he did not understand people, except those he created by his own imagining. If it hadn't been for his own visions he might have felt desperate.

"Did you enjoy yourself?" Mother asked.

"Oh, all right."

"Meet anyone interesting?"

"A mob of kids."

Nothing annoyed their mother more than what she called a "sloppy Australian vocabulary." She was wearing her best blue dress for his return.

"Any girls?" Arthur asked.

"Oh, *yes!*"

He was too tired.

After that Waldo became so thoroughly occupied he hadn't the time to give thought to Dulcie Feinstein. In any case, he convinced himself Dulcie was *de trop*. That was one of several phrases he had picked up recently as weapons of defence. He would have liked to use this one on Dulcie, with her Frenchy, foreign airs, if he had been certain how it ought to be pronounced.

Those last terms at Barranugli High he grew superior, even in his attitude to somebody like Johnny Haynes. Dad was going to speak to a client of the bank whose cousin or something was librarian of Sydney Municipal Library. Dad thought there was every possibility, if he asked, and Waldo passed well, that the library would take him on. It excited Waldo. The only drawback was that the plan might force him into a relationship with his father unconvincing to himself and everybody else.

Thought of all this made him less aggressive. And he studied. He studied in the most obvious place—the train.

Then, the holidays before the end, his parents received a note from Dulcie Feinstein's mother, written in a black, peculiarly angular, foreign hand, suggesting that their boy Waldo should visit them on the Friday to spend a few hours with her daughter "and one or two other young friends."

Waldo noticed Mrs. Feinstein had made a point of not including Arthur, though perhaps that was natural, as Dulcie had never met him, and if her mother had, she would not have connected him with the kind of person Dulcie had described meeting at tennis.

Arthur remarked, "Those Feinsteins have a neat place. At the back there's a brass bell which they keep polished up—like a ship's bell, I think it is—which she told me she rings when she wants to bring the others in."

"*Who* rings?" asked Waldo.

"Mrs. Feinstein. Dulcie's always practising the piano. She plays the piano."

"You went there?" asked Waldo.

"To deliver the order."

How much more Arthur might have told, Waldo would have been interested to hear.

But all Arthur would say was, "Feinsteins are some of the quickest payers. They're fine people."

He had no time for more than to brush the loose hair and dandruff off his shoulders, as Mother had taught him, and leave for work. Otherwise he would have been late at the store.

The afternoon Waldo had to go to Feinsteins' he arrived late to show he wasn't all that keen on coming. Then he got the wind up wondering whether he was expected at all, there was such a withdrawn air about the white-and-green-painted villa. The shutters were not exactly closed, but they might have been. In his uncertainty he went round to the side rather than to the front or the back. That way he had a good look into a large, deserted, but lived-in room, in which an upright piano was more noticeable than the quantities of dark furniture arranged, practically clamped, around it. The piano was obviously Dulcie's, but he could not connect her with the furniture, the dust-coloured tapestry of which was straining to hold the stuffing down. Many people, however, had no connection with their furniture.

Presently Mrs. Feinstein came, and he was relieved to see she expected him.

"You must have wondered, Waldo," she said, and smiled at the shutters she was prodding wider open, "whether we have not returned to Sydney."

There was nothing very extraordinary about Mrs. Feinstein except that her r's made you wonder, and some of her tenses might have been lifted out of a bad translation. She was old, he supposed, though how old he couldn't have bothered calculating. Her skin looked soft, more the colour of skin from an unexposed part of her body. Her nose was of interest.

"As a matter of fact," said Mrs. Feinstein, "we nearly postponed your little visit. The Lembergs and Leonard Saporta are down with a grippe." She was going to be one of those, of irritating habit, who did not explain the persons they were mentioning. "Dulcie, too, has been sick with a cold. She has made herself so miserable. But wanted to enjoy your company."

He did not believe it. And even Mrs. Feinstein's smile wavered.

What could he say to this woman, whose voice smelled of old plush and sounded with slashed cello notes?

Fortunately Dulcie came in. She was in embroidered white today, which made her arms look yellower.

She said, "Hello," and stood applying a ball of damp handker-chief to her inflamed nose.

"Poor Dulcie!" moaned Mrs. Feinstein in suffocating sympathy.

"Oh, Mummy!" Dulcie protested from the other side of her cold. "I am not *dead*!"

Mrs. Feinstein looked as though she could have mourned for her daughter most professionally if she had been.

Instead, she went, it soon sounded, to prepare and fetch food.

"You won't be interested in us," said Dulcie, not particularly looking at Waldo. "Anyway, we're not at all what you'd like us to be. We don't read books—or only occasionally—or discuss interesting topics. My parents are boring."

Dulcie was certainly very different from what he had expected, but he supposed it was the cold having its effect, making her what Mother called "morbid."

"You can play the piano, can't you?" he said.

Because the piano was the dominant object in the room.

"Oh," she said, "I sit down at it. I work at it. I wanted very badly to play, I mean, to show off brilliantly in public. Until I realized it was not for me. I'm really," she said, "a very mundane individual."

She paused as though the language she was using might sound too daring, too much like a dialogue she had rehearsed. It was from the dark role he had expected on the first occasion, when she hadn't played it.

"I'm sorry my cousins didn't come," she said, sitting down on the piano stool and picking at the ivory skin of the exposed keys. "They're very entertaining. Dina can impersonate people," she said, "killingly."

With the result that Waldo grew entranced. He would have liked to think that Dulcie sat in the pepper-pot tower keeping a journal, and that he would succeed eventually in reading it by stealth, after which she would find out and know that he knew.

As though to confirm these possibilities Dulcie broke into the semblance of a piece on the piano, full of clotted notes, which she was creating purely for herself, it was implied, in her sultry, morbid, becolded condition.

"Doesn't Dulcie play nicely," said Mrs. Feinstein, coming in with a trayful of inherited-looking china and a strange black cake.

"Oh, Mummy!" Dulcie protested.

"She will never be a performer, though, and I am glad," Mrs. Feinstein said. "I have heard many of the greatest performers. Acchhh, yes!" After this expression of pain and reverence, she put the tray down and turned quite skittish. "We have been working the *planchette* the other evening," she said, looking at her daughter, "and Dulcie asked it what she will become. Afterwards. In life."

Mrs. Feinstein glanced again, this time obviously for permission.

"No," said Dulcie. "It's too uninteresting."

Her swollen nose aggravated her angry, sullen look. She was really very ugly. The fall of slightly frizzy hair, not long enough to fulfil a graceful purpose, was tied behind her head by a cerise bow.

"Will you take tea, Waldo?" asked Mrs. Feinstein in her kind of translation.

Waldo said all right he would. If it had not been for the dark and interesting cake, again he would have felt sorry he had come.

"This is *Mohntorte*," Mrs. Feinstein said, and cut into the cake as if it were flesh.

"Poppy seeds," Dulcie explained, brightening.

"Is it an opiate?" Waldo heard his cracked voice.

"No, but what a pity!" Dulcie came to life; her face began to lose its swollen look.

Mrs. Feinstein sucked her teeth, as though to defend her poppy cake, and at the same time a little drop of dribble appeared at one corner of her mouth.

"If it were an opiate, then we should float off perhaps," Dulcie said, in such a rich and gliding voice that Waldo looked at her, and seeing her eyes, imagined her dancing, her white dress swirling out from her in waves.

"What ideas!" protested her mother, breathing heavily. "My husband is particularly fond of the *Mohntorte*," Mrs. Feinstein added, turning to consult a gold clock with a partly naked woman reclining beside it under a glass dome.

Waldo bit into the black, tobacco-y cake. As he wasn't sure how he felt about it, he wondered what to tell them if they asked. But they didn't.

"There is mint tea for Dulcie," murmured Mrs. Feinstein, pouring out.

The scented steam added to the slightly dreamy atmosphere, of colds and poppies. Dulcie's frizzy, animal hair had undergone a transformation. Now it flowed, particularly along one of her white-embroidered shoulders where it happened to have arranged itself. And there were her eyes. As she sipped her mint tea, they brimmed and shimmered through the steamy curtain, infused with some virtue he still had to understand. Waldo had no experience of girls, except girls giggling or turning away on trains, or girls leading boys up side streets, to perform acts he knew about at second hand from Johnny Haynes. But Dulcie Feinstein seemed to fit into none of the known categories of girlhood. Perhaps in the end her eyes would give away their secret and all would be explained.

They might have continued in this agreeable state of surmise and abstraction if Mr. Feinstein hadn't come in. At once the gauze was lifted. It was as though a game of billiards were taking place in the wrong room.

"So this is Waldo Brown," said Mr. Feinstein. "How are we doing, Waldo?" Mr. Feinstein asked.

He spoke with a fairly strong Australian accent, to make up perhaps for anything foreign about him. His hand was cold, dry, and firm. His bald head looked as though it might have felt of billiard balls, the click of which was suggested not so much by the words against his teeth, as by the ideas he kept on coming out with.

"I have heard about you, Waldo," Mr. Feinstein clicked. "I have heard about your father. He is, they say, a fine man."

It surprised Waldo that anyone should have heard of somebody so unimportant as his father, let alone imagine him a "fine man."

"A man of independent ideas," said Mr. Feinstein. "The courage of his own convictions. No man today, of any intellectual honesty, could adopt any but a rationalist stand in view of politico-economic developments and the advances in scientific discovery."

Now it was Waldo who had begun to feel important, thanks to Mr. Feinstein's vocabulary and confidences, though he was frightened to think he mightn't be able to live up to them.

"Don't you agree?" Mr. Feinstein asked.

Waldo made what he hoped might sound an acceptable noise.

No one else, he saw, could help him. Mrs. Feinstein sat smiling up at her husband. She had ceased to exist, except as a smile and a dress covered with little steel beads. Dulcie had sucked her lips in. She was looking down at something, probably a crumb, so that he was no longer able to see her eyes.

"We Jews," said Mr. Feinstein, and he attached an almost visible weight to it, "we Jews are not always all that enlightened. But when we are, then we are. Take my old father, who founded the firm—another independent mind for you. My old father had seen the light before reaching these to some extent"—Mr. Feinstein cleared his throat—"enlightened shores."

The lights cannoned off his head onto his daring, curved nose.

Dulcie sighed. She was looking out, though respectfully, into the garden, where a gloom had gathered. She felt the need to dab her soggy nose.

"You will notice I said 'to some extent' enlightened," continued Mr. Feinstein, performing a balancing trick on the tips of the upturned fingers of his right hand. "That is because I don't like to be carried away into dishonest overemphasis in either direction."

Bloody old bore, Waldo decided. If he continued half listening it was only because of the impression of solidity Mr. Feinstein created.

"Take this little cap, Waldo," said Mr. Feinstein, taking a very strange one off the knob of a chair, "this *capple*. Perhaps you haven't met one before. Well," he said, "it is part of the big circus act. But if I wear it—which I do"—and he popped it gravely on his head—"it is not that I am allowing myself to be put through any reactionary hoop. It is because this *capple* happens to protect my nut from draughts."

Here Mr. Feinstein flopped into one of the overstuffed chairs. For a moment the cap seemed to have extinguished some of his conviction. Then he began to shine again, and laugh.

"Eh?" He laughed. "There couldn't be a more practical use!"

And his wife laughed to keep him company.

It was better when old Feinstein showed off some of his other possessions: a walking-stick made from rhinoceros hide, the signed photo of Sara Bernhardt, a ship in a bottle, and the gold clock on the mantelpiece.

"This nude lady," he explained, and winked, "represents Reason keeping an eye on Time. Because of course Time becomes unbearable if you don't approach it rationally."

Waldo looked at the clock, then realized how late it was. Supposing Feinsteins thought he was trying to cadge another meal?

He began to grunt, and redden, and grind a foot into the roses on the carpet. At last he said he ought to go. They did not stop him.

But suddenly Mrs. Feinstein remembered. She was one who smiled almost habitually, it seemed. Mrs. Feinstein smiled and said: "You will come again, Waldo. When Dulcie is recovered. And then you will see the garden."

"There's nothing in the garden," said Dulcie, "but old hydrangeas. And agapanthus."

"Ohhh!" roared her father. "When we pay a man to keep the beds filled with flowers?"

Dulcie put her arm through her father's, and automatically rested her head against his shoulder, but did not answer. Looking at them, Waldo grew guilty for his own foreignness.

When normally you didn't think about her, it was Mrs. Feinstein who appeared to be trying to put him at his ease. Mrs. Feinstein, hovering and smiling, had taken over from her steel dress.

"There is one thing, Waldo," she said, "I would like you to promise. Next time you come I want you to bring your brother."

"Arthur? But you don't know—" he started quickly.

"Oh yes, I do," Mrs. Feinstein answered in an everyday voice. "He has been here. He so enjoyed ringing the bell."

Waldo looked at Dulcie, who at least on that occasion had been inside practising the piano. Now she did not look up, except for a moment to say, "Good-bye," when her eyes expressed nothing but the return of her cold. He could not be sure whether she had already made his brother's acquaintance.

At the prospect of Arthur's introduction into his relationship with the Feinsteins, Waldo found he cherished that relationship more than he was prepared to admit. It was not the Feinsteins themselves who interested him particularly. Old Feinstein, with more or less his own parents' ideas, was frankly a bore, but it was at least something to have become a target for the theories of some-body not his parent, and in another way Mrs. Feinstein, of doubt-ful syntax, and skin with the peculiar uncovered look, confirmed his individual existence as comfortingly as cake. As for their daughter, he was not yet sure of Dulcie, of what part she was intended to play, or whether she despised and rejected him. But he had re-ceived her, jealously, expectantly, into his mind, and allowed her to drift there passively, along with the musty flavour of poppy seeds and the dense little tune on the walnut piano. The Feinsteins were too private an experience, then, to resist Arthur. Arthur would ex-plode into, and perhaps shatter, something which could not be repaired.

So Waldo continued remembering, when circumstances didn't force him to forget. There were fortunately the exams ahead. He had to study; he was, and would remain, weak in maths. There was also the question of the Influential Client of the bank, whether he had spoken; by now it did not seem as though the latter realized how much depended on him. Waldo would wake at night in a sweat. Once he dreamed he was working on the railway as a fettler and had not dared admit his true, his elective work. As he lay there beneath the creaking roof, at home, he thought how safe he would be returning from the books in the library to write his own. Com-paratively safe, anyway. He would still have to face Arthur and his own doubts.

The third occasion on which he came in contact with the Fein-steins, Waldo knew there was no escaping something which was being prepared. Mrs. Feinstein's formal note deliberately arranged it for the Saturday. *"So that you are able to introduce your brother to our circle,"* the writing ended underlined.

Waldo wondered whether he dared pretend he had not received the letter. In that way time, naked but finally rational, might solve his problem.

It was Arthur who decided which line they were to take.

"Saturday," he was telling Mother, "both of us are going up to Feinsteins'. Do you think there'll be a big tea? Will there be other people? Or shall I have an opportunity of making conversation with Mrs. Feinstein?"

Waldo could not decide whether he was hearing what he heard.

"What put it into your head," he asked, "that the Feinsteins are expecting you?"

"The letter," Arthur said, "which you left lying on the dressing-table. I thought you meant me to read it, Waldo, seeing as she's invited me."

Mother did not even correct the grammar, but told Arthur it would be in order for him to go without his coat provided he wore his silk shirt. That was good enough to stand up to any formality.

As they walked up the hill to Feinsteins' on the day, Waldo saw that Mother's present of a silk shirt was much too large for Arthur. It ballooned out on his shoulders, a physical deformity to all the rest. The water, besides, was trickling down the red sideburns from Arthur's attempts to reduce his staring hair.

"I am looking forward to this opportunity," he said, "of meeting Mrs. Feinstein socially."

He was trembling by the time they reached *Mount Pleasant*, whereas it was Waldo who should have trembled, if resentment hadn't tempered him.

Phlox was fluttering in the beds, beside the steps which led from the road, by steep, yet clipped, grassy banks, to Feinsteins' door.

Arthur was gasping.

"We came, all right!" he called from near the top.

As Mr. Feinstein appeared in the doorway.

"You needn't tell me!" The old boy laughed. "And on a Saturday!"

In the hall he took Waldo aside.

"You realize," he said, "this is to bear out a theory I expounded. Do you know, Waldo, it is the Sabbath today? Yet here is your brother blowing like a flame, or spirit of enlightenment, through a Jewish household, with all the doors thrown open."

Waldo only half listened. He was too agonized wondering what Arthur might get up to.

"Shall we have a feast then, Mr. Feinstein?" Arthur called from somewhere behind.

"Oh, yes! It will be all feast!" Mr. Feinstein was shining with laughter. "Once upon a time it was only for a family of Jews mumbling together behind closed doors."

"Shall *we* be your family?" Arthur was gibbering with hope and pleasure.

"Naturally!" Mr. Feinstein could not laugh enough; his stomach was laughing behind the gold chain, to say nothing of his illuminated cranium. "We expected nothing less."

Though when his wife appeared he withdrew, Waldo suspected, for good. It would be for Mrs. Feinstein, rather, to produce the cakes of enlightenment.

Mrs. Feinstein was quite willing. Wearing the same dress as before, she had obviously prepared herself for understanding Arthur Brown. She stuck her most sympathetic smile on her flesh-coloured face.

"You must tell me all about yourself, Arthur," Mrs. Feinstein said.

Fortunately Arthur wasn't taken in by that. He was too interested, in any case, in the room, the same big overfurnished living-room in which they had received Waldo alone on the previous occasion. Arthur was soon walking about, looking at everything as though he must remember forever.

"What is that?" he asked.

"That is a prayer-cap," Mrs. Feinstein explained pleasantly, "which people used to wear in the days when they still have been superstitious."

"Well, that's an idea," Arthur said too thoughtfully. "I never saw anybody praying in a cap."

For a terrible moment Waldo thought he was going to put it on. He might have, if Dulcie hadn't opened the door.

"Did you ever pray in a cap?" Arthur asked as though he had met her before, and she was only, as it were, reappearing.

"It's different with women," Dulcie answered.

At least from that moment Waldo knew that Dulcie was seeing Arthur for the first time. She was so obviously upset. She tried to make it look as though the whole idea of prayer-caps, and superstition generally, repelled her, whereas it was the lumpy look of Arthur Brown slobbering with imbecile excitement. Although Waldo was personally distressed that she should react in this way to his brother, he was relieved to find she was sincere.

"Now I shall be able to remember you in your room, Dulcie,

now that I have seen your face," Arthur was saying, or gobbling, "even if you never want to see me again."

At this Mrs. Feinstein began to protest by noises.

"Why should I"—Dulcie gave a high, unexpected laugh—"not want?"

She ended awkwardly in mid-air.

Because Arthur had gone up too close to her, the way he would with people in whom he was interested, to remember also by touch, it seemed.

"Here, Arthur," Waldo was beginning to say, to interrupt, to drag him off.

But Mrs. Feinstein's smile continued to find the situation reasonable.

"Because we mightn't have enough to say to each other," Arthur said, looking too closely at Dulcie, into her eyes. "I mean, people can say and say, by the yard, but they don't always seem to have learnt the same words."

Then Dulcie appeared to be making a great effort.

"I think, Arthur," she said, "you may be able to tell me a lot I shall want to hear. We may be able to teach," she said, "to teach each other things."

"Will you," Arthur shouted, seizing the opportunity, "teach me the piano? Will you? Can we start now?"

"Oh, yes!" Dulcie said, and laughed with the greatest pleasure and relief.

Waldo knew he must get out quickly. Find the dunny. As he went barging out he heard the discords of music spattering out of the upright piano under Arthur's hands. He knew how Arthur's not quite controlled hands were behaving.

Behind him now, all was music of a kind, and laughter, as he blundered down the passage. He heard at last, against the doors he opened, Mrs. Feinstein following him.

"I want," he mumbled foolishly.

"You want the bathroom?" Mrs. Feinstein asked most sympathetically.

"No," he said, in what he heard was his surliest voice. "The other."

"Here," she said, opening a door.

So that he did not have to go any farther, out through any grass, looking for a dunny. Here was a real porcelain lavatory with mahogany seat, on which he sat down at once and gave way to the diarrhoea which had been threatening him.

And now the music was flowing from unseen hands—they could only have been Dulcie Feinstein's—though under Arthur's influence, he feared. Waldo wished he could have conceived a poem. He had not yet, but would—it was something he had kept even from himself. If it would only come shooting out with the urgency of shit and music. He rocked with the spasms of his physical distress, and the strange drunkenness which the unbridled music, muffled by perhaps several doors, provoked in him. Was Dulcie playing an *étude*? He hoped it was an *étude*. He hoped against hope the Influential Client would soon speak. Then he would walk up the hill to Feinsteins', and present himself, and say: Here I am, an intellectual, working at Sydney Municipal Library—kindness is not enough, you must respect, not my genius exactly, but at least my Australian-literary ambitions.

When Waldo returned at last he was emptied out. He had washed his face, and might have felt better if he hadn't heard a sound of teaspoons somewhere, from kitchen or pantry. Which meant that Mrs. Feinstein was getting the tea. Which meant that Arthur was alone with Dulcie.

The music had stopped now.

As he hurried he was not afraid Arthur would behave in any way violently, oh no, it was rather the violence of what his twin might say.

Entering the room, Waldo made himself appear, he imagined, dry and correct. At least they would not see how he felt. Only he would know.

Arthur and Dulcie were sitting on the twin music-stool, which held the music underneath. They were turned so that they faced each other. Their foreheads appeared almost to be touching.

"What, a *Peerrot* sitting on the moon? On the bottle?"

"A Pierrot painted on the bottle," Dulcie confirmed.

Arthur was entranced by what he was hearing and seeing, and

Dulcie had changed. When he came into the room Waldo felt for the first time this is Dulcie being herself. You couldn't say she was exactly ugly. Or perhaps he was just used to her by now.

"You are right," she was saying, in reply to some remark of Arthur's, though speaking rather to herself. "*Amour* is not the same as 'Love.' *Amour* has a different shape—a different meaning."

Waldo was so horrified he might have expressed his feelings, but fortunately Mrs. Feinstein brought the tea things, and at the same time rain was beginning.

"Oh dear, I do hate thunder!" Mrs. Feinstein admitted, and the things on the tray rattled. "It makes me so afraid! Shut the window, Dulcie, do, please! They say lightning strikes through open windows."

"We shan't be able to breathe," said Dulcie, but did as she was told.

"Arthur and I shall exchange anecdotes to drown the thunder," Mrs. Feinstein promised.

"Is this real cinnamon toast?" Arthur asked, helping himself to two or three fingers and stuffing them buttery into his mouth.

He looked perfectly happy, sitting in a chair shaped like a toast-rack, while Mrs. Feinstein told about her aunt Madame Hochapfel who had sometimes been mistaken for the Empress Eugénie, and whose salon used to be frequented by people of artistic inclinations.

"Every Sunday. Only a *minor* salon," Mrs. Feinstein added out of modesty.

"But to be in business in a small way is better than not being in it at all," Arthur said through his mouthful of toast. "I mean, to have your own. To be independent."

Mrs. Feinstein agreed that her aunt Madame Hochapfel had kept an independent salon.

Dulcie apparently had her thoughts. Waldo couldn't sink into his. He felt as brittle as a dry sponge. Other people had their anecdotes, or the obvious riches of their thoughts. The big drops of rain and fleshy leaves plastering the windows accentuated his unfortunate drought, his embarrassing superficiality.

Yet he knew the theory of it all. It was only a question of time.

It was the *mean* time which weighed so heavily. It made the palms of his hands sweat.

"And Russia." Mrs. Feinstein sighed. "I can only remember the pine forests."

"That's something," said Arthur. "I bet they smelled."

Mrs. Feinstein breathed deep.

"On a visit when I have been a little girl. To another branch. With another aunt—Signora Terni of Milan."

The branch of a shrub, or perhaps an unpruned hydrangea, was scratching the window. They realized the rain was over. Mrs. Feinstein put on her skittish act. Her private-flesh-coloured face appeared less grey.

"Arthur," she decided, "will help me clear the things."

So Waldo saw the garden, as he had been promised, with Dulcie, because she had him on her hands. The leaves were still dripping with moisture. An air of cold showers above had more or less dislodged the green gloom from underneath.

"These are the hydrangeas you told about," said Waldo, although they did not interest him at all.

"Yes," said Dulcie, dully. "And the agapanthus."

From this occasion he would remember her breaking up into the crumbly fragments of greeny-white hydrangeas. Her dress, at any rate. Because she herself was dark brown, and ugly.

"Arthur and Mummy are enjoying themselves immensely," she said. "I think it will take me some time to understand Arthur."

"What is there to understand?" Waldo tried not to shout.

His voice sounded horribly dry and cracked under the dripping hydrangeas.

"Though for that matter," she said, "I don't understand myself."

She had come out in a pimple on one side of her large nose. Which made the dog-silliness of her eyes look more obscene.

He wished he had been taught to do or say something he hadn't been. He could blame his parents, of course. But it didn't help matters.

And soon he and Arthur were walking down the steps, between the painted phlox, out of this Feinstein world which in the end had no connection with them. However sickening and personal the longing, however convincing Madame Hochapfel's features at the moment of introduction, however close the wet mops of white hydrangeas, parting ridiculed them.

Arthur at least knew what to say.

"Good-bye," he was trumpeting. "I had a great time. I'll come back, Dulcie, for the rest of the piano lessons. I'm not going to worry about the theory. I'm going to begin with one of those frilly pieces."

They were walking down the red concrete steps, which had been painted shiny to please Mr. Feinstein, no doubt.

Arthur called back then, as though he had been giving it thought, "I'll have to come back anyway, to tell you what I've worked out."

Waldo was furious, who in the end had not known how to say a thing. Of course those who are sensitive don't.

"What do you mean," he began, choking, after they had gone some way, "what you have *worked out!*"

"Well," said Arthur, "you've got to work out something if you're not happy."

"But *you're* happy, Dulcie's happy! It would only be asking for sympathy to say you weren't."

"She mightn't be," Arthur said.

He wouldn't say any more. He started snorting, and grunting, and finally picking his nose for comfort.

They got home.

And then there were the exams. Waldo passed with Flying Colours, even managed to scrape through maths—where Johnny Haynes failed.

Then there was the letter summoning to the interview. (What price the Feinsteins now?) It turned out Waldo was accepted by Sydney Municipal Library on the strength of his scholastic career at Barranugli High, his suitable appearance—and a favour asked.

In the end the Influential Client forgot to speak. It was Mrs. Musto who got Waldo the job, through Alderman Caldicott, son of her former gardener. Then Mrs. Musto retired, to her house, her shrubs, and her servants. She did not venture very far into other people's lives, because she had been bitten once, no, twice, in the course of human relations, and did not want to risk her hand again.

The preliminaries to dying, to what in the end is the simplest act of all, were so endlessly complicated.

"Mrs. Allwright used to say," said Arthur, "when she did her block at me, when she couldn't find the things she'd put away, or had given somebody the wrong change, she used to say, 'I sometimes wish you'd *die*, Arthur Brown. Then Mr. Allwright would come to his senses and realize how we've been wasting our time.' "

Arthur would assume the voices of those who were addressing him. So that now on the unmade pavement on the Barranugli Road the mother with kiddy in stroller turned round to wonder whatever the old nut could be going on about. One old nut, or two? It was a shame to allow them their freedom. Somebody else always paid the price.

"But it was Mr. Allwright who died," Arthur continued. "Lacing up his boots. Mrs. Allwright took up Christian Science. She'd do anything not to wake up and find she was dead."

"You don't wake up," Waldo reminded.

He wouldn't listen. Only it was not possible not to listen.

"Eh?" asked Arthur.

Though of course he had heard. Arthur always did hear, even with traffic whizzing or lurching along the Barranugli Road.

"Wonder if Mrs. Allwright died. That's the worst of it when people leave the district. Sometimes their relatives forget, or don't know how to put the notice in the column. Or perhaps Mrs. Allwright *didn't* die. By rights, by *logic*—wouldn't you say?—Christian Scientists don't."

"Death, thank God"—Waldo caught himself—"comes to everyone."

Or almost everyone.

He wouldn't listen. He began to count, to name the passing cars: the Chev the Renault the Holden two more three Holdens the Morris Minor the Bentley—that was Mr. Hardwick who'd done a deal with the Council over Anglesey Estate, only it couldn't be proved. Nobody would have known that Waldo Brown, so unmechanical, could name the cars. Perhaps even Arthur hadn't found out. It was Waldo's secret vice.

Arthur who found out everything caused his brother to turn round, to test his face. Arthur, as Waldo dreaded, knew, and was smiling.

"What is it?"

"I waved at the Holden"—Arthur smiled—"and the lady waved back."

Oh well. Arthur was not infallible. So Waldo Brown decided to indulge his other secret vice. If Arthur died. It was not impossible —that dead weight on the left hand. Waldo Brown dragged quicker, if not to effect, to think. He would do how was it he would *blow everything* the first editions of Thomas Hardy the whole Everyman Library quite a curiosity nowadays Mother's spoons with crests on them the emerald ring the Hon Cousin Molly Thourault left in fact one big bonfire the land the developers were after if Anglesey Estate then why not Browns' place Terminus Road see an alderman no alderman was so dishonest you couldn't teach him a point or two approach a minister if necessary the Minister for Local Govt if only Mrs. Musto were alive and say it is imperative imperative was the word that W. Brown of honourable service should end in a blaze of last years.

They were so dry Waldo had to lick his lips. He hoped he wouldn't give himself a heart. His oilskin sounded slithery with speed.

If it was immoral, then he was immoral. Had been, he supposed, for many years. Perhaps always. The million times he had buried Arthur. But only now, or recently, had he perfected his itinerary of islands. He would visit islands first, because they symbolized, if only symbolized, what he craved. Of course he knew about the other things too, the bars and Americans. He would know how to sit in bars and drink, what was it, Pernod Fils, and stick his hand up under the raffia skirt of some lovely lousy brownskinned poster-girl complete with ukulele. And get the pox, and not do anything about it, what was the point at his age, in spite of all the modern drugs.

The Chev the Holden the Citroën quite neat the Holden two six seventeen Holdens one Fiat-2500 flash tripe-hounds. The traffic, he was certain, was sending his temperature up.

Of course, in spite of his intellectual tastes and creative gift, it was the hotels he was craving for. Always had been. He had started long ago writing for the brochures to have them waiting Poste Restante G. P. O. Tore them up after reading and threw them out of the train window before reaching Barranugli. The women would be waiting in the foyers of the posh luxury hotels held down by plush buttons but waiting in their shingled hair, their long cigarette-holders gently balanced. Clara Bow—or was it Marilyn Monroe? And Mrs. Clare Boothe Luce and Mary McCarthy, he wouldn't overlook the intellectuals. To make conversation with the more established intellectual women. Though women, even Dulcie, would suddenly tire him, not so much Mary McCarthy, who was more what you would call a Force. Of course, though, it was the beds he was really looking forward to, the fine linen, or perhaps sometimes silk with monograms, to feel his long limbs had never aged, and now at last, without Arthur, able to lead a celibate life. Spiritually celibate.

Waldo blushed and worked his Adam's apple. Down. Over. Something.

One thing, he decided, he would never do. He wouldn't touch a penny of Arthur's savings, out of delicacy, because he had willed Arthur dead.

"There," he said, looking round.

"What?"

"That's the worst hill done with. So you can stop moaning now."

"I'm not moaning. I've settled down to enjoy a healthful walk."

So faint normally it could have been a refraction from the memory of Arthur's carrot hair, the bluish tinge in Arthur's skin appeared just that much deeper than when they started out, that morning, on a purpose. Abnormally blue.

No, he would not touch a penny of Arthur's wretched account. He would make it over to that skinny Jew boy Arthur Saporta, with brown flannel patches round his eyes. Whatever Arthur Saporta meant. Beyond the fact that he had his mother Dulcie Feinstein's eyes.

If Arthur Arthur Brown died.

But it finally seemed improbable, on that morning or ever, which meant the alternative. Waldo scuttled at the thought. He was still young enough not to believe in his own death. He kicked the nearest of the blue dogs—Scruffy, it was—on deliberate purpose.

"You always hated Scruffy!" Arthur moaned. "Because he was mine."

Waldo could not feel he owned anything—certainly not Runt, his dog, perhaps still his box of manuscripts clippings letters of appreciation, perhaps still Arthur also—if Waldo Brown Terminus Road Sarsaparilla no flowers please ever since the accident he had kept it legibly written out and easy to find if he were inadvertently inadvertently was the word to die.

Paper flowers on the other hand didn't. So he must make sure of his boxful of papers. Sometimes going through the manuscripts the clippings the letters of appreciation he would feel them still warm with the reason which had brought them into existence. The thoughts. Even if he had not produced what you might call a substantial body of work the fragments and notebooks were still alive with private thought. The minds of others appropriating paring hacking rubbing with a sandpaper of lies impairing invariably ossified what had been tenuously personal. Was he vain to have lost faith in public sculpture? Unlike some. Take Goethe, Goethe must have worn a track through the carpet leaping at his notebooks to perpetuate he thought a Great Thought. The vanity was that men believed their thought remained theirs once turned over to the public. All those goggle-eyed women reverent for their own reverence trailing past a sculpture of poetry and epigrams, and earnest young people *fingering* IMPROVING ON because it is ordained that great works of art should be exposed, becoming what they were never intended for: done-by-the-public sculpture.

So Waldo raced the traffic up the Barranugli Road.

"Hey, steady on!" Arthur called bumpily. "What are you up to? What's the point?"

As Waldo raced the traffic towards Sarsaparilla, unfortunately some of it was going in the wrong direction.

But he would arrive, and after they had struggled with that gate, and pushed the grass aside with their chests, because by now in places you might have said they were living under grass, he would go as straight as possible in, and collect the box from on top of the wardrobe, that old David Jones dress box in which Mother had kept the little broken fan and some important blue dress, only in the earlier style, with a pattern of rust where the hooks and eyes had eaten in. The D. J. box was, or had been, the ideal receptacle for papers of a private nature. He had even printed PRIVATE on it, not that it ever helped much. But now he would make it actually his, all those warm thrilled and still thrilling words falling from their creator's hands into the pit at the bottom of the orchard into ash smouldering brittlely palpitating with private thoughts. Because fire is the only privacy the thoughts of great men can expect. Allow them to be turned into sculpture and you are lost.

The wind helped him, and to a certain extent the onward traffic. Arthur was against him of course, as was the opposite stream. But they did arrive at last, on the ramparts of Sarsaparilla, erected laboriously brick by brick, to withstand some hostile thing, by those who had not yet died: the infallible ones with professions and offspring. It was pathetic to think about them. Perhaps like Goethe he was vain, but if small minds could be so obsessed by illusions of permanence, how much less convincing was his own illusion of death?

So Waldo slowed or was slowed down. It is ridiculous, he panted, to think I may pop off, today, or tomorrow, why, I am good for another twenty years, taking reasonable care, keeping off salt, animal fats, potatoes, and white bread.

"What's up?" Arthur asked. "Don't tell me you're running out of energy?"

Because Waldo was standing. Still.

"No," he said, so slow. "I was looking at that rose."

He was too, on another level.

"A good specimen of a rose. I like a rose, a white rose," Arthur said.

It was not its beauty, its whiteness, its perfection, which interested Waldo, it was the solidity of it. Only apparent, however. If he had come closer and alone, he might have torn the rose to show he was that much stronger. Roseflesh on occasions had made him shiver. How much less exposed to destruction was the form of youth, even with time and memory working against it.

Waldo liked that. It made him look rather sly. Now they would go home, and while Arthur was occupied with some bungling business of his own, he would take down the private box, he would take out the current notebook. "Always taking, taking renews, give too much and the recipient expects all." He liked that, he would write it down. For his PRIVATE pleasure. And the bit about "form of youth, time and memory." In that way he would continue living. In the notebooks. In his secret mind. In spite of Arthur. And Goethe.

Youth is the only permanent state of mind. There was no stage in his life when he hadn't felt young—he insisted—except sometimes as a little boy. If growing old is to become increasingly aware, as a little boy his premature awareness irritated his elders to the point of slapping. So there are, in fact, no compartments, unless in the world of vegetables.

Today I am thirty, he had calculated, looking at himself in the glass of the deal dressing-table he shared with Arthur, his brushes and bottles to the right, Arthur's to the left, as he insisted. His face trembled down one side as he tried to accept the incredible. Sometimes he wondered whether anybody realized there was still the little boy inside him, beside his other self, looking out. His eyes, like his mother's, were blue, though his were watered down. It always gave him some satisfaction to acknowledge blue eyes in the street, especially those of women. He made them conspirators. Or members of a select club. Though naturally he would never have informed them. (Brown eyes he blackballed automatically. Ugh!)

It was a penetrating voyage into the glass of the dressing-table (deal for the boys). According to mood, he might take his pince-nez off, blurring the image, allowing his imagination to play amongst the hydrangeas, or alternately he would clip the lenses firmly on, and refuse himself any avenues of escape from that intellectual ruthlessness he knew himself to possess. (He had once described the geography of his face in seven foolscap pages.) The optician's formula made his eyes appear paler, his chin less pronounced, his moustache patchier under the brilliantine, but hadn't the whole botched mess—he was prepared to face it—helped give birth to that proven sensibility?

On his thirtieth birthday he smiled at himself in reflection, for the strangeness of it. Then he shuffled the expanding armbands up his sleeves, put on his workday coat, and went into the kitchen where she was getting his breakfast for him.

"It's odd to think I'm thirty," he said, forestalling the probable question of how he felt about it.

He stood looking down at the pair of eggs, their ruffles edged with a brown frizz.

"I think, dear, you were born thirty," she said.

In her cool voice. Allowing him her cool kiss. She, if anybody, should have known.

His mother was wearing the old blue dressing-gown with the safety pin which failed to disguise the financial truth or her operation. Since Dad died in 1922 she had been dependent on him. (Arthur contributed something.)

Some people would have considered his—*their* mother, dowdy. He could only think of her as timeless, actually so, because she was not taken in by his thirtieth birthday. She, too, realized there were no compartments. Thirty or seventeen.

At seventeen—on his seventeenth birthday, as it turned out—he had presented himself at Sydney Municipal Library, to take up the position he got thanks to Fairy Flour. So it had been hinted. Only the malicious could have ignored the true state of affairs: a spotty youth wheeling trolleys of books between the stacks. Neither light nor air played much part in the sinecure his patroness had bought him. Sometimes the cages were jammed so full, his fellow-suffering and cracking ribs caused him to wonder how easily a person might contract consumption and retire early on a pension. He read one or two works on the subject of that disease. Shoving them back according to numbers, he got to hate the physical presence of books. Never lost his respect for them, of course. But could have hurt any book shoving it back. Occasionally he shoved one so far away from its recorded cell he hoped it would never be found again. The thick porous pages of some of the old public books, ravelled at the edges into lint, clotted with snot, smeary with spittle and nicotine, smelled of old men in greasy raincoats, in hats which their foreheads melted, but which soon set stiff and cold if left standing.

Pffeugh, the books! The injustice necessity had done him was proclaimed by the mirrors of many public lavatories, along with the warnings against venereal disease. He would drop in to wash his hands, though who knew if you mightn't pick up something worse from the tap. Still, you had to wash your hands. There was a period when he couldn't wash them enough.

His purple hands. It was the ink-pads. He was marked from the start. But hadn't he given himself to books? "Waldo is the bookish one, takes after his father in that." And sometimes even then, in the stacks of the Municipal Library, in the sound of dust, and the smell of decaying, aged flesh, he would open a book to dedicate himself anew. And he would stand shivering for the daring of words, their sheer ejaculation.

On one occasion Waldo Brown had found:

> In my dry brain my spirit soon,
> Down-deepening from swoon to swoon,
> Faints like a dazzled morning moon.
>
> The wind sounds like a silver wire,
> And from beyond the noon a fire
> Is pour'd upon the hills, and nigher
> The skies stoop down in their desire. . . .

He shut the book so quick, so tight, the explosion might have been heard by anyone coming to catch him at something forbidden disgraceful which he would never dare again until he could no longer resist. He looked round, but found nobody else in the stacks. Only books. A throbbing of books. He went to the lavatory to wash his hot and sticky hands.

So the life had its compensations, an orgasm in dry places, a delicious guilt of the intellect. It made him superior to poor Dad, whose innocence from a previous age must have denied him even the vicarious sensuality of literature.

Waldo Brown was superior also to Walter Pugh, his superior by eighteen months.

Waldo didn't care for Walter. Pimples were just about the only thing they had in common (if you discounted literature, which, in Wally's case, Waldo couldn't believe in). Waldo was thin, might pass for tall, with thin to disappearing lips, his sculptured chin, good carriage inherited from his mother—*distinction*, in fact, was how he saw it in writing—whereas Wally was thick, to very fat on hot days, a splurge of lips a little open, a little shiny from the bacon he could have been eating a moment or two before, his seams splitting, especially at the thighs of those pants belonging to something else.

Wally said, "I'd give anything for a tart tonight on me way home. Sit all night there at home with Cis and Ern. Sometimes I think I'll bust, Waldo, if I don't get meself a girl. There was one on the ferry gave me the eye. I just on accepted the invite walking up from the wharf. You could do it in that bit of scrub before you get to Permanent Avenue."

"You'd be very unwise," Waldo said.

"Oh, I know," said Wally Pugh. "The pox and all that. Or a kid. But I'll bust, Waldo, if I don't. I'm gunna!"

Even when the glass above the washbasin spelled the warnings out.

"The trouble with you, Waldo, you're cold. Or is it luck? Praps after all you're a lucky bugger."

"It's not what they told me Friday." Waldo felt himself compelled.

His hands folding over the soap enjoyed a sensuality of their own.

"Who?" asked Wal.

"The two of them. I can't say they appealed. Not particularly. Though the one in pink wasn't bad."

"You mean you did them both?"

Waldo was too superior to answer.

"Golly!" Walter Pugh said. "Did you know them?"

"One of them, slightly. The other was her friend."

"What was their names, Waldo?"

"I think the friend was Nell. Yes, Nell. The one I know—slightly—she's called Dulcie."

"And Dulcie's good, eh? You bloody old bugger! You fast old dark horse!"

"She's only what I'd call pretty average. She's a thin, dark, plain girl. She'll never be up to much because of the salt-cellars. She's hairy too, about the arms."

Betrayals brought the gooseflesh out on Waldo. Irresistibly.

"But you got your whack, you old bugger!"

"If that's what appeals, but it doesn't—to me—particularly."

"Go on! Then you *are* cold, Waldo. You're the coldest fish I'll ever hope to meet."

Only superior.

Walter Pugh showed Waldo three poems he had written. Waldo would have called them jingles, rather. When he had written enough of them, as he intended, Walter was going to offer them as a volume and join the ranks of the Australian poets. Waldo's lips fairly disappeared, though he didn't comment. He knew for certain he would never show Wally anything he wrote, he would never show anyone; it was too foolish. Certainly he had confided in Dulcie Feinstein that he was going to be a writer, but then he was only—sixteen, was it? and stupid.

And not long after, Mrs. Feinstein had taken her daughter away. So it was told.

Arthur said, "They're going on a visit to the relatives, so that Dulcie can learn the languages. There are relatives all over the place, like Jews seem to have. And languages come easy to the Jews, Mrs. Musto says. I bet they have a good time. Not Mr. Feinstein. He can't leave the business. But Dulcie and her mother. Mrs. Hochapfel, she'd be too old to go gadding about, but there's still that Mrs. Terni in Milan."

A couple of times Waldo walked home past the villa in O'Halloran Road, not to nurse a sense of deprivation, simply out of curiosity, and the shutters were fastened, and the weeds had grown, as though old Feinstein didn't come there any more, as though the air of Sarsaparilla had lost its savour for him since his wife and daughter went away. On a third evening, Waldo decided to go in, climbing the picket fence because the gate was chained. The grass banks he clambered up no longer seemed to give. Under the hydrangeas, where a steamier, yellower green intensified the desolation, some animal had probably died. His own feet sounded horribly detached on the tessellated veranda, but he had to try to look through the shutters. On fitting his eyes to the slanted slats he couldn't see anything of course, because of the angle; he had more or less expected that before making the attempt. And then the footsteps began approaching along the gravel. From round the side. He stood and waited.

The icy moment finally arrived. It was old Feinstein himself.

"What do you want?" he asked.

He was not wearing the *capple*, but a bowler hat, which made him look and sound more formal. He stood there looking at Waldo as if he hadn't seen him before, although they had met not so very long ago.

Waldo was transformed forcibly into the complete stranger.

"I thought the house might be up for sale. All shut up," he mumbled.

"Well, it isn't," Mr. Feinstein said rather angrily.

As he jolted down the concrete steps which the couch-grass was breaking open, Waldo knew that the owner had continued watching him. The fact that the old man's daughter had given herself to him in his conversation with Walter Pugh seemed to make the incident more icily corrupt.

So much so he would have liked to boast about it to somebody, but there was no one at hand, perhaps never would be, worthy of its subtlety. At tea he merely mentioned, while trimming the fat off his cold mutton, "Saw old Feinstein up at the house. Didn't know he went there any more. Wonder what he gets up to on his own."

Dad suggested he had come to assure himself his property was not deteriorating. Mother thought he might be lonely, and hoped to re-enact some moment before his loneliness set in.

"Trouble with Feinsteins is they're so damn Jewish. That's usually the trouble with Jews," Waldo said, and laughed.

Though he hadn't met—well, perhaps one other.

"I'll trouble you not to speak in those terms," Dad said through a piece of gristle. "Mr. Feinstein's a fine man."

"Oh yes, old Feinstein," Waldo agreed.

He knew his father was not acquainted with Feinstein, but that a lifetime of tolerance was at stake, and he was having difficulty in finding the vocabulary to protect it.

Mother, too, was looking pained.

"I have never met Mrs. Feinstein," she said, "but I'm sure nothing about her calls for such an unprincipled remark. Besides," she said, "I thought you were fond of them."

"I'm not *married* to them!" Waldo said.

The filthy mutton was sticking in his throat. His rejection of the Feinsteins seemed connected with some far deeper, even less desirable, misery. On the outskirts of the lamplight Dulcie hovered, in that same dress, the sleeves of which were embroidered with the bracts of loose hydrangeas. How he resented brown eyes, whether in Dulcie Feinstein, Arthur, or George Brown, whether offering themselves for martyrdom, or like soft brown animals burrowing in, unconscious, but still burrowing.

"Well, I have been guillotined!" said Waldo Brown cheerfully, throwing his knife and fork together on the plate.

For once he was glad he would be leaving for the Library in the morning. For once, too, Arthur was not joining in. Arthur sat munching on his thoughts, his eyelids drooping, so that you could see only the moons of heavy skin. If he had had to face the brown verdict of Arthur's eyes, Waldo suspected the same unhappiness might have risen up inside him to trouble the surface.

In the morning he left for the Library. And then again. Always.

"That girl Dulcie"—Walter Pugh returned to the subject on a later occasion—"what became of her?"

"I had a letter from her. She's in Brussels," Waldo said with the naturalness of inspiration.

"Some people have all the luck! Or spondulicks."

"It's not luck. It's practical, an investment. They've taken her to Europe to learn the languages."

Walter Pugh was breathing hard.

"Not that Dulcie wasn't a cultured girl already," Waldo said. "Plays the Beethoven piano sonatas. Does embroidery, too. Petty point."

After that, Walter invited Waldo to spend the evening at the home of his sister and brother-in-law. Once before Waldo had accepted, and eaten a sociable braise with Cis and Ern—we're going to treat you just as if you were one of the family—and Wally had spoken about his plans for the future, which were uncomfortably familiar.

This time Waldo said, "Sorry, Wal. Too far. All this train travel —I'm played out by the time I reach home."

It was true, too. Everywhere was too far from Terminus Road. From time to time he resented it bitterly, and planned to rent that small room in the city where his thoughts might take finite shape instead of remaining the blurred mess he could never sort out. On the other hand, living under grass down Terminus Road allowed his thoughts their flowing line, to tighten which might mean extinction.

So he continued living too far, soon even farther still. Their Brown world, at the end of the yellow-green tunnel called Terminus Road, contracted before the pressure of events. Because war was breaking, had already broken out. Waldo decided in secret that it shouldn't concern them, though his parents' unhappiness, viewed through the glare of yellow grass, caused him temporary doubts. His father couldn't wait to open the papers, but stood by the road, in his braces, perched lopsided on his surgical boot. His mother used to bring out her knitting, out to the veranda, and sit on the daybed, under the classical pediment. The anger in her flashing needles could not compete eventually with the penumbra easily slicing the classical façade, right through, and the wool, the ineffectual steel, she sat holding.

The Gothic arches of dead grass were taking over from the classical. But he would not, would not let it happen.

Waldo Brown at this stage was becoming a smart young fellow. At the Municipal Library they had put him on the catalogue. So the least desirable part of his life was war and all that it implied. In particular he recoiled from those of the enlisted men who wished to make confidences, to turn out all that was most secret, personal, emotional, painful, as though they were emptying a paper bag. Naturally he disguised his feelings, because under the influence of war nobody would have believed in them, least of all those wide-open faces needing to confess, the country faces cured to bacon tints and textures, the faces of the Boys.

Of course everybody loved the Boys, sang to them, with them, about them. All those blouses full of bust with which the streets were suddenly filled, the cheery young matrons who presided over stalls in Martin Place, and the girls, the girls selling metal badges and paper flags—all of them loved the smell of khaki.

But Waldo hated what he could never in any way take part in. At least his physique would not have made him acceptable. If there were moral reasons for his aloofness he had not yet thought them out. Where the war did concern him in any way personally was through Mrs. Feinstein and Dulcie stranded somewhere in Europe. On one occasion he visualized them as victims of a Zeppelin, but the Zeppelin in his mind's eye was little more than a toy against a paper moon. And he turned his face to the pillow, for the discovery that he could not succeed in transforming his moon into the throbbing flesh which in theory he knew it to be.

Oh God oh God, he repeated, in one of the rare moods of intellectual debauchery he allowed himself.

He evolved a kind of taut joviality with which to counter the confidences in trains, of those who were about to embark. Perhaps if he cut his throat he might atone for his own nature, though he doubted it. To one or two he promised to write from his side of the grave. He would have liked to. Oh yes, he would have liked to. He would have liked to *be*.

Walter Pugh was Waldo's gravest source of disturbance. Wally decided to enlist.

"Like any decent bloke has to in the end. Not that I'm holding anything against those who don't. Or not against you, Waldo. You can't be all that strong."

"I mightn't be very good at it," Waldo answered truthfully.

"Who knows who'll be good at what," Wally said; it was an evening of truths, and he had written poems in his day.

(Wally, in fact, was so good at war he got killed for it, and they sent a medal to Cis.)

Wally, who had become one of the Boys, with a leather strap under his lip, and the smell of khaki, took time off to entertain his pal Waldo Brown, at the expense of Cis and Ernie Baker, before leaving for that hypothetical Front.

Cis had got hold of a boiler and done it up in egg sauce. Afterwards, over the port and nuts, Waldo disclosed that he had a voice. He sang "In the Gloaming," "The Tide Will Turn," and "Singing Voices, Marching Feet"—all light, appropriate stuff. The silkiness of his voice brought the tears to Cis's eyes, and Waldo himself rubbed his pince-nez with a handkerchief between the items. He was smiling slightly for the success of his contribution.

Only Wally sat set stiffer than usual. He had put on weight since the declaration of war, but camp had turned the fat to meat. The pimples were gone, the movements of his buttocks were controlled, and he needed to talk less about the tarts, perhaps had even done one or two of them in the scrub before you got to Permanent Avenue.

He was a good bloke. Waldo might have loved Wally, if that truth had been admitted. As it was, after several beers on the last night but one—the relatives naturally claimed their soldier on the last—they embraced in George Street, furtively, though affectionately, and the stench of khaki was inebriating.

"Do you remember that girl?" Waldo felt it was required of him to ask as they staggered in each other's arms.

"What girl?"

"That Dulcie."

"Oh," said Wally.

Soon after that he was sailing away, and the incident was one to forget.

Waldo had to remember the morning Cis came into the Library. He knew it must have happened, because she was in black. At once he would have liked to look for some excuse in the darker warren of the stacks.

When she had told him, Cis said, "And there's these three or four poems, Waldo. I brought them because you're the literary one. What am I to do with them?"

Everybody was watching.

"Oh yes, Mrs. Baker," Waldo said, when he had been in the habit of calling her Cissie. "I'd take, I'd keep them," he said, "if I were you—well, for the time—wait and see."

So Mrs. Ernie Baker took the three or four poems, which were so unlike her brother, they would in no way help her to realize he had existed. It was reasonable enough, however, it appeared from her face, to suppose the poems might mature by keeping, like wine for instance. She left the Municipal Library in her squashed black hat, her varicose veins just beginning.

Waldo wondered whether anybody listening had expected him to offer nobler advice in the light-coloured, young man's voice he sometimes overheard. He himself was enraged and mortified, not so much by the death of his friend and colleague Walter Pugh, as by the nobler rage which eluded him.

That weekend he went so far as to begin a poem which he hoped might be to some extent expressive of the nobler rage. He wrote:

> Oh to die where poppies shed their blood
> On youths grown faceless in the mud
> For Freedom's effigy to rear its head . . .

(As an old man Waldo Brown discovered these lines amongst his papers, and got a thrill, the "genuine *frisson*," as it had come to be called. It was a pity he hadn't finished the thing. In the same sheaf was that other fragment of his youth scribbled on a piece of official notepaper he must have swiped from the Librarian:

> In my dry brain my spirit soon,
> Down-deepening from swoon to swoon,
> Faints like a dazzled morning moon. . . .

That was it! His hands trembled, and the sheet of paper gave out a stronger smell of enclosure. The light had looked different in those days, keen and expectant, at Sarsaparilla. Not even Goethe, a disagreeable, egotistical man and overrated writer, whom he had always detested, could have equalled Waldo Brown's "dazzled morning moon.")

Towards the end of the war, when it had been on so long people had begun to accept the killing as a clause in a natural law, thus making Waldo Brown feel somehow less responsible for the state of affairs, he walked home one evening by way of O'Halloran Road, to find lights on at *Mount Pleasant*, the jigsaw of partly illuminated lawn looking and smelling freshly mown. He was still wondering, when a woman or girl came out, and stood observing from the veranda. Then, she came running down the steps, at such a speed her bosom flew up and down with the exertion—she hadn't yet set in the formal concrete of womanhood—and there, it was Dulcie Feinstein.

"Why," he said, "I thought you got stuck, over the other side."

"For goodness' sake, Waldo, whatever made you think that?" she babbled in her pleasure. "We came back not long after the outbreak of war. It was a bit hair-raising, I admit. There was a submarine."

Dulcie's formerly frizzy hair was neatly done in a bun at the nape of her neck. She was a very neat, pleasant young woman. There was no mystery, probably never had been. The dark sleeves, ending in narrow white above her elbows, ruled that out. She was too emphatically defined.

"But the house," he said, "looked dead"—when he had meant deserted; he could have kicked himself for using a word so full of recoil.

"Daddy couldn't bear to come here," said Dulcie. "He's been so upset by everything. You remember all those intellectual theories about human progress!"

She would have liked, and did try, to keep it light, giggly, and Australian, but in spite of herself the muted cello notes rose from her thicker throat, as he had heard them also in her mother. Dulcie, though, it was obvious, the matter-of-fact yet still ready-to-become-hysterical young girl, had not yet experienced the full agony of cello music.

"Daddy's not so hardboiled and materialistic, not to say theoretical, as you might think," Dulcie was telling Waldo, while keeping her face turned from him, perhaps so that he shouldn't see her eyes.

Still, there was a touch of velvet.

It had grown darker too.

Perhaps feeling that the temporary circumstances, of whatever colour, were slipping from them, she began again girlishly to babble, leaning over the gate, spitting slightly from between her teeth in her effort to get it all out, but all.

"You must come up to tea. To afternoon tea. And we'll have a good yarn. I've got a collection of postcards I made while we were in Europe. My cousins were sweet to me."

He was wasting his time hanging round this silly girl at the gate.

"But make it Saturday," Dulcie warned. "Because I work in the shop, Waldo, now. In the office. They tell me I'm good at figures. So I have that at least in common with poor old Arthur. How is Arthur, Waldo?" she asked.

He was already mumbling off along the road.

"Give him my love. I do love Arthur."

Shattering Waldo not by throwing a stone.

"I'll tell Daddy," she promised—though why?

"So long!" he called back.

It was the kind of expression Daddy's silly girl seemed to ask for.

So they were going up the hill again to Feinsteins' on a Saturday afternoon. How raw he had been formerly: all fluff and pimples, and food-spots, and the Barranugli High hatband. Waldo touched with the tip of his tongue the hair on his upper lip. It was satisfactorily, wirily male. It shone, he liked to think, with personal magnetism, as well as a dash of brilliantine.

But poor Arthur was almost unchanged and, as things were, probably wouldn't alter much. His shirt-sleeves open at the wrist because the buttons came off at once, he would remain a bigger, shamblier boy, staring this way and that, as if unable to select the detail on which to concentrate. Unless it was numbers. Figures continued to rivet Arthur.

Arthur said, "Thought you knew Feinsteins got back after the outbreak of war. Thought I mentioned it. I must have."

"If you did, you must have mumbled," Waldo said.

They were going up the same O'Halloran Road, where new houses, to spite war, were flaunting the same old signs of life.

"How did you know, anyway?"

"Dulcie's p.c. She sent me a card from some *lake*. An *Italian* lake. I forget. I lost the card. I'm sure I *told* you, Waldo, Feinsteins decided to come back."

"I wish you could remember the name of the lake."

For the name of the lake to be withheld was almost as bad as not having received the card.

"It's too difficult. I'm tired," Arthur said, closing down.

But when they arrived he began to glitter dangerously.

"Oh Mrs. Feinstein," he began, "I am that, I am *so* glad you are receiving us again. In your *salong*."

And pursed up not only his mouth but the whole of the lower part of his face, in an insult to his brother.

Mrs. Feinstein was overjoyed.

"Oh, Arthur," she cried, "I don't know how we can deprive ourselves of the pleasure of seeing you more often."

She couldn't stop hugging him, as though he were only a boy. Which he was.

Events had aged Mrs. Feinstein. Her skin was more than ever of that exposed-private-flesh colour, with a dusting of grey. She had shrunk into herself somewhat, excepting her nose, which hung, suggesting something Waldo wished he could remember.

"What have you got for us to eat today?" Arthur asked.

But Mrs. Feinstein looked sad and grey. She gave a sideways look. She said, "We are a lot older than we were."

When Dulcie brought the tea there was a plate with biscuits from the tin.

Still, Arthur was pleased.

"I could eat the lot," he said, and started by the coloured ones.

Dulcie showed her picture postcards.

"I want to know," Waldo said, putting on a mildly accusatory expression, "the name of the Italian lake."

"Which one?" Dulcie asked. "There are several."

She was bent above her postcards, trying, it seemed, to disguise herself as an absorbed little girl, to whom the names of lakes meant less than their colours and gloss. But for Waldo the withheld name was a source of increasing resentment, as though she had been unfaithful to him intellectually.

> "Como, Lugarno,
> Have a banarno. . . ."

Arthur began to sing; he loved to join in the singing in the streets.

Waldo was afraid his brother would become dangerous that afternoon, particularly when Arthur suggested to Mrs. Feinstein that he should take the tray out to the kitchen. Waldo waited for the crash.

It had not yet happened, when Arthur burst back into the room, wearing, his shouting seemed to emphasize, the *capple* Mr. Feinstein had kept as a symbol of his emancipation.

"Who am *Ieeehhh*?
Guess! Guess! *Guesss!*"

Arthur hissed rather than sang.

Waldo could only sit holding his kneecaps, from which sharp blades had shot out on Arthur's reappearance.

Arthur sang the answer to his question without waiting for anyone to try:

> "*Peerrot d'amor*
> At half past four,
> That's what I am!
> How the leaves twitter—
> And titter!
> No one is all that dry,
> But *Ieeehhh!*"

Mrs. Feinstein, who had behaved so *piano* since her welcome, with hands in the sleeves of a coat she was wearing although it wasn't cold, began to shriek with laughter.

> "I am the bottom of the bottom,"

Arthur sang,

> "But shall not dwell
> On which well.
> Might see my face
> At the bott-*urrhm!*"

There he stopped abruptly, and his face, which had become impasted with the thick white substance of his song, returned to what was for Arthur normal, as he hung his ruff together with Mr. Feinstein's *capple* on the knob of a chair.

"What a lovely song! Where did you learn it?" Dulcie finished laughing, and asked.

Her upper lip was encrusted with little pearly beads.

"I made it up," said Arthur, primly.

Not so prim as Waldo.

Waldo said, "I think you'd better sit down. Otherwise you'll overexcite yourself."

Arthur obeyed, and when he was again seated, they heard Mrs.

Feinstein's throat settling itself back, as though to suggest they were all as they were in the beginning.

Presently Waldo asked Dulcie, "Don't you still play the piano?"

"Yes," she answered guiltily.

"Can you play us the 'Moonlight Sonata'?"

Now, he thought, he'd show her up.

"It might be disastrous," Dulcie said, but got out of her chair to prepare for it.

It seemed as though they were all under compulsion, with the exception of Arthur, who had contributed enough to their dissolution and fallen asleep, masticating a few last crumbs of Arnotts' biscuit.

The moon was rising, however jerkily, as Dulcie began to play.

Waldo at once knew how wrong he had been to encourage her to make an exhibition of herself. Needn't have accepted, of course, if she hadn't wanted to. But it was going to be a heroic struggle. Not in the beginning, not in the Adagio what's-it. There she could lay the atmosphere on, and did, in almost visible slabs. Dulcie's ever so slightly hairy arms were leaning on the solid air, first one side, then on the other. Building up her defences against inevitable suicide somewhere along that road which was never moonlit enough. Her shoulders, however, were getting above themselves. If she had started humbly, the music had made her proud. It was kidding her all over again into becoming the genius she was never intended to be, dissolving the bones in her arms with a promise of release, offering a universe of passion instead of plunkety-plunk on the home upright. For moments Waldo was truly tortured by that innocence in others to which he was periodically subjected. He could, at last, have been responsible.

Not Mrs. Feinstein. She was responsible for nothing. She was beating time, chasing the tail end of a tune, out of her fur sleeve.

Waldo frowned. He wished he could remember what Mrs. Feinstein's nose . . .

He yawned. They had entered on a boring stretch, during which he watched himself opening the Private Papers on a Sunday—such an abuse, but Sunday was the day of abuse—taking out his pen to immortalize a false moment, bottling the essence of Dulcie Feinstein's *sostenuto*.

When a succession of little pure notes trickled from her fingers into the living room, suddenly and unexpectedly, but right. He could have sunk his teeth in the nape of her neck where the little curls were unfurling, from beneath the bun, with the logic of notes of music on the page.

With less logic than tenacity Dulcie began to shape the Allegretto. The paper moon was dangling. Unwisely she allowed herself to indulge in coy skips and pretty sidesteps for the Allegretto, and did not recover her balance in time for arrival at the precipice.

Dulcie plainly wasn't prepared, and never would be, for Beethoven's prestiferous night. It made her lunge at the piano as if to crack, to tear the walnut open. Her arms lashing. Her fingers clutching at the keyboard. From the muscles in her neck, her throat must have been swelling, knotting, reddening, strangling with the poetry which had got into it.

Would it escape without his assistance? Or someone else's? Waldo could only look at her back and wonder. By now his pants were a network of creases. He thought he loved Dulcie, increasingly, if moodily.

But her back presented itself as a wall which had to be scaled. Was he strong enough? A weak character—oh no, no character is weak if the obsessions are only strong enough. Besides, his obsession was acquiring the surge of Beethoven's proposition. B. was certainly strong enough, if a mightily unpleasant old man writing music on a lavatory wall.

At that moment Waldo Brown realized Mrs. Feinstein's nose reminded him of the uncircumcised penis of an Anglican bishop he had noticed in a public lavatory. The connection was too obvious, too obscene to resist, and he was forced to bring out his handkerchief to sneeze.

So much for Dad, he decided. And the Jews. He was sorry about Dad, the brown burrowing but never arriving eyes, and the twitch of a moustache on your skin years ago.

Dulcie broke off just then, saying, "I can't go any farther."

Immediately afterwards she turned round, her appearance dishevelled, as though she had walked out between storms. Branches still wet and aggressive had hit her in the face, without however breaking her trance, deepening it even, by making her gasp and swallow down the black draught of sky which otherwise she might have shuddered back from. As she sat looking out at them from her irrelevant body with such a pure candour of expression Waldo saw it was he who had lost. He might never be able to forgive her the difficulties she put in the way of loving her.

"I bit off more than I could chew," she admitted with that same awful honesty.

"It was my fault, I'm afraid," Waldo answered politely.

It could have made it worse if Dulcie hadn't been so cool and reasonable, hands in her lap, still seated on the carpet-covered music-stool. Because of this innate reasonableness, which was another surprise silly, frivolous, mysterious Dulcie had sprung on him, he would have liked to counter it with something really good, of such truth, simplicity, and directness, say, "Der Jüngling an der Quelle," that he would have shamed her further, even deeply, for her pretentious performance of the Beethoven. But he feared Schubert might not collaborate in this. He would have to rely on a few ballads to decorate his passable voice.

For he sensed that Mrs. Feinstein was about to invite him to take his turn at showing off.

"Don't you in any way perform, Waldo?" she asked in what he heard to be a disbelieving voice.

So the moment had arrived. He said he would sing a few songs.

"Though I warn you, I accompany myself very badly, with little more than one finger!"

"Oh," said Dulcie, "perhaps I can help."

And did when she heard the titles. He sang them "In the Gloaming," "The Tide Will Turn," and "Singing Voices, Marching Feet." At once he regretted denying his own skill at the piano, for as he glanced down Dulcie's neck, and at her dexterous hands, he realized he was putting, not so much no expression, as the wrong one, into the words he was singing. Because how could Dulcie have learnt the accompaniments, if not at some sing-song for the Boys? Thumping out worse, no doubt, in a vulgar low-cut blouse, as the bacon-faced men, smelling of khaki and old pennies, propped themselves up on the piano. Anyone coarsening so early as

Dulcie, in both arms and figure, could only have acted openly. The authentic AIF brooch she must have worn would barely have held her breasts together.

After this discovery he confessed his voice was dry.

"You will tire yourself, giving so much." Mrs. Feinstein sighed.

And Dulcie said, "I never realized you had such a charming tenor voice."

With the result that it almost rose again, silkily, in his injured throat.

But the afternoon, like the lolling Arthur, had just about exhausted itself. As the others sat nibbling at a few last crumbs of conversation, his head rolled without waking, and for a moment Waldo noticed with repulsion the whites of his brother's upturned eyes.

If he had not been making other discoveries he would have woken Arthur. Instead he noticed Dulcie was wearing, not the AIF brooch, but a Star of David on a gold chain.

"Are you religious?" he asked, as brittlely as the question demanded.

She pulled an equally brittle face. He might have teased her some more if Mrs. Feinstein hadn't wandered off at a tangent.

"I am so sorry," she said, "you will not have had the opportunity of meeting Leonard Saporta. On another occasion he was to have come, but he had the grippe or something, I seem to remember. This time he has been too impulsive. He slammed a door, and cut his hand on the glass knob."

"Is he a relative?" Waldo asked.

Mrs. Feinstein said, "No."

The mention of relatives set her off again, and he hardly dared, though did finally, inquire after the Signora Terni of Milan.

"Old, old." Mrs. Feinstein protested against it. "Very agèd."

Then Waldo grew more daring.

"And Madame Hochapfel?"

Mrs. Feinstein was desolated. She emulated Arthur in showing the whites of her eyes.

"Before we have reached Europe," Mrs. Feinstein replied in a voice from beyond the grave.

"Aunt Gaby had lived, Mummy," Dulcie suggested.

Her idea was to stanch the cello music, but it sounded, rather, as though she had turned her mother's lament into a duet.

When Mrs. Feinstein began to take herself in hand.

"I don't know what Daddy would have to say to so much Jewish emotionalism. I was thankful we did not have him with us, either in Paris or Milan. Poor things, *they* are devout." Mrs. Feinstein smiled for the sick, though it could have been she enjoyed the sickness. "Of course we did whatever was expected of us while we were there. We did not have the heart to tell them we have given up all such middle-aged ideas, to conform," she said, "to conform with the spirit of progress. Daddy, I am afraid, who is more forceful in his expression, would have offended."

After that she disappeared, trailing the outdoor coat she was wearing. It was so out of place. It was also so shapeless it might have been inherited.

Waldo would have woken Arthur, only he saw that Dulcie, in some distraction, had thrown open the glass doors and was holding her handkerchief to her upper lip, while breathing the rather fetid air of their wartime garden.

"Aren't you well?" he asked.

"Oh, yes," she said, "I am *well*! Didn't you gather I am very healthy?"

Suddenly he knew he would like to say: Dearest, dearest Dulcie —taking her hands in his hands with a suppleness not peculiar to them.

Instead he continued standing stiffly, against the prospect of staggy hydrangeas, their leaves yellow and speckled from neglect.

Dulcie, he realized, had begun to cry. Very softly. Which made it worse.

"What is it?" he asked, in a tone to match—worse and worse.

"There is so much I don't, I shall never be able to grasp," she said abruptly, in a comparatively loud and shocking voice.

At the same time she held out her arms, not to him, but in one of the ugly gestures with which she had fought Beethoven, again in an attempt to embrace some recalcitrant vastness.

Fortunately Arthur woke, and it was clearly time to go.

"Then you can have a proper cry," Arthur advised through a yawn.

"I've done all the crying, proper or improper, I intend to do," Dulcie said.

She sounded so very practical.

"Give my regards, Arthur," she said, "to your mother. I hope one day we shall meet."

Arthur was dawdling his way through the garden. He could have been feeling depressed.

"Oh. My mother," he murmured. Then: "You mightn't like each other," he called back.

As it was too probable to answer, Dulcie went inside, closing the door, against the glass panels of which Waldo saw her figure pressed, very lightly, fleetingly. He remembered seeing a fern pressed under glass, the ribs more clearly visible.

Then he and Arthur were going away. Arthur was holding him by the hand.

Anything so unassessable, and in a way he did not wish to assess their relationship with the Feinsteins, was liable to suffer from the more positive occurrences. The Poulters, for instance. The Poulters arrived in Terminus Road perhaps about 1920; anyway, Dad had retired, but had not died. Waldo remembered with difficulty the occasion of his first setting eyes on the Poulters. All too soon there were the heap of bricks, the matchsticks of timber, but before that, yes, he could remember the day the man and woman trampled round and round in the grass, more like cattle let loose on fresh pasture. Then the man appeared to be pacing out dimensions. Mother went inside, saying she had heartburn, but Waldo stayed to watch, in spite of the felted chug-chug from somewhere in the region of his throat or heart. The man was a thin one. The woman, more noticeably fleshed, had stupid-looking calves, which Waldo thought he would have liked to slap if he had been following her up a flight of stairs. Slap slap. To make her hop. After a bit the strangers went away, driving in a sulky with a sweaty horse, lowering their eyes to avoid the glances of those who had the advantage over them by being there already.

"They hired that horse and trap for the day," Arthur informed the family as they sat at tea eating the salmon loaf.

No one any longer asked how Arthur knew. (He had, in fact, gone across the road, to look closer and ask.)

"They're from up country," he said. "Mr. Poulter was a rouse-about, Mrs. Poulter helped at the homestead."

"But why have they come down here?" Mother wondered.

"To be more independent," Arthur explained at once.

Waldo laughed. He had begun to feel gratifyingly superior.

"But why Terminus Road? Why directly opposite us?" Mother couldn't leave it alone.

"They had to go *some*where," Arthur said.

"What have we got to hide, Annie?" Dad asked.

Only Mother and Waldo knew.

And the Poulters came.

Bill Poulter, who remained scraggy, and awkwardly articulated, began to build the home. There was someone, some lad out of Sarsaparilla, giving him a hand. They were putting together the blank box, very quickly, it seemed, so much so the grey flannel undervests hung darker from their shoulders to their ribs. In the end the structure looked less a square house than an oblong house-boat.

All this time Mrs. Poulter had been living in a tin shed on the site. She cooked on an open fire, and the smell of burning wood floated up and crossed the road, together with the smells from her boiling pot, or, more accurately, half a kero tin.

Mrs. Poulter herself began to come across the road. She borrowed a cup of sugar, a cup of rice. She was the high-complexioned decent young woman they got to know, who put on a brave red hat to walk up Terminus Road to Allwrights' or the post office. Sometimes Arthur brought the orders home for her; sometimes, if it was closing time, they walked down together, Arthur carrying the brown-paper bags and the newspaper parcels. She seemed to take to him, or at least she didn't mind, as some women did.

From the beginning Mrs. Poulter gave the impression of wanting to perform some charitable act.

"If you was ever sick, you know, you'd only have to give us a shout, Mrs. Brown, and I'd come across and do what I could. Sit with you at night, or anything like that. Or if it was the men, Bill would. I think Bill would," she was careful to add.

Waldo knew how this sort of thing embarrassed their mother.

Mrs. Poulter told Mother the war had got on Bill's nerves sort of, not that he had been gassed or shell-shocked, or gone overseas even, but from being in a camp. Afterwards he couldn't settle. That was one of several reasons why they had come to Sarsaparilla. Where she hoped to keep a few hens, and grow flowers, she loved all flowers. Bill was going to get taken on by the Shire Council. Only temporary. Because Council labourer wasn't much of a job for a man. Bill could kill, milk, fell trees, he had once entered for a woodchopping competition though he hadn't won. It was terrible dry up country where they had come from. That was Mungindribble. Her own people came from Numburra. Her auntie had started having the indigestion, they thought, when it turned out to be cancer. They said, said Mrs. Poulter, there was a cure for it from violet leaves. If only she could make certain, she would perhaps grow the violets, and post the leaves in a moist parcel.

Mother decided after that not to encourage Mrs. Poulter. Though you couldn't say Mother wasn't always polite, not to say kind. She gave Mrs. Poulter a piece of lace insertion.

Sometimes when his wife crossed the road, to borrow, return, or yarn, Bill Poulter would come down to the grass edge of their side, and stand looking across, squinting because of the sun. His arms, usually exposed as far as the armpits, for he had had her cut off the sleeves, were stringy rather than muscular, with prominent veins. He never had much to say, not even, it seemed, to his wife.

Although the material wasn't promising, Waldo began to wonder whether he could make Bill Poulter his friend. He walked springily at the prospect, deciding how he should go about it. He had never really had a friend of his own sex, unless you could count Walter Pugh, for whom he could never have really cared, because of those ridiculous literary ambitions. But take Bill Poulter—virgin soil, so to speak. He might turn Bill into whatever he chose by cultivating his crude manliness for the best.

So, if Bill Poulter happened to be hoeing or hewing within easy distance as he passed, Waldo took to flicking his head sideways at him, as he had seen other men, and sometimes his neighbour would flick back, nothing more, in recognition. On other occasions Bill just didn't seem to see. Waldo used to walk quite prim and virginal, wondering whether Bill would recognize or not. It began to matter a great deal.

Until he knew he must take the bull by the horns, as it were, if he intended to influence their neighbour's mind and future. He might, for a start, lend him a book, something quite simple and primitive, Fenimore Cooper, say, they still had *The Deerslayer* in the Everyman edition. Waldo made his decision returning from the Library on a Friday night. That Sunday morning he went across to Bill Poulter, who was splitting a pile of wood for the stove. (Mrs. Poulter had gone up the road to church or chapel, or whatever brand of poison she took.)

Waldo opened by flicking his head. Then he squatted down, to watch in silence, as he had learnt from seeing other men, or comment knowledgeably on the weather.

Bill Poulter chopped. He nearly always had a sucked-looking cigarette butt hanging extinct from his lower lip. Though sometimes he would pause to roll a fresh one.

"So you think it's gunna rain, do yer?" Bill responded antiphonally as he rolled his next cigarette. "Could do," he dared add. "Clouds are comun from the right direction."

The situation couldn't be called desperate. The climate was too positive. A smell of male exertion on the air encouraged Waldo to come to the point.

"Ever go in for reading books?" he asked very cautiously.

"Nah." Bill swung the axe and split the knottiest chunk of wood. "Never ever have the time."

"I'd lend you a few decent books," Waldo offered.

Something had made him boyish.

"If you read the paper," he coaxed, "and I see you do take the *Herald*, you might find you had time for a read of a book."

"Nah," said Bill. "Wife reads the paper. But what's the point? Don't know anybody down in Sydney."

Waldo's long wrists hung between his squatting thighs as he watched Bill Poulter chop.

"Then there's nothing I can do for you," he said at last.

Bill didn't deny that. He was flinging the wood into a barrow, piece by piece, as he split it, and the fuller the barrow the more wooden the thud.

Bill said through his ugly teeth, "Don't find time enough for thinkun, let alone gettun littery."

Waldo refused to feel humiliated. He continued squatting for a little, smiling a shallow smile at the chunks of wood, at the knots split apparently by light.

Soon after this Bill Poulter got taken by the Council and Waldo saw less of their neighbour, as their movements did not coincide. On occasions when he did catch sight of Bill, the stringy rather than muscular arms with veins so prominent as to become obtrusive, he no longer flicked his head sideways. And Bill did not even look, forcing Waldo to remember the day he had offered the books. It had become so sickeningly physical. It was as if he had been snubbed for making what they called in the papers an indecent proposition.

But Waldo did not hate Bill, not exactly, or not yet. You could only despise ignorant, suspicious minds. Or the simple, wide-open ones. That Mrs. Poulter, for example, with her puddings, and her hens troubled with the white diarrhoea. Not that he spoke to her. Not that he saw her, even. But knew she was there.

Arthur used to keep him informed. "Mrs. Poulter let me taste the lemon sago pudding. When I brought the order down. She has a hen, she says, will bust herself from laying eggs the size she does. Mrs. Poulter says there was a goat she knew at Numburra ate a basinful of yeast. The goat blew up."

"Why," Waldo asked, "do you have to listen to that stupid, babbling cow?

"I don't just listen. We tell each other things."

"I'm sick to death of the very Name!" Mother said at last.

Arthur told quietly after that, but told. "When I was over there Sunday afternoon she was washing her hair. In a kero tin. She makes a lotion out of bay leaves. She showed me the leaves. You never saw such lovely hair. But it's not what it was. It used to reach down below her waist."

"You have your job, son," said Dad in some difficulty—he had begun by those years to gasp. "Why don't you concentrate on that?"

Arthur kept quiet.

And Mrs. Poulter remained the same young woman, of firm flesh and high complexion, her hair glistening in certain lights. There was nothing you could have accused her of. Nothing. Except perhaps her living in the boat-shaped erection immediately opposite, with the fowl sheds and wire netting behind.

Arthur began to go very carefully, to speak very softly.

"She took me over the hill," he no more than breathed. "We saw the Chinese woman standing under the wheel-tree. You ought to see a wheel-tree flowering. I would never have seen without she took me."

Waldo shuddered.

He used to feel relieved starting for the Library while the greeny-yellow light reflected off the arching grass was still too weak to paralyse. He was glad of his job on the catalogue. At least Dad had retired, and buses had replaced the train which used to run between Sarsaparilla and Barranugli, so Waldo could give himself to the more pneumatic bus, and reflect bitterly on his relationship with his father. His mother too. She who might have conceived him in more appropriate circumstances must expect to share the blame.

On several occasions, when she was old and preparing to die, Waldo tempted his mother by asking, "Why did you marry Dad?"

Her teeth were giving her difficulty, and she would not always answer at first.

"Because, I suppose," she once replied, managing her old and complicated teeth, "we were members of the Fabian Society. And your father was a good man. Oh, yes, I loved him. I loved him. The way one does."

She was determined not to be caught out.

But Dad. In that dark street. With the Baptist chapel at one end.

After he retired, Dad would sometimes recall, in the spasmodic phrasing which came with the asthma, his escape by way of Intellectual Enlightenment, and the voyage to Australia, from what had threatened to become a permanence in black and brown, but in the telling, he would grow darker rather than enlightened, his breathing thicker, clogged with the recurring suspicion that he might be chained still. Waldo was not sure, but had an idea his father had turned against him because he, of all the gang, had escaped.

Dad would look at him and say, "Anyway, Waldo, you have had the opportunity. I gave it to you at the start." (As if he had, but that was what the poor devil liked to think.) "Nothing ought to hold you back. Although, I admit, your brother will be a handicap."

You could see that behind the words their father was really hoping his son Waldo might be recaptured, to remain chained to the rest of them. Waldo had to have a quiet laugh. As if *he* were the one a shingle short! He wouldn't stay chained to Arthur, or anyone else. He was only marking time, and would create the work of art he was intended to create, perhaps even out of that impasto of nonconformist guilt from which Dad had never struggled free and was so desperately longing to unload on someone else. The irony of it would be that Dad should inspire something memorable, something perfect. But first Waldo must cultivate detachment.

In the meantime it amused him to see his colleagues at the Library remain unconscious of what was hatching. Unquenchable mediocrities, their only experience of genius was on paper.

Not the least subtle and satisfying moments of his life at that period were those of his return to Sarsaparilla, by exhausted summer light, or breathtaking winter dark, his thought so lucid, so pointed, so independent, he could have started—if he had had a pencil and notebook, which he never had—there and then at the Barranugli bus stop to rough out something really important.

It came as a shock on such an evening when the voices of two men cut in.

He knew the men by sight, one of them a Council employee, a fellow called Holmes, of bad reputation, generally pretty far gone in drink, the other a stooge to his companion of the moment.

Holmes was saying, "Sawney bugger!" He laughed without mirth. "Now don't tell me Bill Poulter isn't a sawney. Because I know. Know why 'e went sick last week?"

"No. Why?" his companion asked because it was expected of him.

"It's 'is missus. 'Is missus is leading 'im by the nose."

"Go on!" said the other, smaller, beadier, perking up. "A fine class of woman if it's the one I think."

"I dunno which you think," Holmes continued, "but I could do with a slice of Bill Poulter's missus meself. Not that she'd come at me. Seems to got pretty funny ideas."

"Ah?" His companion was again only formally interested.

The man Holmes, rocking on his heels, had lowered his chin to resist the intensity of an experience.

"Seen 'er making through the scrub with that bluey nut Arthur Brown."

"Go *on!*" said the other, soaring to astonishment.

"Even in the street. Seen 'er 'olding 'im by the hand."

The little beady person had whipped his head around, the better to visualize a situation, or actually to watch it happening on the screen of Holmes's face.

"Mind you," said Holmes, "for all they say, that Arthur Brown, I don't think, could do more harm than a cut cat."

The little one nearly peed himself.

"You can't be all that sure," he said, "the knife 'as done its job. Sometimes they slip up on it, eh?"

"Yer might be right," Holmes answered. "And a woman like that, married to such a sawney bastard, she wouldn't wait for 'em to put the acid on 'er."

Then he looked round, and stopped, not because he noticed, let alone recognized, Waldo Brown, but because his story was finished except in his thoughts.

All the way in the Sarsaparilla bus Waldo could have thrown up. And at tea. He pushed his knife and fork to the side. The pickled onions had never smelt more metallic.

Later on, he decided to have it out with Arthur, though he couldn't think how he would put it.

Arthur was in the kitchen, mixing dough for a batch of bread. His shoulders rounded over the bowl. His hair alight. The tatters of dough with which his hands were hung made them look dreadful—webbed, or leprous.

Then it all came out of Waldo, not in vomit, but in words.

"I want to talk to you," he gasped. "This woman, this Mrs. Poulter business, if you knew what you were up to, but it's us, it's us too, ought to be considered, if you did you wouldn't traipse through the scrub, or in the street, the *street,* holding hands with Mrs. Poulter!"

Arthur had never looked emptier. His face was as clear as spring-water.

"She takes my hand," he said, "if I'm having difficulty. If I can't keep up, for instance. If I tire."

The bread, which was his vocation, had begun to grow difficult. The long, stringy dough was knotting at the ends of his fingers.

"Then," he added, "Mrs. Poulter is my friend."

Waldo laughed out loud through the sweat which was bouncing off his face.

"Oh yes!" He laughed. "So they're saying! That's the point. Whatever the truth, that's beside it. Don't you see? And you're degrading *us*! Even if you're too thick-witted to be hurt by what other people think and say."

When suddenly the bread grew simpler. Arthur had freed his fingers.

"Mrs. Poulter," he said, "says we mustn't go together any more. Her husband got offended."

If you could believe that people were so simple, and Waldo couldn't quite, but hoped. Dignity is too hard won, and lost too easily.

"Well, if you've decided it like that, between yourselves," he said, "I congratulate you, Arthur."

It made him feel like Arthur's elder brother, which in fact he had become.

While Arthur's overgrown-boy's face was consoled by this simple arrangement. He went on simply to fill the greased tins with dough.

Not long after, Waldo overheard in the bus that Mrs. Feinstein had died. It was a shock to him, not because he had felt particularly close to Mrs. Feinstein, but the unexpectedness of her death found him abominably unprepared. (He would have felt equally put out if Mrs. Feinstein, if anyone, Arthur even, opened the bedroom door without warning and caught him in a state of nakedness examining a secret.) At first he felt he didn't want to overhear any more of the rumour the bus was throwing out at him. Then he decided to listen, and perhaps turn it to practical account.

To be precise, Mrs. Feinstein had died several weeks ago, the informant was continuing, and old Feinstein and the daughter had now come to sort out their things before disposing of the house, it was only understandable, what would a man, a widower, want with one house in the city and another at Sarsaparilla.

The bus ran on.

Waldo was relieved Arthur hadn't found out about Mrs. Feinstein's death. He couldn't have. He would have announced it immediately.

So Waldo kept quiet. He would have to write, he supposed, although, when you came to consider, he had barely known the woman. Even so, Waldo composed several letters, none of which was suitable, one being too literary, another too matter-of-fact, almost bordering on the banal, a third, though addressed to the father, suggested by its tone that it was intended for the daughter.

So Waldo decided to walk over to O' Halloran Road quietly one weekend. It was a Sunday, as it turned out, which made his decision more discreet, formal in a way. As he walked, it even began to appear momentous. Could it be that this was one of the crucial points in his life? His mouth grew dry at the idea. He had, if he wanted to be truthful with himself, thought vaguely, though only vaguely, once or twice, that in the end he might decide to marry Dulcie Feinstein. Now her mother's death was helping a decision crystallize by introducing a certain emotional compulsion and inevitability. It was obvious they had both been waiting for some such occasion to drop their defences and accept an arrangement which could only turn out best for themselves.

As he walked along the roadside, thoughtfully decapitating the weeds, Waldo went over the ways in which he would benefit by marriage with Dulcie. On the financial side they might have to skimp a bit at first, because he would refuse to touch anything Dulcie brought with her until he had proved himself as a husband. Nobody would be in a position to say theirs was not an idealistic marriage. The ring—they would decide on something in the semiprecious line, of course, though he would not suggest an opal, as some women were foolish enough to believe opals bring bad luck. Then, the home. Undoubtedly he would benefit by having a home of his own. A bed to himself. And the meals Dulcie would prepare, rather dainty, foreign-tasting dishes, more digestible, more imaginative and spontaneously conceived. Because food to Mother was something you couldn't avoid, and which she had always offered with a sigh. But it was his work, his real work, which would benefit most. The atmosphere in which to evolve a style. The novel of psychological relationships in a family, based on his own experience, for truth, illuminated by what his imagination would infuse. One of the first things he intended to do was buy a filing cabinet to install in his study.

It was all so exhilarating. He wondered whether Dulcie would affect surprise. More than probably. He doubted whether any woman, faced with that particular situation, ever came out of it completely honest.

When he arrived at the house Waldo was surprised to find it didn't look any different. He had feared it might be wearing an oppressive air. As it wasn't he felt relieved, though he couldn't help wondering a bit about the Feinsteins. They had *seemed* very fond of the old girl.

He went up, and into the long room in which his relationship with the family had grown. Now there was a smell of dust, of furniture disturbed, of new, glaring packing-cases. Waldo almost protected his eyes. And heard his breath snore backwards down his throat on discovering his brother Arthur seated with Dulcie on the sofa. They were facing each other, their knees touching. Waldo couldn't help noticing Dulcie's, because her skirt was drawn up higher than usual, exposing the coarse calves which filled her black stockings. For at least she *wore* mourning.

Dulcie and Arthur looked round, out of some intimate, not to say secret, situation in which they had been discovered.

Dulcie couldn't help laughing, which made her look, you couldn't say pretty, but healthy.

"Poor Waldo has seen a ghost!"

Arthur too laughed a bit.

"He got a shock because it's me."

It was certainly a shock. Arthur was wearing a coat besides, which he almost never did, and his hair was darkened to a deep chestnut by the watering it had undergone.

"Anyway," he said, "I'm going now, because I've done what I came for. I still have a lot of messages to run, and you like to have

Dulcie to yourself. Waldo," he told her, "is just about the jealousest thing you'll find."

Waldo could get nothing out but a mumbling "I I I," at the same time propping himself against one of Feinsteins' obscenely physical chairs.

But Arthur and Dulcie were again ignoring him.

"Arthur, dear," Dulcie was saying, "thank you again. I am so touched."

She was looking into her hand. She could hardly express herself, it appeared, as she sat on the sofa, in her black dress, turning her face at last towards Arthur. Although her mother had died, Dulcie's was not a mourning face. Her expression, rather, attempted to offer joy to those she addressed. Her eyes shone, no longer like those of a suppliant spaniel, but like those of a woman, Waldo feared, of some experience and certainty.

"You can tell if you like," Arthur said. "Otherwise people may feel hurt."

"I shall have to make up my mind," Dulcie answered.

She was offering her face almost as though for a kiss. Waldo forced himself to concentrate on the ugly shadow of Dulcie's encroaching moustache.

"For the moment," she was saying, "I'd like to keep it as something between ourselves."

"That's up to you," said Arthur.

He was trying to imitate a man giving his permission, but had to finish it off with a boy's wriggle of his fat neck. After that, he left.

Waldo was embarrassed, not only by the situation, but by the shambles of a room, the clutter of old newspapers and the packing-cases, which Dulcie, apparently, had been filling dutifully with ornaments and books.

"I'm sorry if I interrupted," Waldo felt he ought to say.

He was glad he hadn't composed a speech to suit his intention, because certainly he would have forgotten it.

"It was nothing," said Dulcie, "nothing."

It didn't sound convincing, and she got up and emptied her hand into a little tortoise-shell box, which she took out of one of the half-packed cases, and which Waldo had noticed in a cabinet in the days of false permanence.

"What I came to say was really of no importance either." Perhaps that was going too far. "I mean," he said, "it is not of immediate importance, because Mrs. Feinstein, and nothing I can say in sympathy will help," he said, "either you, or your father. Or Mrs. Feinstein."

He was pleased with that, its humility.

Dulcie had begun to bite her lip. She was after all a loving daughter. Or was it a dutiful one? Waldo thought he might prefer a dutiful to a loving wife. It was not that he was cold, exactly, but would have to give so much time to his writing.

"Mother was unhappy towards the end," Dulcie was saying. "Her aunts meant so much to her. She resented their being carried off. Then there was the matter of her conscience. But I can't very well go into that. One's conscience is one's own affair."

The word "affair" sounded ill-chosen. Otherwise he was impressed by her rational approach.

"How I agree!" he said quickly. "Nobody should meddle with another's conscience."

He looked at her to see what line he should take next. But Dulcie apparently wished to talk about herself.

"Everybody has been so kind," she said. "Since it happened— that was too terrible to tell about—I haven't felt unhappy. I never expected the death of somebody I loved could make me happy. But it has, Waldo. It seems to have made the living more accessible. Arthur, for instance." Dulcie paused. "He was right, I see now, in suggesting I should tell others what he has done for me, given me. He brought me"—she paused again—"one of his glass marbles."

Waldo was astonished, then horrified, at the strangeness of it.

"He calls them—" she was continuing.

But there Dulcie hesitated longer, as though she were not yet ready.

"Yes! Yes!" Waldo got it in quickly, so that she would understand, either that he knew, or that he didn't want to be told. "Poor Arthur!"

He was in fact deeply relieved to discover Dulcie was such a compassionate girl. Her acceptance of Arthur, her interest in his brother helped him to visualize himself in sickness. She was cool. She had a soothing, practical hand.

"I always wanted, Dulcie, to understand you," Waldo said, "and today I believe I can. What I have found," he stammered, "is exactly what I hoped to find."

Dulcie was looking at him, obviously wanting to hear more. As a student of human nature, he knew that nobody, however modest, could resist being told something more about his or her character. Ladies, moreover, were the livelihood of fortune-tellers.

"Dear Dulcie," he said, "my feelings for you are based on what you truly are. You are what I need, and I hope what I can offer will be what you feel you want. We have music and literature in common. Taste, I like to think. There can't be religious differences, because each of us has seen the light. We expect nothing of life but what we can humanly make of it."

If only the Feinsteins' room hadn't grown so still. He had begun to hear the silence. Dulcie in her black dress was at her very very stillest. She could perhaps be waiting to break out in some demonstration of love. Modesty no doubt had imposed restraint, until she could feel she had received the last inch of encouragement. Or had he offended? Was it about religion? Which was always and unexpectedly liable to raise its ugly head.

Then Dulcie, suddenly, was overflowing with what, in spite of faith in his own proposition, he had hoped to postpone hearing. He would have much preferred to see it in writing, because, after all, situations of such a nature could only be of the embarrassing sort.

She began shaking her head in what appeared a convulsion of passion. He was surprised at the strength of her hand, and wondered how he would manage her.

"Oh, Waldo, Waldo!" Dulcie was almost crying. "It never entered my head that anyone else could get hurt!"

Then she sat down again, bringing a *crump* out of the sofa, and the smell of dust, but it had to be remembered the Feinsteins had spent only part of their time at the house at Sarsaparilla.

"Anyone," he said, "anyone at all sensitive expects to suffer in love. That is what refines it."

"But," said Dulcie, sinking her chin, swallowing some recurrence of emotion.

Although the scene was going to his head he didn't forget he must not lose touch with a lower level, and balanced himself accordingly on the sofa beside her. He would not stare, but was immensely conscious of her eyes brimming with a love she was still too timid to express. Tender Dulcie!

"I am not in love, though," she said. "At least," she said, "I am afraid," but there she halted.

"There is nothing to be afraid of."

He said it in a tone not suited to his voice, but felt he carried it off.

Then Dulcie had begun again in a strain which repressed emotion was making exceedingly dry. The springs in the dust-coloured sofa groaned.

"I'm afraid, Waldo, that what I want to say is: I can't love you in the way you seem to want me to."

Sympathy swam on the surface of her eyes, he began to realize with disgust, watery sympathy, or worse still, poisonous pity, yet in their depths Dulcie's eyes appeared to remain passionate.

"Because I am in love," she said.

If only their attitudes had been less awkward. But the angle at which he was placed on the sofa made sitting downright painful.

"I'm in love with, I'm engaged to, Len Saporta."

He remembered her saying on a former occasion, "I'm really a very mundane individual," and now she had tried to inject her announcement with something of the same banality, but there Dulcie failed. Her voice reverberated. The pity she was offering him shone with what she was unable to share. Her bosom, the riper for experience, filled not not, he hoped, with indecent impatience. He looked down fascinated at her breasts. He was never quite sure of that part of the anatomy, of what it might contain.

"It's a pity," he said, "your mother will never know."

That a daughter became engaged while a mother was still high in her coffin, he prevented himself from adding.

"Oh, but she did! She knew," said Dulcie. "She half agreed. There was only this dreadful business of conscience. Though that was only on account of my father."

Dulcie was quite prepared to let nobody's conscience rest, except apparently her own. Waldo did not greatly care by now.

"Leonard, you see, is a practising Jew. And our darling, neat-and-tidy rationalist parents are apt to throw fits over principles."

Gongs could not have sounded louder in Waldo's ears.

Dulcie looked down.

"I am making it sound frivolous," she said, "because I can't convey the importance of the step I'm taking. There are times," she said in a suddenly metallic voice, her tongue acting as a quivering clapper, "when I am deaf, dumb, and blind with it."

Or besotted, as women become, he had read, with some man. For this one coming into the room. For this Jew. For there was no doubt the young man, of physical, not to say vulgar appearance, now entering, was Mr. Saporta.

What hell!

Dulcie looked, and Waldo avoided her dazzlement.

"This is my fiancé, Waldo," she recovered herself and added.

They were again in Australia.

"I've never stopped hearing about you, Waldo," Leonard Saporta said.

He gave one of those big laughs, which come up deep, leathery, but most respectful, from the region of the pocketbook. He also gave his hand, fleshy, but firm flesh, promising a warmth of male comradeship. Leonard Saporta was obviously designed for clubs, if a club would have admitted him.

"And now we meet!" Again ox-eyed Saporta laughed, sweating at the roots of his nose. "Whatever prevented us till now? Fate, eh?"

Waldo could not think of a better answer than Saporta's own—unless a glass doorknob and the flu. It was thoroughly ridiculous what all three of them were going through. Even Saporta, probably an athlete, as well as the returned soldier his badge proclaimed, worked only by consent of hinges. These allowed him to incline just so far in the direction of his new-found, valued friend. In slightly different circumstances Waldo could have been the object of his courtship, Waldo felt. Well, he wouldn't have fallen for it.

Dulcie stirred, and the springs in the sofa remonstrated anomalously.

"I was hoping you would come yesterday," she said, in a private tone intended only for her lover.

Since his arrival, her throat was permanently raised, to whatever he might do to it.

"Saturdays are out of the question," Leonard Saporta replied, sweating yellower round the nose, and explained with awful earnestness to Waldo, "I attend the synagogue Saturday."

Both Dulcie and Saporta needed to explain a lot. They were both of them proud and shy to do so.

"Leonard is a carpet merchant. He inherited the business from his father."

They were doing it all for hurt Waldo, who was not so hurt he couldn't pity in turn. It was their illusion of strength which made their dependence pitiable.

With the fag-end of her intelligence Dulcie could have sensed this. She began to complain about humidity, while staring at her lover's wrist; he was wearing a gun-metal wristlet watch. Finally, falling vaguer still, she sat removing a stray hair from her tongue.

"Well," said Waldo, getting up, "I am not one to mow the lawn on Sunday, but," he positively insisted, "know when I ought to make myself scarce."

Having launched his joke, he laughed slightly.

Mr. Saporta was easing the sleeves of his business suit down from where they had rucked up, over his rather muscular forearms.

"If you ever care to look me up. In the city, Waldo. My number, Waldo, is in the book." He meant it, too—he was so earnest.

Waldo had never before heard his name repeated enough to grow ashamed of it.

He got out quickly after that. But Dulcie followed him into the garden.

"You see," she said, "how unavoidable it was. I know, Waldo, you will understand."

The Star of David, glinting from between her breasts, gave him the clue he should have followed in the beginning.

"We should all be ready," he said, "to admit our mistakes."

Not least his own: the many fragmentary impressions of Dulcie Feinstein, elbowing her way through the lashing rejoinders of ungovernable music, in loose embroidery of white hydrangeas, and flashes of gunpowdery flesh, merging only now into the mosaic of truth—of a rather coarse little thing the carpet merchant was leading back into his ghetto of ignorance and superstition.

In the convention of human intercourse he threw in automatically, "Mr. Saporta, I'm sure, is a very reliable man."

Dulcie winced, and tormented her upper lip.

"I would like to think you could come to us," she said.

Lowering her head she groped her way out from under the hydrangeas to stand exposed at the top of the steps, and continued standing as he went slack-kneed down.

"That you could feel our door was open. However you may want to accuse me for what I was incapable of being. Don't you think it better," she finished, "for all of us, to accept the past out of which we've grown, out of which we're still growing?"

He did look back just once at Mrs. Saporta, increasing, bulging, the Goddess of a Thousand Breasts, standing at the top of her steps, in a cluster of unborn, ovoid children. This giant incubator hoped she was her own infallible investment. But she would not suck him in. Imagining to hatch him out.

"I'm past the incubation stage!" he called.

So much for Dulcie Feinstein Saporta and her lust for possession. He was tempted to look back again, to see whether his scorn had knocked her bleeding to the steps. He resisted, however.

And after he had turned the privet corner, which in theory chokes those who are susceptible, her eyes continued to follow him, to engulf in the light of conquest, or love, and he did then choke momentarily. He regretted not being years younger, when he might have run some of the distance home, churning up the dust for a disguise. Or cried less dry and secretly. For the tragedy of this ugly girl. Wiping his eyes with the back of his hand instead of his pince-nez with a handkerchief.

As soon as he got back, Mother said, "Your father is far from well, dear. You ought to go in and talk to him."

"Oh, Mother," he protested, "when did that do anybody any good?"

If, on hanging up his hat, his conscience twitched for his parents, he knew from experience that Dad would be listening intently to his own thoughts, nor did their mother always seem to hear since they had become the furniture of the house in which they had been placed.

Dad had retired a year or two early on account of his health. They were loyal about it at the bank. They presented him with an engraved watch. There were other considerations. But none of it seemed to compensate for some indignity of life which hung about, haunting him.

George Brown had to suffer. The threads of his breath tangled in his chest, or visibly, smokily, smelling of saltpetre, in the room in which he spent his nights. He rarely succeeded in cutting the tangle. (Nor could Waldo use blotting-paper for years after his father's death without the sensation of anxious distress.)

After his retirement George Brown mostly sat.

"Where is your book, dear?" Mother used to ask; it would have been pointless to name the book.

He cleared his throat before replying, "Thank you, I'm resting my eyes."

In the beginning, faced with the luxury of years to spend, he had promised them jokily, "I'll have time now to give Gibbon another run."

He sat, at least, holding a volume or two. On a wet afternoon he opened the Countess Martinengo-Cesaresco, but complained that silverfish had eaten the introduction since he had been there last. If opening a book was an occupation, closing one became a relief.

Waldo fortunately did not have to wonder what he might do for this man who was also by accident his father, because so clearly he didn't expect anything to be done. If passion stirred in George Brown, it was for the more unassuming manifestations of nature. On an expedition to Barranugli he bought a rain-gauge, which he set up on a patch where, for some reason, the grass refused to grow. The rainfall he noted down at the back of an old ledger. He would knock on the barometer beside the hatstand, and read the thermometer nailed to the classical veranda. He collected seeds of all kinds, to put in paper bags, which he hung by the necks and forgot. Though what appeared to be his favourite occupation was the watch he kept on the flux of light, which required him to do nothing about it.

Only sometimes in the gentle recurrences of light and dark, he seemed to gather hints of some larger, cataclysmic plan. Then his Gothic shoulders would arch more acutely, and his already inactive hands turn to stone. He would cough the cough his family had come to recognize as having no outlet.

"Where is that Mrs. Poulter?" he would ask between the coughing.

Arthur grew soft, and didn't know.

"Haven't clapped ear to *her* since Tuesday," Dad used to say, making it sound contemptuous because he had developed a weakness for her.

He loved her because she paraded the minutiae of flesh and blood while always keeping them under control.

Mrs. Poulter would come and say, "When we was at Mungindribble they allowed us the quarter of a sheep, and some of the offal if we was lucky. Bill got so as he couldn't stand the sight of offal. From the regular killin'. Threw it to the dogs. Lovely fry. I like a nice lamb's fry before it loses its shine on a slab."

Mrs. Poulter's moist, young-woman's lips would glow with no more assistance than she got from contemplating the desiderata of life.

Then there were the mysteries.

Mrs. Poulter said, "There was a feller cut 'is own throat down the line beyond Numburra. We women went down to lay out the body. We all of us took something—scones, or a soda loaf, there was one person took a basin of brawn. All shared, like. There's more what they call community spirit up country." She sighed. "And we had to come down here. But we're happy."

She let down her eyelashes then, afraid she might have said too much.

Mrs. Poulter, who had faith also in food, used to bring dishes to George Brown. It amused Mother.

"Here is a macaroni pudding, Mr. Brown," Mrs. Poulter might say, lowering the basin for him to look inside. "Nice," she coaxed. "Nutmeg on the top. You must eat, you know, to keep your strength up."

It was more than advice. That, too, she tried to turn into a mystery.

"Making a sacrament of food. 'Take, eat' is what she would *like* to say," said Dad, laughing for his own joke at the expense of the churches and Mrs. Poulter.

Waldo frowned, not for any lack of taste or feebleness in his father's joke, but for the flickering memory of some feebleness in himself the day of his meeting with Leonard Saporta and parting from Her. He still heard the slash of that lawn-mower running itself deliberately against the stones.

And Dad, darkening, began to cough. He could never forgive the Baptist Church. Its chocolate campanile, "leaning a bit, but not far enough," stuck in his mind. He couldn't let it rest.

"It's a pity you weren't born a Quaker," Waldo said. "There would have been less architecture. And you could have left them just the same."

But Dad didn't care for other people's jokes on serious matters.

"There's too much you boys, reared in the light in an empty country, will never understand. There aren't any shadows in Australia. Or discipline. Every man jack can do what he likes."

Because he wanted to believe it, he did believe—if not of himself.

Towards the end he appeared to have repaired the deficiencies of his sons enough to refer to them in the abstract.

"Whatever else," he once said to Mrs. Poulter, "the children are our testament."

Then, remembering, from hints she had dropped, that their visitor might die intestate, he gave her an old raincoat.

"There's still plenty of wear in it," he gasped. "Your husband will find it useful."

The effort tuned up his cough as he limped a little way along the path.

When their father died at last but suddenly, Waldo was determined that the shock would not prevent his enjoying their mother's company and the secrets she had been waiting to tell. Family matters of an exalted nature had always been stirring in his mind. If he resisted toying with the possibility of his not being his father's son, it was because a twin brother denied him that luxury. Though Waldo might have been better got, Arthur's getting and fate could hardly be improved upon. Still, there were certain details of their mother's breeding which reserve—and possibly breeding—

had prevented her telling, and for which Waldo intended some time in the future to ask. In fact, it didn't turn out quite like that. His father—of all people, Dad—hadn't altogether let go. There were the paper bags filled with the seed he had left, and which nobody ever thought to take down. The paper bags continued hanging by their necks, rattling the husks and seed inside them whenever a wind blew, and sometimes disagreeably, after dark, coming into dry collision with a living face.

What is more, Mother changed, as though the moral responsibility of protecting a marriage with a man not her social equal had at last been lifted. So she lifted at last the grave structure of her face, roughened red over milky skin. She rearranged the straying grey of her hair, for whom it was difficult to tell.

Not for Waldo, he discovered almost at once.

"Tell me," she said, "about the book you are writing."

He could feel the flesh shrivel on his bones.

"What book?" he asked.

Her question, her look had been practically indecent.

"You needn't tell me," she said, "if you don't want to."

And continued smiling at him in the way of those who know through hearsay or intuition that something is being hushed up.

As he had to live with it, he decided to ignore her indiscretion, while hiding his private papers in another place. No book, certainly. His life was his book, until at some point in age and detachment it wrote itself logically into the words with which his mind and notebooks were encrusted.

In the meantime, his mother smiled at him, and worse still, forgot.

"I can never remember," she complained, "whether I have paid the rates. At least they won't cut us off, as I am told can happen to those who go in for telephones and electricity."

It had been decided years before that neither of these advantages would enrich their lives. Lamplight emphasized the family circle, and they could go across the road to ring for a doctor in the event of sickness, as they had been forced to also in their one experience of death.

In the beginning Waldo had been tempted to remark: The progressive spirit surely doesn't eschew the telephone. (He was fond of "eschew.") But on thinking it over, he did not exactly dread, he had doubts about the inquisition the telephone might have subjected him to. So he kept quiet.

"To return to the rates," Mother harped, "now that Dad is gone, you boys—*you*, Waldo," she corrected herself, "ought to take them on as one of your responsibilities. You pay for the things, anyway."

He liked *that*! And hoped she would forget about it along with other threats.

For so many years she had been saying, "You are men now," as though she were in doubt.

On the other hand she would fly into passions if they brought her letters from the box.

"You boys must never collect my letters!" Her own commands made her tremble. "That is one small pleasure you must allow me to enjoy. Besides, you might drop a letter somewhere in the rosemary. That wretched, thick stuff! A letter might lie in it unnoticed for years, and disintegrate in the weather."

But she loved the rosemary when it was not against her. She would crush it with her trembly fingers, and sigh.

"Next week—next week definitely, there will be a letter from Cousin Mollie."

She was convinced she was psychic, and would have liked to see a ghost, though she did not believe in ghosts on principle. Premonitions were a different matter; they were scientifically acceptable.

When her science let her down, it was agreed that "Mollie has always been an unreliable correspondent."

In the absence of letters Mother got considerable pleasure out of prospectuses and catalogues. She collected election circulars, to fold into spills, after studying the photographs of those who had heard the call to office.

She would have liked to take out old family photographs, but misalliance had deterred her from keeping any.

"The faces on my side," she mentioned, "were too cruel. On his, too mean."

Waldo couldn't remember faces. He recollected scents and sensations: of the flowering, steely, soft, and prickly perfumes in the dark of wardrobes; of an old woman's cushiony hands in their mail of rings; of geranium disinfecting with its pink a heraldic urn in which a cat had shat. The chocolate campanile, swooning earthwards from the too green, the too daringly transcendental touch of dusk, often recurred on the screen of his mind. Had he actually experienced, or had he selected out of hearsay, the icy vision of the blue woman about to descend the stairs? In blue, it could only have been his mother, though the diamonds must have choked her principles. For that reason she had "gone over." But her conversion to sacrificial love and socialism had convinced neither side. The ice-blue ancestral stare, and the little black rats of eyes gnawing at holes in fogged lace, were at least united in chasing her away.

"We used to drive down to Tallboys—that was before the family —before anything happened," Mother liked to tell, and joined her hands closer on the kitchen table. "It was quite a journey. Mama could not endure carriages for any distance. They upset her pug. Poor Grumble! Grannie was so kind to *dogs*. The gardeners were always setting the stage, it seemed, as we arrived. Nothing ever grew. It was potted out. The shrubs were sculpture which never got finished. Oh, and dogs, more dogs!" Her eyes would shine after sherry, particularly after she took to the four-o'clock sherry. "The willowy, bronze and golden breeds, snoozing on the steps, amongst the lichen! And Mollie. Mollie remained good, better than most who accept the *status quo*. She had a hundred dolls, I believe. I believe we counted them. Once she allowed me to tear up a Japanese doll because I decided I wanted to. It was the nanny who made a scene."

Mother scarcely ever laughed over any of her pictures, even when they gave her pleasure. They were far too serious, even the funny ones, for laughter.

"Always when we arrived they would take us in, and fortify us with cups of soup, flavoured, I should say, with port—with port wine."

This reminded her of her sherry, and although it was only half past four and she had put the bottle back, she would take it down again, to refresh her tumbler.

"After you had gone upstairs," Waldo sometimes had to assist.

But she grew vague, with sherry and memory. She did not care to describe elaborate interiors. They yawned too dark in her mind.

Not that he needed reminders. He had dared reconstruct the house, room by room, and add it to his other experience of life.

Sometimes Mother, under the influence of four o'clock, would add a detail, a cupola or tower, and he would lean forward to visualize, and formally preserve.

"Tallboys was an omnium gatherum! A shocking architectural muddle!" How he loved the language her mouth was conducting through a ritual of elaborate slovenliness. "The façade was Palladian. They used to pour out elderberry wine for the huntsmen on frosty mornings. Lord, it was cold! You could almost hear the stone crack."

She poured herself another.

"But Tudor, the original Tudor, Mother."

Still so far to go, he grew anxious for the end of it.

"Oh, Tudor! Tudor was too down-to-earth, too much like human beings living and loving and stabbing and poisoning one another. Tudor got pushed back hugger-mugger behind the stone. The *kitchens* were in the Tudor part of this great baroque treadmill. When I say 'baroque' I only mean it fig—figuratively, I think."

She formed her hands into a globe above the waning gold of sherry.

"Wasn't there also the Gothic," he dared, "The Gothic folly?"

"Oh, the Gothick folly!" she laughed, or sniggered, and they shared in the knowingness. "Uncle Charlie always pronounced it with a k. That was Waldo's Folly."

She needn't have told him. He had been there, gloved and sensual, attended by salukis and an Arab.

"*Waldo,*" she said, pronouncing it as though it were someone else's name, "Waldo had such peculiar vices they were kept locked up, behind a grille, in the library."

Those peppercorns! He knew. He had fingered the reseda silk through the bars.

But Mother's voice was dwindling with the sherry.

"He died at Smyrna, I think it was. They brought him home, rather smelly, so they say—the Greeks hadn't done a proper job—and put him in the tomb he had built for himself. In marble from

Paros. Beside the lake. Mollie and I liked to play there in August. It was so—cool. And full of echoes."

Round about five her mouth grew slobbery on the glass, and she would glance sideways at his abstemious thimbleful.

"They are all dead now," she said drily, "I suppose." Adding quickly, however, "When Cousin Mollie writes she will tell us the symptoms." And more meditative: "A pity your father died. He would have enjoyed hearing. Of course you never knew your father. For a frail man he was strong. Strong."

Suddenly he hated that strength, and his parents' withdrawal into a room of their own. Resentment lingered, forcing him on some mornings to deliver lectures.

"Mother," he said, "I want to talk to you."

"Oh, yes?"

She did so hope he would. She was raising her face to receive helpful advice.

"The sherry is all very well. In moderation. It is moderation which makes life bearable."

Her little knotted laughs remained the most youthful sign in her.

"Sherry is the last perquisite!" Then, making an ugly mouth: "The perks! The cooking sherry! The cook wouldn't have crooked her *finger*. The housekeeper wouldn't have *gargled* with it."

Waldo said, "I forbid you, Mother!"

He admired the sound of her kind strong son.

"My dear little sherry wine!"

And it continued to trickle in.

"Poor soul! What else has she got?" was Mrs. Poulter's argument.

"Here's an odd one, Mother, that I brought back from the store, because it's Saturday, and it helps you when you're feeling sick."

Arthur made Waldo sick. He was glad he had the Library, even though a doubtful blessing.

Because Crankshaw had started playing up.

Crankshaw said, "Mr. Brown, can you truly answer for the accuracy of these references?"

"Why should I falsify them, Mr. Crankshaw?"

Did he hear a simpering note in his own voice? Sometimes, to his horror, he thought he sounded like a maid in a Restoration play.

He waited for the titters.

Which did not come.

Only Crankshaw grumbling: "I wouldn't say you *falsified*. Only that you might have got them wrong."

He was a heavy man, with a family at Roseville.

"Who can say," Mr. Brown said.

He was only certain that Crankshaw had it in for him.

But, as an alternative to Crankshaw, he had to take the train, the bus, home.

"She *is* sick," Mrs. Poulter told him. "You ought to get the doctor to her."

"My health is my own affair," Mother insisted, making it easier for him. "To the end I shall keep it so. I shall know when it is the end."

She knew, apparently, it would be a long time from then, because she died ten years after George Brown her husband. Anne Quantrell was carved out of stone, the true Gothick. At least Waldo had that satisfaction, although it caused him to suffer before he could inscribe her name on what he always hoped was the authentic dust.

"Mother won't die easy," Mrs. Poulter became of the opinion.

Mrs. Poulter didn't actually like Mrs. Brown, because Mrs. Brown would not allow her to. Mrs. Brown didn't actively dislike Mrs. Poulter, she simply resented encroachment of any kind. Waldo Brown *couldn't* like Mrs. Poulter, because of, well, everything. Whether Arthur had loved Mrs. Poulter or not, in this one instance he had listened to reason, sensed the shocking anomaly of it, and choked her off. So that human relationships, particularly the enduring ones, or those which we are forced to endure, are confusingly marbled in appearance, Waldo Brown realized, and noted in a notebook.

He knew also he dreaded his mother's death, in which event, he would be exposed to Chankshaw, and not exposed, but left to Arthur. Perhaps he dreaded Arthur most of all, because of something Arthur might tell him one day.

But for the moment Mother showed no signs of dying, she only grew more difficult.

She would flare up on the edge of a room in which he was thinking, or making notes. At night, by lamplight, her hair was terrible. It got out of control. It looked like an old grey gooseberry bush. More often than not, she was dangling a bottle by its neck.

She would barge in, shouting, "Waldo, it's time you decided to marry. What about the little Jewess? That Miss Finkelstein. We were all Jews, weren't we, before we stopped to think? Or was that somebody else?"

Waldo hunched himself over his papers.

"Miss Feinstein? She's probably a mother."

"All to the good. What would you have done without your mother?"

"Dulcie has a little boy," said Arthur, "and a little girl some years younger. That was what they wanted."

His mother and brother had come in on purpose to add to the litter of his room, the desperate untidiness of his thoughts, which blew at times like old newspapers or straw round packing-cases which never got packed. They had come in deliberately to conjure up Dulcie. He knew that if he spoke he would deflect nobody from his predetermined actions. He alone was free to choose. The one choice he would never be free to make was that of his relationship with other people. So he ground his fists into his ears, he hunched his shoulders, and squirmed on the needle-points of his buttocks. He must cling to his gift.

Mother would go presently. He heard her opening other doors. She would walk as far as, and no farther than, the house allowed her, before sitting down to finish the bottle. She would end up cold on the bed, the old blue gown parted on her jutting legs, the long lovely Quantrell legs in which the varicose veins had come. And he would draw the curtains of her skirt, shivering for the hour, or an offence against taste.

Mother could be relied on to drop off. But Arthur stuck. Standing by the lamp, head inclined, staring into one of those glass marbles. Watching the revolutions of a glass marble on the palm of his hand.

"If you have to stay, don't fidget, at least!" Waldo ordered. Arthur raised his head.

"Mother is real sick. Didn't you know?"

"Is it necessary to speak like that? It doesn't come naturally to you."

"It comes natural to me to speak natural in a natural situation," Arthur said.

The porcelain lampshade was jiggling, Waldo heard. He could feel the frail old kitchen chair reacting badly to the stress of emotion.

"Mother is not sick!" he shouted. "We know her weakness. I will not be bullied into thinking that what isn't is!"

"Ssshhe's asleep! You might wake her, Waldo, if you shout."

Arthur had turned, and was towering, flaming above him, the wick smoking through the glass chimney.

But his skin, remaining white and porous, attempted to soothe. Arthur put out one of the hands which disgusted Waldo if he ever stopped to think about them, which, normally, he didn't.

Arthur said, "If it would help I'd give it to you, Waldo, to keep."

Holding in his great velvety hand the glass marble with the knot inside.

"No!" Waldo shouted. "Go!"

"Where?"

There was, in fact, nowhere.

And the Poulter woman kept nagging at him. She appeared one evening, out of the waves of grass, and said, "Waldo—Mr. Brown, I've come to have a word with you. It's time we saw things realistic." From *Mrs. Poulter*! "It's no business of mine, I know. I would think twice if I was a friend, but I'm worse than that, only a neighbour."

He looked at this woman who had aged across the road from them. It was terrifying to see the way other people aged.

"Your mother lying in bed all these months," Mrs. Poulter said, "and nothing to do for her."

"She's comfortable enough."

"Oh yes, I'm comfortable," Mother called, whose hearing would reach farther, through doors and windows, the longer she lay living. "Since I didn't have to think about the salmon loaf I'm comfortable."

Mrs. Poulter lowered her voice. "She's used right up. Eaten up. It's the poison's got into her veins."

Then Waldo invited their neighbour to leave.

"Who helped pour it into them?" he shouted at her down the path.

"Whoever you kill, Mr. Brown," she turned and shouted back, "it won't be me! I'll only die by the hand of God!"

She saw immediately, however, that she had cause to feel ashamed.

"I'm always here as you know," she said in her usual voice, "and can telephone the doctor—the minister," she said, "if you can't come at doing it yourself."

The minister made his flesh creep.

How long now, he tried to calculate, had their mother kept to her room? He used to go in to her at night and read her *The Pickwick Papers*, which she didn't much care for, but was used to.

"It's stuck to us, hasn't it?" she said. "That makes it all the better as a plaster."

With so much reading, and the kind of conversation they made, time passed.

Then suddenly he noticed, or the inexorable Mrs. Poulter had, the eyeballs were lolling, the long yellow teeth were protruding from their mother's skull, her fingers, to which Arthur would attach the figures of cat's-cradle, stuck out like sticks at the ends of her arms.

Noticing him stare at her, Mother said, "At least we have our health, whatever else is taken from us."

Waldo Brown blundered out, the grass catching at his ankles, the moths and one of his father's paper bags hitting him in the face. Crossing the road he heard to his surprise its foreign surface under his feet—of the road beside which they had lived their lives.

"Yes, Mr. Brown," Mrs. Poulter said. "I'll be only too happy."

Mrs. Poulter brought the doctor. And the minister, as she had threatened. Amongst them they arranged for Mrs. Brown to be removed to something called a Home of Peace. They sent for Waldo, but before he could arrive his mother was gone, fortunately too drugged to realize the damage to her principles.

Waldo said he wouldn't go in. He did not care to look at her, because what was the point. Dead, he said, is dead. One had to be realistic about it.

Arthur, whom he hadn't allowed to accompany him, dreading the almost inevitable scene, murmured that he would speak to somebody who'd know what ought to be done about their mother. In the special circumstances, it did not seem improbable, and Waldo let him.

So Anne Quantrell—never a Brown in spite of her love for that sallow little man with the gammy leg—was cremated by arrangement.

Waldo was surprised to hear Arthur had been present.

"Who arranged it all?" Waldo asked somewhat cagily.

"Mr. Saporta."

Nothing more was said. Arthur's incomplete mind must have included compartments in which delicacy predominated. Or he may have sensed intuitively something of the hurt Dulcie had done Waldo by not respecting his intentions, by refusing to accept his sacrifice, and devouring instead that vulgar commercial Jew, Saporta. So at least dotty old Arthur kept quiet, until a couple of years later when, perhaps through no fault of his, though seemingly by somebody's prearrangement, the ghastly meeting between Waldo and the whole Saporta family was staged on a corner of King and Pitt. After the accident, in which Waldo lost his pince-nez, and decided it would be more practical to replace it with spectacles, Arthur did recapitulate, inevitably, the whole Feinstein-Saporta history. Waldo forgave him. There was too much else to disturb Waldo, then, and over many years.

There was Crankshaw first and continuously.

It was difficult exactly to put a finger on what difference in mediocrity distinguished the Librarian from the mediocre. Mr. Crankshaw was several years his junior when appointed the superior of Mr. Brown. For anyone so heavy, such a bear in pin-stripes, Crankshaw trod remarkably gently round the sensibilities of those who were officially inferiors, without ever, but ever, failing to bruise.

From time to time Waldo considered opening a special notebook in which to analyse the character of Chankshaw, working up his observations into a portrait, a detail eventually of some vast corrosive satire on the public services. (Fortunately such victims were always too vain or too obtuse to recognize themselves.)

Poor Crankshaw, he was almost obliterated by brisket and a jutting forehead. He had the hands of one who had felled timber, without having known the feel of an axe, except the one he used, by law of gravity, on those beneath him. He had read several books, and was personally acquainted with that priest who wrote *Around the Boree Log*. Crankshaw's pet subject, however, was Numbers of Readers. Poor Turnstile Crankshaw! Would receive an obituary, anyway, as a public servant in an unassailable position. He had a wife who reeked of the dry-cleaner's, and three or four girls in white hats, who gave shower teas for their friends, without ever being showered upon themselves. Poor Crankshaw.

Waldo might have felt magnanimous if he had not been persecuted. But one of the juniors would come tapping on his desk. "Mr. Crankshaw, Mr. Brown."

Crankshaw would heave himself creakingly round in his bucket chair. He was so heavy.

"Mr. Brown," he began, on the first of several progressively intensifying occasions, "we are starting a welfare drive. Do you find you have time enough to digest your sandwich?"

There was a catch in this, for Waldo bought nuts from the Health Food in the arcade, and chose a banana, very carefully—just on the turn—at Agostino's.

"I would not," he replied, looking at Crankshaw with that degree of steeliness he had forgotten practising as a little boy, on the advice of a booklet on *How to Succeed*, "I wouldn't have, if I hadn't given up sandwiches years ago, the quality of Sydney bread being what it is."

Crankshaw lowered his eyes to look at the folder he was holding.

"Any draughts?" he asked peculiarly.

Was this some obscure reference to the mistake he had made in that report on damage to *The Golden Bough*? That was years ago, and, Waldo hoped, forgotten.

Contempt might in time have transferred itself to his mouth in sounds, but Crankshaw was not interested to wait.

"Very well, Mr. Brown," he said.

Then looked up. That jutting forehead, split down the centre of its louring bone, the cleft hinted at again in the chin, which, it was said, is the sign of a lover. Waldo almost sneeze-laughed. Love me, Cranko, in a white hat!

And Crankshaw looking.

"Are you a Catholic?" the Librarian asked very gently.

If it had not been so subtle, if Waldo had not been keyed up to match his wits against Crankshaw's question, he might simply have turned and gone out of the room. Instead, he modified his disapproval.

"Technically, I think, Mr. Crankshaw, I am not required to answer," Waldo said, and added, by inspiration, he congratulated himself afterwards: "I prefer not to confirm what you have already in your folder."

Crankshaw looked so wry-mouthed. He could only end the silence with a laugh, and dismiss his superior subordinate.

So much—this time—for Crankshaw, said Waldo, brushing a few nuts off his own table. He was relieved to return to his corner. He had the trimmest collection of pencils. Was sweating under his collar, though. And knew that his spectacles would have left those white marks, where the metal had eaten into his skin, during a distressing incident. The odder part was: Crankshaw himself must have been a Catholic, considering his intimate friendship with the priest who had written *Around the Boree Log*.

Priests in white hats. You never could tell.

This was the year Waldo Brown began what became a considerable fragment of his novel *Tiresias a Youngish Man*. He was invited, too, in a roundabout way, to address the Beecroft Literary Society, and did, or rather, he read a paper on Barron Field. Afterwards over coffee and *petits beurres* a solicitor congratulated him on the thoroughness of his research. Modesty forced Waldo to admit that the subject was a minor one, but he hoped and felt he had left no stone unturned. Finally, a lady novelist of the Fellowship had asked him to an evening at her home, to which he hadn't gone, for scenting sexual motives behind her insistence.

With all this, it was incredible to think a second *war* had broken out, though of a different kind. For men were tearing one another to pieces in a changed ritual. Mother would not have been in the race with Cousin Mollie's Japanese doll.

Waldo couldn't help noticing a certain ferment in the streets. Arthur wouldn't have let him ignore it.

Arthur said, "Over in Europe they're dragging the fingernails out of all those Feinstein relatives. They're sticking whole families in ovens."

"What's that to do with us? We don't put people in ovens here."

"We didn't think of it," Arthur said.

Arthur had a pen friend who was a soldier. He sent his friend a comb, short enough to fit inside the envelope. It began haunting Waldo, the young corporal combing his hair in a desert, singing "Yours" to a red sunset. The wretched Arthur would not leave anyone alone. Though of course the censor would never allow the comb to arrive.

Waldo was relieved to think that not everybody was irresponsible. Only at night his doubts would return, when the waves of yellowing grass thundered down Terminus Road, to break against what, in spite of the classical pediment, was a disintegrating wooden box, and the great clouds rolled down out of Sarsaparilla to collide in electric upheaval over his undeserving head. Thus pinpointed, he stood accused of every atrocity over and above the few minor ones he had committed unavoidably himself. If it had not been for the insufferable mental climate occasioned by the war, and his incidental, though demanding, public career—to say nothing of his ever-present family problem—he might have committed to paper that metaphysical statement for which he felt himself almost prepared. One great work, no longer question of an *oeuvre*. As it was, the war killed *Tiresias a Youngish Man*. Its substance was bound to return, of course; creative regurgitation would see to that. But in the meantime, in this state of perpetual night and frustration, Waldo would throw himself on the knife-edge of his body in the bed in which they slept, or his twin Arthur did—he himself was more often than not incapable of sleep for dreaming.

Not long after Dad died Mother had said: There is no reason

why you boys shouldn't have this larger bed, after all you are men, and I shall take the bed and room you have outgrown. So they moved into what had been their parents' bed, where Waldo gradually overcame his distaste. It was not for Arthur, Arthur was inescapable. It was their father's limp disjointing his thoughts, it was, even more, the great baroque mess of their Quantrell heritage, which Waldo loved to distraction, its crimson rooms and stone corridors extending through the terrors of sleep and war. By comparison, their own immediate Tudor imbroglio was a mere bucket of blood.

On one occasion, during the night, during the despair, Arthur had comforted Waldo.

"You had the blues last night." Arthur yawned.

You never knew what distortion of fact he might come out with. But Waldo could not feel concerned on such a clear morning, himself a man of responsibility and discretion, almost of action, as he dashed at his hair with a touch of brilliantine. His hair lost that dusty look. He settled the expanding armbands on purposeful arms.

"By gosh," he said quite boyishly, "the old Municipal's fairly going to hum."

"How?" asked Arthur out of a yawn.

As he grew older he liked to take it easier. He would lie in bed until he heard the fat spitting. Then he would rise, in a flurry of iron joints, a ringing of brass balls.

"Matters are coming to a head," said Waldo, but would not explain beyond: "It concerns our friend Crankshaw."

"You'll have my blessings," Arthur said, "as you gather round the boree log."

Actually Waldo was surprised he had succeeded in forming any kind of plan during the years of anxiety and stress through which he had been living. Quite apart from everything else he had always been expecting Cissie Baker to return clutching those few poems perpetrated by her dead brother and his former colleague, Walter Pugh. He could not have borne the first sight of her black figure creaking through the turnstile.

That morning the old Municipal, as if regretful of having provided a setting for what Waldo had catalogued as *Inquisition of a Living Mind*, was spreading snares of nostalgia and regret. Even ugliness has its virtue in the end. Certainly Waldo's corner was darker than ever, but it had driven him on occasions to pour light on obscurity, just as the stench of disinfectant on that morning sternly assaulted a wretched catarrh and stripped the last vestige of doubt from his intention. He was so spare and purposeful as he went and stuck his nose for the last time in one of the linted books, which, ever since his youth and the patronage of the late Mrs. Musto, had reminded him of the stink of old putrefying men in raincoats. Smelling them for the last time he laughed out loud in the deserted stacks.

Then he sat down and wrote several drafts before the final version.

He let it be eleven before knocking on the Librarian's door. There was still a mouthful of muddy tea in Crankshaw's cup, and he had not yet started looking for something to do. The room smelled, as always, of the beastly treacle in an old and bubbly pipe.

"What can I do for you, Mr. Brown?" Crankshaw asked, ever so affable, moving a box of pins from A to B.

Little realizing how he would be pricked.

"Mr. Crankshaw, I have decided to resign," Waldo said, coming to the point. "In fact, I am tendering my written resignation."

And he fetched the paper round on Crankshaw's desk with a frivolous twirl, unrehearsed, which reminded him once again of the maid in a Restoration play, though this time he did not care.

Crankshaw was obviously stunned.

"Have you given it all possible thought?" he asked between bubbling into his filthy pipe.

Waldo appreciated the "all possible." Thoroughly characteristic.

"I have been thinking it over for years," he said not quite accurately.

"Made any plans?"

Waldo said no he hadn't, though he had but wasn't going to tell.

The Librarian looked at Waldo, who was again conscious of the cleft chin, which, so it was said, is the sign of a lover.

"If there is any way in which I can assist," Crankshaw offered.

It was the exact tone of his dictation.

"We have never, it seems, got to know each other, not, I mean, as human beings, and everyone, I expect you will agree, has the potentialities." So Crankshaw uttered. "I would have liked to see you out at Roseville. We might have had a chat. But apparently I was slow in asking."

Tell that to the priests and the white hats! Waldo smiled the smile which left the token of a dimple in his lean right cheek. He could not be caught so late in the piece.

He went out and took down his homburg. They would think the Librarian had entrusted him with business of a confidential nature. So he escaped without further embarrassment from the scene of Cissie Baker's offering him, in another war, her soldier-brother's poems.

The streets were full of soldiers now. Waldo Brown could have outmarched the most virile of them, up King and along Macquarie, to the big new Public Library they had opened a couple of years before, and where he began without delay offering his services.

Time thus spent is not life lived, but belongs in a peculiar purgatorial category of its own. Waldo got used to it, and even detected in his face signs of moral purification. If any, his religion had become a cultivation of personal detachment, of complete transparency—he was not prepared to think emptiness—of mind. In this way he suffered no immediate hurt, and would only remember years afterwards fragments of conversation overheard.

For instance, from during his petitioning:

"This Brown cove—this *Waldo*—sounds nutty enough to me."

"Oh, Crankshaw agrees. But advises we should give him a trial. Says he's a glutton for continuity."

"All very well for old Crank."

"He's an honest man, Mr. O'Connell."

"Except when it comes to his throw-outs. No man can afford to be honest then."

(This part alone made Waldo Brown inclined to lose the faith he didn't have in human nature.)

"Ah well, fit him in somewhere, I suppose. Waldo *Brown*. Somewhere amongst the introverts. Some corner. They like that.

Let him sharpen his pencils and sweep up the crumbs of his rubber in peace."

Such was the texture of mind he had cultivated, Waldo only saw this dialogue printed black on its transparent screen perhaps six years afterwards, and immediately realized O'Connell was somebody to hate.

Arthur's dog helped him reach his conclusion.

One Saturday morning when Allwright had allowed him to knock off early, Arthur had gone in to Barranugli and bought from the pet-shop a blue pup. Waldo found his brother seated on the edge of the veranda, grunting apparently with joy, kneading the formless lump of fat, gazing at it, snout against snout, staring into the animal's rather unpleasant marbles of eyes.

The puppy, grunting or growling back, bristled up on seeing Waldo.

"Don't tell me!" the latter rattled. "I thought we had this out last time you did it. You were younger then, Arthur. But look at you now, an old man!"

"Fifty-six," Arthur said.

He could not cuddle the puppy less.

"Well, then," said Waldo. "At your age. You won't outlast that dog. And what am *I* going to do with one? Arthur? Quite apart from that, what about his biting the postman, shitting in corners, or not even corners? What it will eat, too, a large dog, at postwar prices. At cheapest, stinking horseflesh, fetching in the blow-flies."

"Keep the meat in a bucketful of water. Under the coral tree."

Arthur's hands grew noticeably gentler wrapping the pup in enormous velvety flaps of dough. The pup was either grinning back, or waiting to sink its teeth in Arthur's not too human snout.

"But all that yellow fat on horseflesh! Ugh! There's something about an old man with a dog. Arthur? Now, young children. Parents, I've read, often invest in a pup to teach their children the facts of life. That's unpleasant in itself, though practical. You can't say it isn't *normal*. But later on it's the people who are in some way denied or denying—sexually frustrated women, selfish, childless couples, *narcissists*—who keep dogs. People in some way peculiar."

Waldo's voice continued on a curve with no prospect of coming full circle. When Arthur interrupted.

"I am peculiar," he said.

So dreamy since shutting the pup to sleep in his arms, this old man was looking peculiarly awful.

"I warn you," Waldo said irrelevantly.

Anyway, this time Arthur refused to return the pup.

He called it Scruffy, and might have created what he named. Arthur present, the dog's attention was all for Arthur, its large tongue lolling out of its smaller mouth, its nose perpetually swivelling. In Arthur's absence, the marble-eyes were fixed on distance and some abstraction of the man.

Once when Arthur wasn't there Waldo tried kicking Scruffy, and the dog growled back but, realizing its own inferiority, did not attack its punisher. Waldo was satisfied. It occurred to him then to go to the bucket where they kept the horseflesh, he couldn't get there quick enough, to cut off a strip of the submerged meat, and dangle the purple spongy stuff under the puppy's frantic nose. The animal gulped, would have eaten more, but was content instead to slobber over Waldo's hands and wrists. Waldo, too, was content, but to feel so immensely superior.

He couldn't resist telling Arthur at least the conclusion of the story.

"It ate from me," he said. "It took some meat."

"Natural thing for a dog to do."

Then Arthur began to look sly.

"Waldo," he said, "how about letting Scruffy come and sleep in the bed? So as we'd all be together."

Waldo almost spat, the way elderly, ignorant people used to spit at a bad smell to keep disease out of their mouths.

"What do you think a bed is for?" he asked.

His question inevitably turned him prim.

"For dogs to lie in, of course," said Arthur.

But he did not try it on again.

And Waldo waited, before confessing a plan of his own. For it was about this time that he allowed himself to remember a dialogue of the Public Library overheard six years earlier. The confirmed perfidy of Crankshaw, not to mention O'Connell, perhaps recommended the honesty of dogs.

So Waldo in turn grew sly.

He finally said, "What do you say, Arthur, if I get a mate for Scruffy, one which will be really mine, as Scruffy is obviously yours?"

"What, and breed together? That would be whacko! Nobody's breeding down Terminus Road."

"My dog will not be a female." Waldo was very firm.

"Any dog will be one more," said Arthur. "Would you like me to choose it?"

"I shall choose it," Waldo said, "because it's going to be my dog."

Waldo brought back his pup. It could not have been much younger than Arthur's Scruffy, though rather smaller.

"That dog might be sick," said Arthur.

"That's because it isn't yours," Waldo replied. "The sort of thing people say when they grow resentful. It may be smaller than Scruffy, but, I should say, tougher."

From clinging to life, perhaps. Though Waldo would not have admitted it at first. His dog, a shade of blue similar to that of Arthur's Scruffy, had a staring coat, plastered in places from confinement in the pet-shop window. It had a mattery eye, and its barrel-belly, swollen by the knots of worms probably inside it, gave surface shelter to a busy race of fleas.

But Waldo proposed to love his dog the way man does, according to tradition.

"What are you going to call him?" Arthur asked.

"Runt," said Waldo, on a high note, and immediately.

His own honesty cut him painfully. For it was not the dog he was humiliating. To atone for dishonesty in other men, in Crankshaw, not to mention O'Connell—he had thought it out, oh, seriously—he would mortify himself through love for this innocent, though in every other way repulsive creature, his dog. At least Arthur neither applauded nor discouraged Waldo's moral strength. To give him his due, there was a strain of delicacy in Arthur.

As for Runt and Scruffy, they accepted the fatality of their arbitrary relationship, gnawing, licking, tumbling each other over. They enjoyed the luxury of each other's farts.

And Runt grew fat. His glossy blue glimmered at its best like star sapphires. He would catapult suddenly at Arthur, always greedy for the taste of his hands. Or less impulsive, but no less desirous, the creature would roll over on its back, exposing its belly and a slight erection.

"Whose dog *is* this?" Waldo complained, jokily at first.

Then it became a serious matter. Runt was really Arthur's dog. Nor did Scruffy care particularly for anyone outside the triangular relationship chance had constructed, out of himself, with Runt and Arthur.

Waldo got to hate Runt. He got to hate both the dogs, on account of all the tenderness—the *tendresse,* to quote the French, which sounded much more tender—he had promised himself, and been denied.

"Dogs, in the end," he said, "are much like human beings. That is not a platitude, exactly. What I mean is, they lack perception. When one had heard differently."

"The poor buggers," said Arthur, "are only dogs. I love them!"

The rangier, the more shameless they grew, lifting their legs on furniture when men weren't looking, or even when they were, the more often was Arthur driven to scrabble on the floor amongst them, to grab himself an armful of dog, to plant his nose in one or another of the moist-blackberry noses so that he and dog were one.

Then Waldo would rush into their midst, putting the boot into those dogs.

"Do you think this is what we got them for?" he took to shouting.

"What did we get them for?" asked Arthur.

A big, porous, trembly lily, he was terrified for the fate of their dogs.

"What?" moaned Arthur.

Waldo could not always answer.

He once gasped, "Obviously not for copulation."

Then when his panting had subsided, and he had thought it out, "Why," he said finally, "to protect us from those who, those who," he said, "make a habit, or profession, of breaking and entering."

On that occasion Mrs. Poulter was forced across the road, hands in the sleeves of her cardigan, to speak.

"You two men and your dogs!" she said. "To listen to you, any-one'ud think there was still a war on."

Waldo's guilt at being reminded was not less than his irritation at somebody else's facetiousness.

The Peace, he remembered, had caught up with him a couple of years after his momentous transfer to the Public Library. The new building was still smelling of varnish and rubber. By comparison with those of the old Municipal, the books themselves appeared new, or at least, the condition of their readers had not been ground into them. So Waldo could only feel quietly pleased. Particularly did he appreciate the discreet, the hallowed atmosphere of the Mitchell attached—all those brown ladies studying Australiana, and crypto-journalists looking up their articles for the Saturday supplements.

For a short time before, and especially during, the brief and ecstatic orgasm with Peace, Waldo's faith in man revived. Several of his colleagues at the Library appeared to be discovering the subtler qualities in Mr. Brown as they strolled with their lunchtime cigarettes, along the railings, or into the gardens and a glare of public statuary. Merely by their choosing them, such intellectual concepts and moral problems as they happened to discuss were at once made urgent and original.

"What does Mr. Brown think?" Miss Glasson might inquire, to draw him in.

And Cornelius and Parslow, also, seemed to expect his participation.

There were mornings, fuzzed with gold, splotched like crotons, when Waldo found difficulty in breathing the already over-pollinated air, and would return to his table almost spinning on his heels, stirring the change in his pocket, slightly more than intellectually excited. It was the times in which they were living, of course. Because at his age, whatever he noticed in the behaviour of a certain type of gross business minotaur, to entertain sexual expectations would have been neither prudent nor dignified. Consequently, when Miss Glasson, so well balanced in her golfing shoes, and protected by her grubby fingernails, asked him to her flat at Neutral Bay to drink coffee and listen to Brahms, he refused after giving it consideration. It was too far from Terminus Road, he could always explain. Miss Glasson blushed, and Waldo appreciated at least her sensibility. He was sorry about Miss Glasson.

Whose two or three stories had been accepted by *The Bulletin*. (She had asked him to call her Honor, but he couldn't.)

Cornelius, that rather ascetic Jew, heard that Mr. Brown lived at Sarsaparilla, and wasn't he perhaps acquainted with a certain family . . .

Waldo interrupted to explain that his own family had made too great a demand on his time.

And Parslow. Parslow, who remarked that by next Sunday he should have wangled petrol enough to drive out through Sarsaparilla, with Merle, and perhaps look in, Parslow had to be choked off. Because Mr. Brown of the intellectual breathers in the Botanic Gardens must never be confused with the subfusc, almost abstract figure, living on top of a clogged grease-trap and the moment of creative explosion, under the arches of yellow grass, down Terminus Road. Waldo Brown, in whom these two phenomena met on slightly uneasy terms, would have suffered too great a shock on looking out, from behind his barricade of words and perceptions, to discover some familiar stranger approaching his less approachable self—as happened once, but later.

So Waldo, who was in frequent demand, continued to refuse, on principle, by formula.

To submit himself to the ephemeral, the superficial relationships, might damage the crystal core holding itself in reserve for some imminent moment of higher idealism. Just as he had avoided fleshly love—while understanding its algebra, of course—the better to convey eventually its essence. He had the greatest hopes of what they had begun to refer to as the Peace. Remembering Miss Glasson's success with *The Bulletin* (though you could never tell; she might have been somebody's cousin or niece), Waldo almost wrote, not an article, more of an *essay*, embodying his reactions to the Peace. Searching the faces in the streets for reflections of his own sentiments, he almost composed a poem. But men were either dull or dazed, incapable of rising to the ecstasies of abstract more-than-joy—*die Freude*, in fact—which he could not help visualizing as a great and glittering fountain-jet rising endlessly skyward—never, till then, plopping back into reality.

He was so exhilarated.

Then the Peace, the crucial moment, came, and naturally it

brought its disappointments. It had its mundane aspects. It was a grand opportunity for everyone to get drunk as though they hadn't done it before. Waldo accepted to drink a glass of something at a pub down near the Quay with Parslow and Miss Glasson, though he had not cared for Parslow since his colleague's projected, practically immoral, assault on his private self. As he chose a port wine, Waldo wondered whether Parslow realized the degree of his forgiveness.

On that night, when he unavoidably missed his usual train, swamped as he was by the chaos of drunken faces, hatched and cross-hatched in light and lust, laughing right back to their gold, singing, sweating, almost everybody dancing as though it came naturally to them, Waldo was accosted by a woman in Bent Street. On such an occasion, he decided, he must return at least a token civility by listening to her. But how relieved he felt that Arthur was not present to pervert an already dubious situation.

It was not a question of listening, however, for the woman, of vague age and positive colours, her face and body blown up overlifesize by drink and emotion, fastened her greasy lips on his mouth, and, as though she had been a vacuum cleaner, practically sucked him down. Waldo had such control of himself he was able to laugh afterwards while readjusting his hat.

The reeling woman refused to believe in failure on such a night.

"Come down by the water, brother," she invited with her body as well as with her tongue, "under oner those Moreton Bay ffiggs, and we'll root together so good you'll shoot out the other side of Christmas."

But Waldo declined.

And so did the Peace. Though not at once. On his way home from work some weeks later, still intellectually drunk on that idealism which an almost blank future can inspire, Waldo bought the doll for Mrs. Poulter. Certainly it was cheap, considering its size, and rather ugly. Nor did Mrs. Poulter come spontaneously to mind, more the desire to exercise his generosity on some unspecified human being. Then, who else, finally, but Mrs. Poulter? There could not have been anyone else.

All the way home in the train Waldo was conscious of the huge doll lying on his lap, and of the eyes of his fellow passengers boring through paper wrapping and cardboard box. Long before Lidcombe he resented buying what had started as a bargain and a gesture. The dolls were being offered at one of the stores to demonstrate the versatility of plastics. So that he might enjoy the reality of plastic flesh the young lady at the counter had even undressed the doll for Waldo, and buttoned her up again in what she referred to as "the little lass's bubble-nylon gown." Waldo's first qualms set in. The continued weight of the doll on his crotch did not lighten them. Nor was it probable that the idealism or the outlay of his gesture would be appreciated at the other end.

Mrs. Poulter, less firm than fleshy now, warier of spontaneity, still lived in the house across the road built by her husband and the lad from Sarsaparilla soon after their arrival. The speed and necessity of its construction had possibly given it that abrupt look, not so much of house, as of houseboat moored in a bay of grass. Never putting out in its semblance of boat, the alternate illusion of house had been strengthened by fuchsias and geraniums springing up to dare the waves.

Even so, several times a day, Mrs. Poulter used to come on deck, and lean upon the gunwale of her boat, in her capacity as captain and lookout. It would have been tempting, Waldo thought in rasher moments, to ask Mrs. Poulter what she had done with her telescope. Although not exactly inquisitive, her eye clearly yearned to see farther than it could.

On the evening Waldo brought the doll down Terminus Road, Mrs. Poulter was, as a matter of course, leaning on her gunwale. Whether Bill Poulter was at home or not, Waldo had no time to consider. The speed of events was carrying him along, and the obscure, by now half-frozen desire to present the wretched doll. He was appalled by Mrs. Poulter's cheeks alone, which by this period had started turning mauve.

"Good evening, Mrs. Poulter," Waldo said.

And then stood. Time had stuck for the two of them. Nor did their familiar surroundings offer for the moment any sign that it might be set going again.

It was Mrs. Poulter's smile which released them both, for it could not be stretched indefinitely, but snapped back into its normally perished self.

"I brought"—Waldo began to eruct—"I lugged this thing all the way down Terminus Road, and think you had better have it as—well, there isn't anybody else."

Mrs. Poulter did not retreat, for after all it was a good-will offering, not a bludgeon, he was handing, or thrusting, over the gunwale.

She had turned practically puce. She was licking her lips for the brown parcel. Her fingers were fiddling to no effect.

"What—a present, Mr. Brown?" she said. "I don't know what I done to deserve it. Not a present."

Waldo could not have felt more foolish if he had been sure Bill Poulter was inside. Or Arthur behind their own hedge. What would Arthur, what would anybody think? When, after all, there was no cause.

While Mrs. Poulter, clutching her parcel, was again overtaken by paralysis.

"I don't know, I don't really."

Presently he got away, and Mrs. Poulter went inside, but although he waited behind their protective hedge in the dusk, there was no indication of what she might have felt on unpacking the huge plastic doll.

Nor was there ever any. Never.

Mrs. Poulter continued to come on deck, and nod and smile, her hands hidden in the sleeves of her cardigan, above the fuchsias and geraniums which attempted to disguise her houseboat. The sight, and the thought of it all, made Waldo sweat.

So he got to resent Mrs. Poulter, and everyone else who made mysteries as the Peace declined. He began to hate the faces leering and blearing at him in the streets. He hated, in retrospect, Crankshaw and his priests. He hated his brother Arthur, although, or perhaps because, Arthur was the thread of continuity, and might even be the core of truth.

Some years later, when they got them, he hated Arthur's dogs—though technically one of them was his own. If anyone, thinking of his good, had been interested enough to accuse Waldo Brown of neglecting his responsibilities to his fellow men, nobody could have accused the dogs of neglecting theirs: in being, in reminding at least one of their owners of the exasperation, the frustration of life, in farting and shitting under his nose, in setting beneath his feet traps of elastic flesh and electric fur, to say nothing of iron jaws, in chewing up bank notes, and far more precious, the sheets of thoughts which escaped from his mind—lost forever. So the whole purpose of the dogs, together with Arthur, seemed to be to remind, constantly to remind.

Then there was the visit, more ominous still, because less expected, more oblique in execution, undoubtedly malicious in conception.

It was a couple of years after they got the dogs that the strange man pushed the gate which never quite fell down. It was a Sunday, Waldo would remember, the silence the heavier for insects. The thickset man came up the path. He was the colour and texture of certain vulgar but expensive bricks, and was wearing tucked into his open shirt one of those silk scarves which apparently serve no other purpose than to stop the hair from bursting out. If it had not been for his vigour, the burly stranger, who inclined towards the elderly by Waldo's calculating, might have been described as fat. But with such purposefulness animating his aggressive limbs, "solid" was the more accurate word. Waldo had begun to envy the artificial gloss which streamed from the stranger's kempt head, and the casual fit of his fashionable clothes, so that it came as a relief to spot one of those zips which might one day get stuck beyond retrieve in some public lavatory, and to realize that, with such a build, in a year or two, a stroke would probably strike his visitor down.

If visitor he were. And not some busybody of an unidentified colleague. Or blackmailer in search of a prey. Or or. Waldo racked his memory, and was racked.

He found himself by now in the dining-room, that dark sanctuary at the centre of the house, from the safety of which on several occasions he had enjoyed watching with Mother the antics of someone unwanted, Mrs. Poulter for instance, roaming round by congested paths, snatched at by roses. Only now, with Mother gone, the game had lost some of its zest, he had forgotten some of the rules. The Peace, moreover, had so far receded he couldn't help wishing the dogs hadn't gone trailing after Arthur, that they might appear round the corner, and while Scruffy held the stranger up, Runt tear the seat out of his insolent pants.

For the man had begun to knock, and ask, "Anyone at home?" then growing braver, or showing off, to rattle, and shout, "Anyone in *hiding*?"

Waldo sincerely wished Mother were there to deal with things, especially as a woman, more of a female, whether the stranger's wife or not, was following him up the path. She walked with the quizzical ease of a certain type of expensive woman Waldo had never met, only smelt, and once touched in a bus. She walked smiling, less for any person, than for the world in general and herself. Which was foolish of her when you knew how the axe could fall.

"Perhaps you've made a mistake," the woman said rather huskily, touching her hair, and looking around at nothing more than a summer afternoon.

She was wearing a lime-green dress of more than necessary, though diaphanous, material. Raised to her hair, her arm, exposing the dark shadow of its pit, was a slightly dusty brown. Under his dressing-gown, Waldo got the shivers.

"No, I tell you!" the man insisted.

He continued rattling the doorknob, till he left off to thwack a windowpane with the crook of one of his blunt fingers.

"I can't believe anyone really *lives* in it," said the woman in her inalterably husky voice.

Waldo was sure he had heard somewhere that huskiness of voice was an accompaniment of venereal disease. So however good the stranger might be having it with his wife or whore, there was retribution to come. Waldo nearly bit his lip.

But much as he regretted the stranger's presence and relationship, he thrilled to the evocations of the woman's voice as she stood amongst the lived-out rosemary bushes, humming, smelling no doubt of something exotic, *Amour de Paris* out of the Pierrot bottle, holding her head up to the light, which struck lime-coloured down, at her breasts, and into her indolent thighs. The result was he longed to catch that moment, if he could, not in its flesh, oh no, but its essence, or poetry, which had been eluding him all those years. The silver wire was working in him ferociously now.

At least the long cry in his throat grew watery and obscure. Mercifully it was choked at birth.

Again memory was taking a hand. He remembered it was that

boy, that Johnny Haynes, they could have cut each other's throats, telling him behind the dunny to watch out for hoarse-voiced men and women, they were supposed to be carriers of syph.

Waldo might have continued congratulating himself on this piece of practical information, if the man hadn't just then shouted at the woman, "But I *know* it is! It's the place all right. I'd bet my own face. There's that erection they had my old man stick on top because they wanted what Waldo's dad used to call a 'classical pediment.' I ask you!"

But the woman apparently did not care to be asked. She remained indifferent. Or ignorant.

It was Waldo who was moved, not by the materialization of Johnny Haynes, but by the motion of his own life, its continual fragmentation, even now, as Johnny, by his blow, broke it into a fresh mosaic. All sombre chunks, it seemed. Of an old blue-shanked man under his winter dressing-gown, which he wore because the house was dark and summer slow in penetrating.

So it was only natural he should continue hating Haynes, clopping like a stallion with his mare all round the house, staring vindictively at it from under his barbered eyebrows—what vanity—as though he intended to tear bits of the woodwork off. Waldo remembered reading some years earlier, before the demands of his own work had begun to prevent his following public affairs, that Johnny Haynes was going to the top, that he had become a Member of Parliament—if you could accept that sort of thing as the top—and been involved in some kind of shady business deal. Exonerated of course. But. You could tell. Only gangsters dressed their women like that.

Then, edging round the secure fortress of the dining-room, Waldo saw that Johnny had come to a stop in the yard. After kicking at the house once or twice, to bring it down, or relieve his frustration, the visitor appeared the victim of a sudden sentimental tremor.

"I would have been interested," he grumbled, "to take a look at old Waldo. And the dill brother. The twin."

Waldo had never hated Johnny Haynes so intensely as now, for trying to undermine his integrity in such seductive style, and when Johnny added, "I was never too sure about the twin; I think he wasn't so loopy as they used to make out"—then Waldo knew he was justified.

O God, send at least the dogs, he prayed, turning it into a kind of Greek invocation as he was not a believer, and, no doubt because of his blasphemy against reality, the dogs failed to come.

Instead, the mortals went.

"The Brothers Brown!" Johnny snort-laughed.

"If they ever existed," the woman replied dreamily.

Then she shuddered.

"What's wrong?" Johnny asked.

"A smell of full grease-trap," the woman answered in her hoarse voice. "There are times when you come too close to the beginning. You feel you might be starting all over again."

At once they were laughing the possibility off, together with anything rancid. They were passing through to the lime-coloured light of the front garden, where the woman's body revived. The mere thought of their nakedness together gave Waldo Brown the goose-flesh, whether from disgust or envy he couldn't have told. But his mouth, he realized, was hanging open. Like a dirty old man dribbling in a train. Whereas Johnny Haynes was the elderly man, asking for trouble of the lime-coloured woman, wife or whore, who was going to give him syph or a stroke.

Anyway, they were going out the gate. Most indecently the light was showing them up, demolishing the woman's flimsy dress, as the Member of Parliament passed his hand over, and round, and under her buttocks, which she allowed to lie there a moment, in the dish where those lime-coloured fruits had too obviously lain before.

More than anything else these dubious overtures, such an assault on his privacy, made Waldo realize the need to protect that part of him where nobody had ever been, the most secret, virgin heart of all the labyrinth. He began very seriously to consider moving his private papers—the fragment of *Tiresias a Youngish Man*, the poems, the essays, most of which were still unpublished—out of the locked drawer in his desk to more of a hiding place, somewhere equal in subtlety to the papers it was expected to hide. Locks were too easily picked. He himself had succeeded in raping his desk, as an experiment, with one of the hairpins left by Mother. Arthur was far from dishonest, but had the kind of buffalo mind which could not restrain itself from lumbering into other people's thoughts. How much easier, more open to violation, the papers. So it became imperative at last. To find some secret, yet subtly casual, cache.

In the end he decided on an old dress-box of Mother's, lying in the dust and dead moths on top of the wardrobe, in the narrow room originally theirs and finally hers. Choked by quince trees, the window hardly responded to light, unless the highest blaze of summer. A scent of deliquescent quinces was married to the other smell, of damp. The old David Jones dress-box lay in innocence beyond suspicion. Heavy, though, for its innocence. Waldo discovered when he took it down some article which had been put away and forgotten, something more esoteric than could have come from a department store.

It turned out to be one of Mother's old dresses shuddering stiffly awkwardly through his fingers, and the scales of the nacreous fan flopping floorwards. He would have to investigate. Afterwards. Arthur was out roaming with the dogs. Waldo almost skipped to transfer the papers, so easily contained: his handwriting was noted for its neatness and compression—in fact he was often complimented.

Then, as though the transfer of the papers had been too simple on an evening set aside for subtlety, he remembered the old dress. He stooped to pick up the little fan. One of the ribbons connecting the nacreous blades must have snapped in the fall. The open fan hung lopsided, gap-fingered. But glittering.

In the premature obscurity which quince branches were forcing on the room Waldo fetched and lit a lamp, the better to look at what he had found. Rust had printed on the dress a gratuitous pattern of hooks and eyes. Not noticeably incongruous. Age had reconciled their clusters with the icy satin and shower of glass which swirled through his fingers creating a draught. It was a dress for those great occasions of which few are worthy. He need not mention names, but he could see her two selves gathered on the half-landing at the elbow in the great staircase, designed by special cunning to withstand the stress of masonry and nerves. Standing as she had never stood in fact, because although memory is the glacier in which the past is preserved, memory is also licensed to improve on life. So he became slightly drunk with the colours he lit on entering. How his heart contracted inside the blue, reverberating ice, at the little pizzicato of the iridescent fan as it cut compliments to size and order. Disorderly in habit, because the years had gradually frayed her, Mother kept what he liked to think of as a sense of moral proportion. Which he had inherited together with her eyes. There were those who considered the eyes too pale, too cold, without realizing that to pick too deeply in the ice of memory is to blench.

Merely by flashing his inherited eyes he could still impress his own reflection in the glass—or ice.

Mother had died, hadn't she? while leaving him, he saw, standing halfway down the stairs, to receive the guests, the whole rout of brocaded ghosts and fleshly devils, with Crankshaw and O'Connell bringing up the rear. Encased in ice, trumpeting with bugles, he might almost have faced the Saportas, moustache answering moustache.

When his heart crashed. So it literally seemed. He was left holding the fragments in front of the mirror. Then went out to see. A lamp he had disarranged on the shelf in taking the one for his own use had tumbled off. He kicked at the pieces. And went back.

To the great dress. Obsessed by it. Possessed. His breath went with him, through the tunnel along which he might have been running. Whereas he was again standing. Frozen by what he was about to undertake. His heart groaned, but settled back as soon as he began to wrench off his things, compelled. You could only call them things, the disguise he had chosen to hide the brilliant truth. The pathetic respect people had always paid him—Miss Glasson, Cornelius, Parslow, Mrs. Poulter—and would continue to pay his wits and his familiar shell. As opposed to a shuddering of ice, or marrow of memory.

When he was finally and fully arranged, bony, palpitating, plucked, it was no longer Waldo Brown, in spite of the birthmark above his left collarbone. Slowly the salt-cellars filled with icy sweat, his ribs shivery as satin, a tinkle of glass beads silenced the silence. Then Memory herself seated herself in her chair, tilting it as far back as it would go, and tilted, and tilted, in front of the glass. Memory peered through the slats of the squint-eyed fan, between the nacreous refractions. If she herself was momentarily eclipsed, you expected to sacrifice something for such a remarkable increase in vision. In radiance, and splendour. All great occasions streamed up the Gothick stair to kiss the rings of Memory, which she held out stiff, and watched the sycophantic lips cut open, teeth knocking, on cabuchons and carved ice. She could afford to breathe indulgently, magnificent down to the last hair in her moustache, and allowing for the spectacles.

When Waldo Brown overheard: "Scruff! Come here, Runt! Runty? Silly old cunt!"

Arthur's obscene voice laughing over fat words and private jokes with dogs.

As the situation splintered in his spectacles Waldo was appalled. The chair legs were tottering under him. Exposed by décolletage, his arms were turning stringy. The liquid ice trickled through his shrinking veins. Shame and terror threatened the satiny lap, under a rustle of beads. Each separate hair of him, public to private, and most private of all the moustache, was wilting back to where it lay normally.

Was he caught? Breathe a thought, even, and it becomes public property.

Only the elasticity of desperation got him out of the wretched dress and into respectability. His things.

When Waldo came out carrying under his arm the ball of some article, Arthur said, so ingratiating, "I know you won't be angry, Waldo, but the self-raising had arrived, and I took Mrs. Poulter the couple of pound she wanted. Mrs. Allwright asked me to. And what do you know, I found her dressing up a big doll! Mrs. Poulter! And she began to rouse on me, as if I was to blame. She said she was going to throw the silly thing away, but I told her better not. Not a valuable doll of that size."

Waldo went outside to the laundry, to the big copper, behind which nobody had ever cleaned, because it was too difficult to reach. He threw the dress behind the copper, and there it stayed.

Now at least he was free, in fact, if not in fact.

When he returned he said, "It serves you right, Arthur. It must have embarrassed you to intrude like that on someone else's privacy."

But Arthur didn't answer. He was mooning about, polishing one of those glass marbles. Arthur *seemed* content, though of course he couldn't possibly be.

Waldo was relieved tomorrow was another weekday and he would return to the safety of the Library. He inhaled the smell of polished varnish. And Miss Glasson, Miss Glasson had promised to lend him the unexpurgated edition of something, he couldn't for the moment remember what.

His public life became an assurance. Nobody of his group would be expected to strip in public, unless in a purely intellectual sense. (He had to admit that recently they had caught him out over *Finnegans Wake*, but Parslow, he knew for certain, hadn't got beyond page 10, and Miss Glasson, for all her scruples, sometimes forgot she had skipped the middle volumes of Proust.) Nakedness was not encouraged, or eyes were decently averted whenever it occurred. All the necessary or compulsive exhibitions were reserved for Terminus Road, which he loved because of Memory's skin, and where he could always ignore Arthur's burrowing through the long grass in search of that vicious ferret, the other truth.

Waldo had sat down one evening in the corner he would have reserved for himself if choice had been possible, at the little table of knife-nicked limping legs, on the surface of which his boyhood had spilled its blobs of scalding sealing-wax, and was as usual collating and correcting in the Japanese ink he preferred to ordinary blue-black—it had always seemed to him that black-black would perpetuate where blue-black might fail—when Arthur came and dumped himself on the edge of the lamplight, hunching and mumbling, playing with one of the glass marbles. As usual Waldo erected his hand as a wall in front of what he was working at.

Even so, he remained unprotected. For he soon noticed Arthur poring over a sheet of paper, one of the private papers, moreover, which he must have picked up from the floor.

"Tennyson wrote some pretty good poetry," Arthur said.

"What of Tennyson?" Waldo asked.

"This about the 'silver wire.' The one you copied out, Waldo."

The paper in Arthur's hand was making a scratching noise on the air.

Waldo could tell his lips were draining. He watched the wall of his hand, which he had raised uselessly in front of his work, grow transparent and unstable. He was trembling.

"How do you know about Tennyson?" he asked.

"I learned to read, didn't I? I read some bits in that old book of Dad's, the one the wadding's bursting out of."

It was too brutal for Waldo.

"Tennyson," he said, "is, I suppose, everybody's property. Tennyson," he added, "wrote so much he must have had difficulty, in the end, remembering what he *had* written."

"Oh, I'm not saying I've read *all* of Tennyson. I wouldn't want to. Anyway, I couldn't—could I?"

Waldo continued his automatic writing. Wasn't most of anybody's? After all.

"What else do you read, Arthur?" he asked, dreading to hear.

"Shakespeare."

"But you can't *understand* Shakespeare?"

"The stories. Anyone can understand people killing one another. It's in the papers every day."

"That's only the bare bones. The blood and thunder. It's the language that matters."

"Yes. Language is difficult. But a word will suddenly flash out, won't it, Waldo?—for somebody who doesn't always understand."

Indeed! He was blinded by them. So much so, his eyes were dropping tears of Japanese ink, whether for himself or Arthur he decided not to ask.

Just then Arthur dropped the marble with which he had been playing, and began looking for it, crawling about the room, snuffling in dark corners.

His brother! This obscene old man!

More than ever it was necessary for Waldo to leave for the Public Library, in which, for all he knew, other obscenities sat hunching over the tables, but clothed.

One day, after he had had time to forget, at least enough, Miss Glasson was standing at his elbow.

She said, "I'd love to show you an old bloke who's catching up on his reading. He asks for the most extraordinary things. Sometimes at the desk they nearly split themselves. The *Bhagavad Gita*,

the *Upanishads*! He's interested in Japanese Zen. Oh, and erotolog-
ical works! Of course there's a lot they don't allow him. Mr. Hayter
vets him very carefully. He might overexcite himself. Some old
men, you know!"

Miss Glasson of Neutral Bay sniggered, and it did not fit her
face.

Waldo stared frowning down at his sheet of addenda. He would
have liked to plug his ears with stones, when he only had his
fists.

"What's so very funny?" he asked.

"No," she said. "It was wrong of me." She could sound rather
wistful. "But I thought it might have appealed to your sense of the
grotesque. Such a funny old man."

In Miss Glasson's more unguarded moments there was a lot
which appeared "funny old" and "quaint."

Waldo hoped she would leave him, but she wouldn't, goaded on
an empty morning, it seemed, by a longing to witness rape.

"Today his tastes are comparatively simple," she persisted. "He's
back on *The Brothers Karamazov* and *Through the Looking-Glass*.
Oh, I do wish"—this time Miss Glasson only half-giggled—"I do
wish you'd let me point him out. I'm sure you'd find it rewarding.
Just a peep. I shan't show myself. I sometimes talk to him, and it
would be such a shame if he felt he could no longer trust me."

Waldo did not want, but knew he had to.

On reaching the reading room Miss Glasson led him about a
third of the way down, through the law students and the cut
lunches in waxed paper. Waldo was deafened by his own squelching heart and the sound of other people's catarrh.

"There!" hissed Miss Glasson, nudging, half pointing at the figure in a raincoat at the other end.

Waldo was relieved to feel she was preparing to abandon him to
his fate.

He went on. Long before it was possible, he identified the smell
of the old man, which was that of the overloaded stacks in his
youth at the Municipal Library. He went on, into the remembered
smell, but before arriving at the form Miss Glasson had conjured
up to disgust his curiosity, and which he was planning to skirt discreetly round, he became convinced he would recognize the heart

pulsing like a squeezed football bladder under the old man's dirty raincoat. Still some way distant from the climax of disgust, Waldo was listening to his own breathing stretched beside him in the bed at night.

Rage shot up through his drought, not only at Miss Glasson, but at all those human beings who were conspiring against him with his brother. But he went on.

Coming level with the raincoat he confirmed that Arthur was inside it in the flesh. On such a fine warm day it was not surprising he was glittering with white sweat. The reason his brother had worn the raincoat could only have been to deceive his brother.

There he sat, exposed, though, under the dismal grease-spots. Munching and mumbling over, of all things, a book. Playing with a glass marble. How it would have crashed, shattering the Public Library. But never smashed. Arthur's glass was indestructible. Only other people broke.

Having to decide quickly what action to take, Waldo pulled out an excruciatingly noisy chair and sat down exactly opposite. His attitude at the table was so intense, he was so tightly clamped to the chair, he realized at once he might be giving himself away, not only to Miss Glasson, but to all those others who would be watching him. At least he had the presence of mind to relax almost immediately.

Arthur, as soon as he had swum up out of his thoughts, closed his mouth, and smiled.

"Hello, Waldy," he said rather drowsily.

Waldo winced.

"You have never called me that before. Why should you begin now?"

"Because I'm happy to see you. Here in the Library. Where you work. I never looked you up on any occasion because I thought it would disturb you, and you mightn't like it."

This was so reasonable a speech Waldo could only regret he was unable to squash it.

"Do you come here often?" he asked.

"Only on days when I run a message for Mrs. Allwright. Today she sent me to fetch her glasses, which are being fitted with new frames." He felt in his pocket. "That reminds me, I forgot about them so far. I couldn't come here quickly enough to get on with *The Brothers Karamazov*."

Arthur made his mention of the title sound so natural, as though trotting out a line of condensed milk to a customer at Allwrights'.

"But," said Waldo, ignoring the more sinister aspect of it, "is there any necessity to come to the Public Library? You could buy for a few shillings. In any case, there's the copy at home. Dad's copy."

"I like to come to the Public Library," said Arthur, "because then I can sit amongst all these people and look at them when I'm tired of reading. Sometimes I talk to the ones near me. They seem surprised and pleased to hear any news I have to give them."

He stopped, and squinted into the marble, at the brilliant whorl of intersecting lines.

"I can't read the copy at home," he, who had been speaking gently enough before, said more gently. "Dad burned it. Don't you remember?"

Waldo did now, unpleasant though the memory was, and much as he respected books, and had despised their in many ways pitiful father, his sympathies were somehow with Dad over *The Brothers Karamazov*. Which George Brown had carried to the bonfire with a pair of tongs. Waldo found himself shivering, as though some unmentionable gobbet of his own flesh had lain reeking on the embers.

"I think he was afraid of it," said Arthur. "There were the bits he understood. They were bad enough. But the bits he didn't understand were worse."

All the loathing in Waldo was centred on *The Brothers Karamazov* and the glass marble in Arthur's hands.

"And *you* understand!" he said to Arthur viciously.

Arthur was unhurt.

"Not a lot," he said. "And not the Grand Inquisitor. That's why I forgot Mrs. Allwright's glasses today. Because I had to get here to read the Grand Inquisitor again."

Waldo could have laid his head on the table; their lifetime had exhausted him.

"What will it do for you? To understand? The Grand Inquisitor?"

Though almost yawning, he felt neither lulled nor softened.

"I could be able to help people," Arthur said, beginning to
devour the words. "Mrs. Poulter. You. Mrs. Allwright. Though
Mrs. Allwright's Christian Science, and shouldn't be in need of
help. But you, Waldo."

Arthur's face was in such a state of upheaval, Waldo hoped he
wasn't going to have a fit, though he had never had one up till
now. And why did Arthur keep on lumping him together with almost all the people they knew? Mercifully he seemed to be over-
looking the Saportas.

"The need to 'find somebody to worship.' As he says. Well,
that's plain enough." Arthur had begun to slap the book and raise
his voice alarmingly. "That's clear. But what's all this about bread?
Why's he got it in for poor old *bread?*"

He was mashing the open book with his fist.

"Eh? Everybody's got to concentrate on something. Whether
it's a dog. Or," he babbled, "or a glass marble. Or a brother, for
instance. Or Our Lord, like Mrs. Poulter says."

Waldo was afraid the sweat he could feel on his forehead, the
sweat he could see streaming shining round his eyes, was going to
attract even more attention than Arthur's hysteria.

"Afraid." Arthur was swaying in his chair. "That is why our father was afraid. It wasn't so much because of the blood, however
awful, pouring out where the nails went in. He was afraid to worship some thing. Or body. Which is what I take it this Dostoevski
is partly going on about."

Suddenly Arthur burst into tears, and Waldo looked round at all
the opaque faces waiting to accuse him, him him, not Arthur. But
just as suddenly, Arthur stopped.

"That's something you and I need never be, Waldo. Afraid. We
learned too late about all this Christ stuff. From what we read it
doesn't seem to work, anyway. But we have each other."

He leaned over across the table and appeared about to take
Waldo's hands.

Waldo removed his property just in time.

"You'd better get out," he shouted. "This is a reading room.
You can't shout in here. You're drawing attention to us."

Arthur continued sitting, looking at the book, mumbling, seeming to suck up some last dreg.

"But I don't understand. All."

"You will leave this place, please, at once," Waldo commanded in a lower voice. "Please," he repeated, and added very loudly, "sir."

Arthur was so surprised he looked straight into Waldo's face.

"Okay," he said, his mouth so open it could scarcely form words.

"But the Inquisitor," he said, recovering himself.

And again looking down, he began to tear several pages out of the book.

"You have no right!" Waldo screamed, and snatched at what he discovered afterwards he had stuffed in his own pocket.

"This is a public library," Arthur mumbled.

Whom Waldo was shoving running in something approaching the professional manner through the inner swing doors.

Arthur did not look back, but walked in his raincoat, over the inlaid floor, through the hall. Nor did the Lithuanian attendant, from some charitable instinct, attempt to arrest the offender, for which Waldo was afterwards thankful.

In the meantime Miss Glasson had come running up.

"Oh dear!" She was panting. "What a scene! How embarrassing for you! And I feel I'm the one to blame. But you came out of it splendidly. I was afraid he might grow violent. One can never be certain of any of these peculiar old men. I am so relieved," she said, "you are not in any way hurt."

He was in fact only hurt that Miss Glasson did not appear to see. But what could you expect of her, or anybody else?

He began to sleek back into place his thin, but presentable hair, and to pull down the sleeves of his coat, which had rucked up towards his elbows and stuck.

And later on, as he was passing, O'Connell came out of his office and congratulated Mr. Brown on his neat handling of a vandal, not to say madman. Waldo would have liked to enjoy praise, but in a flash of frosted glass and closing door he suspected he saw, seated on leather, at the other end of O'Connell's room, Crankshaw, was it? and a priest.

The rest of the day was not quite in focus. In the evening he returned as usual to Sarsaparilla, carrying a small parcel of New Zealand cod he had bought for their tea. As the train rocked his bones the hoardings were proclaiming a millennium. He was too tired to contradict, even in his hour of personal triumph. He was so tired he would not have been able to resist the figure in the old raincoat, for he realized the other side of Lidcombe that his brother was sitting ahead of him. Arthur either remained unaware, or made no attempt to approach, anyway, there and then.

For at Barranugli he came and sat, equably, silently, beside Waldo in the Sarsaparilla bus, and they remained together after getting down.

As they walked down Terminus Road, Waldo realized that, somewhere, he had left his parcel of New Zealand cod. He was too tired to care.

The children running along behind them—as would often happen, on account of Arthur—were playing a game dependent on a string of screams from which occasional words would dangle.

"One a one makes two,"

the children seemed to scream.

Screeeeee they went on the evening air damp with nettles.

"One a one a one,"

they sang,

"Two a two is never one."

Perhaps understanding they should not advance beyond the pale, the children dissolved on seeing the Brothers Brown enter Terminus Road.

And when there was silence, Arthur took Waldo by the hand.

"Whatever happens," Arthur said, "we have each other."

"Yes," said Waldo.

Who was otherwise too weary. As his brother led him along and down their familiar road he was too tired to cry.

The incident at the Library did not exactly wind up Waldo's career, for it happened two years before his retirement, and in the time left he presented himself regularly for duty. He could not feel he was running down, and nobody ever suggested it. He was content. He would himself have admitted to the incidental signs of age: red rims under watery eyes, papery skin which, if pinched up, remained standing in a blue ridge, his tyrant bladder. But the physical, the superficial, was of minor concern. He was still young and twitching at the level where the Incident—the incidents, were continually being re-enacted.

Arthur continued remarkably active. After the death of Allwright in 1951, the widow had kept him on. He was necessary to her, especially for the deliveries, and because he remembered the prices she forgot. At home as usual he baked the bread three times a week. And made the butter twice, from whichever cow. Waldo never remembered the names, the number in the series. He hated cows.

All this while the mutton fat was curdling round them in skeins, clogging corners, filling bowls with verdigris tints and soft white to greyish fur. You couldn't be bothered to empty the mutton fat out. Like a family, it was with you always. Set.

And dogs. The dogs had reached what was probably their prime. They would lay themselves out in glistening sleep on warm bricks, or, coming to, would narrow their eyes at the sun, and lick their private parts, and contemplate the flavour. The young strong dogs loved each other in the end, which was strange, considering. Scruffy used to wander off in search of sexual excitement, and once Waldo came across him locked in a little bitch outside the Sarsaparilla post office. Waldo hurried in to buy his stamps, not wanting several ladies to connect him with Arthur's dog.

Scruffy returned on that occasion, as on many others, holding his tail at an angle, fulfilled, and yet respectable.

Runt was less inclined to stray. Though he was Waldo's dog he waited longing for Arthur to return. He preferred games of mounting, rounding his eyes, twitching his impeccable tail. Runt and Scruffy loved each other.

Then suddenly Waldo Brown was retired. All that had to be said was said, the documents and the objects received, the addresses exchanged. He realized that Miss Glasson, Cornelius, Parslow, Mr. Hayter—who had never joined them in the intellectual breathers on the edge of the Botanic Gardens—even O'Connell himself, had grown brittler, if jollier, their silences deeper, their vision in-turned. Though there was none of them who would not ignore his own involutions, looking up in friendship even after he had been caught out picking his nose the moment before.

Waldo said good-bye to them all. They made arrangements to meet, to discuss Bartok, Sartre, the milder statements of Picasso—it was so important to keep abreast—and Waldo smiled, agreeing, while knowing he would not care to. Not now that he was retired. He had work to do.

He said to Arthur, "A good job the Widow Allwright is selling out. Because it's time you retired too."

There was no reason why his brother should be let off.

"I, of course, shall find a lot to look into," Arthur said. "But what about you, Waldo? What will you do?"

Knowing that Arthur's contradictory eye was on him, Waldo answered, "I have my work."

As if it wasn't twitching inside, barely contained by, the dress-box on top of the wardrobe.

"Oh yes," said Arthur, satisfied, "the book you're going to write."

As if Waldo, and all those in collaboration, hadn't been writing it all his life. Now that he was retired it was only a matter of settling himself, of sifting and collating the evidence, of A progressing to B.

So, they were retired.

When the two old men returned from the walk which wasn't Arthur's last, pushing at the gate which had not yet fallen down, pushing with their chests in places at the grass which had swallowed up shoes, crockery, sauce bottles, salmon tins, anything of an incidental or ephemeral nature, including the sticks of rose-bushes and stubborn trunks of long-dead rosemary, they came to the house in which they must go on living. For the moment at least, Waldo saw, Arthur could not die. If they hadn't been knotted together by habit he might have continued resenting Arthur's failure to accept the plan he didn't know about. As it was, Waldo could even make a compensation out of the prospect of prolonged mutual habit. Habit in weaker moments is soothing as sugared bread and milk.

Arthur was now preparing to go in and make that bread and

milk, faintly sweetened, which soothed away the flapping of acidulous stomachs after walks. He used to serve it out in pudding basins, and they would take their basins and eat from them in whichever room they wanted to be. Sometimes they would find they had chosen the same room, or Arthur had flopped down in Waldo's, there was no escaping, nor from the *glup glup* of someone else's bread and milk. The louder Arthur glupped, the more ingeniously Waldo managed his spoon. He could feel his teeth, in self-defence, moving like the false ones of some over-refined female in a businesswomen's luncheonette, though his own teeth, he knew, were still sound as nails, and when alone, and there was no need to set an example, he would worry food like an animal, his pleasure increasing with the violence of the physical act.

In his brother's company he felt compelled to wipe his mouth, and fold his handkerchief, and say, "If you could listen to yourself eating bread and milk you would hear the tide turning in a sewer."

Arthur didn't mind. He very rarely cared what people said.

"Why don't you care?" Waldo used to ask because it exasperated him so.

"I dunno," Arthur said, sucking a tooth. "I think it was that time at the Public Library, before we retired, when you called me sir. After that I didn't bother. I don't care what people say."

Waldo couldn't be expected to remember every word which had ever been uttered, certainly not those it did your health no good to remember.

So he insisted, "But you should. You ought to take a pride in yourself, and care what other people say."

Arthur continued sucking his teeth.

"Don't you care if people don't like you?"

"No," said Arthur. "Because they mostly do. Except Mrs. Allwright. And she went away to Toowoomba."

Waldo hated his brother for moments such as these. While knowing he should be thankful for Arthur's insensitivity.

The day they returned from the walk on which Waldo had decided Arthur should die, the latter chose to remain in the kitchen after the bread and milk was served. Waldo was spared listening to the *glup glup* for the noise the dogs were making as they crunched, or gnawed, or dragged along the floor the mutton flaps on which they were feeding. It was from such treatment that the kitchen boards, which had sloughed their linoleum years ago, got their rich polished look.

The *scrape scrape* of the mutton flaps, together with the steady crunching of bone, made at a distance a fairly companionable sound.

Waldo was sitting with his legs apart. He was sitting in the room in which their mother had lived her last illness. He ate by full, openly greedy, quickly swallowed mouthfuls, because now of course he was on his own, and the closeness of his collected works in the dress-box on top of the wardrobe gave him a sense of affluence. If he sometimes bit his spoon between the more voluptuous acts of swallowing, it was for remembering how he had contemplated burning his papers during those panicky moments on the walk.

He was so annoyed at one stage he called out to Arthur, "You shouldn't have given them the mutton flaps now. Kept them till evening. It's only middle of the day."

"Yes," called Arthur through his bread and milk, "I forgot it's only middle of the day."

If Waldo did not criticize further, it was because they did forget. They both forgot. Sometimes the light reminded them, but the light could not tell them the day of the week. It could not remind them when they had been born, only that they were intended to die.

Why were they always dragged back to this? Or he, Waldo. He was afraid Arthur didn't think about it enough, which could have accounted for his unconcern when faced with signs and accusations.

Just then Arthur came into the room, and caught his brother wiping out the basin with his fingers, which annoyed Waldo considerably.

Arthur stood looking at him.

"I want to talk to you, Waldo," he said.

"What is the schoolmaster, the *head*master, going to announce?" Waldo grumbled.

"We can talk to each other, can't we? We are brothers, aren't we?"

Then Waldo saw it printed up as HA! HA!

He only grunted, though, and looked with distaste at the empty basin. He would have liked to complain about the bread and milk he had just eaten, but there isn't much bread and milk can lack.

Arthur, the mountain in front of him, finally asked, "Do you understand all this about loving?"

"What?"

This, perhaps, was it, which he most dreaded.

"Of course," said Waldo. "What do you mean?"

"I sometimes wonder," Arthur said, "whether you have ever been in love."

Waldo was filled with such an unpleasant tingling, he got up and put the pudding basin down. One of the dogs, it was perhaps Scruffy, had come in to gloat over him.

"I have been in love," Waldo said cautiously, "well, I suppose, as much as any normal person ever was."

By now he suspected even his own syntax, but Arthur would not notice syntax.

"I just wondered," he said.

"But what a thing to ask!" Waldo blurted. "And what about you?"

At once he could have kicked himself.

"Oh," said Arthur, "all the time. But perhaps I don't love enough, or something. Anyway, it's too big a subject for me to altogether understand."

"I should think so!" Waldo said.

I should hope so, he might have meant.

"If we loved enough"—Arthur was struggling, kneading with his hands—"then perhaps we could forget to hate."

"Whom do you hate?" Waldo asked very carefully.

"Myself at times."

"If you *must* hate, there's no reason to pick on yourself."

"But I can see myself. I'm closest to myself."

Then Waldo wanted to cry for this poor dope Arthur. Perhaps this was Arthur's function, though: to drive him in the direction of tears.

"I don't know what you're talking about," he said, to offer his driest resistance.

"Love," said Arthur. "And that is what I fail in worst."

"Oh, God!" Waldo cried.

The light was the whitest midday light, of colder weather, and Arthur was standing him up.

"If," said Arthur, "I was not so simple, I might have been able to help you, Waldo, not to be how you are."

Then Waldo was raving at the horror of it.

"You're mad! That's what you are. You're mad!"

"All right then," Arthur said. "I'm mad."

And went away.

Although he was trembling, Waldo took down his box intending to work, to recover from the shocks he had had. After all, you can overcome anything by will. If the will, the kernel of you, didn't exist—it didn't bear thinking about.

So towards evening he retied the strings round the bundles of unresponsive papers. He didn't know what had become of Arthur. He went out and walked round and about, mowing down the tall grass, which stood up again when he had passed, because he was light-boned and old.

So he returned to the house in which they lived, and Arthur was standing, beyond avoiding, in the doorway, waiting for him. Arthur was looking old, but seemed the younger for a certain strength. Or lamplight. For lamplight rinses the smoother, the more innocent faces, making them even more innocent and smooth.

Except Arthur was not all that innocent. He was waiting to trap him, Waldo suspected, in love-talk.

So that he broke down crying on the kitchen step, and Arthur who had been waiting, led him in, and opened his arms. At once Waldo was engulfed in the most intolerable longing, in the smell of mutton flaps and dog, of childhood and old men. He could not stop crying.

Arthur led him in and they lay together in the bed which had been their parents', that is, Waldo lay in Arthur's vastly engulfing arms, which at the same time was the Gothic embrace of Anne Quantrell soothing her renegade Baptist. All the bread and milk in the world flowed out of Arthur's mouth onto Waldo's lips. He felt vaguely he should resist such stale, ineffectual pap. But Arthur was determined Waldo should receive. By this stage their smeary faces were melted together.

But so ineffectual. Waldo remained the passive, though palpitating, plastic doll in Arthur's arms, which he didn't even attempt to undress, for knowing too well, perhaps, the wardrobe of garments, the repertoire of flesh. Mrs. Poulter, who had knitted the sweater Arthur was wearing, must have experienced, if not pleasure, at least satisfied curiosity, probably even a cauterizing fear, in undressing and dressing up her doll. But Arthur, it seemed, was unafraid of anything, and Waldo only afraid of time now that it had begun to slip.

As they lay in the vast bed time was swooping in waves of waves of yellow fluctuating light, or grass. The yellow friction finally revived their flesh. They seemed to flow together as they had, once or twice, in memory or sleep. They were promised a sticky morning, of yellow down, of old yellowed wormy quinces.

Until in the grey hours Waldo not exactly woke, he opened another compartment to find that Arthur had rolled over, onto his back, snoring with a grey, thistly sound, and he, Waldo, was again the dried-up grass-halm caught in the crook of Arthur's sweater. He began almost at once to twitter, for Arthur's illusion of love and a greyed-up grass-halm. If the moustaches had mingled—Arthur was smooth—they should have run off a string of little flannel-eyed boys, and girls with damp ringleted hair. But that was the way it hadn't worked. The carpet Jew had wrapped them (un)fortunately up.

Presently Waldo creaked out of bed and began stealthily washing up the dirty bowls and things, which normally they left till cement had formed. This morning he was making use of them. To ignore the thoughts Arthur might otherwise pounce on when he woke. So Waldo had to work with care, not to avoid making a noise, but to prevent himself from giving room to his thoughts. Noise never woke Arthur. He would lie there well into light, and then, still half asleep, stay picking the dead skin off the soles of his spongy feet, waiting for an opportunity to barge in on other people's thoughts.

That morning, when Arthur woke finally, he called out to

Waldo, "I dreamed about you, Waldo. You had lumps of Pears soap trying to come out of your nostrils. You seemed upset. I wonder what it means."

Waldo was revolted. He broke a basin.

"Perhaps it means," said Arthur, "you're afraid of having a baby."

"I think," said Waldo, "I needn't have any such fear by now."

"Did you know Dulcie had two miscarriages? She was more upset than I've ever known her."

Arthur came shambling in. In that dreadful sweater on a puce theme Mrs. Poulter had knitted for him.

"She loved them I believe," Arthur said, "more than the real children she had."

"Miscarriages"—Waldo snorted—"are more than real. I know that!"

Arthur sat down, scuffling up his old-man's hair, in which stains of his fiery youth were visible still. If you hadn't known Arthur, his bare feet would have looked peculiarly gentle.

"What are we going to do today?"

"We're going for a walk."

"What walk?"

"The same."

Arthur and Waldo were observing each other.

Then Arthur said, with that fluency and lucidity which his crumbly face would suddenly produce, "That's all right, Waldo. Because we'll be together, shan't we? And if you should feel yourself falling, I shall hold you up, I'll have you by the hand, and I am the stronger of the two."

So there was nothing for it but to go.

Every morning, sooner or later, they went for the walk, longer, and then longer, Waldo always hoped. They would return about midday, later if it had been longer. They returned to the basins of bread and milk.

Meat they ate also on occasions: a lump of beef, mutton flaps, rather rubbery from the dangers boiled out of them. Or sometimes they would tempt fate, they would join in stuffing a mutton flap, with the old bent aluminum skewers always taking on fresh shapes, or raining on the floor, as hands fought to contain a sculpture of dough, or torture dead meat into submission. As they slapped and pinned, during their joint effort, they might begin to laugh, probably for different reasons. At least they had the meat in common. While the skewers threatened to pierce their hands.

If Arthur made no other attempt to convert Waldo to the love he preached, it was perhaps because love in the end becomes an abstraction like anything else. From meat to Bonox in several acts. Anyway, brown.

It troubled Waldo no end the night he woke to discover the worst had happened. Sinking low is never sinking low enough. Since he had not yet recovered his vocabulary, he could only call faeces shit.

Or shout and bellow.

When Arthur had lit the lamp he said, "All right, Waldo. Don't we know? I know I'm responsible for a lot."

As he fetched the basin he added, "But have never jibbed at mopping up."

Muttering still: "To go back to what I told you. To let Runt and Scruffy in the bed. Then we'd be all of us together."

Waldo thought he couldn't allow himself to fall asleep ever again. And find *that*. Only walk, which is another kind of sleep.

Which they did every day.

Once he looked at Arthur and said, "At least it must be doing us good."

Arthur said, "Yes, it's obviously doing us good."

So that Waldo flung himself at the dress-box almost every afternoon with such passion he had torn off one of the cardboard sides. He sat with his papers spread out round him, weighted with stones when the wind blew. Mostly he corrected, though sometimes, as his throat rustled dryly, he would also write.

On one occasion he wrote: In the extreme of his youth, which was fast approaching, Tiresias suffered difficulties with his syntax and vocabulary. He found that words, turning to stones, would sink below the surface, out of sight.

He did not care for that, but kept it. He kept everything now, out of spite for Goethe, or respect for posterity.

When Arthur produced something he had found.

"What is it, Waldo?"

"An old dress of Mother's."

"Why was it behind the copper? She must have forgotten."

"Put it away!" Waldo shouted. "Where it was!"

To Arthur, who was holding in front of him the sheet of ice, so that Waldo might see his reflection in it.

Arthur threw away the dress.

Which turned into the sheet of paper Waldo discovered in a corner, not ferreting, but ferreted. On smoothing out the electric paper at once he began quivering.

"Arthur," he called, "do you know about this?"

"Yes," said Arthur. "That's a poem."

"What poem?"

"One I wanted to, but couldn't write."

Then Waldo read aloud, not as menacingly as he would have liked, because he was, in fact, menaced:

> "my heart is bleeding for the Viviseckshunist
> Cordelia is bleeding for her father's life
> all Marys in the end bleed
> but do not complane because they know
> they cannot have it any other way"

This was the lowest, finally. The paper hung from Waldo's hand.

"I know, Waldo!" Arthur cried. "Give it to me! It was never ever much of a poem."

He would have snatched, but Waldo did not even make it necessary.

When his brother had gone, Waldo went into the room in which their mother used to sit at the four-o'clock sherry. He took down the dress-box and began to look out shining words. He was old. He was bleeding. He was at last intolerably lustreless. His hands were shaking like the papers time had dried.

While Arthur's drop of unnatural blood continued to glitter, like suspicion of an incurable disease.

Waldo was infected with it.

About four o'clock he went down, Tiresias a thinnish man, the dress-box under his arm, towards the pit where they had been accustomed to burn only those things from which they could bear to be parted. He stood on the edge in his dressing-gown. Then crouched, to pitch a paper tent, and when he had broken several match-sticks—increasingly inferior in quality—got it to burn. The warmth did help a little, and prettiness of fire, but almost immediately afterwards the acrid years shot up his nose.

So he stood up. He began to throw his papers by handfuls, or would hold one down with his slippered foot, when the wind threatened to carry too far, with his slippered foot from which the blue veins and smoke wreathed upward.

It was both a sowing and a scattering of seed. When he had finished he felt lighter, but always had been, he suspected while walking away.

Now at least he was free of practically everything but Arthur.

After he had lain down on the bed he began to consider how he might disembarrass himself, not like silly women in the news who got caught out through falling hair or some such unpremeditated detail, but quick, clean, and subtle, a pass with the tongue he had not yet perfected, but must. As he lay, he raised himself on one creaking elbow, because of the urgency of his problem.

That was when Arthur came in and saw him.

"Waldo!" Arthur was afraid at last. "What are you trying to do to me?"

When Waldo had always wondered, fainter now, whether Arthur noticed the hurt which was intended for him. Or Dulcie. He had never shown her he had noticed that moustache. And Dulcie's moustache might possibly have been the means of her destruction.

But Arthur so practically smooth.

Through the pain of destroying Arthur he noticed more than heard Arthur's last words.

"I know it wasn't much of a poem." Arthur was shaping his defence. "Oughter have destroyed it at once. Apologize, Waldo."

The warmed stones of words.

"That poem? That disgusting *blood* myth!" Waldo gasped to hear his own voice.

"I would have given the mandala, but you didn't show you wanted it."

"I never cared for marbles. My thumb could never control them."

He was entranced by Arthur's great marigold of a face beginning to open. Opening. Coming apart. Falling.

"Let me go! Wald! *Wald-o!*"

As dropping. Down. Down.

THREE

ARTHUR

IN THE BEGINNING there was the sea of sleep of such blue in which they lay together with iced cakes and the fragments of glass nesting in each other's arms the furry waves of sleep nuzzling at them like animals.

Dreaming and dozing.

The voices of passengers after Cape Town promised icebergs to the south, two-thirds submerged.

He looked but only saw the sea in varying depths of light and blue. Sometimes in the stillness of a wave he heard a seabird mewing which might have accounted for his sad stomach. He wasn't sick. He hadn't been sick. Waldo was the sick one, they said, Arthur has always been strong. So he must continue to be.

Then suddenly he noticed for the first time without strain, it seemed, the red-gold disc of the sun. He was so happy, he ran to reach, to climb on the rails, reaching up. His hands seemed to flutter his breath mewing with the willing effort.

Voices screaming lifted him back, and he noticed he had been scratched by ladies.

"You must never never climb on the rails at sea!" said Mother. "You might fall over, and then you would be lost forever."

He looked at her and said, "Yes. I might. Forever."

Feeling the cold circles eddying out and away from him.

Mother was soon calm again, sitting talking to the lady who, arranged from head to toe in veils, became always more of a silkworm the tighter the better she arranged her veils.

"Yes, he is very different," Mother agreed, and laughed. "But they are honestly twins. I can vouch for it! The other one, Waldo, has gone with his father to make friends with someone—the Chief Engineer, I believe. Neither George nor Waldo likes engines, but perhaps they feel it is manly to try."

The Silkworm said she could not bear the ship, there were cockroaches in the Ladies, she could not bear the passengers, they were so common, she could not bear the voyage, it was too unnecessarily long.

"Never again round the Cape!" The Silkworm shuddered inside her cocoon. "All the nicer people travel via the Canal. But Mr. Viney-Smith—my husband—says we wouldn't stand up to tropical heat."

"Yes," Mother said, and sighed, "it is long. But we have come this way because it is cheap. And I don't expect we shall ever travel by any other route. When we arrive, we shall have to stay where we are put."

That night there was to be a ball. So presently the Silkworm went, to get herself up as the Primrose Pompadour, and win the prize.

Arthur was glad to be alone with Mother. He held the back of her hand to his cheek and rubbed it with the only ring she wore.

But Mother ignored him, or at least half. She half spoke to the setting sun.

"We mustn't exhibit ourselves," she said.

"We mustn't what?"

"We mustn't show off. I have given the most disgusting exhibition of false humility. To which I know I am prone."

Then she looked at him again, and this time it was only for him.

"Promise me never to show off."

She was all for promises, and he was always promising, even those promises he would have to break.

Because he knew he loved to exhibit himself. He loved it when other people showed off. He loved the feel of the velvety seats.

"How do you like being in a box, Arthur?" It was Granny asking.

They were all for asking how he felt, and he could not have answered, except that he was sleepy and excited. He could only run his hands along the velvet edge, of what was not, except jokingly, a box, floating in the sea of music.

Everybody talked a lot in the box while the ladies in the huge lit scene were singing against one another.

Again it was: how do you like? what do you make of?

This time it was the person who was Mother's Uncle Charlie leaning over the back of his chair.

"Well, what does the young fellow make of *Götterdämmerung*?" Uncle Charlie asked.

To that Arthur could only try to stroke his left shoulder with his cheek. The answer would have been too velvety, too foolish.

"It's a wonder Anne allowed us to carry off her brat to this unrewarding experiment." Uncle Charlie yawned.

"Poor Anne! She's too harassed," said Cousin Mollie Thourault, smelling so flowery, "too upset by the other one's being ill."

Uncle Charlie, Arthur could feel, had become in some way interested again. He could feel his relative's hand on the nape of his neck. He would have liked to throw the hand off, but was afraid of disturbing Uncle Charlie's thoughts. For his fingers were thoughtful as his voice increased.

"Wouldn't you have thought, Adelaide," he said to Granny, and against the singing his speaking voice sounded enormous, "she might have suspected some irony of intention? You wouldn't expect it of Him. Irony is not for Baptist-rationalists even when it kills off a few more unacceptable gods."

"How brutal you are, Charlie!" Granny said laughingly. "Men are more brutal than women, and far more complicated."

Arthur could not tell, but found out later Granny was right, that even dogs are less brutal than men, because they are less complicated.

For the time being, lapped so deliriously in linings of dark red velvet, sleep was carrying him off. Or music. Who and where were the gods? He could not have told, but knew, in his flooded depths. Tell Waldo about the lady in the brass helmet. The primrose pomp. If the crimson flood of music had been of Waldo's world.

"Wake up, darling!" Mother said.

And of course they were sitting on the deck. The dying sun had turned them cold.

"You funny boy!" she said. "Falling asleep just anywhere. Perhaps it's a blessing," she added.

Again she was looking out to sea. And he loved her.

He would have loved to see the icebergs, but never ever did they pop up, not even though he looked to the line which divided sea from sky. Only in sleep the icebergs moaned, and jostled one another, crunching and tinkling. The moons of sky-blue ice fell crashing silently down to splinter into glass balls which he gathered in his protected hands.

Somehow at least he knew from the beginning he was protected. Perhaps it was Waldo. Not everybody has a twin. He must hang on to Waldo.

"You're a funny pair," said the woman at Barranugli when she brought in the big brown teapot. "Are there many others like you at Home?"

"I should hope not," Waldo answered; it had made him angry. "I should hope we are different from just anybody."

The woman went out. She didn't seem to understand their speech.

Arthur had not contributed because he mostly left it to his brother, who was quick at answering questions. Perhaps if things had made him angrier Arthur might have answered back more often, but he was lazy enough to leave it to Waldo.

They lodged at first with those people at Barranguli, Mr. and Mrs. Thompson—he was a joiner who hadn't taken to them. But it was convenient because of Dad's job at the bank. Arthur and Waldo went to school only a couple of blocks away, where nobody understood them until they managed to learn the language. Even so, Waldo, then and always, preferred to speak English because, he said, it had a bigger vocabulary. Arthur did not care. Or he did. He developed the habit of speaking mostly in Australian. He wanted to be understood. He wanted them to trust him too. Waldo, he knew, was suspicious of men, though Waldo himself was inclined to call them Australians.

Dad was at the bank then. They looked in to see him whenever possible, to be made a fuss of by the young ladies, and Mr. Mackenzie would give them things, sometimes even sixpences. Best of all Arthur liked to go upstairs to the residence. He loved other people's houses, and never quite succeeded in breaking himself of a habit, it shocked Mother terribly, of opening cupboards and drawers to look inside. Mother continued shocked even after he pointed out it was the best way of getting to know about the owners.

"It's a form of dishonesty," Mother said.

"It's not! It's not!" Arthur shouted.

"I shouldn't like to think you were dishonest."

He could feel inside him the rush of words which wouldn't come.

"What's dishonest," he blathered, jerking his head against the gag, "when all you want is know, talk to people? I can talk better if I know them better."

"People tell you as much as they want you to know."

"Is that honest?"

"Don't excite yourself, dearest. It isn't good for you. We do know that."

It wasn't good for him. But Mother could also be unjust.

So at least he didn't look inside any of the cupboards or drawers at the bank manager's residence. It would apparently have been too humiliating for Dad. Whenever they were taken upstairs Arthur had to content himself with the sound of silence, the brown shadows, and the mystery of the bank manager's wife.

"Mrs. Mackenzie is bedridden," Mother explained.

"What?"

"She's delicate. An invalid. She has to stay in bed."

"What's wrong with her?"

"That's something we don't ask."

Waldo said, "I think Mrs. Mackenzie is a pressed flower," and giggled.

It was of the greatest interest to Arthur. Certainly Mrs. Mackenzie's hand had the dry cool scratch of clean writing-paper or pressed flowers. And yellow, she was yellow, in her still, brown room, with a blowfly that had got inside, and the little prayer-desk, or *pre-dew*, she called it, which she was no longer strong enough to kneel against.

"Perhaps," suggested Arthur, "if you wore a surgical appliance."

But Mrs. Mackenzie appeared too delicate to see any point. She only wet her lips.

So Arthur didn't collect Mrs. Mackenzie, although he was the one interested in people. Waldo was more interested in words and all that Waldo was going to do. Natural enough—Waldo was the clever twin.

It was not till towards the end of their stay at Barranugli, on an occasion when Waldo had gone behind the counter to give his views to two of the clerks sitting at their ledgers, that Arthur decided to go up alone to the residence, and if things had turned out otherwise, might even have started looking through the cupboards and drawers. But it did not happen that way.

The residence above the bank was laid out rather unusually. Almost at the top of the stairs there was a little half-landing where you were offered a choice of directions. Arthur had never been there long or unencumbered enough to discover what lay beyond the right-hand turn, beyond the brown linoleum and the thick brown light.

On the morning when he should have found out, he was, so to speak, arrested. He was approaching the little landing, when he stood, and held on to the banister.

For precisely at that moment, Mrs. Mackenzie the manager's wife, yellower, brittler than ever before, flew or blew across the landing in the sound of her own starchy nightdress. He could hear the sound of her long, rather fine, but yellow feet, just scratching the surface of the linoleum, somewhat sandpapery in effect.

On seeing Arthur, Mrs. Mackenzie, too, was arrested. On the little landing. She stood looking down at her own toenails. He was surprised to find her so tall. Far taller than her tobacco-y husband. Perhaps it was from lying in bed.

Then Mrs. Mackenzie said, still staring at her toes, which were curling upward to meet her gaze, "My husband has taken the trap, and gone to Wilberforce for the day."

Arthur wished he knew what to say.

"It is business," she said. Then she laughed out of pale gums. "Men are a business to themselves."

The nightdress looked quite solid compared with skinny Mrs. Mackenzie.

Suddenly she said, looking straight at him, and he recognized the look, "I am sick, you know. Didn't they tell you? I shouldn't have left my bed. My husband will be so upset. When he returns from Wilberforce. If he doesn't find me arranged."

She began to drift back to her room, trailing the sound, not of flesh, but of skin and crumpled starch.

"All right, Mrs. Mackenzie," Arthur felt he had to call out as she flitted, "I only know as much as you've told me."

It was disappointingly true, for he never found out whether the manager's wife had some important secret, or whether he had simply caught her on the way to break into a pot of jam.

Just then Waldo started calling from the bottom of the stairs, and he had to go down, when he would have liked to stay and at least watch Mrs. Mackenzie arrange her invalid arms in the right position on the counterpane. He loved the ladies, and even though they didn't take him seriously, knew quite a lot about them. On the whole he didn't require the confirmation of cupboards and drawers.

About this time they bought the land down Terminus Road. On several occasions Dad had been out there on his own. He had met a storekeeper, a man called Allwright, who told him Sarsaparilla was a coming place.

"Not that we're interested in that sort of thing," Dad warned them when he got back from one of his expeditions. "What we want is to live to ourselves don't we? with a minimum of nosy parkers. Well, Mr. Allwright believes Sarsaparilla will never lose its backwaters, though the greater part of it is bound to open up."

"Oh dear," Mother was beginning, she seemed afraid of something. "Do you think Mr. Allwright is trustworthy? You know you are too trusting, George."

"Any major move," said Dad, "is a leap in the dark. And you, Mother, were the biggest leap of all."

Mother kept quiet, as Arthur got to know, when Dad confused the issues.

Soon they all went out to Sarsaparilla on the train, to see the land and meet Mr. Allwright, so that Mother would be convinced.

"But it's so *far*, George!" she complained in the swaying train. "Imagine after a day at the bank!"

Because Dad did not answer and looked so grim they knew it was all going to happen. While the train strewed their laps with smuts.

Mr. Allwright met them at the siding with a buggy. Arthur did not look at him closely, and years afterwards, trying to remember the first time he set eyes on his employer, wondered why the first occasion had left so little impression on him. Mr. Allwright can never have been a particularly young-looking man. He was tall and fairly broad, oblong like a bar of chocolate. His full moustache, his thick glasses, his waistcoat over his shirtsleeves, all made you feel he was an honest man. Perhaps the reason you didn't at first notice anyone so solid was that you knew he would still be there, he would keep till later. Anyway, Arthur hardly bothered to look, but was staring in all other directions, at Sarsaparilla, which lay glittering with early summer.

Mr. Allwright, who didn't say an awful lot, drove them in the buggy, and pointed out to Mother the convenience of *their* road. It was already theirs. It was already called Terminus, because of being close to the station, practically planned, in fact, for Dad.

As they drove down Terminus Road they passed a ruined house standing amongst fruit trees which had been allowed to go wild.

"What is that?" Waldo asked.

"Ah," said Mr. Allwright, "there's a story attached to that."

"What story?" Arthur could hear Waldo insisting.

"Ah," said Mr. Allwright, "something for a winter evening. Too long for now, and we're nearly there."

Arthur knew this meant Mr. Allwright wasn't willing to tell, just as he knew Waldo was put out.

"If you don't tell it now," Waldo said, "how do I know you won't have forgotten it?"

Arthur laughed. He was enjoying himself.

"It doesn't matter, Mr. Allwright," he said. "If you don't tell, my brother will make the story up."

Mr. Allwright flicked his whip, and turned to Dad.

"Young fullers"—he pronounced the "fell-" to rhyme with "gull"—"young fullers," he said, "are a bit too sharp. Too much imagination could get them into trouble."

But Dad who was already living down Terminus Road did not answer. He had stuck out his jaw. He had taken off his billycock hat. He sat showing the mark where the leather band had eaten into his forehead, and for quite some time he had forgotten to shift his bad leg.

So that before very long they were living really and truly on the land they bought from Allwrights down Terminus Road. First, of course, there was the house to build, and they used to come out from Barranugli on Sundays to supervise the building by Mr. Haynes and a couple of men, and Arthur would play with a big randy dog belonging to one of the labourers.

Arthur loved the classical façade of the brown weatherboard house. He learned there was something about the Classical which Dad called "sacrosanct—in a manner of speaking."

After Waldo had pestered him enough, and fetched the book, Dad would read them the Greek myths. While pausing every few weeks to remind them: none of this is real, none of this is true. Whatever he meant by that. In the strong sunlight of Sunday mornings, or the more fruitful evenings, seen through leaves, Arthur could not even care. He loved Demeter for her fullness, for her ripe apples, he loved Athene for her understanding.

There was an occasion when Dad put down the book and said, "Sometimes I wonder, Arthur, whether you listen to any of this. Waldo can make an intelligent comment. But you! I've begun to ask myself if there's any character, any incident, that appeals to Arthur in any way."

Arthur couldn't answer Dad, or not in full.

"Tiresias," he said, to keep him quiet.

"Why on earth Tiresias?" asked Dad.

And Waldo had begun to stare.

But it was too difficult to explain to their father even if Arthur had wanted to. He could not explain the diversity of what he partly understood. He was too lazy. It was too long. Nor would his family understand. How could he tell them of his dreams, for instance, except as something to laugh about. They would laugh to be told how shocked he was for Tiresias when Zeus took away his sight at the age of seven—*seven*—for telling people things they shouldn't know. So Arthur kept quiet. He was only surprised they didn't notice how obviously his heart was beating when Zeus rewarded Tiresias with the gift of prophecy and a life seven times as long as the lives of ordinary men. Then there was that other bit, about being changed into a woman, if only for a short time. Time enough, though, to know he wasn't all that different.

So when Waldo stared at Arthur stupid Arthur, who couldn't answer Dad's question, Arthur simply plaited his too pliable fingers, and sat looking down.

Brown Brown Arthur Brown? he heard them at school, but the other side of his own more interesting thoughts. He heard the voice of Mr. Hetherington who, after a little, realized, and did not keep him in.

The headmaster was Mr. Heyward, with whom at first there was a spot of trouble. It was not so much over the green Junior Scripture Books which Mr. Hetherington doled out. You didn't need to bother with those. You could look at other things beyond the page. The trouble began over the half-hour segregation, when the clergyman, the ministers came.

Dad wrote Mr. Heyward a note:

Dear Sir,
    As my twin boys are convinced unbelievers I must request you to exempt them from religious instruction. I myself was born a Baptist, but thought better of it since.

Yours truly,
Geo. Brown

Mr. Heyward sent a reply:

My dear Mr. Brown,
    The problem is a simple one. All agnostics are classified automatically as C of E. You can rest assured the Rev. Webb-Stoner will not assault your boys' convictions.

H. E. Heyward
(Principal)

Then Dad thought of a tremendous joke.

Dear Mr. Heyward,
    What if I should reveal that a pair of Moslem boys are attending your very school?

G. Brown

The Brothers Brown were pestered no more, but allowed to moon about the yard. Waldo kept a book hidden on him. But Arthur used to play with the marbles he had earned. Arthur in particular longed for the half-hour segregation. Which did seem to set them apart. It got round Sarsaparilla there was something queer about the Browns, over and above one of them a real dill. It did not worry Arthur. Dill in the engravings looked like fennel, which grew increasingly wild down most of the side roads at Sarsaparilla.

Of course Mrs. Allwright, so well placed at the store she always heard about everything, had suspected in the beginning there was something wrong with Browns, though from goodness of heart, on their coming out Sundays to supervise (I ask you!) Mr. Haynes, she had provided a cold tomato, a wet leaf of lettuce, and a slice of beef, with sometimes perhaps a hard-boiled egg as an extra.

Mrs. Allwright said, "Fred, I knew you were acting unwise selling land to such as them. *My* land, too, though I don't propose to harp on *that*."

Land was one of the several reasons Mrs. Allwright was superior to her husband, Arthur learned in time. But now he had just come into the store to buy humbugs with one of the sixpences Mr. Mackenzie the manager had given.

"I have a feeling," Mrs. Allwright was saying, "that the Browns are on our hands for always. Mind you," she said, "I have nothing against the English in general, the decent, churchgoing ones who you wouldn't mind sitting down at table with. But *these*!"

"These are human beings, Ivy," Mr. Allwright said.

"Human beings," said Mrs. Allwright, "are all very well."

Then Arthur declared himself.

"Mrs. Allwright," he called, chipping on the counter with the sixpence, "I don't want to interrupt, but have come for humbugs if you've got them."

Mrs. Allwright came out from behind. She was that red. She was wearing a little watch which you could pull out to the end of its chain, to tell the time conveniently.

"Not humbugs," she said, as though she wouldn't have had them on the place. "Not humbugs, but bull's-eyes. They're the same."

"They aren't really," said Arthur, "but I'll take the bull's-eyes. I never really cared for bull's-eyes."

Mrs. Allwright began to weigh them out.

"Why," she said, "what a trick you are!"

"How would you feel, Mrs. Allwright," Arthur asked, "sucking a bull's eye?"

While Mrs. Allwright was twisting the corners of the paper bag.

"Come along," she said. "I haven't time for argument."

"You wouldn't feel good," said Arthur, taking the paper bag and the change.

Mrs. Allwright didn't answer, she only breathed.

"That's a pretty nice watch," Arthur said, to sweeten her. "Will you let me pull the chain?"

But Mrs. Allwright said, "I would of thought, Arthur, your mother would of taught you that ladies don't appreciate bold behaviour in little boys."

So Arthur Brown realized that Mrs. Allwright did not like him. It did not disturb him, however, nor that she should continue to dislike. It was Mr. Allwright who mattered.

On a later occasion, going to the store for some article of less importance, Arthur looked through what must have been the storekeeper's bedroom window, and there was Mr. Allwright down on his knees in a blaze of yellow furniture. Arthur was fascinated, if not actually frightened, by his friend's face sunk on his chest, by the hands which he held out in front of him, pressed straining together as stiff as boards. It puzzled Arthur a lot.

"Mrs. Allwright," he said at the counter, "I saw Mr. Allwright down on his knees."

Mrs. Allwright blushed and pursed up her mouth.

"He is praying to his Maker," she said, as though that explained everything.

"His maker?"

He liked the idea, though, of the wooden man, freshly carved, and sweet-smelling.

"To the Lord Almighty."

As Mrs. Allwright elaborated, she very discreetly lowered her eyes.

If Arthur did not altogether understand, the wooden man began to put on flesh.

And then Mr. Allwright himself came.

"Well, young fuller," he said, which continued to fascinate Arthur. "I bet you've found out something else since yesterday."

But Arthur had grown shy, for some power which Mr. Allwright possessed.

Then the grocer rummaged in the calico bag in which he kept the change from when he went round delivering.

"Did you ever see a lead florin?"

Arthur couldn't touch it enough.

"Was it *made*?" he asked.

"It was made, all right," said the grocer. "A brum two-bob—like anything else."

Then he took the hammer and struck the coin into a disc of blurred metal.

"That'll cost you a whole two bob!" Arthur was enjoying it.

While Mrs. Allwright stood wincing, as though suffering it in her own flesh.

"Somebody," she said, "always has to pay the bagpipes."

Though she made pretty sure, as a rule, that she would not be somebody.

Arthur eventually added Mr. Allwright to what he knew as truest: to grain in wood, to bread broken roughly open, to cow-pats neatly, freshly dropped. If he did not add Mrs. Allwright it was because she did not fit into that same world of objects, she never became distinct, she was all ideas, plots, and tempers. In myth or life, he never ever took to Hera.

Johnny Haynes, the boy at school, asked if Browns were really pagans as was said. Arthur didn't know what they were.

When Johnny found that Arthur Brown could solve mathematical problems, Arthur was in some demand, and began earning the glass taws.

Arthur the dill, and Waldo the dope, Johnny Haynes used to saysing. Nothing could have hurt Arthur. Arthur only feared for Waldo.

At least they allowed Waldo to go down behind the dunnies with them. They did not suggest that Arthur. They did not want One-Ball Brown.

He was different, then, in several ways. But did not mind since he had his marbles.

However many marbles Arthur had—there were always those which got lost, and some he traded for other things—he considered four his permanencies. There were the speckled gold and the cloudy blue. There was the whorl of green and crimson circlets. There was the taw with a knot at the centre, which made him consider palming it off, until, on looking long and close, he discovered the knot was the whole point.

Of all these jewels or touchstones, talismans or sweethearts, Arthur Brown got to love the knotted one best, and for staring at it, and rubbing at it, should have seen his face inside. After he had given two, in appreciation, or recognition, the flawed or knotted marble became more than ever his preoccupation. But he was ready to give it, too, if he was asked. Because this rather confusing oddity was really not his own. His seemed more the coil of green and crimson circlets.

Waldo the twin used to scoff at the marbles.

"Who'd want to lug round a handful of silly old marbles!"

"You would not," said Arthur, undisturbed.

"You'll bust your pocket, and lose your old marbles. What'll you do then?"

"Nothing," said Arthur. "I shan't lose them."

But he went cold knowing that he might. He knew, too, that Waldo hoped he would.

Waldo who loved kissing. No, rather, he liked to be kissed, and forget that it had ever happened. Coming in from school Arthur had caught him kissing the mirror.

"Fancy kissing a looking-glass!"

"I never did!" said Waldo, the moment already buried in his face.

But they would lie together, and the dark bed was all kindness, all tenderness towards them, the pillowed darkness all feathers. Skin was never so velvety by day. Eyelashes plait together in darkness. As Venus said, in the old book Arthur came across years later: I generate light, and darkness is not of my nature; there is therefore nothing better or more venerable than the conjunction of myself with my brother.

But darkness could descend by daylight in one black solid slab.

"Don't speak to me!" Waldo would shout, as they sat dragging socks over toenails, and Arthur had forgotten how to lace up his own boots.

It was the kind of moment when Arthur sensed he would have to protect his brother, who was too clever by half, who read essays aloud in class, who liked books, and who was said to be their mother's darling. Because of it all, Waldo needed defending from himself and others. It was all very well to hang on to your brother's hand because Waldo was accepted by the tight world, of tidiness and quick answers, of punctuality and unbreakable rules. Even Johnny Haynes and the boys who went behind the dunnies to show what they'd got, accepted Waldo by fits and starts, because they were deceived, from some angles, into seeing him as another of themselves. But poor Waldo was so different, and so frail.

Arthur could never take time off like his brother reading books. He would never have been able to protect Waldo if he, too, had so exposed and weakened himself. Arthur could only afford to look up a book on the sly. In time, he thought, he might, perhaps, just begin to understand.

In the meantime there was his family. All the members of his family were frail. As he went down to milk, there they were, sitting on the classical veranda: Mother who knew better than anyone how things ought to be done had sliced her finger doing the beans; Waldo who knew how to think was screwed up tighter than his own thoughts; and poor Dad, very little made him sweat under his celluloid collar.

So Arthur had to go carefully. He tried to prevent the bucket from clanking. He was glad of the opportunity to give Jewel's udder a punch—holding up her milk as per usual—and bury his head in their cow's side.

But when he returned along the path of trampled grass, he would have liked to cry. If they wouldn't have seen it. For there they were. Still. With Waldo going to write some old tragedy of a play.

Arthur had by some means to distract.

So he stood the bucket, and said more or less, "I'll act you my tragedy of a cow."

For nobody would be able to accuse him of not fully understanding a cow. And they sat looking at him, almost crying for his tragedy. As he stamped up and down, pawing and lowing, for the tragedy of all interminably bleeding breeding cows. By that time his belly was swollen with it. He could feel the head twisting in his guts.

Everybody had begun to share his agony, but that, surely, was what tragedy is for.

When Mother suddenly tried to throw the expression off her face, and said, "Oh Arthur, we understand your tragedy without your showing us any more."

And at that moment he felt Dad turn against him. It was some question of afflictions. Except in theory, the afflicted cannot love one another. Well, you couldn't altogether blame Dad. With his aching leg.

"I wish I knew how it felt," said Arthur.

"Why?" asked Dad, biting his moustache.

"It would make it easier, wouldn't it? if I understood."

Dad didn't seem to think it would. And Arthur knew that he was right. Their limping and lumbering together would not help. For his father it would have been detestable.

As for Waldo, Arthur was closest to his twin when silentest, the moment before falling asleep, or walking down the side roads at Sarsaparilla, or in the class early, after seeing their father off. Dozing awake amongst the quickly solidifying rows of desks, they sat propping each other up.

Except on the morning when Waldo accused.

"You're just a big fat helpless female."

Arthur did not tell him: If that's the way you want it. He simply said, "I'm that tired."

He laid his face sideways on the desk, and dreamed a short, unsatisfactory dream about someone he was on the point of meeting.

Then Waldo punching. Waldo shouting.

"Wake up, you dope! They're coming in!"

"They've seen us, haven't they? before, Waldo?"

Waldo gave him that extra punch for luck.

"Waldo the dope and Arthur the dill," Arthur chanted as the kids came in.

He gave the performance they expected of him. They seemed to like him for it. Arthur was only wretched for betraying Waldo so easily.

Nobody could remember, not even Arthur Brown himself, when he developed his head for figures. The gift was found growing in him, as naturally as hair for instance. He was safest with numbers. The steel springs of clocks could not be unwound so logically. Arthur's awkward fingers would become steel tentacles reaching out for the solution of his problem. What Waldo called those messy-awful melting-chocolate eyes would set hard in the abstraction which should have been foreign to him. How did he do it? He just knew. And immediately after, was laughing it off. The brown sloppy awful eyes had a squint in them too, or in one of them.

"Music and mathematics have something in common," Mother was happy to remember.

Arthur would have liked them to. But it was Waldo who learned to play, with care, from Miss Olive Fischer of Barranugli, "The Raindrop Prelude," "The Turkish Rondo," and "Fur Eliza."

That was later on, however. Till then, Waldo grumbled, "When can I have those real lessons?"

"When the money has been saved up," said Mother, "you shall both have lessons."

"What! Arthur?"

"Why not Arthur?" Mother said. "Arthur may be a musical genius."

Waldo went so silent he must have been offended.

But Mother was determined Arthur should be a genius. She sat beside him remembering all that she had learnt—sometimes of an evening she would flop down on that hard stool and play the Paderewski minuet, crossing her wrists at the moment they were waiting for—but sat beside Arthur stiff and stern to supervise his scales. Arthur's hands became ungovernable then. He could not manage the angular scales, though of course he could hear, he could *see* in advance the splotches of sound. If he could only have moulded music as he knew how to work butter and knead the dough. Or add up the notes until they made a musical whole.

He couldn't. And Mother gave up. She grew sad, though not, she said, on account of that. Instead, they entered deeper into their conspiracy of butter and bread. Only she and Arthur were to understand the mystery they had to celebrate. Arthur was only too glad to adopt the rites she imposed on him. By lamplight he and Mother became their own closed circle in the kitchen.

This development gave Arthur Brown a satisfaction more intense than any he experienced before the coming of Mrs. Poulter.

In the meantime they decided schools were wasted on him. Arthur Brown was taken on by Mr. Allwright about the time Waldo began at Barranugli High. Arthur Brown's apprenticeship was arranged quite quickly and easily, in spite of, he learned at once, the opposition of Mr. Allwright's wife.

He went to the store, and on finding himself the right side of the counter, grew more serious for a bit, took to damping down his orange hair, got the hiccups frequently, and would stand alone waiting for custom, twisting an invisible ring on his little finger.

If he stood alone it was because his employer would be out delivering the orders, and his employer's wife inside, pouring tea for her sister Mrs. Mutton, who was almost always visiting behind the shop.

"You must realize, Arthur," Mrs. Allwright explained, "my sister depends on my support. She has never been the same since Mr. Mutton passed on. You must just do your best, and make your mistakes, and learn things, like all of us, the painful way."

When Mrs. Allwright said painful she meant painful, that he knew. He knew Mrs. Allwright and Mrs. Mutton were sitting out there on the closed-in veranda waiting for him to make those mistakes. Like the incident of Mrs. Musto's change. That sort of thing was what gave him the terrible hiccups. On one occasion Mrs. Allwright administered so large a drink of vinegar it shrivelled his inside and left him winded. From the way she laughed he must have looked comical.

His own solemnity did not last too long. He learned too thoroughly the extent of Mrs. Allwright's stock, and could tot up so quick she herself got sarcastic about it.

"Oh dear!" she shrieked. "Don't you put me to shame, Arthur! I'll have to watch out while you're around. You'll catch me out, won't you?"

"You're not all that mathematical, Mrs. Allwright," Arthur had to admit.

Which made her turn nasty.

"I never cared for brass," she said, "in particular from subordinate young men."

"Sub-what?" he asked, hiccuping.

But Mrs. Allwright had returned to Mrs. Mutton.

Even before he learnt to drive the buggy his outside duties were more diverting. To run outside and chase away the dogs when they began pissing on the overflow produce. To stack on the veranda the cases delivered by farmers' wives, almost all of whom enjoyed his jokes. Sometimes he would simply lean against a post with the empty theatre of the distance spread around him, no sound but the hooting of a train in the cutting or a chattering of sods in the coral tree, as he took out one of those glass marbles left over from the school yard. Not to play with. It had developed into something more serious than play. For the circle of the distant mountains would close around him, the golden disc spinning closer in the sky, as he contemplated the smaller sphere lying on the palm of his hand.

He would put it away quickly, though, on hearing anyone approach from behind. He was less afraid of theft, or even total destruction, than he was of damage by scorn.

Once or twice Mr. Allwright descended on him before he could hide the marble. But it did not seem to matter. For Mr. Allwright's smile slid around and away from it.

He would make a remark such as: "Mare cast a shoe other side of *Ferndale*. Remind me Thursday morning, Arthur, to take her up to Harry Booth's."

Mr. Allwright was so discreet.

Even if he had been able to explain to his employer the mystery of his glass marbles, it was possibly unnecessary. As for Mrs. Allwright, there was no question. She was a voracious cat who could not digest half of what she gobbled up. He left her to the pleasures of Mrs. Mutton's company. Her elder sister, all in black, sat on the glassed-in veranda, sipping Indian tea, and masticating pumpkin scones.

After the storekeeper had taught him to drive the buggy, and he was allowed to go round delivering the orders, Arthur felt more independent than before. To flick the flies off Treasure's rump, as the bay mare clumped and snorted down the empty roads, her rear opening curiously like a passion fruit. The yellow dung went *plop plop*. Arthur Brown would roll on his seat in time with the buggy long before its motion called for it.

Waldo decided in later years: Arthur is an unconfessed volupu-tuary.

Arthur liked that; it sounded in itself voluptuous.

He liked best of all to arrive with Mrs. Musto's order, crunching round the drive to the back, where Louie presided over the girls, behind the Virginia creeper and the plumbing. After he had scrambled down, and gone inside with the deal case full of groceries, they would feed him cherry conserve, or peaches in brandy, or, if he could get there early enough, voluptuous slices of boiled ham.

"I shan't forget how to live, eh?" With difficulty he forced it out, through his stuffed mouth, past his fatty lips.

"Spare the masters, feed the servants. That's my motter!" Louie used to say.

Then when the old girl got on the tube: "That's 'Er. No one need spare 'Er. Not Fairy Flour."

"Yes, madam. Oh no, madam," Louie breathed into the mouth-piece. "There is the ham, madam, for luncheon, as we 'ad agreed, hadn't we? Oh yes, madam. After the consommy jelly in *tasses*. And the celery sticks will taste lovely stuffed. And the Marsala bomb to finish off with. Yes, madam."

"No bomb would finish '*Er*," Louie said after she had stuck the stopper in the mouthpiece.

She and her mistress had been quarrelling it out for close on twenty years.

After the grocery items had been checked, more often than not Arthur would get up and wander past the green baize door to the inner parts of Mrs. Musto's house. He had never been denied access to them. Everyone was mostly too busy: dusting, digesting, looking for somebody who couldn't be found, sulking, making it up, or preparing to give in their notice yet again. He would plunge deeper through the high rooms, fingering the blind busts, and books nobody ever read, the unused china, and the photographs of those who had ceased to matter. Mrs. Musto seemed on the whole to prefer to know people only slightly. They were always preparing her crammed house for the entrance of someone she hadn't yet got to know.

The morning he went so far as to explore an upstairs room Arthur was surprised to find Mrs. Musto standing in her bloomers and camisole. Mrs. Musto, too, was surprised. It appeared as though she had just finished having a cry. Her impulse was to scream, until she realized who it was.

"Oh dear, Arthur," she said, "it is you! I am sure yer will understand."

Then she flopped into a chair, as though she could not have stood any longer, her ankles and emotions swelling as they were, and sat like a half-filled bag of flour.

"What is it, Mrs. Musto?" Arthur asked, not only because he was curious to know, but because she obviously wanted him to.

"As you are interested," she said, "it is, well, it is Him. Stubbens, I mean."

Then she rearranged her arms, from which the skeins of flesh were dangling over the arms of the chair.

"It is that *creature*," she said. "Nobody could call me difficult, but I am not wax in *anybody*'s hands."

Remembering the blunt but well-kept hands of the elderly chauffeur who had been a groom, Arthur couldn't help remarking, "Wouldn't mind betting he manicures them."

But Mrs. Musto ignored it.

"If my husband," she mumbled, as she bungled her thoughts, "if my husband was only available."

Arthur waited, because he saw it was intended.

"Ralph—" Mrs. Musto picked her way. "I lost me husband, Arthur, in Palermo. We had gone there against advice. It was already too late. Too hot. Perhaps you know I suffer from the prickly heat. And *She*—this woman from Boston—carried Ralph off by the scruff of the neck—in her teeth, yer might say, if they hadn't been a denture. Out of a *cathedral*!"

Mrs. Musto was so upset.

"Ralph could charm the ladies just by lecturin' to 'em. He had fagged it up—out of books—for no other purpose. He could talk to 'em about the Crusades. He told them about those chastity contraptions. I can hardly bear to hear the term, let alone use it. Because, indecency apart, Ralph had assaulted their chastity before they ever guessed he had the key."

All this was most mysterious but rewarding to Arthur Brown.

"How did things turn out in Boston?"

"I never cared to inquire. Or Cincinnati. Or Denver City. Ralph always had to play for higher stakes. He never stopped to think whether he had lost the game before. Me, I wouldn't have let 'im lay a finger on the business. His head," Mrs. Musto explained, "his *business* head was abominable. Otherwise, Ralph was a personable man. One of the sculptured men." Her voice added to it.

"And do you happen to have a photo of your former husband, Mr. Ralph Musto?" Arthur asked. "I mean, it's nice to keep some memento, even of the duds."

He so much liked to see how other people looked, particularly the husbands of the wives and the wives of the husbands—to work it out.

Mrs. Musto grumbled and frowned. Her bosom boiled inside the camisole.

"Ralph," she said, "was not worth the silver to stand 'im in."

And opening her mouth she cried out, out of the back of her throat, out of her matrimonial past.

But shut up pretty quick. As though she had realized something for the first time.

"Come to think of it," she said, "this other one—this *creature*—is the dead spit of Ralph!"

She might have begun hollering again, but remembered enough to gather up her slackness from the chair.

"Oh dear," she said, "there's this mob I'm expectin'. Evelyn and Bertie are motorin' up, with some divine Peruvian contralto, if she can be got out of bed bi luncheon."

At once Mrs. Musto rushed at the pots on her dressing-table, and began to smear, and dab, and hit herself hugely with a powder puff, her bottom sticking out behind.

So Arthur knew he was dismissed.

He meandered down through the cool house, where slavery was

made to look the most enticing freedom. He went touching such objects as he passed: the loaded sceptres of tuberoses, a crystal bird, the little Moorish torchbearer, the marbles of Mrs. Musto's solitaire board.

Something was nagging at him in the library. He began dawdling through the books, some of them almost too heavy to lift. Some of them. Then his nostrils dilated, with pure animal conviction, or else that psychic sense his mother hoped she possessed. His hair bristling. His blood racing him, his heart thundering, breath thicker. In no time he was all prickly, looking through the books from which Mr. Ralph Musto had learnt more than was good for him. What they would have said at home made him swallow a mouthful of guilt.

He had found, but only just, what he must have been supposed to find, when Mrs. Musto came downstairs.

"What," she said, "Arthur, I never suspected," she said, "that you were another one for books."

"Yes," he said, and: "Not exactly."

Now too guilty even to read.

"Well, I wouldn't touch one," Mrs. Musto said vehemently, "not if I was carried off by a second Deluge, with books instead of animals."

He could only stand there foolishly, weighed down by the certainly open but trembling book.

"Tell me," she said, more sympathetic, or inquisitive, "what are you having a read of in Ralph's encyclopaedia?"

She wasn't laughing, so, lowering his head, he read out loud, pushing the words well forward with his lips, because he almost doubted he would be able to form them, he was so excited.

" '*The Mandala is a symbol of totality. It is believed to be the "dwelling of the god." Its protective circle is a pattern of order super—imposed on—psychic—chaos. Sometimes its geometric form is seen as a vision (either waking or in a dream) or—*' "

His voice had fallen to the most elaborate hush.

" '*Or danced*,' " Arthur read.

He was so thunderstruck he was relieved to feel that Mrs. Musto, in spite of her inquiry, was preoccupied.

She said, "Evelyn, I think, is on a diet. Oh, dear!"

So Arthur was able to put the encyclopaedia away, and give his most joyful attention to his friend and protectress Mrs. Musto.

She was wearing a great hat, on which stiff bundles of feathers had been laid, in the manner of ears of corn in a shallow basket. Although it was still only late morning Mrs. Musto was shimmering with moonlight, from her net insertion right down to her ankles, which, it seemed, were hobbled by what looked like a pair of Turkish pants. It was most dazzling. Even her arms, which the fringe of sleeve above the elbows allowed to escape from custody, were too decently powdered to offend.

"Do yer like me?" Mrs. Musto asked, and smiled.

"Oh yes!" said Arthur.

He did so genuinely.

Then again a thought appeared to cross Mrs. Musto's face. Perhaps it was the shimmer of her dress which caused her thoughts to flicker on and off, or dart fishlike to the surface.

"Poor Waldo," she said. "Something must be done about yer brother. I am goin' to give a tennis afternoon, and ask a mob of youngsters. But yer mustn't tell," she warned sternly. "You understand?"

"Yes," said Arthur, as he heard the melancholy sound of his relationship with Mrs. Musto snapping.

"I shall ask that Feinstein girl," she decided. "Does it work, though? A *couple* of lost souls."

Arthur did not know how to say it often has to.

He said instead, "I'd better be getting back to the mare. She's restless when she's finished her nosebag. By the way, Mrs. Musto," he said, turning in the doorway on a little mat which was threatening to shoot from under his feet, "there isn't any Demerara."

But she was running, hat down, at a big bowl of roses, and didn't hear.

Arthur only half resumed his round, for thinking, as he clacked at Allwrights' mare, how bitter it was the Feinsteins also, who might have become his private property, were being given to his brother Waldo. If the thought didn't grow unbearable, it was because, as Mrs. Musto had pointed out, Waldo was in need of a kind. What this need could be, Arthur was not yet certain, much occupied as he was in working out his own needs and relationships.

Then the thought of the mandalas made him begin again rocking on the buggy seat. If only the curtain on his mystery hadn't stuck halfway up.

That Sunday he decided to ask help from somebody—Dad, or Waldo, either of whom was naturally better informed. Over what remained of the salmon loaf, by then reduced to a pink dribble and the little white rounds of crumbly bone, Arthur was rehearsing his speech: Now tell me, Waldo, you will know. But suddenly he knew his brother wouldn't. Which relieved him somewhat. Because he would not have cared to ask an intellectual favour of Waldo's face. That left their father. Why he did not propose to ask their mother, he wasn't sure, only that their relationship depended more on obscurity and touch. So there was Dad. Cleaning his moustache of salmon.

When the others had withdrawn to their own more private corners in the house, Arthur began.

"Tell me, Dad," he said, "there's something I want to ask you."

George Brown looked at first as though he had been hit.

Then he let out his breath, and said, "If you can't ask me, son, I don't know who you can."

Dad did not always sound convincing. But Arthur had begun to enjoy it.

"What," he asked, "is the meaning of 'totality'?"

Again George Brown might have been recovering from a blow.

"Well," he said, "it is one of those words so simple in themselves as to be difficult of explanation. So very simple," he repeated.

Clearing his throat, freeing his teeth, finally blowing his nose.

Then, as he marched out of the room, Arthur of course had to follow, bumping one or two things in the hurry. In fact, together, Dad and he were shaking the whole house.

Dad took the dictionary down.

"Accuracy in the first place can only be called a virtue," George Brown recommended. "Always remember that, Arthur."

Arthur said yes he would, while concentrating on holding his breath for what might come.

Dad read out: "Totality is 'the quality of being total.' "

He looked at Arthur.

"That is to say," said Dad—he could not clear his throat enough

—"it means," he said, " 'that which is a whole,' " adding: "Spelt with a w—naturally."

Then Arthur realized Dad would never know, any more than Waldo. It was himself who was, and would remain, the keeper of mandalas, who must guess their final secret through touch and light. As he went out of the room his lips were half open to release an interpretation he had not yet succeeded in perfecting. His body might topple, but only his body, as he submitted the marble in his pocket to his frenzy of discovery.

Arthur discovered Feinsteins too.

Whenever he went up the slope to *Mount Pleasant*, climbing Feinsteins' red concrete steps, usually the morning was at its finest stage of glitter. Sometimes there had been rain, and the droplets were still hanging. Or music. There was often music, and if Arthur did not march in time, as he would have liked to, it was because it wasn't that kind. Cheerful enough, but music which could suddenly knife. There were glossy mornings when he was bleeding trickling through the mouth.

Round the back Mrs. Feinstein, a decent sort of woman, used to come out—they did not keep a maid, either from wanting to act modest, or because they only lived there half the time—she would receive the groceries herself.

"You must tell me your name," she said in the beginning, and ever so naturally replied, "Arthur Brown? That is a name I shouldn't forget!"

"No, Mrs. Feinstein," he said, "and I'm glad you won't."

So gallant. The ladies liked that—though not all of them.

Mrs. Feinstein liked it so much she gave him a cool drink in the kitchen.

"This is ice-cold lemonade," she said, explaining its virtue.

It was certainly ice-cold, and scented, if rather weak.

"You should drink it slowly, and concentrate," Mrs. Feinstein advised. "Then you will extract the *prana* from this lemonade."

"The what?"

"It is Indian," she said, "for 'vital force.' "

It made her grow thoughtful.

"Of course we don't know exactly if this is a practice which has been *scientifically approved of,* but it's a nice idea, don't you think?"

It gave her so much pleasure, Arthur could only share it. He lost his breath on the lemonade.

Once she let him pull a ship's bell, and it clanged against the music with which the house was filled.

"Ssshhh!" she warned, holding a finger to her large nose.

If he was not encouraged to explore their house it was perhaps because of the young girl inside. Practising.

It added to the mystery of *Mount Pleasant,* and Arthur liked to leave by the other path, when he could look, at first carefully, then pressing his face against the glass, at Dulcie Feinstein's back.

She never looked over her shoulder, although, considering the strength of his interest, it was difficult to believe she could not feel his presence outside. As she played and played—the prickly scales, or the *etoods,* the polkas and gavottes, which would never be for him—his flesh pressed against the pane must have been turning that sickly-plant tone of green, of faces forcing themselves behind glass. From time to time his stomach accepted a delicious thrust of misery. In the Feinsteins' moist garden. In which music broke and scattered, or lashed back, tail to fang, like snakes or thoughts.

Once Mrs. Feinstein came out and caught him, and looked the other way so as not to appear annoyed. She was determined, it seemed, though politely, to prevent him from seeing more of her daughter. Though he had, he thought, once, at the store: a skinny girl with a dark shadow on her upper lip, standing probably having the sulks beside a bag of potatoes. But that was different. This would have been the real Dulcie swaying the music out of her body and shaking back her dark hair, if her mother hadn't been determined to keep her a faceless mystery. She succeeded too. Dulcie Feinstein never turned round. Only the smell of lanoline drifted sometimes as far as Arthur.

Once in the course of his humdrum yet complicated relationship with Mrs. Feinstein he dared mention his brother, and she said yes she knew of Waldo, but delicacy or something prevented Arthur from encouraging her to add to her uncommunicative reply.

So he was able to keep the Feinsteins, and particularly Dulcie, as part of his own secret life, which was naturally so unsuspected nobody tried to enter it. What irritated some of them was when a withdrawal into himself drew attention to the luminous edges of his face, where at any time the skin was of a whiteness to suggest blue.

More than anyone Mrs. Allwright would grow resentful if she could tell by his expression that he was absent without leave.

"That boy—'man' I shall never hardly bring myself to say—is not *logical* from one minute to another," Mrs. Allwright remarked to Mrs. Mutton over the pumpkin scones.

Leave alone someone else's logic, Mrs. Mutton had trouble in mastering her own wind.

"I hope the scones are good, Mrs. Mutton, Mrs. Allwright," Arthur said, coming round alongside the glassed-in veranda. "Because it would be too bad if they weren't."

Then Mrs. Allwright had to titter.

"You can't help laughing!" she used to say.

Sometimes Arthur would do his best to give the old girls a real good laugh. On one occasion he had even begun to caper and sing:

> "It's my guess if the laugh
> Is on the right side or the wrong side
> Of my girlie's face.
> If it's on the right side
> It's all all right,
> If it's on the wrong side
> It's too too bad to be true!"

At that point Mrs. Allwright averted her face as if it were too full of scone, and spoke sounding thick and soggy.

"You will hear more about this, Arthur, from Mr. Allwright," she glumphed, and swallowed.

While Mrs. Mutton looked at the window, through and away, managing her teeth.

Arthur did not expect to hear any more, nor did he, on account of the understanding which existed unexpressed between himself and Mr. Allwright on the subject of Mr. Allwright's wife.

And then there was his meeting, the first official, socially ratified meeting with Dulcie Feinstein, not that she needed to exist more completely than she did already in his mind. It was only that Dulcie, he knew, had to turn round and face whatever it was in Arthur Brown.

Arthur had the shakes by the time they reached the house. It was impossible to gather to what extent Waldo was already established at the Feinsteins'. Much as he admired his brother for his scholastic brilliance, his knowledge of the world, his self-sufficiency, he had begun to fear for Waldo, for some lack of suppleness in his relationships with other people. There were moments when Waldo was as rigid as a closed cupboard, which no one but his brother had learnt the trick of jerking open. So he trembled for Waldo on the way to Feinsteins', for fear that Waldo had been there too often alone.

He was somewhat reassured, however, by the sight of Mr. Feinstein gleaming in the doorway. Old Feinstein sometimes gave Arthur a bob or two. And then the appearance of Mrs. Feinstein, in her rustling, metal-beaded dress.

"Why, Mrs. Feinstein, you do look good! Like oil on water," he was moved to say.

It was a good beginning, with all the indications of a love feast.

If only Dulcie would declare herself.

Then she came in. In that white, loosely embroidered dress, a flurry of white hydrangea heads. If he was at all flustered it was because of her beauty and the movement of the flowery flowing dress. He was, in fact, so overcome he began to babble all that silly rot about her father's old *capple*, a performance which Dulcie obviously found distasteful, it was showing so clearly on her face.

He continued babbling, he heard, "Now that I've seen your face. Even if you never want to see me again."

At the same time he knew, of course, that this could not be true; Dulcie herself let him see it. When he went up to examine her more closely, by touch as well, he saw her suddenly closed face open out again as it must in response to music. In spite of the natural shyness of any young girl, she accepted his entry into her thoughts.

"Oh yes," she seemed to be, and was in fact, saying, "we shall have so much to exchange, to share."

More than anxiety, fear that something precious might escape her, was making her take him by the hand.

"Of course I shall teach you the piano!" Dulcie agreed, laughing with a joyful relief.

They couldn't get down to it quick enough, regardless of anyone else present.

Dulcie would play a scale, or form the shapes of fully fleshed music, or explain the theory of what she was doing. While in between Arthur was glad to splash around with his unmanageable hands, which, he now realized, she would never notice. Why should she? She understood his sudden splurges and sallies of music.

It was the most exquisite fulfilment Arthur Brown had experienced yet.

He hardly noticed when Waldo shot out of the room, nor did he more than half see that his brother had returned looking pale.

For Dulcie was telling Arthur about the *Pierrot d'amour* on the scent bottle in Mrs. Musto's bathroom where, in spite of his familiarity with the house, he had never been.

"That's interesting now, Dulcie," he said. "*Amour* sounds different from 'love.' Eh? Doesn't it?"

"Oh yes," she agreed. "The words are different. They have a different shape. Probably even a different meaning."

He would have liked to give it further thought, but this was after all a social occasion.

When the tea came, and the rain, when they were all sitting round behind rain-pelted windows, eating the buttery cinnamon toast and exchanging anecdotes, Arthur knew how to retract what some people considered his aggressive personality. He knew how to lick his buttery fingers with the daintiness required. Most delicious of all, because most apparent, were the tales Mrs. Feinstein had to tell of Europe. He could see the lights of the prescribed cities like the bottles in a chemist's window. He could smell the forests of Russia which Mrs. Feinstein had visited with an aunt.

"To think," he said, "that the world is another mandala!"

"Another what, Arthur?" Mrs. Feinstein asked.

But already she was thinking other thoughts.

Like poor old Waldo. It should have been Waldo's afternoon, afterwards at least, under the dripping hydrangeas with Dulcie, while Arthur helped Mrs. Feinstein clear away the things. Instead of Waldo's afternoon, it would become Waldo's tragedy, because he wouldn't know how to act. Only Arthur and Dulcie in the end would know the parts they and others must act out.

Only Arthur knew that Mrs. Feinstein was planning to take Dulcie overseas. On a cold day in early winter Mrs. Allwright and Mrs. Mutton had sent him to Sydney to execute some small commissions.

"Mummy and I are going to slip away," Dulcie informed him, "without telling anybody. Leave-takings are rather painful when they are not absurd."

Arthur began his stumbling. The cold light made the situation look so serious. He and Dulcie were walking together in the park, over the dead grass, along the edge of the wild lake. Dulcie was carrying a little muff, and wearing a collar of the same fur.

"But we decided we should tell you," she added. "Because—" she paused in thought—"in case you might fret."

He was so moved as Dulcie spoke, and by the lights in her dark, shimmery fur, that his jaws were munching for every word.

"Don't mind me, Dulcie!" he said. "After all."

He could not hobble gratefully enough.

"Have you got a stone in your boot, perhaps?" Dulcie asked.

"No," he said. "I don't know."

"Don't you want to look?"

"No," he said, and laughed.

He was laughing at the swamp-hen strutting blue-enamelled through the reeds.

"Shall you send me picture postcards?" he asked.

She would, of course. Written in coloured inks. In all the languages she proposed to learn.

Together they were making a joke of it.

"And Russian?" he asked.

"Too untidy for postcards!" Dulcie laughed.

So they were happy together, rounding the empty shelter with its broken glass, and back the other side of the lake. Each moment was the happiest for their passing through it. They were the long-legged lovers, confidently offering their faces to receive each other's gentleness as they moved in perfect time, in absolute agreement, against the flesh-coloured trunks of the paperbarks. Even when they were silentest, and he listened to Dulcie's skirt dragging its hem through the wintry grass, and he could smell the smell of cold mud, he reckoned his face wouldn't have collapsed yet into its normal shapelessness.

"Say a blind person married a blind person, do you think it would matter to them not to have seen each other?" Arthur asked.

"I've never thought about it," Dulcie said.

She was walking with her head raised, looking so far into the distance, she had already left him.

She kept her promise and wrote him, if not several postcards— you could not expect too much of people when you were not there to remind them of you—at least the card of the Italian lake, the name of which he was unable to read, nor did it matter, nor the foreign languages she had promised, and in which she did, in fact, write:

14 April 1914

Es ist hier sehr nett u. freundlich bei unserer kleinen Pension where we are staying the two of us after being suffocated amiably by relatives. It is so beautiful eating trout beside the water. *Je ne peux croire qu'il y aura guerre*—as the know-alls promise—*il y a trop de soleil. Mio caro Arturo,* we visited a villa, or small castle, out on the lake, and the walls of one of the rooms were studded with rock-crystal! I thought of Arthur—*e tutte nostre cosi chiare conversazioni. Affetti!*—D.

The foreign languages failed to obscure Dulcie Feinstein focussed as she was in the crystal of his mind. Long after he had lost the card, he had only to revolve the marble in his pocket for Dulcie's lake with the crystal-studded castle to reappear.

When war broke out, which was important enough for those who became physically involved, it was more important that the Feinsteins should return, to the life which in fact they had never really left, in the house on the edge of the park. They came. And they appeared older. It continually amazed Arthur Brown that other people were growing older. Mrs. Feinstein was older, and sadder, perhaps for this very fact of age. Dulcie was older, different, unexpected—for one thing she was unable to remember what she had written on the postcard.

"Shall we walk in the park," he suggested, "like we did before you went away?"

"Not today," she said, frowning slightly.

"Why?" he asked, though there was not much point, and his hopes had never been high.

"I have a headache."

It must have been the airless room. The windows of the Feinsteins' town house were more often than not sealed.

"I'll open the window," said Arthur.

But she did not seem to think it might help.

"It is not that. I am not in the mood. It is not a day for walking," she added. "And besides, there are the railings. We should have to go so far along to get to a gate."

The railings had existed before.

Soon after the remark, he went away, deciding not to admit to Waldo what could only be counted as defeat. In fact, he wouldn't mention the return of Dulcie and Mrs. Feinstein. For some reason, for the moment, he was less able to communicate with them, though if he hadn't lost the art, he would not have known exactly what he wanted to say.

He happened to pass by the music store, where old Feinstein, who was following the war in the paper, received him more jovially than might have been expected. Normally it pleased Arthur to look through sheets of music, at the notes of music he would never be able to read.

Today he asked, "What are these?"

"Those are some songs which nobody will buy. Those songs were born to fly-specks and the remainder counter," Mr. Feinstein answered, gloomily turning back to the news.

The *Pierrot d'amour* on the cover certainly conveyed less expectancy, less of the slightly scented breathlessness of the afternoon when Dulcie had explained about the *Pierrot* on Mrs. Musto's bottle. So Arthur sat, and as the clanking tram flung the passengers together, composed his own version of a song, ignoring all those faces with which, in normal circumstances, he would have begun an intimate and, more likely than not, illuminating conversation.

When Waldo realized Feinsteins were back after meeting Dulcie at the gate one evening, and he and Arthur were invited up to

Mount Pleasant on an afternoon which turned out not a bit as Arthur had hoped and expected—Waldo's rather than Arthur's, and instead of something squishy to eat, a few of Arnotts' hard old biscuits—it was this rather fly-specked version of a Pierrot song, composed to the clanking of a crowded tram, which Arthur rendered in Mrs. Feinstein's "salon." It was really a song for Dulcie, which she alone would understand; she would see behind the words, and the deliberately ridiculous convulsions of his face.

Even though she said, "Oh, what a lovely song!" like some lady arriving for luncheon at Mrs. Musto's, he thought Dulcie understood.

So he was able to flop down afterwards, and not exactly sleep, retire behind his eyelids, leaving the field to Waldo. This didn't mean he didn't experience Waldo's torture of Dulcie when he provoked her to music, and all of that episode in the garden, first as Waldo, then as Dulcie, very intensely. He could smell the smell of rotting as they stirred up the dead hydrangea leaves. He could even smell the almond-essence smell of the vegetable-bugs on which they trod. Suffocating. Exhausting in the end. All the answers he could have foretold while the others were still looking for them.

Somewhere at some point Mrs. Feinstein had remarked to Waldo, "I am so sorry you will never have had the good chance of meeting Leonard Saporta."

"Is he a relative?" silly old Waldo asked.

Was he a relative! Leonard Saporta was a born relative.

Arthur had met this Mr. Saporta, coming or going, never by arrangement, at Feinsteins' other house. In Arthur's life there were the convinced, the unalterable ones, such as Mr. Allwright and Leonard Saporta, as opposed to those other fluctuating figures, of Dulcie, Waldo, his parents, even Mrs. Poulter, all of whom flickered as frightfully as himself. Whereas Mr. Allwright and Leonard Saporta must have kept the solid shape they were moulded in originally. Arthur was grateful for knowing they would never divide, like the others, in front of his eyes, into the two faces, one of which he might not have recognized if it hadn't been his own.

It was during the First War that Arthur visited Mr. Saporta in his shop. It must have been towards the end, for the merchant himself was there, discharged. Leonard Saporta had enlisted, gone overseas, and returned with several shrapnel wounds which he did not care to talk about. (It was while he had been on leave in France that Leonard had sent Dulcie the little Star of David, which she afterwards wore on a chain round her neck, and which would have become a source of jovial mirth to Mr. Feinstein, if his wife had not implored him, with all the resources of her face and muted cello notes in her voice, to desist, for Dulcie's, for everybody's sake.)

Anyway, Mr. Saporta had returned, and the day Arthur went to his shop, approached with the appearance of a merchant receiving a genuine customer—certainly business was pretty slack—and clapping his hands together, asked, "Well, Arthur, may I show you a few first-quality Oriental rugs?"

Altogether Arthur felt too large, too shy, drifting sideways amongst the piles of rugs, which the merchant was preparing to turn over as though they were the pages of a book.

"No, thank you," Arthur said, and giggled, "Mr. Saporta. I'm really only wasting your time."

However often he had been invited to drop the "Mister" in favour of "Leonard," Arthur had not been able to—something to do with the respect in which he held the merchant's solid foundations.

Not that Mr. Saporta was particularly rich in goods, it seemed, and his appearance was undoubtedly what Mother and Waldo would have described as "loud": the suit too flash, the shoulders too broad, the teeth too gold, the moustache too clearly parted under the great curve of his nose. Yet you could not have caught the merchant's eye without suspecting him of gentleness and honesty. Perhaps, also, he was slightly, if only very slightly, stupid. For Arthur sensed on his way through life that only the very clever and the very stupid can dare to be dishonest.

On this occasion the merchant went on turning over his rugs for the pleasure of showing them off, only occasionally straightening his back on account of the twinges caused by the shrapnel, when Arthur started pointing with his toe.

"That! That! That is it!"

"That," Mr. Saporta agreed, "is a very fine Turkish rug. From Panderma."

Arthur scarcely heard, and certainly he did not need the name.

"It has the mandala in the centre! But don't you see, Mr. Saporta?"

"Don't know about the mandala," the merchant said.

He obviously did not want or need it.

"Have you seen Dulcie?" he asked.

"Yes," said Arthur, looking up.

He was suddenly certain this was a secret he would not mind the merchant's sharing.

Mr. Saporta's glistening eyebrows looked very grave, as though he could not make up his mind how much depended on him personally, and how much could be expected to happen in spite of himself. Fearing his friend, at this, if only at this point, might be in need of assistance, Arthur began to chatter on what probably sounded too high, too irrelevant a note.

"One morning—one Saturday—I'll come down from Sarsaparilla, Mr. Saporta—to give us more time—and you shall show me all your rugs."

But Mr. Saporta hesitated.

"Not Saturdays," he said. "Saturdays I am otherwise engaged. I go to the synagogue," he reminded. "And my family expects me afterwards."

He sounded sombre, but a sombreness of such rich dark colours and vibrating harmonies, Arthur was at once reassured.

Seeing his friend thus enclosed he went away soon afterwards, and in the street realized for the first time that the Star of David was another mandala, and that Dulcie's marriage to Mr. Saporta would be arranged.

In his joy and distress he sang one of those shapeless songs: joy that the person he loved most—after Waldo—would be made round, as he saw it, distress that he could not relieve Waldo of his ignorance. Waldo could only relieve himself.

All the way down Terminus Road Arthur's twitching throat kept up a shapeless, practically a wordless singing.

And then the Peace came. He had always loved the excuse for

singing in the streets. He bought a rattle. He bought a blower which unravelled as far as a pink feather on its end. He went to Sydney, to the streets for which celebrations are created, and for the occasion he composed a song:

> After the fireworks the fireworks
> after the gas the gasworks
> I shan't mind my chop chop chop
> after a day in the shop shop shop
>
> no no no no no no no no NO!
>
> Love is the biggest firework of all
> don't be afraid when its bursts
> don't be afraid if it hurts
> it's the best the fieriest way
> to go off BANG
>
> oh oh oh oh oh oh oh oh OH!

"Fuckun mophret!" A man spat.

And a girl shrieked, "Don't let him touch me! That orange nut!" before disappearing as fast as her new button-boots and the crowd would allow.

But many of them kissed Arthur Brown. They seemed to want a mascot of some sort. They got him drunk. Who blew out his blower with the pink feather on the end, to stroke suddenly familiar features. In particular, he enjoyed the retreat of the sterner noses. Always when his blower had recoiled, again, there was someone to kiss him on his large face, slobbery with the joy of fulfilment, of recognition. Everybody was being and doing.

When things had settled down again he heard that Mrs. Feinstein was dead. Although she had been his friend he didn't exactly grieve for her, realizing that she had in fact died on her last trip to Europe. But again he went to the city, this time in search of Dulcie, in the house at Centennial Park. Some woman relative told him where she was, and that Mr. Feinstein was too disconsolate to receive even those he knew intimately. Arthur found Dulcie sitting on an upright chair, on the edge of a room, wearing the black dress.

She smiled at him, and he saw that grief had destroyed her face, all except the bones, which were a polished yellow. Even so, she shone with a grave, ivory beauty of her own.

"Sit down," she said, in someone else's voice. "Was the train full?" she asked, as though he had arrived for some other purpose.

"Yes," he said. "Yes, Dulcie."

"They always are at this time of day."

That seemed to upset her. She would obviously have liked to cry, only she had dried up inside, there was nothing there but a rack of coughing.

He sat comforting her by stroking the back of her hand with one of his forefingers.

"Hasn't Mr. Saporta been?" he asked.

"Oh, I think so. Yes. Of course."

If he had not known her to be genuine, her manner could have appeared false. Perhaps, it now occurred to him, Dulcie herself had not yet realized. Otherwise, she must surely have found the means for grief out of her love for Mr. Saporta.

It was then he conceived the idea of giving Dulcie Feinstein one of his solid mandalas. Supposing he had been wrong, that she was not intended to marry the carpet merchant, that she would never sit down with her children at that overcrowded, overladen family table after the service at the synagogue—then without his help she would have no means of relieving her continued drought, of filling her dreadful emptiness.

They sat together for a little. They talked about the price of flowers, and in greater danger, the migration of birds. The room had been abandoned by all those ever connected with it.

Dulcie leaned forward at last, and wiped his mouth with her handkerchief. Perhaps her kindness was to soften an expression which suggested she wanted him to leave.

When he had got up, she said, "I shall let you know when you are to come. Probably at Sarsaparilla. Daddy, I expect, will sell *Mount Pleasant*. There is not what you would call point in it now."

She kissed him when he left soon after.

Then—he did not want to think it—she forgot.

Even after it was known they were at Sarsaparilla to collect their belongings and sell the house, he hardly dared wonder at the reason for Dulcie's neglect. Waldo even had found out Feinsteins were there, though naturally Waldo made no mention of a death. Waldo had begun looking at himself in the glass. So Arthur decided not to delay. He went up to *Mount Pleasant* uninvited.

Dulcie said, "Oh, Arthur, I am so glad! We made an arrangement, didn't we? I forget exactly what. But now you've come. So perhaps I'm not so much to blame."

If Dulcie had been different, again he might have suspected her of putting it on. She was still dressed in black, though. She was standing amongst the packing-cases, in the smell of dust from a dismantled room.

"Why, Dulcie," he said, in his excitement over a genuine discovery, "I didn't know we have the same colour of eyes!"

"Yes," she said—like that.

Whereas on the previous occasion Dulcie Feinstein's face had been whittled down to the yellow bone, this afternoon she was restored to flesh, out of which the eyes were shining, not, he saw, with the dry fever of wordless grief, not inward-looking, but steady with a lovely confidence.

"Come and let us sit down," she said, pushing aside a packing-case.

So that Arthur, too, grew confident.

When they were seated on the sofa, knee to knee, Dulcie could not suppress a little, passing, unexpectedly humourous whimper.

"My poor darling mother," she said, "it has turned out exactly as she always expected it to!"

With her hand she might have been smoothing Mrs. Feinstein's perpetual earth.

"I mean, she predicted I would decide to marry Leonard Saporta," Dulcie said, looking straight at Arthur.

There was now no need, he saw, to offer the mandala, but he would, because he still wanted to, because they were all four, he and Dulcie, Mrs. Feinstein and Leonard Saporta, so solidly united.

"I want you, and Leonard has agreed," said Dulcie, "I want you to come to our wedding, Arthur."

"Oh, no!"

He had to sit back. She could not have been more astonished.

"Oh, no!" he repeated. "Waldo would be far too—far too *shocked.*"

She drew her mouth in rather uglily, against her teeth, down against her gums. She could have been sucking a lemon the moment before.

Then she said, averting her face, "Waldo is only your brother, you know. At least he's no more than that to me. Arthur's brother."

"Oh no," said Arthur, "he's more than that."

She hung her head.

"It's necessary to escape from Waldo."

"Necessary for you. Not for me."

It was too obvious. But Dulcie had made her own escape. For the moment at least she did not see very clearly.

"I know you'll be kind to him, Dulcie."

"Oh," she said, "by nature I'm not *at all* kind!"

Shaking herself with a little frilly movement he would have loved less if it had meant more.

"Yes," she said, biting her lip, still not looking, "I know I shall be kind because you want it."

Then Arthur took the mandala out of his pocket. It was the blue taw which Norm Croucher had traded for liquorice straps. The mists rolled up, to be contained by the perfect, glass sphere.

"Dulcie," he said, "I brought you this."

Scarcely moving his hand he worked it into motion on the open palm.

"It's one of the solid mandalas, the blue mandala," he explained.

"Oh," she cried, lowering her head.

He had always known the blue mandala would be the one for Dulcie. Her beauty would not evaporate again.

Though first she had to denounce herself, saying, "I have always been—particularly lately—hideously weak. You," she said, gasping for breath above the glass marble, "were the one, Arthur, who gave me strength—well, to face the truth—well, about ourselves—in particular my *own* wobbly self."

Then she was laughing for the riddle solved. She was holding up her full throat, the laughter rippling out of it.

Exactly when Waldo walked in, perhaps neither of them saw. Dulcie, on noticing, tried to strangle her laughter, but she couldn't.

They both sat looking at Waldo, who had put on his blue serge, and was wearing one of the butterfly collars. He must have been working on his glasses with the shammy for them to shine with just that expression of inquiry. His smile was tight. It had almost reached the point where the twitch began.

So Arthur decided to say the one or two necessary things, and go. He, who could not help himself, could not have helped his brother now. *Arthur is the backward one.* That was the way the relationship had been arranged. Of the twins. The twin brothers. Waldo had wanted it. *Waldo is the one who takes the lead.* Joining them together at the hand. And because Waldo needed it that way, only the knife could sever it.

Like Mother's breast.

The year the Poulters came to live down Terminus Road, Mother had gone into hospital in Barranugli for the operation Waldo would not talk about.

"What operation?" he hedged, and decided almost at once: "It's something that isn't mentioned, do you hear?"

So Arthur had to tell Mrs. Poulter.

"Our mother has lost one of her breasts."

"That need not be so serious," said Mrs. Poulter, herself a serious and kindly woman.

"But a breast!" he said, wrinkling up.

He could not help looking at their neighbour, so full and firm.

"I expect women are pretty attached to their breasts," he said.

Mrs. Poulter looked the other way. She began to tell about her sick turkey.

Because of its firm whiteness, its generosity at least in theory, he would have liked to discuss the breast with their mother, but as though she knew what to expect she always quickly silenced him.

"Mrs. Poulter says," Arthur said.

"I can't bear to hear the Name," said Mother.

"Why?"

"Repetition becomes monotonous."

He was considering that.

"Besides," she said, "a grown man—nearly twenty-eight—surely I don't have to tell you, Arthur, where your thoughts should and shouldn't lie?"

"I can't help it," he said, "if she's started to live here."

"Oh, no, it can't be *helped*," Mother agreed. "But one does wonder—why *here*?"

Soon after their arrival he had gone across the road to speak to the woman in the iron hut, to ask her, among many other things, why they were living down Terminus Road. If her answers varied, he accepted the variety; there were several answers to most questions. He took it for granted he would be allowed to squat outside her hut yarning, and eventually, when it was built, he used to barge into her kitchen, though only when her husband wasn't there. The reason for that was too obvious. Mr. Poulter didn't like him.

"Why did you marry Mr. Poulter?" Arthur asked over the tea she had poured out in thick white cups.

Mrs. Poulter laughed, and thought.

"Well," she said, "there was his hands. Bill had lovely hands. A man's hands, mind you," she said.

Arthur looked at his own.

"Of course," she said, "he's mucked them up by now. Couldn't help it. A working man. Times when he worked on the roads, too. But I must have fell for Bill's hands."

"Can he play the piano?" Arthur asked.

"Bill would have a fit!" Mrs. Poulter was certain.

At that moment Arthur wanted so badly to play the piano, he knew he could have done it, only Mrs. Poulter did not own one.

"Here," she said, "you'll think I'm a funny sort of woman."

Suddenly anxious, she came and sat down opposite, at the kitchen table.

"Bill's hands! I married Bill because he was the only thing I could ever think of. And because he needed me," she said.

She leaned so close, almost crouching over the table, he could see the moisture on her sunburnt skin, he could see down the crack between her breasts.

"I expect he must have needed somebody," Arthur said, serious and interested. "The darning and all that."

"Yes," she said.

Her rather blunt white teeth were showing in her smile.

"Bill couldn't put on a mutton-flap to boil."

She was that firm and pretty, with her smooth arms, and wedding ring.

"I wonder why I'm telling you all this?"

"Because that's the way people have a yarn."

"Yes," she said, laughing. "But a man!"

"A man isn't all that different," he said, sipping the disinfectant-coloured tea, which had turned pretty mawky by now.

"Not different in himself, I suppose," she said *"Some* men. Oh, I dunno!"

Her doubt was not deep enough to last.

"Ah dear," she said, "it might have been lonely here." She went and stood against the window. "With only your mum opposite."

"Mother's good," Arthur said.

"Ah yes," Mrs. Poulter agreed. "I didn't say Mrs. Brown wasn't good."

Mrs. Poulter loved her potplants. She would keep on poking at them, ruffling them up, tweaking them as she talked. From time to time she would stand back to get a better look.

"Do you like boiled fruitcake?" she asked.

"Too right I do!" said Arthur.

"One day I'll boil a fruitcake. Ah, dear," she cried, remembering, "there's a lady at Mungindribble has a lovely recipe for boiled fruitcake. If I only knew."

"You could write for it, couldn't you? Eh, Mrs. Poulter?"

"Yes," she said, as though she wouldn't.

She was tweaking her cerise geranium.

"It's that long," she said, "since I got a letter. I knew a girl—one of the housemaids at the station—used to write letters to herself. They took her away in the end."

"What, to Peaches-and-Plums?"

"What's that?"

"That," he said, and laughed, pleased because he was able to tell, "why that's the nut-house down at Barranugli. They planted it out so lovely with flowering things that people call it Peaches-and-Plums. See? People come from all round when it's the right season."

She was delighted.

"Well I never!"

It was the embroidery of life on which they were engaged. They followed no particular pattern and could seldom resist adding another stitch.

That Arthur Brown. Harmless enough. Nobody could ever accuse you.

From her house, like a houseboat moored in the backwaters of grass, Mrs. Poulter would often beckon. To tell. To show.

Once she showed him a bloodstained finger she had found in a matchbox, in the grass beside the road. Arthur was so upset he had to sit down on Mrs. Poulter's step.

"In the grass?" he panted.

"Go on!" she cried. "Don't be silly! It's a trick I learned!"

Which, in fact, it was: Mrs. Poulter's own finger, got up with red ink, stuck through the end of the matchbox, lying on a bed of cottonwool.

"Golly," she said, "you're a kid," she said, "Arthur, at times!"

She had to touch him to comfort him.

And once at dusk, when her husband had gone up the road, taking the cow for a late service, Arthur Brown had jumped out at Mrs. Poulter on her way back from the dunny to the house.

"*Urrrhhhh!*" she screamed.

"Ha! Who got a fright?"

She had, too. She had broken out in the trembles.

"Thought I was going to criminally assault!"

Even after they had pushed inside her house Arthur couldn't get over his joke.

"That's the sort of thing I don't go for. Not a bit of it, Arthur. Never ever do it again," Mrs. Poulter said, switching on the light.

Then he was afraid his friend might have stopped liking him.

"Are you honest?" she had to ask.

He was so afraid, he hoped the light would show her he was.

"Don't you know me, Mrs. Poulter? Eh?"

"I thought I did," she said.

"When shall we go for a walk, eh? For another walk?"

"That depends," she said, "on a lot of things."

Her eyelids would not let him make sure.

"Now," she said, taking up a book, "I'm going to settle down. By myself."

Mrs. Poulter liked to read the paper for the deaths and ads. She did not care for books, though she owned two. She owned the Bible and Pears' Cyclopaedia. Sometimes she would sit with one or the other, which meant, he discovered, that she had begun to get sick of him.

"I'm going to settle down, and have a read of the Cyclopaedia," she was telling him now.

Of course it was inconceivable that Mrs. Poulter shouldn't want him to walk with her. He knew this as he went away. Or did he, though? Arthur was sweating, he was crying, as he crossed back over Terminus Road. Too many pictures of contentment flickered in front of his mind's eye. She had a little black pig which ran rootling round the back yard. She could lift the combs out of the hives without ever bothering to put on a veil. She stored pears on high shelves, the burn fading out of her skin towards the armpits.

Once Arthur dreamed the dream in which a tree was growing out of his thighs. It was the face of Dulcie Feinstein lost amongst the leaves of the higher branches. But Mrs. Poulter came and sat on the ground beside him, and he put out his hand to touch what he thought would be her smooth skin, and encountered rough, almost prickly, bark. He would have liked to wake Waldo to tell him. In the morning of course he could barely remember.

And in the morning, it was a Sunday, Mrs. Poulter said, "What about that walk, Arthur, you and me was going to take? Oh," she said, "not *now*! Morning's for church, isn't it?"

So he had to wait.

For the rather sultry, still stately afternoon, while people were either asleep, or holding their full stomachs, or totting up the past with a relative. He saw Mrs. Poulter looking up and down, still dressed in her churchgoing clothes.

"Where shall we go?" she asked.

"I dunno," he said, and sighed.

So they went.

They crossed paddocks, they stalked like turkeys through belts of thinned-out scrub, they visited a plopping creek where neither had ever been before. Arthur picked up the dry cow-pats and sent them spinning through the Sunday air. If neither spoke they were not so far absent, it seemed, from each other's thoughts.

"Funny none of you Browns never ever went to church," she said.

"I suppose they went in the beginning. Till they found out."

"Found out what?"

"That they could do without it."

"Ah, but it's lovely!" Mrs. Poulter said.

"They began to feel it wasn't true."

"What isn't true?"

He saw her raise her head, her neck stiffen.

"Oh, all that!" said Arthur Brown, spinning a cow-turd. "About virgins. About Him," he said.

"Don't tell me," said Mrs. Poulter, as prim as Waldo, "that *you* don't believe in Our Lord Jesus Christ?"

"Don't know all that much about Him."

For the moment he cared less for her.

"How do *you* know, anyway?"

"It's what everyone has always known," she said. Then, looking at the toes of her shoes as they advanced, she said very softly, "I couldn't exist without Our Lord."

"Could He exist without *you?*" It seemed reasonable enough to inquire.

But she might not have heard.

"Mother says Christians are all the time gloating over the blood."

"Don't you believe they crucified Our Lord?" she said looking at him angrily.

He had begun to feel exhausted.

"I reckon they'd crucify a man," he said. "Yes," he agreed, trundling slower. "From what you read. And what we know. Christians," he said, "are cruel."

"*They* were not Christians," Mrs. Poulter said. "Men are cruel."

There was a wind starting. A raw sun was sawing at them. They had gone too far.

"Here!" he called. "How long is this walk gunna last?"

He reached out for her hand, and she allowed him to take it.

"You're surely not tired?" she said, but he could tell she was not giving it thought. "A big man like you!"

There wasn't any malice in it. She continued speaking very gently.

"Fancy," she said, almost for herself, "if you was my kid, Arthur. I wonder whether you'd like it."

"Yes," he answered.

He would have liked it for the pleasure it would have given her, and because nobody could have objected any more to his being with her.

"When are we going for another walk, Mrs. Poulter?" he asked, and lagged to put a weight on her hand.

"We haven't finished this one yet."

But suddenly they had. They had taken a short cut neither of them had suspected, and there they were, plunging down on Terminus Road.

"Well now," she said, "here we are home without any of the trouble!"

"Yes," he said, gloomily.

That night he dreamed he was licking the wounds, like a dog. He wondered whether he had been doing right, to lick up nonexistent blood. Fortunately Waldo, who was sleeping, need never know. He had reached out and touched him to make sure. He reached out to feel for the mandala, his own special, on top of the po cupboard, but heard it roll, scamper out of reach. It would have involved too much to retrieve it, so he lay there miserably conscious of the distance between his desire and perfect satisfaction.

Even the walks with Mrs. Poulter were not all that satisfactory, because it was only natural to talk, and you kept on coming up against a wall, if not religion, something else.

"Did you never ever have any children, Mrs. Poulter?" he asked.

"No," she answered.

From where he was walking, as mostly, a little behind, he thought it sounded sulkily.

"Do you mind?"

"Oh," she said, "life isn't just children. I've got my husband."

"Does he like you?"

"What a funny thing to ask!"

"Well," he said, "you always wonder what a person likes."

This time it was a holiday, and she was not wearing her church dress, something clean though, and cottony. He liked to watch it moving close to her full, but still quite firm body. It surprised him to realize Mrs. Poulter was younger than himself, nor did he altogether want it. He preferred it when he could forget about ages, when Mrs. Poulter could grow into the larger-sized wise woman she really was, telling of cures for illnesses.

"This isn't half a slope," Mrs. Poulter complained, grunting.

"It's that all right!" he agreed, and giggled.

But suddenly they had climbed out, panting and dazzled.

"Oh, look!" she called, pointing.

"That's a wheel-tree," said Arthur.

He could tell because Mrs. Musto had shown him one. Still panting, he stood smiling, proud of the treeful of fiery wheels.

And under the tree was standing the Chinese woman, whom he often remembered afterwards. They stood looking at one another. Then the Chinese woman, so little connected with them or their other surroundings, turned, it seemed resentfully, and went behind some poultry sheds. There was no great reason why he should remember her, except as part of the dazzle of the afternoon. For that reason he did.

Soon afterwards they plunged on down into the blackberries, and were grabbing the enamelled berries by the handful to drop into Mrs. Poulter's little can, and scoffing them besides, till their faces were inked over.

"What a sight you are, Arthur!" Mrs. Poulter sounded quite pleased.

"Speak for yourself!" He pointed, and laughed.

It suited her, and the shadow from her hat. Her face might have been mysteriously tattooed.

Afterwards they sat down on the grass, in a bay formed by the blackberry bushes. Their few bits of luggage were spread around. It was peculiarly *their* ground once they had staked their claim. It was so well protected Mrs. Poulter, after glancing round once or twice, announced rather nicely, "I tell you what, Arthur, I'm going to take down my hair, and nobody will see or think it strange."

It was sensible enough, he thought, because you couldn't hardly count himself. Besides, he had watched Mrs. Poulter washing her hair in the kero tin, in the days when she was living in the iron hut.

"There!" she said, when she was sitting in her long hair.

He loved watching her as she sat inside her shiny tent. He half closed his eyes, out of pleasure, and against the sun, and from then on all that was spoken and acted was as inescapable as conviction and dreams.

Shaking the veil of hair from where it hung across her face, Mrs. Poulter said, "Sometimes I used to think I'd go into service, proper like. In some big house in the city. Where the lady did a lot of entertaining. All the ladies in fashionable gowns covered with jewellery. And I'd be going round, handing the eatables, or changing the glasses, with nobody taking any notice or wondering what I was thinking. Then, while I was offering the vegetables at table, there would be one man of some importance, a bank manager, say, or a doctor, who would look up into my face and realize I was different. I'd be waiting for him when he came to fetch his coat, and we'd walk off together to catch the tram."

Arthur listened, who was grinning with the glare and the mass of jewellery.

Mrs. Poulter said, "It's funny I went on having that sort of ideas long after I'd married Bill." She paused, then she did not ask, but said, "It isn't wrong to think about what will never happen. I love Bill," Mrs. Poulter said.

Arthur loved Mrs. Poulter. He loved her jewellery.

He said, "Will you let me touch your hair, Mrs. Poulter, just to feel?"

She looked round, not at him, but over her shoulder.

"It's a funny sort of thing to do," she said, "but you can if you like."

So he crawled just so close that he could put out his hand and stroke the tips of her shiny hair. Warmed by the sun, it seemed to be leading a life of its own, like some kind of sleepy animal.

Till in his turn Arthur suddenly realized what was intended of him.

"I'm going to dance for you, Mrs. Poulter," he said. "I'm going to dance a mandala."

He knew she was preparing to laugh, but wouldn't, because she had grown fond of him.

"The mandala?" she said, soberly enough. "I never heard of a dance called that. Not any of the modern ones."

He did not attempt to explain, because he felt he would make her see.

So Arthur Brown danced, beginning at the first corner, from which he would proceed by stages to the fourth, and beyond. He who was so large, so shambly, found movement coming to him on the hillside in the bay of blackberries. The bands of his shirtsleeves were hanging open at the wrists. The bluish shadows in the less exposed parts of his skin, of his wrists, and the valley between his breasts, were soon pearled over.

In the first corner, as a prelude to all that he had to reveal, he danced the dance of himself. Half clumsy, half electric. He danced the gods dying on a field of crimson velvet, against the discords of human voices. Even in the absence of gods, his life, or dance, was always prayerful. Even though he hadn't been taught, like the grocer, to go down on his knees and stick his hands together. Instead, offering his prayer to what he knew from light or silences. He danced the sleep of people in a wooden house, groaning under the pressure of sleep, their secrets locked prudently up, safe, until their spoken thoughts, or farts, gave them away. He danced the moon, anaesthetized by bottled cestrum. He danced the disc of the orange sun above icebergs, which was in a sense his beginning, and should perhaps be his end.

While Mrs. Poulter sat looking, playing with the tips of her dark hair. Sighing sometimes. Then looking down.

In the second corner he declared his love for Dulcie Feinstein, and for her husband, by whom, through their love for Dulcie, he was, equally, possessed, so they were all three united, and their children still to be conceived. Into their corner of his mandala he wove their Star, on which their three-cornered relationship was partly based. Flurries of hydrangea-headed music provided a ceremony of white notes falling exactly into place, and not far behind, the twisted ropes of dark music Waldo had forced on Dulcie the afternoon of strangling. There she was, the bones of her, seated on the upright chair, in black. And restored to flesh by her lover's flesh. The inextinguishable, always more revealing eyes.

Dulcie's secrets, he could see, had been laid bare in the face of Mrs. Poulter, who might otherwise have become the statue of a woman, under her hair, beside the blackberry bushes. Though she was swaying slightly as he began to weave her figure into the appropriate corner. In Mrs. Poulter's corner he danced the rite of ripening pears, and little rootling suckling pigs. Skeins of golden honey were swinging and glittering from his drunken mouth. Until he reached the stillest moment. He was the child she had never carried in the dark of her body, under her heart, from the beat of which he was already learning what he could expect. The walls of his circular fortress shuddered.

Mrs. Poulter was at that point so obviously moved, she would have liked to throw the vision off, or stop him altogether, but he would not let her.

He had begun to stamp, but brittlely, rigid, in his withering. In the fourth corner, which was his brother's, the reeds sawed at one another. There was a shuffling of dry mud, a clattering of dead flags, or papers. Of words and ideas skewered to paper. The old, bent, overused, aluminum skewers. Thus pinned and persecuted, what should have risen in pure flight, dropped to a dry twitter, a clipped twitching. He couldn't dance his brother out of him, not fully. They were too close for it to work, closest and farthest when, with both his arms, he held them together, his fingers running with candle-wax. He could not save. At most a little comfort gushed out guiltily, from out of their double image, their never quite united figure. In that corner of the dance his anguished feet had trampled the grass into a desert.

When Mrs. Poulter leaned forward. She was holding her hair by handfuls in knots of fists, he could see—waiting.

Till in the centre of their mandala he danced the passion of all their lives, the blood running out of the backs of his hands, water out of the hole in his ribs. His mouth was a silent hole, because no sound was needed to explain.

And then, when he had been spewed up, spat out, with the breeze stripping him down to the saturated skin, and the fit had almost withdrawn from him, he added the little quivering footnote on forgiveness. His arms were laid along his sides. His head hung. Facing her.

He fell down, and lay, the rise and fall of his ribs a relief, to say nothing of her eyes, which he knew could only have been looking at him with understanding for his dance.

Arthur must have dozed, for when he got up, Mrs. Poulter was putting the finishing touches to her hair. Her head was looking so neat, though her nostrils were still slightly flared, from some experience recently suffered.

Then Arthur knew that she was worthy of the mandala. Mrs. Poulter and Dulcie Feinstein he loved the most—after Waldo of course.

So he put his hand in his pocket, and knelt down beside her, and said, "I'm going to let you have the mandala, Mrs. Poulter."

It was the gold one, in which the sparks glinted, and from which the rays shot upward whenever the perfect sphere was struck by its counterpart.

"Ah, that's good! Isn't it, Arthur?" Mrs. Poulter said, inclining over her open hand. "I *would* like to have a loan of that!"

"I want you to keep it. Wouldn't you like it?"

She looked up, and said, "Yes."

After that they began to walk home.

The perfection of the day saddened him in retrospect. He knew it could never recur. At meals the members of his family were already avoiding, composing. It was only a matter of time. If he mentioned his friend Mrs. Poulter, Mother would start murmuring against "the Name." Waldo did more than murmur. Waldo exploded finally.

"If only you saw the *obscenity* in such a situation! I ask you! And my brother!" The forked veins in Waldo's forehead were bursting blue.

It was a good thing perhaps that Arthur was mixing the bread. That on its own might have helped establish his honesty if Mrs. Poulter herself had not contributed.

"Mrs. Poulter has decided," he was able to tell Waldo as he folded and refolded the dough.

One evening shortly before, he had gone across the road, in

hopes of exchanging a word or two, or not even that—of being together. The dishes were stacked beside the sink, for her husband had eaten his tea and gone inside. Bill Poulter spent much of his spare time lying on the bed, either nursing an ulcer, or listening to the walls, waiting for a doubt to be confirmed. While his wife finished whatever had to be done.

Now Mrs. Poulter was straining the milk. She was looking stern, Arthur noticed. While holding her head delicately, she was frowning at the cow-hair in the muslin. He realized almost at once that he, and not the cow-hair, was the cause of it all.

"What's up?" he asked.

"Oh," she said. "Nothing," she said, tilting the strainer this way and that. "That is," she said, "we shan't be going on any more walks. Not from now."

She sounded so cool.

"Mr. Poulter doesn't like it," she said. "*They* don't like it. So you'll have to lump it, Arthur."

She was making herself sound brutal—he could hear that—so as he would not be hurt by the brutality of what they called life, only by her. He would realize she was a coarse and brutal woman unworthy of his trust.

"So there we are," she said, looking at him for the first time, slamming the strainerful of hair and muslin back into the empty bucket.

"All right," he said. "All right, Mrs. Poulter"—trying to work out his steps towards the door. "I don't have to tell you I'll be sorry, though."

The night of his outburst Waldo congratulated Arthur on the decision he and Mrs. Poulter had come to. Waldo was obviously pleased by what he called its *"ethical rectitude,"* though immediately gloomy over a situation he had read about but not experienced. Perhaps Waldo was a bit jealous, as well as contemptuous, of Arthur's miserable affair. If he had not admired his brother, Arthur might have felt hurt.

What did hurt Arthur was the attitude of Bill Poulter, who, every time they ran across each other, turned his face away from the obscenity Waldo had brought to light.

All of this lost its importance the morning their father died.

The metal of the bucket as Arthur milked was too obtrusive. The too clear morning clanked. Waldo, he knew, would be prowling round outside the house in his shirtsleeves and armbands, before putting on his coat, before leaving for the Library. Arthur stood up, giving the cow's voluminous velvety belly a push. For the time being she was only a thing. He had already begun to pant for what must have happened. He ran through the grass, slopping the milk.

Waldo by then was running off, away from the house, into the garden. It was much as Arthur had expected.

And finding their father in the dark room. Because touch was his approach, Arthur touched George Brown's head. Before pushing his way through the house. Before bursting out on the classical-tragic veranda.

The words were shouted out of him: "Our father, our father is dead!"

Not that George Brown had done more than withdraw from Arthur a second time. Who would bear it now as before. Perhaps their afflictions, which had caused the withdrawal, helped him to.

Or Waldo's running away.

Soon Waldo was coming back along the path, and Arthur had to control his own unhappiness. He had to take Waldo in his arms. Pity replaced admiration. Not that he would have admitted it, or not more than occasionally.

Arthur would have liked to admire their mother less. He would have liked her to continue loving him, but she had no time, from living in her own thoughts. Excepting the morning George Brown died. She needed him then. To get them breakfast.

"Yes, darling," she sighed.

It was like somebody turning in bed, turning, waking, returning to your arms, asleep.

"You shall get it for me," she breathed. "Wouldn't you like that?"

Of course he liked it. Anything to keep on the move. To keep her eyes on him. He brought the warm milk in her favourite bowls with the pattern of camomile sprigs. He couldn't help it if he couldn't manage the skin of boiled milk. If the skin swung from his lip. It brought an expression to her eyes, out of the depths. She was wincing, her eyebrows pinched together, for their father dead in another room, or the string of burnt milk.

"It always burns," he apologized, "if you so much as turn your back."

But neither Waldo nor Mother had ears for it. They were too busy translating their own thoughts. Waldo used to say Dad was teaching himself Norwegian to translate his thoughts into a language which could not be read.

So Arthur said, "I'd better be making tracks. Allwrights will be wondering."

Then Mother's: "I'd hoped you would stay with us."

Though her voice made him interpret it as "me." He was afraid that, on finding himself left out, Waldo might feel hurt.

"Today," said Mother.

If only today. It was only today that Arthur was the big brother, or lover. When she was stroking back his damp, his ugly old hair, he moved his cheek, his neck, just so much, against his shoulder, to catch her hand in the hinge. And she didn't even cry out. She went on looking into his face for someone else.

And soon her voice lost its satin. The milk was standing cold in the bowl under the wrinkle of skin. She no longer needed Arthur.

Until she needed him again for the sherry. He would bring the occasional bottle in case she had forgot, and ask Mrs. Allwright to chalk it up. It was the only thing he bought on credit.

"You'll rot your liver, Arthur, if you're not careful," Mrs. Allwright said. "I'm surprised at a man, otherwise steady, like you."

"Every person's got their vice," Arthur quoted Mrs. Poulter.

"I like to think I haven't," Mrs. Allwright said. "I like to feel I have dispensed with vice. Anyone can who tries. To live up to the advice we are given in the Gospels."

Of course Arthur knew that Mrs. Allwright knew. It was all over Sarsaparilla. *What'll happen when she's filled the gully with her bottles?* Mrs. Allwright knew all right, but enjoyed this game of not knowing. That was how she got her pleasure, though she wouldn't have admitted it, even with her hand on the Gospels.

For another, for Mother, another pleasure.

"Here's a drop to help out," Arthur used to say, or: "Thought you might be going short."

At such times she would hardly turn her cheek, let alone look over her shoulder.

"Thank you, dear. It was thoughtful of you."

As though she scarcely needed him.

He would hear her crinkle up the foil, however. And sometimes the corks were terribly tight.

"My wrists are losing their strength," she complained.

Needing him.

"You couldn't do without me. Eh? Could you? Eh?"

"Hardly," she had to admit.

His strength of wrist, if not of principle, as Mrs. Allwright insisted, often made him laugh.

"Everyone's got their uses."

"Almost everyone," Mother said.

Then she would sit down to nursing the bottle. She was going to make it last till tonight. Oh, yes. You could if you tried. You stood a chance up to the first third.

But at the first third Mother would have to begin.

"Tell me, Arthur," she would say, "tell me if you feel I've failed you."

The importance of it made the sherry slop over the glass.

"No!" she said, quickly, in her own defence. "Don't tell me! Nobody normal ever enjoyed settling their accounts."

She would grow louder, annoyed too, at spilling the good stuff in her glass.

"All good money," she complained. "But don't tell me. Nobody likes to be told. That they've got a spot. On their nose. On the night of the ball."

Insects in the air made it sound more fretful.

"At least," she said, "once upon a time—when people observed the conventions—all that sort of thing was avoided. Nowadays it isn't considered realistic. Then, it wasn't good form."

"Oh," she said, shaking her hair, "we would dance, though! In the mornings the lawns used to swim up under the windows. We would swim out, just as we were, against the mist. The ladies, of course, were at a disadvantage because their hems were filled with dew. Heavier than anyone would believe. To sink a punt. If one hadn't felt so light with light. The men in kilts came off best. I never cared for the nubbly knees of black Scots. Strong men can be boring in their aggressiveness. And weak."

She could not forgive them their strong legs.

"But if you could have seen us *dancing*! And dancing on the lawns, amongst the topiary, on the mist which was pouring out of the lake. That," she said, sinking her mouth in the glass, "was before I married your father. It was all utterly rotten. But how deliriously memorable"—working her mouth around it—"after the mutton fat has dragged one down. Do you know, Arthur," she said, looking at him, "I believe you inherited your love of dancing from your mother."

"What dancing?"

"Let me see," she said. "I don't know *what* dancing. At least," she said, "nothing *formal*. Movement, though. Dancing," she said, "can compensate. Cure, in some cases. Victims of infantile paralysis recover, they say, the use of their limbs by dancing. Or swimming."

He would have liked to give her his third mandala, but realized in time their mother could not have used it.

Against his better judgment Arthur offered Waldo the mandala during their mother's last illness.

"Mother is real sick," he said.

The lamplight seemed to draw them into its circle.

"Mother is not *sick*!" Waldo shouted.

All this sickness, of their mother's, of the old weatherboard house, with its dry-rotten tremors and wooden tick-tick, seemed to concentrate itself in Arthur's stomach, till from looking at his own hands, soothing, rather than soothed by, the revolving marble, he realized that the knot at the heart of the mandala, at most times so tortuously inwoven, would dissolve, if only temporarily, in light.

And it seemed as though the worst could only happen for the best. It was most important that his brother, shuffling his papers, looking for a sheet mislaid, or just looking—that Waldo, too, should know.

"If it would help I would give it to you, Waldo, to keep," Arthur said.

Offering the knotted mandala.

While half sensing that Waldo would never untie the knot.

Even before Waldo gave one of his looks, which, when inter-preted, meant: By offering me a glass marble you are trying to make me look a fool, I am not, and never shall be a fool, though I am your twin brother, so my reply, Arthur, is not shit, but shit!

As he shouted, "No, Arthur! Go, Arthur!"

But Arthur was rooted. His hand closed on the icy marble. If he had not been his twin brother, would Waldo have hated him?

There was too little time those days to nurse suspicion. Arthur was too busy playing cat's-cradle with their mother, arranging the string round her fingers, since she was no longer able to work them into the required positions.

"Doesn't this entertain you?" he asked.

"Infinitely," Mother said.

It was important—Arthur was convinced she agreed with him—that Waldo shouldn't know their mother was dying. That might have turned out unbearable.

When, suddenly, Mrs. Poulter, the doctor, and the minister, had her removed.

When she was dead Arthur went to Mr. Saporta, who, because he was in business, knew how to have her disposed of. Although the whole of him was racked by the part which had been ampu-tated, Arthur was fascinated to watch the coffin jerking down the ramp towards the curtain. What if it, if they all, stuck?

However, he would be careful to hide from Waldo, who had not, of course, been to the funeral, any of his own fears and suspi-cions.

On one occasion Arthur did slip up.

"Do you approve of the Hindu custom of burning people who have died?"

Waldo's hand was stiffening in his hand. They were walking up Terminus Road, up the last hill before Sarsaparilla.

"It's hygienic, at least," Waldo said.

"So is cremation, isn't it?" said Arthur. "I was thinking of the smoke, only. It must be beautiful to watch the smoke. Don't you think? Uncurling out of the fire?"

"Picturesque is perhaps the word," Waldo said from between his teeth.

He sounded like somebody biting on a pipe, though he, for that matter neither of them, had ever learnt to smoke.

After Mother's death their twin lives would not have diverged all that much if Arthur hadn't developed his sense of responsibility towards the Saportas. Of course Waldo could not be told about that. If Arthur usually got possession of what Waldo did not tell, it was because he had his sense of touch, and from lying beside Waldo in their parents' bed, on nights when his brother needed comforting. Arthur's spongy largeness, not to say, at some times, cloudiness of mind, became an asset then. To envelop the unclouded terrors of night.

So, it was not so much because he didn't have the clothes, as out of sympathy for Waldo, that he didn't go to the Saporta wedding. He had to control his disappointment. For he would have liked to watch Dulcie standing with Mr. Saporta under the canopy-thing, he would have loved to experience the breaking of the glass.

That was already as far back as 1922, the year George Brown had died. Dulcie and Leonard got married, and on the occasions when Mrs. Allwright sent Arthur to the city for something unobtainable in Barranugli, he would visit the Saportas in their house on the edge of the park. It was really Mr. Feinstein's house, where they had gone to live with him after he had his first stroke, after the death of his wife.

The Feinsteins' house looked enormous because of the many flourishes it made—battlements and turrets, spires and balconies, bull's-eyes and dormers, even a gargoyle or two, which the weather was cracking and chipping too soon. Although it looked like a partly fortified cement castle, with veins in it after the leaves of the Virginia creeper had fallen off, it was a fairly normal, human house inside. From the beginning Dulcie didn't allow the inherited furniture to take over. It was she who pushed it around, often into unpremeditated groups. She was also a director of the music house, while Mr. Saporta remained in rugs—as it should have been. The Saportas were pretty substantially established.

Arthur Brown visited them all through the two children and several miscarriages. Sometimes he sat in company with others, elderly Jewish ladies and uncles, who eventually overcame their surprise.

They respected Arthur. Perhaps, for some obscure reason, they even valued his presence amongst them.

When he played with his glass marbles, and explained, "These are my two remaining mandalas," they sat forward, expressing the greatest interest and pleasure, and on one occasion one of the elderly uncles remarked, "There, Magdi, I told you this young man is in some way phenomenal."

Naturally Arthur was pleased. Though not deceived. He waited to be alone with Dulcie, when they might resume that life which they alone were permitted to enjoy. His thighs would quiver in anticipation of blissfully joyful union with his love.

For Dulcie's beauty had increased with marriage, was more outflowing, her eyes more lustrous in communication. She would often put her hand in Arthur's, particularly during pregnancy.

"You know," she would say, and laugh, looking down at her swollen figure, "I am a slave to *all this*."

He noticed she failed to blush, although he realized it embarrassed her to take her belly outside the family circle, and that she would blush more often than not at the comments made by aunts. With him alone she was composed, as though, in their common mind, they could contemplate in peace the child curled and sprouting like a bean.

Once, before the birth of their first, Dulcie said, "Today, I think, when he comes in, Leonard is going to tell you something."

"Why Leonard?" Arthur asked, and began to sweat.

He was afraid something might be spoilt.

"It's the kind of important thing," said Dulcie, "which I think the man ought to tell."

Then she smiled, and Arthur saw it was because her husband had entered the room and was making his way amongst the mounds of inherited furniture.

"I shall leave you together," said Dulcie, heartlessly, Arthur felt. "I shall go up to Father."

She went out from them in full sail.

Arthur was horrified and disturbed.

Thickened by marriage and good sauces, huskier of voice from the many excellent cigars he had smoked, Mr. Saporta was prepared to tell.

He said, "Arthur, when this kid is born—this boy," because that was what they had decided it would be—"we want, both of us, to call him 'Arthur.' "

"Why?" said Arthur.

He was more than ever disturbed.

"Because of all you mean to Dulcie," Mr. Saporta said.

Arthur sat tingling in his thighs. He realized his watery mouth was hanging open, but knowing did not help him close it.

"What about when this boy gets to know whose name he's saddled with?" he asked.

"It will not be his only name," Mr. Saporta said, and his glance hoped he had found an acceptable solution. "We shall also call him 'Aaron.' That will be his Jewish name. But for everyday purposes—'Arthur.' "

Arthur was relieved to think he might be blamed less bitterly.

"Aaron."

After trying it out he was tolerably content.

Though he would not wait for Dulcie to return. Taking Mr. Saporta by the wrist—the latter no longer wore the little gun-metal wristlet-watch, but a large golden disc which showed practically everything—Arthur confirmed that it was time for him to leave. Even though Dulcie was coming down the stairs, though he was close enough to hear the sound of her skirt after she had finished calling to him, he neither looked back nor answered, but hurried throbbing spongily along the street.

Sometimes on arrival at the house he would go up unannounced to old Mr. Feinstein, who had chosen to live in a narrow maid's room, or attic, when his daughter and son-in-law moved in. There he was spending his last days, between newspapers and tobacco, taking refuge from what he referred to as the Jewish Reaction. Although his speech had not been made unintelligible by his first attack—that happened only with the third—his tongue was noticeably clumsier, and his right arm had withered on its trunk.

"I will not deny they thrive on superstition"—Mr. Feinstein referred to his children—"but it could also be the extra food. Because Jews, Arthur, use their religion as an excuse to overeat."

Mr. Feinstein continued going to the store until the third stroke prevented it.

On the last occasion Arthur saw his friend, the old gentleman had been sat up in one of those armchairs which continue to survive their owners.

"I shall leave you to talk to him," Dulcie said practically.

"Why?" asked Arthur.

"Because the baby is singing for his supper."

Old Mr. Feinstein appeared fairly satisfied by now with everything which was done for him. To the centre of his chest they had pinned a card, with the words, the phrases, and the names he was most likely to need, and he would make his rather suffocated sounds, and scratch at the card with the less withered of his hands.

As the old man snuffled and gasped Arthur leaned forward to read what was printed there, but could not decide which of it all might suit what his friend wanted to say.

Arthur, he saw, and: Aaron. Good for business. I want the chamber please. The word Torah puzzled Arthur.

"What's this Torah?" he had to ask, though without the greatest expectations.

Then Mr. Feinstein scratched at his chest, at the print which hardly served to explain.

Changeable weather, Arthur read.

He would have liked to do something for this old man whose strings had tangled and trussed him. But he himself could only shamble round the narrow room, looking for help from the old gentleman's possessions. It was a relief to discover on a cluttered shelf the little Star of David he had seen Dulcie wearing round her neck.

"See this, Mr. Feinstein," he said, "this, this *thing*," he said, "this is just another mandala."

This time Mr. Feinstein did not attempt to scratch a reply, but sat still, looking at Arthur. Waiting, it seemed.

Then Arthur knew he could never explain what was too big, an enormous marble, filling, rolling round intolerably inside his speechless mouth.

He had sat down opposite the old man, so that they were knee to knee. He was holding Mr. Feinstein's cold claws in his own warmer, spongy hands. Otherwise there was nothing he could do.

"The mandala," he was trying to say, and did, but mouthing it so idiotically, he too might have had a stroke.

Then they sat looking at each other from opposite ends of the tunnel, in a light of such momentary intensity, Arthur at least was too confused to know exactly what he saw.

On the next occasion when he visited the Feinstein-Saporta castle he found Dulcie in their big square living-room, seated without her shoes, on a mattress, on the floor. She was wearing a dress in flowing black, the folds of which, together with the lights in her neck and her rounded limbs, made her into something of a statue.

"My father died, Arthur," she explained, as though the old man had tottered out only a moment before, into the park. The only unusual part of it was: they couldn't expect him back.

Then, when she had gathered up her knees inside her arms, and laid her face against her shoulder, she began dreaming, as she rocked.

"Oh yes, I've mourned for him, and shall continue to mourn. But my father was always embarrassed by what he used to call 'Jewesses indulging themselves by tearing their clothes and emotions to tatters.' We were only ever allowed to love him on his own terms. I think on the whole that made him unhappy, but any other behaviour would have offended against his principles. A complete surrender to love might have let in God. Of course, in the end, he did. When they were shut up together in a room, he couldn't avoid it. I saw. My father died peacefully."

Dulcie raised her head.

"You, Arthur," she said, "are you, I wonder, the instrument we feel you are?"

Whatever she intended to convey, he was glad not to grasp it, and lowered his eyes to the level of her breast, from which the milk had trickled, through the black dress. She noticed at once, and covered herself with her scarf. With the same slow but natural motion, she covered her head.

As he continued to visit the Saportas over the years with some regularity, Arthur did not particularly notice Dulcie's greyness or her glasses, nor that Mr. Saporta was setting in fat, because friends and lovers enjoy a greater freedom than their bodies: they are at liberty to move out of them, and by special dispensation communicate with one another through far-sighted eyes.

It was Waldo who suffered, Arthur regretted, from his meeting with the whole Saporta family in Pitt Street, in middle age. The shock of recognition had sent Waldo temporarily off his rocker, with the result that he was knocked down farther along, his pince-nez damaged beyond repair. It was not Arthur who had arranged the meeting, though Waldo seemed to think it was.

All the way to his brother's bedside Arthur had suffered for Waldo's suffering, more particularly for Waldo's fear of death. The crisp perfection of the sister colliding with the weakness of his stricken brother sent him almost frantic. It put him in a most difficult position: to pacify the bossy sister by keeping quiet, while convincing Waldo he couldn't afford to let him die. Careful regulation of his conduct at last persuaded her they might be left, and at once Waldo sounded less afraid. Though Arthur continued to blub a little to show his brother he needed him. Love, he had found, is more acceptable to some when twisted out of its true shape.

Not that Waldo would accept much. He was too busy with his problems, of libraries, and Mr. Crankshaw. Arthur realized he had a problem of his own when Waldo joined the staff of the big new Public Library, where Arthur himself was inclined to read. Fortunately Waldo, in occasional flight through the reading room, was too preoccupied to notice anyone beyond the outskirts of his mind.

He barely noticed the war even, the second one which was going on. In the First War, Arthur Brown had been all fireworks and singing. He wore a patient gravity for the Second. Too much had happened down Terminus Road and in other parts. Although still a boy, he went more slowly, nursing his jammed fingers, expecting the next kick in the pants.

On the night of the Peace, when the singing was let loose, the vomit, the piss, the gobs, and the little girls with their wicked bums and flouncing hair, Arthur couldn't make up a song, until at last a couple of lines—or three:

> No more dying only the dead
> love is lying in the parks
> and lying and lying . . .

He smiled, though, for all those pairs of twins, and no word between them to express the truth.

When a lady approached him, violet over grey, and fetched out a screech from away back near her uvula: "You big *man*, where have you *bin*?"

He replied, simply, sadly, "Madam, I am not your cup of tea."

He wondered where Waldo was. He was glad it was he, not his brother, involved in such a tasteless incident.

Related in more than flesh, Waldo had become by then the first of his two preoccupations. Since his discovery of the spirit, Arthur could not go too softly, offering, as it were, this other thing, where his body might repel. He realized he could not run the risk of Waldo's refusing something less material than glass. Glass was shattering enough. In his left pocket, certainly, he continued to carry Waldo's mandala, though for the most part he avoided taking it out. He preferred to contemplate his own, in which the double spiral knit and unknit so reasonably.

This solid mandala he held in his hand as he sat, whenever possible, in the reading room at the Library. For the Books became his second obsession. To storm his way, however late, however dark the obscurer corners of his mind. So he sat twirling the solid mandala, and by shuffling the words together, he made many if not all of the permutations of sense. Admittedly, in flashes of desperation, crushed grass and his own palpitating lump of flesh convinced him more.

Arthur wrestled with the Books. He wrestled with his obstreperous mind, which disgusted far too many by its fleshly lumbering round their thoughts. He knew he must look a real old faggot in the raincoat he wore, not so much for the weather as to cover up his shortcomings. Perhaps, after all, Hindu smoke was the only true and total solution. As for the lotus, he crushed it just by thinking on it.

On one occasion, in some book, he came across a message. Pinned to the back of his mind, it rattled and twitched, painfully, hopefully, if obscure:

As the shadow continually follows the body of one who walks in the sun, so our hermaphroditic Adam, though he appears in the form of a male, nevertheless always carries about with him Eve, or his wife, hidden in his body.

He warmed to that repeatedly after he had recovered from the shock. And if one wife, why not two? Or three? He could not have chosen between them. He could not sacrifice his first, his fruitful darling, whose mourning even streamed with a white light. Nor the burnt flower-pots, the russet apples of his second. Or did the message in the book refer, rather, to his third, his veiled bride? Heavy with alternatives and hoarded wealth, he sat back on the heels of the creaking library chair, opened his raincoat, scratched through his flies, rubbed at his rather cushiony chest.

When the chair collapsed under Arthur Brown he wasn't hurt. It was such a joke.

"You must take care!" It was the young lady, that Miss Glasson. "At your age. Once you start falling. Public property, too!"

When Arthur had got himself another chair he went and took *Through the Looking Glass*. He loved that. His mouth still watered for sweets of any kind. He would shake back his hair before entering.

Or he would glance up. And sometimes Miss Glasson was hovering over her hermaphroditic Adam. If she only knew. On one occasion he decided to tell. And decided not to. Although Miss Glasson was good for a smile, she mightn't have been on for a laugh.

In any case, it was time. It was time to return to Terminus Road. So frustrating. If only he could have retired—but they needed him more than ever, Mrs. Allwright and Mrs. Mutton, since Mr. Allwright died—he would have been able to give all that extra time to his reading.

To *The Brothers Karamazov*. Wonder what Dad would have said!

But there were days, whole weeks, Arthur couldn't help feeling, when he remained congealed, possessed by Terminus Road, and Waldo—it was Waldo. When the great basalt clouds were piled up over their heads, the fragments of shale restlessly flying, the yellow loops of wet grass setting traps for ankles, Waldo had to be comforted. Arthur accepted his duty. Their life was led down Terminus Road. Of course they went to their jobs, they had been so regulated they couldn't have helped going. But their actual life was the one which continued knotting itself behind the classical weatherboard façade. Sometimes Arthur wished Dad hadn't burnt his copy of *The Brothers Karamazov*, so that he could have got on with it at home. Then he realized it mightn't have been desirable: to introduce all those additional devils into their shaky wooden house.

Once, at the height of a storm, when the rain was coming down aslant, in slate-pencils, against the roof, the water coming through the rusty iron, in that same place, into the basin, in the scullery, and the quince twigs squeaking against, the rose thorns scratching on, the panes, Waldo shouted, "I wonder what you damn well think about, Arthur!"

"Well," said Arthur slowly, because it was a difficult one to answer, "what most people think about, I suppose."

"Nothing!" Waldo shouted back. "That's the answer!"

"Or everything," Arthur only mumbled, because Waldo seemed so put out.

"You think about nothing!" Waldo had begun to cry. "No worries on your mind!"

"If you want to know, I was thinking about Tiresias," Arthur said to interest him. "How he was changed into a woman for a short time. That sort of thing would be different, wouldn't it, from the hermaphroditic Adam who carries his wife about with him inside?"

Then Waldo took him by the wrists.

"Shut up!" he ordered. "Do you understand? If you think thoughts like those, keep them to yourself, Arthur. I don't want to hear. Any such filth. Or madness."

Waldo might have wrenched Arthur's hands off at the wrists if only he had been strong enough. But he wasn't.

Instead he sat down rather hard, and Arthur went to him, to comfort him, because they had only each other. Waldo knew this. He put his head on the table, under the falling rain, and cried.

Waldo was such a terrible problem to Arthur, their love for each other, that there were whole visits to the library when he couldn't bring himself to take down *The Brothers Karamazov*. He preferred Alice.

But he had to return to what had become, if not his study, his obsession. There was all this Christ jazz. Something of which Mrs. Poulter had explained. But he couldn't exactly relate it to men, except to the cruelty some men practise, in spite of themselves, as a religion they are brought up in. Reading *The Brothers Karamazov* he wished he could understand whose side anyone was on.

Who was the Grand Inquisitor?

Then quite suddenly one morning at the library Waldo was sitting at the same table, opposite him, making that scene. Afterwards Arthur could not remember in detail what was said. You couldn't exactly say *they* were *speaking*, because the remarks were being torn out of them helter-skelter, between tears and gusts of breathlessness, like handfuls of flesh. The raw, bleeding remarks were such that Waldo kept looking around to see who might be noticing. As for Arthur, he did not care. Their relationship was the only fact of importance, and such an overwhelming one.

"I shan't ask if you've come here, if you're making this scene, to humiliate me," Waldo was saying, "because the answer is too obvious. That has been your chief object in life. If you would be truthful."

"Why hurt yourself, Waldo?" Arthur was given the strength to reply. "Kick a dog, and hurt yourself. That's you all over."

"For God's sake don't drag in the dogs! And who, I'd like to know, wanted the miserable animals? And why?"

"We both did," said Arthur, "so that we could have something additional—reliable—to love. Because we didn't have faith in each other. Because we are—didn't you say yourself, Waldo?—abnormal people and selfish narcissyists."

Waldo was looking in every direction at once, and especially at that Miss Glasson, who, although standing at the far end of the room, might have been holding a telescope. She had that kind of eye.

"Afraid," Arthur was saying, and now he did begin to feel a kind of terror rising in him. "Like our father. I mean Dad. Not the one they pray to. But Dad putting Dostoevski on the fire."

He knew the flames of argument must be colouring his face in the way which distressed strangers, even Waldo, most. But for the moment he was almost glad he couldn't control himself.

"Afraid of the blood and the nails, which, as far as I can see, is what everyone is afraid of, but wants, and what Dostoevski is partly going on about. Do you see, Waldo"—he was bursting with it—"what we must avoid?"

Suddenly Arthur burst into tears because he saw that Waldo was what the books referred to as a lost soul. He, too, for that matter, was lost. Although he might hold Waldo in his arms, he could never give out from his own soul enough of that love which was there to give. So his brother remained cold and dry.

Arthur stopped crying almost at once, because the reason for his beginning was so immense it made the act itself seem insignificant. He was ashamed.

"But we've got to keep on *trying*, Waldo, just as we get up every morning and lace our boots up again."

I don't know what you mean, Waldo could have been on the point of saying. At that moment he looked so lost, Arthur had to lean across the table and try to take him by the hands. He, the lost one, taking his lost brother by the hands.

When Waldo started snatching back his property.

"You're drawing attention to us!"

Arthur did not understand at first.

"You will leave this place," Waldo was commanding, and very loudly: "*Sir!*"

Indicating that he, Arthur, his brother, his flesh, his breath, was a total stranger.

It was then Arthur began to tear the Grand Inquisitor out of *The Brothers Karamazov*, he was so confused. And Waldo shaking him like any old rag, which he was, he admitted, he was born so, but not to be bum-rushed against and through the swing-doors. As if you could get rid of your brother that way.

He walked across the hall, steady enough, and out the main entrance, his shadow following him in the sun, as he carried away inside him—his brother.

In the circumstances Arthur was glad they had the pups—or dogs they were by then—to return to, to cherish, though Waldo would never have admitted to cherishing anyone or anything. The dogs used to rush out on Arthur, their supple, flashing bodies, their strong white teeth revealed in pleasure, and he would go quite passive, though wobbly, allowing them to lick his hands. By the time their saliva had dried on his skin, he was usually restored. Then he would potter round a bit, talking, or grunting, to his dogs. Mostly in little pleased noises or phrases of gasps. Though on the evening of his scene with Waldo, he announced from the depths of him, "I got a proper flogging today."

Waldo never talked to a dog, and on his arriving home, they would prowl round him, lifting their pads as though they were sprung, and whining through their sharp-looking noses.

"Those dogs of yours," Mrs. Allwright used to complain when they followed Arthur to the store, "I wouldn't trust them an inch. Not on my heels. On a dark night. Not by day neether. Look, Arthur! *Arrrrrhh! Arthur?*" she would call, stamping, her voice rising. "Dogs! Dogs!" she would moan. "Filthy brutes! Soiling the produce!"

And the dogs would growl back, but make off across the paddocks, home.

Mrs. Allwright was not in a position to create about the dogs as much as she would have liked, because, on the death of her husband, she became too dependent on Arthur at the store. When Arthur needed a day at the Library, she didn't even dock his wages. If she complained a certain amount, well, complaint was in her nature.

"I shan't let you down, Mrs. Allwright," Arthur promised. "Not in other ways. I owe it to Mr. Allwright since he died."

"Mr. Allwright didn't die," his widow used to maintain. "He is all around me."

Then Mrs. Mutton her sister would suck her teeth, and ejaculate, "It's a mercy you have your faith, Ivy."

It was fortunate Mrs. Allwright had her faith in faith, for she hadn't any in man or dog, and on her deciding to sell the store, and retire to Toowoomba with her sister and her Christian Science, Arthur's only regret was that he had never got to know Mr. Allwright; he had been saving it up for the future when his employer died. If he hadn't got to know Mrs. Mutton either, it was because there was nothing to know. Mrs. Mutton was more a monument than a woman.

So Arthur retired, and the convenience of it was: his twin brother Waldo began his retirement at the same moment.

If it had not been for the dogs they might have succumbed to the silence of their suddenly unfamiliar house. It seemed as though the house had grown elastic with time, and they would have to accustom themselves to its changing shapes. The rooms which they had used before, or not, according to their needs, began using them. So much of what they had forgotten, or never seen, rose up before their eyes: the dusty paper bags still hanging by their necks as Dad had left them, rattling with husks when the wind blew or they hit you in the face; a simple deal chair suddenly dominating the shadows; the smell of old milk rags, of turps, and rotted quinces, mingling and clotting so thick as to become visible in memory's eye, a string of solid glossy days to chase the pong out of the present; dates of years ago turned to fly-shit on the calendars; a ball of Mother's hair in the corner of a dressing-table drawer; a dress of Mother's. For a long time Arthur had been afraid to touch the dress in case it stood up in a crash of remonstrative beads.

So the dogs were a blessing. And the walks. Waldo did not take to walking till later, because at first his papers demanded too much of his time. He was putting them in order.

"A disorderly life, a disorderly mind," Waldo said. "You won't understand, Arthur, the mental handicap physical disorder can become. You don't need to. In my case an absence of method could undo the plans of a lifetime."

He continued fussing over the old cardboard box in which Mother's dress used to be.

Arthur went out. He liked to moon across the paddocks with the dogs. It was very soothing. On keener mornings he would put on that old coat in stained herringbone tweed, which had belonged to Uncle Charlie, and which was still wearable in spite of moths. When he grew tired he would sit on a log and only at first wonder what he had come there for. The morning was reason enough— breaking into phrases of sound bursts of light threads of thought. He would sit in some sheltered bay of dripping blackberry bushes, the winter wire of which whipped him to greater appreciation of all he had experienced in the past. While in the present the dogs sat licking their pads, or, jacked on their sterns, lavished respectful tongues on the blue perfection of their balls.

Arthur laughed, for all roundnesses. He took out the marble and looked at it.

One year he went up to look at the wheel-tree, again in the season of its second flowering, and, as though by contrivance, the Chinese woman was standing beneath it. Only the crackle of her surface more pronounced, her bones more obviously breakable. On this occasion she turned even quicker, and went somewhat angrily behind the sheds. Perhaps seeing him on his own, without the benefit of Mrs. Poulter. Well, he expected that sort of thing. But the wheel-tree fairly sizzled with fire, burning its way back through time to the other afternoon.

He shivered, remembering the feel of hair, skin smelling ever so faintly of struck flint.

Waldo said, "If ever I catch you hanging round that woman."

He had not explained what he would do, but out of respect for Mrs. Poulter, and to avoid any risk of her humiliation, Arthur did not see her again. That is, they no longer walked together along the unseen, the secret paths. For it was impossible to ignore the sight of Mrs. Poulter, in this cardigan or that, pulling a weed, or wiping the pollard off her hands.

He developed the habit of calling out across her picket fence, "How are we, Mrs. Poulter? Eh?"

And Mrs. Poulter would reply, "Good, thanks, Mr. Brown."

Looking, rather, at the weeds.

"And Mr. Poulter keeping good?"

"Good enough, thanks. Yes."

Exploring the soil with the toe of her shoe.

They lived opposite each other for many years without a change in the recognized climate.

Then one evening he had gone in, taking the two pounds of self-raising which Mrs. Allwright said Mrs. Poulter was inquiring for. He had barged right in the way it had been customary in their youth. Banging the gauze door. Had gone on into the house drunk with the scent of beeswax and overpowering cleanliness.

"Mrs. Poulter?" he called. "Where are we?"

On that evening he was so happy.

In the empty, half-darkened house he had come across her, through the bedroom door, standing over against a chest. Doing something of a private nature. Mrs. Poulter, he realized, was dressing, or undressing, an enormous doll.

"Go on!" he almost shouted. "Where did you get that beaut doll?"

He would have trampled farther into the bedroom, but saw he had caught her out cruelly in what she was doing. She stood there holding the naked doll against her bosom, half looking as though the plastic were turning molten in her arms and she wanted to shoot it out across the carpet.

"You've no right," she began to stutter, "barging in. Into people's houses. A lady's bed—bedroom. They should of learnt you *that*, Mr. Brown!"

They might never have known each other. For he too was becoming a stranger, in the forbidden doorway, holding a packet of flour in his arms.

"Okay," he said, "Mrs. Poulter."

But she continued creating.

"Ugly thing!"

She flung the doll into a drawer, where it made the sound of a body thudding, and gave out a cry of mechanical anguish.

"Nobody," she panted, "ever wants half of what they're given!"

Crumpling into a ball the doll's dress and knickers which, in her hurry, she had overlooked.

"Okay, Mrs. Poulter," Arthur said, "you can give it away to some kiddy."

Then Mrs. Poulter, who was standing by now in the centre of the room, said something, something surprising, still squeezing up the doll's clothes.

"I wouldn't contaminate any kiddy," she said. "I mean, I'd encourage her to think most kiddies can expect better than dolls."

And he could see the knots forming in Mrs. Poulter's throat, like a goitre. Age had made her fat and rather purple. He would have liked to comfort the stout woman.

Instead he said, "I brought the flour."

"Thank you, Arthur," she said, coming forward, and leading the way into the kitchen.

"You ought to switch on the light," he advised. "For company. That way you won't get morbid."

"It's more economical to go without the light," she said. "I'll switch it on when Bill comes in and I give him his tea."

By now Mrs. Poulter was quite restored, and they stood together, just a moment, unconfessed, over the packet of flour. He was surprised how their hands had swollen since he had been forced to dance his mandala, on an afternoon flowing with fire.

Never again had he danced out of fulness, though sometimes on winter mornings, after the grass had been released, and the sunlight was dripping through the steel mesh of blackberry bushes, he would execute one or two movements. He would hang his head to one side, he would extend his herringbone arms, the fingers dangling in bundles of thawed flesh, and the dogs would stop their licking to watch.

Never did any of them feel that these were amongst the inspired moments. He would go off home, followed neatly by the blue dogs.

In the beginning he had wondered how to fill the time. Of course there was the bread and milk they ate, and on Sundays the salmon-loaf habit which they had inherited from Mother. They ate mostly boiled stuff, because Waldo had ordained.

"Boiled food prevents ulcers," he said, "and as much as anything else helps ensure longevity."

And there was the butter-making besides, and bread. Arthur used to clean the lamps, an activity he associated with that of churning or baking, the outcome so lucid.

He wrote his poems too, on mornings full of sun and blue dogs scratching at their fleas. Though why he wrote, or for whom, he could not have told, nor would he have shown. But sat with the pencil, the paper on his knee. He wrote the poem of the daughter he had never had, and of the wives he carried inside him. The writing of the poems was the guiltiest act he had performed since starting to look up in the dictionaries, to read the books, his mind venturing through the darkened theatre in which the gods had died in the beginning.

Until Waldo would stick his head out the window and shout, "Can't you *do* something, Arthur? Haven't you an occupation? Take those dogs for a walk at least. I can't think for having you around."

Poor Waldo, his neck stuck out like that of a hen about to be decapitated.

"Good God, Arthur," he used to shout, "do I have to think for you as well?"

Poor Waldo, in spite of himself, called on God more often as time went on.

Thus dismissed, Arthur would shuffle off—it was all the same, and nothing could hurt—taking with him his papers, his dogs, and his mandalas. He would wander for hours.

He only first realized how old he was when he caught sight of his reflection nose-picking in Woolworth's plate-glass window. He might have come home ashamed if he hadn't remembered halfway down Terminus Road moments of other people's shame: Mrs. Poulter for her doll, his brother for his brother.

The night Arthur, dogs at heel, brought the flour to Mrs. Poulter, Waldo was acting or celebrating something. The wreath of roses, the banksia roses, made a frame for Waldo in the blue dress. If they had been less intimate, if Arthur had not experienced already some such translation in himself of his brother's personality, then he might have suffered a greater shock, from Waldo's white, plucked arms, and the shattering torrent of glass beads. Breathing alone stirred the beads. Or tilting of a chair. As Waldo squinted between the slats of his fan. Or stroked his bit of a raggedy moustache. All the family were gathered in the glass: Dad and Mother, Uncle Charlie, Cousin Mollie and "Adelaide," all huddled in the darkened box, waiting to see, not only what might offer itself for killing, but how their own blood would run.

Oh he might have cried, if he hadn't laughed, through the beads and roses, at himself in Waldo's blue dress. Bursting out of it. His breasts were itching.

So Arthur had begun to scratch, and call.

"Come here, Runt! Runty?"

To call or laugh, "Silly old cunt!"

When he went inside he told how he had delivered the flour,

sensing that in the circumstances the return of Mrs. Poulter and Waldo's hatred of her might take his brother's mind off other matters.

But all that was long ago.

Now the dry woodwork ticked the rusty iron creaked or responded to mere claws or rain-scurries at night the water dripped in the scullery basin plant life was reflected in the thinnest smear of sunlight on the walls and ceilings of the house in which not everyone had died.

Arthur didn't intend to die. He couldn't afford to. He had his duty towards his brother. If not to perform for Waldo the humblest tasks, to allow him to believe himself superior to anything proposed. It seemed fitting to Arthur that the house which had been built in the shape of a temple should be used as a place of worship, and he took it for granted it would continue to fulfil its purpose, in spite of timber thin as paper, fretting iron, sinking foundations. Like the front gate, it would hold together by rust and lichen, or divine right. At least there was that about age: there were others in the conspiracy.

The gentleness of it appealed to Arthur. It was his brother who kicked. Or turned his face away. That night, for instance, the worst happened in bed. When Waldo got the diarrhoea.

"What are you doing to me?" he bellowed.

Almost as though Arthur were responsible for the act as well as for the mopping up.

"All right, Waldo. Don't tell me. I know I'm the cause of a lot. But I know my responsibilities."

Glad to perform the humblest act of all.

Waldo's breathing sounded pacified at last.

It was Arthur who bit his breath the morning he got the shock, the morning his ticker didn't actually stop, but ticked over slower bumping grating paining. He put his hands to his side, as if trying to hold in them, to protect and prolong, the first apple he was ever given.

If it was Arthur who got the shock, it was Waldo who took fright. You could see that. Even when there was no longer any reason for it, the fright persisted. Waldo had prescribed the walks to show them they were still good for something. As, of course, they were. After the warning, Arthur had never felt fitter. It was Waldo who shrivelled up, bluer, thinner than if he had been— what was it? *collating* his notes, or writing a novel.

"Do you think," said Arthur, "we ought to be taking these walks?" but looked at Waldo, and added: "At least they must be doing us some good. Yes," he said, because Waldo was looking so furious, "they're doing us good."

When even the aged dogs had begun to have their doubts. Runt had refused once or twice. Scruffy had turned the other side of the service station.

"Those dogs are going to die on us," Arthur complained, "and what are we going to do then?"

Waldo laughed.

"We shall have each other."

They had their memories. Sometimes a memory would assume a more convincing shape than any present flesh. If Arthur picked up from behind the copper that old dress, embroidered with rat-pellets and the light skeleton of a small bird, it was not an act of malice, but because the past forces itself on those who have participated.

"What is it, Waldo?" he asked.

Of course he knew. He only wanted to hear it said. You can never really confirm too often.

But he saw at once Waldo was hurt.

"Put it away," he shouted, "where it was!"

"Why," asked Arthur, "should we keep what hurts?"

Though he knew the answer.

He threw away the dress. Which turned into that poem.

Now the poems were about the only part of him Arthur would not have revealed to his brother. The mandala, the knotted man-dala, he would have given, had kept, in fact, for that purpose, had offered even. But not the poems. There was no blasphemy at the centre of the mandala. Whereas, in certain of the poems, there was a kind of blasphemy against life. Which Waldo exaggerated quite horribly and deliberately on finding the crumpled poem unfortu-nately fallen out of an overstuffed pocket.

"all Marys in the end bleed"

Waldo's voice was reading, deliberately blaspheming,

"they know they cannot have it any other way . . ."

In spite of mornings shouting with light, and faces of women receiving the truth.

"I know, Waldo!" Arthur cried. "It was never ever much of a poem."

Because, more than his own, written words, his brother's voice was convincing him of his blasphemy against life. Not so much against God—he could understand God at a pinch—but against the always altering face of the figure nailed on the tree.

"Give it to me, Waldo!"

Waldo made it unnecessary. Waldo was tearing the poem up.

That his brother continued to suffer from the brutality of their revelation was evident to Arthur when, in the course of the afternoon, he looked through the trees and saw Waldo carrying his boxful of papers towards the pit. Knowing he had probably destroyed his brother did not help Arthur to act. Through the trees he could smell the burning papers. He stood around snivelling, sniffing the fumigatory smell of burning. But he was not in any way cleansed.

When finally he went into their room, he found Waldo lying on the bed. Waldo raised himself on an elbow.

And Arthur saw.

He saw the hatred Waldo was directing, had always directed, at all living things, whether Dulcie Feinstein, or Mrs. Poulter, or the blasphemous poem—because that, too, had life of a kind—the poem which celebrated their common pain.

"Waldo!" Arthur was afraid at last. "What are you trying to do to me?"

Arthur was afraid Waldo was preparing to die of the hatred he had bred in him. Because he, not Waldo, was to blame. Arthur Brown, the getter of pain.

Then Waldo, in the agony of their joint discovery, reached out and grabbed him by the wrist, to imprint him forever with the last moment.

"Waldo! Let me go! Wald."

Big and spongy though he was, Arthur Waldo's big dill brother could go crumbly as one thing for love and now the death of it.

Waldo was lying still, but still attached to Arthur at the wrist.

When Arthur saw the murder he had committed on his brother he began to try to throw him off. He did not immediately succeed, because the fingers of this dead man were determined, in their steel circlets, to bring him to trial. So he had to fight against it. And finally snapped the metal open.

Then Arthur went stampeding through the house in which their lives, or life, had been lived until the end. It was a wonder the cries torn out of him didn't bring the structure down. Before he slammed a door on the shocked faces of dogs.

FOUR

MRS. POULTER AND
THE ZEITGEIST

YOU COULDN'T say she wasn't comfortable. He kept the home painted up. Bill never showed his age. Lucky to still, in spite of his quirks, have his strength. Took a few jobs on the side to make the something extra. Like grass-cutting and pruning roses. For the few extra luxuries. You had to keep up with the times. They had bought the plastic awnings for the front. She had the electricity, she had the phone. Sarsaparilla wasn't on the sewer of course, and Bill wouldn't come at a septic, but she had her health, in spite of one or two aches, and what was a few steps across the yard to the dumpty. Altogether you couldn't say she wasn't comfortable. She had the radio, but no longer used it all that much, not since they got the telly, or anyway began the payments, like most else since recently. Bill said people had never in history had it so good, and well, she admitted, you couldn't say it wasn't pretty good. You couldn't complain. Not with the electric frying-pan—never used her oven now—not with the phone, and two doctors. And the telly. If she didn't have any friends without the ones she yarned with over fences, in buses, or the street, she didn't need any. She had the telly, the nice announcers, and world figures in your own lounge. She could afford to mind her own business, without Mrs. Dun reminding her of it. That Mrs. Dun was something of a disappointment. Cold. A dash of Scotch somewhere there. There was nothing like the Scotch for keeping their distance. Well, you couldn't blame them, you couldn't blame nobody for how they were made. And the Duns, both, were what the magazine articles call neurotic. From living with Bill she could tell neurotic, oh yes, even in the bus. Still, you couldn't say no to Mrs. Dun. Company becomes a habit, if only the journey in the bus, and mucking around Davy Jones, or seeing a big new feature picture at the Roxy, you wouldn't ever go on your own, it was something at least to know who it was breathing in *one* of the seats alongside of you. So you developed the habit. But there was nothing intimate with Mrs. Dun, such a yellow little person, knotting up her scarf tighter still, those brown silk scarves, or buff, and the cameo brooch her auntie from West Maitland left. You couldn't say Mrs. Dun wasn't a refined-looking lady, only somewhat cold, and never a dash of colour, that old black velour which must of been renovated, it was the niece who did it, more than once. But that was Mrs. Dun's business.

At sixty-seven Mrs. Poulter still liked a bit of colour. She knitted herself the cardigans. She loved the latest, her watermelon cardigan. Even though it had just come in through High Fashion and the magazines, without boasting, she had thought of it herself years ago. Watermelon. On chilly evenings she would tuck her hands inside the cuffs, and draw the wool down over her bust, and walk to the gate, and back to the steps, and down to the fence, to look, just to see. Of course she never expected anyone, and nobody ever came. It wasn't necessary. She was that snug in her watermelon cardigan. And soon she would go inside, to get Bill's tea, and watch the telly after he had eaten whatever it was, chops usually, or else a braise, and laid down.

Mrs. Poulter was still quite bright of countenance. Her skin had gone to rags of course, at her age, but she had her health, her colour, which she helped out with Cyclax, more discreet than the other brands. More refined-smelling, more like a kind of ointment for the skin. No one could object to a person doing something for her chaps. Of course she couldn't alter herself. She was born brownish and healthy-looking. If she cracked up like some old enamel pot, it was what happens in time.

When Bill asked her, her skin had been as smooth as plums. She was not, you couldn't say, pretty, but without being vain, nice-looking, in those cotton frocks she made up from the patterns, buying the stuff at Mrs. Fat's. And a gay hat. She waited for the ones they used to send up to Fats' from Sydney. She was not what they call sophisticated then, none of them was in those days, at Numburra or at Mungindribble. Bill would drive in in the trap. They would drive down by the river, there was nowhere else to go, but in good seasons it was lovely, flowers to pick, the trees was lovely, big smooth-barked gums standing straight and cool by the river. That was where Bill asked her, and she accepted so quick—how could she not of?—she felt a bit ashamed wondering what Bill. Oh, well. She loved a handsome man, and never looked at another. It was his teeth, it was his hands, yes, above all it was his hands that she could never stop looking at, or wrists, a man's wrists never seemed to know their own strength, but then a man never seemed to know. So she could afford to keep on looking. What of it, if you love a person? That was what the Bible told you. It was only with the ministers that sin came in, but they didn't always understand. She loved, she had loved Bill. Wearing his hat that way, and in the Army afterwards. She had only to look at Bill and would have melted if he had wanted. But. Bill wasn't one of those with only the one thought in their heads. Bill was not uneducated. Could write a stylish letter. You weren't at everybody's mercy with a man like that around. Could use educated words. He was not just rouseabout and Council labourer start and finish. No one altogether realized that. Not those Browns. Waldo walking that stiff with all he was supposed to know you would of thought he had the piles. Poor Arthur you couldn't very well expect.

Stringing fresh green beans sprayed her with the same chill smell as when she thought the name. Arthur Brown. That was different. That was years afterwards.

In the beginning there was Bill. It was of course a white wedding, and such a dusty day, but they had their photo took, with everybody all standing in the dust. There was no honeymoon, because Bill couldn't run to it, and she didn't complain. When they were together in the back room she tried to show it made no difference to her. She was not happy, she was more than happy, knowing what she had got. Well, there was nothing wrong with it, was there? She lay back wondering about the laundry, but grew too tired to wonder long, and everyone knew about it, anyway.

Those first years she could have eaten Bill. It wasn't right. He had his principles, it seemed. It made her proud. And him such a manly man. She loved his throat. It was wrong perhaps, but she loved where the hair began and ended.

She loved him, her husband.

She loved him. Oh my darling, she said between mouthfuls. His legs like a pair of scissors would cut her short.

How terrible the war was, only a woman could of known. She received his letters, of course, while he was at Liverpool and down the coast, but it did not ease her body growing softer for him.

They took away the little girl she lost. First the sister let her look. In after years sometimes she would cry, thinking how nice it would of been, to have her little girl to tell things to.

Bill never mentioned it. Well, you couldn't expect him to. She was the woman. Sometimes she felt she embarrassed him.

Anyway, he had changed when he returned. While remaining her husband.

At least she had her faith, which Bill didn't altogether approve of, but it was what she was brought up to, if she didn't always understand, but hoped to in time, not through the ministers, she would never of dared ask, but somehow. She had her Lord Jesus. Who was a man. By that she meant nothing blasphemous. Humankind. That was what they turned him into, wasn't it?

Mrs. Poulter would lick her lips thinking it out, with very slight Cyclax. She knew herself by the glass to be what they call highly coloured.

My darling, she would say, walking amongst the white chrysanths, she would say to the little black curly pig. No one could lift the combs out so gently as she. In winter she stood saucers of sugar outside the hives.

At first she used to cry when the pigs were dragged out squealing, to be hitched up by one leg, and bled. Later on she changed. Bill asked how could you live without butchers. There's the vegetarians, she said. The vegetarians are nuts. So, if men could only live normal by butchery, then she accepted it.

But would go in quickly beyond range of squealing, and switch on the radio, or better, after they got it, the telly. She loved the telly. It made her sit forward, holding her elbows, not exactly tense, but waiting, most of all for the *real* programmes, when they let off one of the bombs, or an aeroplane caught fire at the moment of crashing, or those guerrillas they'd collared, of course they were only Orientals, and once it showed you the bodies they'd shot. The news made the rubber eat into her, she would hear herself wheeze, the news items so real, you only sometimes overheard the squeals of a stuck and bleeding pig.

One midwinter evening the squealing got so bad, she went and slammed the window shut, although it had only been open a crack. She broke a nail, they was so brittle, she got the indigestion, she couldn't concentrate on the telly for all that old sadness returning. Couldn't breathe, not in what they call them now the step-ins. The sister had said perhaps it was all for the best. But only to make it easier. All the while they was firing on a mob of squealing Orientals, in Singapore, or some such place. You wouldn't believe.

Mrs. Poulter sat and hiccupped for a misborn child and a plastic doll writhing on the square of gelatin.

That bally doll, why she should remember she didn't know, or why Waldo Brown had bought her the doll. Even so, she had wanted to keep it and dress it nice, until poor Arthur found her out. With a big lump of a rubbery doll. She wasn't half ashamed. If you came to think there was a lot of things, the loveliest, made you ashamed by remembering them. Those first days with Bill, which were lawful and sacred, she had behaved so natural perhaps it had put him against her, only because she loved, and could not learn enough about him. Anyway. That nasty doll she had took down the gully with the spade and buried it in the loose bush soil beside the creek. And felt a little easier. For a while only. Because after the rain she had dared look and there was its legs, dimpled too, and mulberry nylon skirt, sticking out of the sand and leaves, like a corpse they find at Frenchs Forest. She kicked the thing. She got the hiccups. In that chilly hollow of yellow draining floodwater it was too sad to stay thinking of what was done with. She couldn't scramble quickly enough up and over the rocks. Must of strained her back.

Sundays of a morning she went to church, unless she had a throat, or her leg was hurting. She took it easy up the road to church, because Bill never got a car, she could understand, it was his nerves, nor came with her, most of Sunday morning he lay on the bed, it was not exactly that Bill didn't *believe*, she suspected, but like most men he left it to the women. It was anyway too delicate a matter for men. Not that she knew what it amounted to herself, not all of it, but knew. It was her own breath, her own body, the blood quicker in her own veins. But she wished she could see more clearly. She wished she could *see*. Recognize the face they spoke about.

In the days when she had gone with poor Arthur lovely walks through the paddocks and blackberrying in season as far as the Chinese farm she had almost seen or at least known so intimately so many details vein of leaf blade of grass sound and silence funny enough by Arthur's being there his head a fire amongst the blackberry bushes Arthur got cured of his trouble anyway on that day to dance the thing the mandala she still had the marble but too afraid to take it out for fear of facing what though on the day she had known there was never no need for fear with her and Arthur cured of all.

Of course she knew he was a nut. Though he wasn't. They'll say anybody's a nut. They said about Jesus.

So the bonfire of Arthur's head had never quite gone out for Mrs. Poulter. Even though she never addressed him after. Unless addressed. In the moments of years. It was the only secret Bill wouldn't ever get out of her, if Bill was to ask for all. It was too difficult. Unlike their own lovely-fitting grooved love of the beginning, it could not be fitted to word or hand. If she and Arthur was answerable for the day in the blackberry bushes, where in a moment or two they had gone through more than you live in years, they was answerable only to the Lord God, to who the last answers are made. She was no know-all, but she did know that.

So Mrs. Poulter, on cold evenings, after the telly had closed down, would roam far and wide through her wooden house and up the yard, crying softly, above grief: My darling, my curly pig, there is an end to blood and squealing if only we can remember how.

For she could never quite remember what they had seen and understood there below the Chinese farm.

But got at last to remembering she had not seen, she had not seen Waldo, she had not seen Him—Arthur—since when.

It was a Saturday, a Saturday afternoon, when Mrs. Poulter, trying to mind her own business, failing to outstare the hedge opposite, decided to bake a nice custard. After all, someone could be sick, and neighbourliness was another thing to curiosity. It put fresh heart, fresh life into Mrs. Poulter to bake the custard. She put on her watermelon cardigan.

However many times she had crossed the road to Browns' she had never got used to it. Her flesh grew prickly for the crunched sand. That gate, which they never mended for not knowing how to, poor things, a matter of upbringing, was standing open. Which was unusual. Somebody had forced it back so hard on its hinge it had stuck in the grass. No sign of dogs neether.

"Scruffy?" she called, for courage. "Runt? Runty? Where's the boys?"

All those old wormy woody quince trees were pressing against the house, against most of the windows. Mrs. Poulter went round the side, carrying as a protection her baked custard, but her heart and the silence were getting too big for her.

She wasn't going to not exactly look, but glance, to see whether one of the gentlemen was in their room. Sick. She was almost sure of something by now. She was glad she had brought the lightly flavoured vanilla custard.

Then Mrs. Poulter looked. She couldn't quite see at first for their never cleaning the windows. Then it was Mr. Waldo she saw, laid on the bed in the closed room, through the curtains of dust, and that was their Scruffy sitting, unusually, on the bed. Waldo in that old dressing-gown fallen open. No longer sick, Waldo.

Mrs. Poulter almost was. She had to stand the custard on the ground. She could feel her own cries stuck in lumps in her stiffened throat. And the other dog, Runt, crouching on the floor. Swallowing down. Runt swallowed and glared growled at Mrs. Poulter out of his almost blind eyes.

All of them almost blind by now. Waldo Brown stiff with blindness. Mrs. Poulter blind with loathing. She had known for days almost, and wouldn't admit, only there are some things you can smell—Waldo dead.

Or worse than dead.

His throat open on the gristly apple. Torn by the throat.

Then their Scruffy sitting on the bed, he hadn't even noticed her, lowered his head, pulling at that other part of Waldo Brown, she wouldn't have hardly dared look if it hadn't stopped being real, as Scruffy pulled, pulled at the old soft perished rubber.

Mrs. Poulter trod on the edge of her custard dish. She could not scream. The sounds were knotted up inside her.

And when she turned, beginning to run, she wasn't so much moving, as moved along the brick path by moments, over the clumps of grass, her legs in half-frozen motion. Running. Tumbling inside her soaking clothes.

At the gate she did cry out, "*Urrrrhhhh!*" only there was nobody to hear.

Mrs. Poulter continued running. She did not believe she had seen what she had seen, but again, believed. She would not believe. That is, she believed in everything now under the bruised and bursting sky. Not to say *heaven*.

For the clouds were building up, from beyond and over Sarsaparilla, for the Armageddon of which Mrs. Poulter had read and heard. She knew now. All the films, all the telly, all the black-and-white of the papers was turning real, as the great clouds, the great tanks, ground up groaning over Sarsaparilla. To lock together. Men burning in their steel prisons. Mrs. Poulter went zigzagging over the ruts, along the road, along the banks, over the tussocks, to save those who need not die. But age had made her topheavy. Hope was faint. She knew now. The flat faces of all those Chinese guerrillas or Indonesians, it was the same thing, dragged out across the dreadful screen. All those Jews in ovens, that was long ago, but still burning, lying in heaps. Lone women bashed up in Mosman, Maroubra, Randwick, places you went only in your sleep. Little girls held to the ground. The bleeding wombs of almost all women.

Mrs. Poulter lurched, but ran, her watermelon cardigan flickering, up Terminus Road, through the rainy green.

And He released His hands from the nails. And fell down, in a thwack of canvas, a cloud of dust.

It was not Arthur. Arthur would never ever of done that. He was not God. Arthur was a man.

Just this side of Duns' Mrs. Poulter's heel came off.

So that she went racketing round the back, lurching worse, smashing the fuchsias, crushing a lobelia border, grabbing the back doorknob, which, although highly polished, was not all that secure.

Mrs. Poulter stood rattling the knob. The door was locked, on account of it was bowling day, and Mrs. Dun, she knew, was nervous on her own.

"Mrs. Dun!" Mrs. Poulter called in her highest voice.

She would never of dared call Mrs. Dun Edna. What she would tell, she couldn't think. She was still living it all.

Then Mrs. Dun came through the house to the glassed-in back veranda. She had not had time to put her teeth in. She looked to be suffering from neuralgia, though that, with Mrs. Dun, was not the case. It was her normal look. With something added by the rattling of the knob.

Mrs. Poulter, who longed to share her terror with someone, saw that her friend Mrs. Dun was already far too terrified.

"What," said Mrs. Dun, "what is it?"

Her lips so pale behind the glass.

"I got to come in, Mrs. Dun," Mrs. Poulter shouted, "then I'll tell."

"No, you don't!" Mrs. Dun croaked back. "I said: What is it?"

The flaps of her lips flew in on her empty gums.

Mrs. Poulter realized she would never succeed in reaching Mrs. Dun, but continued, for continuity's sake, rattling the old brass doorknob. Even if she broke it off. As Mrs. Dun had broken their always fragile relationship.

"Mr. Brown—Mr. Waldo Brown is dead," Mrs. Poulter said in spite of all. "I can't tell exactly what 'as 'appened. Who done it. I don't know. But something funny. Something. Dead," Mrs. Poulter rattled.

"Ring the police," Mrs. Dun hissed, you could see the spray on the glass door. "That's what you do. Don't you know?"

"Yes," Mrs. Poulter said, while continuing to rattle the knob.

Then suddenly she felt quite exhausted.

She began to recede, like Mrs. Dun, as through water, only it was glass. Both backing. Mrs. Poulter smiling, because she didn't know what else to do. To hear and feel the fuchsia sticks, so frail, snapping against her body. Cool at least the leaves were. And Mrs. Dun backing through her always darkened house into the deepest darkness of it. Her lips clamped to her gums. Perhaps Mrs. Dun would be too terrified to open even to Mr. Dun, when he returned, carrying his bowling kit.

Mrs. Poulter manoeuvred past the fuchsias. To ring the police. At least she could thank her friend for reminding her of the obvious, though even so, she was not so very grateful. For the moment her leg was hurting more than her thoughts. The rain didn't exactly wet, but warned, out of the purple-looking clouds. The light had deepened until it was sort of moss-colored.

She began running again through the heavy landscape, through which she had meandered formerly with Arthur Brown. Now she whimpered for the sparkle of it, the long-lost bird-shot silences.

Then she fell down. She lay amongst the cold mossy-coloured grass at the side of the road, extended, not so much injured by her fall, as bludgeoned by this moment at which the past united with the present, her own pains with those of others.

When she got up, her stocking down, her right knee grazed blue and bleeding, Arthur should have been standing beside her. As she ran on, he was that close to her thoughts, without putting out her hand she could feel the shape of his.

For a moment, on her own gate, she hung gasping like a stranger about to ask a favour of the house. Then she went in to the telephone.

"Yes," she said. "Mr. Waldo Brown. The dogs," she could not say. "Mr. Arthur Brown is not, he isn't anywhere about. Mr. Arthur Brown didn't do it," she said. "He couldn't of. Not Mr. Arthur."

Sergeant Foyle, a decent fellow, must understand.

When she had shuffled the phone together, she turned round and there He was, dressed as some old hobo. Which of course was how he always had been. Only you forgot.

"What have you done to yourself?" she asked, raising the kind of joky voice a person might expect. "You look as if you was dragged through a tunnel!"

"Yes," said Arthur. "I had a shock."

He sat down, and she went to him.

When he had run out of the room, out of the house, slamming doors, he had at first some intention of escaping a murder he had committed. So he ran down across the paddocks, into the thin remainders of scrub. An escaped cow he had chased as a boy flickered around him as he listened to the lunging and crashing of his own body. With a recurrence of houses, and people staring over fences, he had to walk, to appease the faces. While failing to appease Waldo's eyes. He began to suspect he might never escape the hatred of which his brother had died.

Waldo had always hated people, but always rather, well, as a joke. Waldo had done his block at Arthur, but always more or less as a brother. Till it was made plain as a bedstead that the life, the sleep they had shared, must have been jingling brassily all those years with the hatred which only finally killed.

Arthur walked chafing his killer hands, big blurry lips blubbing through the streets for what he had caused.

"Who is this crazy old bugger going or gone off his rocker?" people were asking one another.

Without ever addressing Arthur, at most an animal, at least a thing.

This was possibly why he had been moved to take the bus, the train: to lose his name, if not the hateful load of his body. Streets are full of guesses which rarely develop into questions. Certainly in the days when the city had been celebrating with relief and joy the ends of wars, people had plastered themselves all over him, boozily expecting to discover a new style of love. No one, fortunately, was overanxious to investigate grief or terror. So now he went unmolested. Provided it was dark enough, he was free to enter where he liked, to prepare himself for putrefaction. Several dark corners dedicated to garbage might easily have assimilated his bundle of old torn clothes and older aching flesh. Collections thrice weekly removed the possibility of a too obtrusive stench.

Arthur Brown did in fact enter a narrow printer's lane, and got down alongside the cold-smelling bricks, in the corner in which drunks, evidently, came to piss.

He began to hear a pair of these, streaming and calling to each other as they stood buttressing the wall.

"Is it Friday ter-morrer?" one of them asked.

"At this time a night," the other replied, "you couldn't christen it any bloody day at all."

"We done our best!" laughed the first, belching, and shaking the drops off his end.

Then he fell to tripping and cursing.

"God sod the bastard!" he shouted.

"What's up, Leslie?"

"A body."

"A dead body, Leslie?"

"Wouldn't be surprised."

They walked away, leaning and laughing, and buttoning their flies.

But Arthur, who had known at most times, even after his attack, even after Waldo had walked him and walked him and, yes, walked him, knew again that he was not intended to die. Though an immensity of darkness in the printer's lane almost overwhelmed him. He would have liked to be a little boy, staring at the sky through hydrangea leaves. But couldn't manage it. All his family gone, he was threatened with permanent manhood. Or protected by his permanency. The sound of dogs gnawing at rib-bones, the faces of women exploring his face or weighing his words, eased him gently towards the future.

Snivelling for this considerable prospect he pulled out the ribbon of grey lint, which was what his handkerchiefs always became. And heard the sound of a glass marble, leaping, out of his control, away. At once he began the search which ended nowhere but in filth and darkness.

Only when reduced to nothing he remembered that one mandala must be left, and rummaged through the other contents of his pockets. The first and sleaziest ray of light from the entrance to the lane showed him the whorled marble lying in the hollow of his hand. The knotted mandala was the one he had lost.

Nursing his survivor he lumbered farther, moved by no specific desire, napping on his feet by moments, till the morning, it seemed, was noisily clattering amongst the leaves of the Moreton Bay figs, feathering the water, breaking and entering on all sides, only stopping short at the depths in early-opened eyes.

How many days Arthur Brown walked his guilt he didn't think to calculate; time was all of a piece, and meat pies, and snatches of sleep on the slats of benches. He began to feel his age at last. If he continued experiencing guilt while the sorrow drained out of it, it was because he knew Waldo would have been ashamed of sorrow.

Waldo had always been ashamed. Himself, never, but the cause of shame in other people.

Catching sight of that interminable face in shrivelled kid, as he did now, in what wasn't even a fun-fair mirror, he was sorry about it. For being the cause of everybody's shame. If he could only have revealed himself glistening in a sphere of glass.

At one stage in his limping progress, he squared his shoulders, he put on the cloak of an air, and swirled inside the Public Library, squelching over the polished rubber, trailing his identity round the room in which he had begun the struggle to find it. If he no longer felt moved to take down a book, it was because in the end knowledge had come to him, not through words, but by lightning.

They, however, were not much struck. They came and told him he must leave. He was distracting the readers. In any case, everyone he had known was gone, or dead. Only the incident at the table, between himself and Waldo and the Karamazovs, lived by virtue of *his* imperishability. He prepared to leave, though, as he had been asked to. Now, as then, nobody arrested him.

That was something they were saving up.

In the meantime he strewed the streets with peanut shells. He stole a book called *How to Relax the New Way*, not because he wanted to read it, but to try out the criminal tendency so recently acquired. Only very occasionally now he derived comfort from remembering: I am Waldo's dill brother of whom nothing is expected.

Then, on a street corner, he found himself standing crying, for what, he had forgotten. Unless because it was getting dark too soon.

That night he took the bus out to Dulcie's place, hoping he might find he had been invited.

The house on the edge of the park increased in possibilities at night. Darkness, by dissolving its ironwork, its gingerbread columns, its cement shell, had made it more truly a castle, the electric stars screwed into silhouetted battlements. All the shutters had been thrown open, as if the secret of the precincts might be shared, if only then, and only from a distance. Although the gate squealed piercingly as Arthur worked himself inside, it was easy enough to clamber up the yielding lawns without giving himself away. But cold. He farted once. The nerves twittered inside him as the sound of voices singing swelled the already gigantic house. Manœuvring through the outer wall of shrubs, avoiding the webs of light both hung and spread to catch any such intruder, he succeeded in reaching a window, and in clinging to a rope of creepers.

There he hung awhile. As the singers withdrew their breath the upright candle flames made the room look vast and black. The Saportas were preparing to dine, amongst their children and their children's children. Several shabbier relatives, unexpectedly younger than their hosts, were assisting at the ceremony. Only her beauty still aglow inside her revealed Dulcie in the old woman of fuzzy sideburns and locked joints, caged by her own back. Leonard Saporta's skin was draped in greyish-yellow folds, though age had not lessened his conviction when he spoke.

" 'She stretcheth out her hand to the poor; yea, she putteth forth her hands to the needy.' "

Arthur longed for Dulcie to put out her hand to him, while knowing she would not, she could not. She lowered her eyes to avoid meeting with approval. But as she sat in her violet dress, her painful claws with their smouldering of rings twitched to receive the homage her family was paying her. It was, after all, her right.

" 'She openeth her mouth in wisdom,' " continued the husband in his wife's praise, " 'and the law of lovingkindness is on her tongue.' "

Arthur longed to hear Dulcie speak, but it wasn't yet her moment. She knew, and was content to wait, while her husband blessed the wine, which their son, their Aaron-Arthur, held. Mr. Saporta, it appeared, was afflicted with the permanent trembles.

After the washing of the hands, the old bungling, and the small determined ones, after the bread had been uncovered, after all this, oh dear, endlessness of songs, and prayers, and blessings, the chatter broke above the dishes, above the golden steam, the scent of cloves, and he did not hear his darling speak. Her eyes accepted the situation, as her lips moved, expressing approval, but of others.

While Mr. Saporta trembled worse than ever, to assist a grandson measuring out his drops for him.

Practically built by this time into the network of steel vines, the intruder had been numbed. If he could have freed himself, and climbed in to test their lovingkindness, they would surely have kissed him, and fed him, and put him to sleep in linen sheets. But looked at him with surprise and disbelief. Or they might not have recognized somebody their lives had left behind. Just as he himself could no longer identify some of the Feinstein furniture.

So he went away without attempting to storm their fortress, and on the following day he felt the sun burning between his shoulder-blades, he felt a resistance leaving him. He would have liked to lie down and rest his head on the grass, if all the grass in those parts hadn't been worn to scurf. Remembering the springy green cushions grass can become as it collaborates with sleep, he decided to take the train back. To Mrs. Poulter, naturally. Whose need was as great as his. Who had sat with him on the grass, under the great orange disc of the sun, and burned with him in a fit of understanding or charity. So the drowsily revolving wheels, of trains, of buses, carried him back, as he sat twirling the solid mandala in his pocket.

When he got there she turned round. Her voice, overcoming surprise, might have been expecting him. He sat down, and she went to him.

"Where have you been?" she asked. "What have you done?"

Stroking his hair with the continuous motions of a younger woman. Only her skin, which was dry and withered, kept on catching.

"Eh?" she asked. "All this time?"

"I ran away," he said, "because I got a shock."

"Yes, yes," she said, stroking. "We know. You must of. You needn't tell, Arthur. Do you hear?"

It was so much what he had hoped for, he had to protect her from her innocence.

"After Waldo died—after I killed him—I ran away."

She did not even stop stroking.

"You didn't kill Waldo, Arthur. Waldo—do you hear?—was ready to die. He only took such a time dying."

"I don't think, Mrs. Poulter, I could live without my brother. He was more than half of me."

"Oh no," Mrs. Poulter said. "No more than a small quarter."

She was breathing hard, holding his head against her side.

"I was the one who should have died," said Arthur. "In the beginning. They never told me."

Mrs. Poulter was rocking, bruising what had been his head before she had taken possession of it.

"Only Waldo told me. In the end. When it was too late. I'd killed him. I killed Waldo in the end."

Then Mrs. Poulter threw away his head. She went to the window where the plants were choking out the light. She began to part the big swollen geranium heads.

"I don't believe you, Arthur," she said, "any more than Sergeant Foyle will believe, who is here now."

Arthur realized he was hearing the approaching, then the halting, motorbike. It was very still inside the reflected red of the geraniums.

"He's over the road," she said. "Constable Kentwell with him in the sidecar. The both of them going to investigate. Afterwards they're bound to come in here, and what you have to tell him Sergeant Foyle will never believe."

"If it's the truth," Arthur said.

"There's a truth above truth at times. That," Mrs. Poulter said, "is what a person, if she's honest, believes."

"That's okay for you," he said. "You're safe. You've got your religion to believe in."

"I believe in you, Arthur."

So she did, this man and child, since her God was brought crashing down.

Then they heard the shot, the second shot.

"What are they shooting?" he asked.

When she did not answer, the aged man or crumpled child began to whimper, so she went to him again, because it was necessary to take him in her arms, all the men she had never loved, the children she had never had.

"It is something that had to be done," she said groggily, because she was an elderly shaky woman, stiff in the joints, and the positions of love did not come easy to her. But she slid down painfully to her knees, along his side, until by instinct she was encircling her joy and duty with her arms—ritually, as it were.

And Arthur was considerably comforted when she was kneeling against him. The shots, which had at first pierced his heart and paralysed his spine, continued on into the duller regions of memory.

"They were too old." She tried to sound convincing. "You will feel happier," she said.

"Yes," he agreed, to please her.

He had the sniffles, however. So she wiped the nose of her little boy, her old, snotty man.

"What will become of me?" he asked, when he had recovered, and got his breath.

"Well," she said.

She had to think.

"They'll take you somewhere," she said, "where they'll look after you. Perhaps to some home or other."

She was not so soft as to say: I will keep you forever—though that was what she would have done for choice, carried him forever under her heart, this child too tender to be born.

"It won't be the Home of Peace," said Arthur. "I'm not ready for the Home of Peace."

"Oh dear, no!" she said. "You're not! We've life to live yet," she said.

She did honestly believe it. Since her Lord and master Jesus had destroyed Himself that same day, she had been given this man-child as token of everlasting life.

"I know," Arthur said, hesitating too, because it was a serious admission. "They'll probably take me to Peaches-and-Plums."

It sounded so inevitable she rested her cheek against his cheek.

"That will be nice, won't it?" she asked.

"Yes," he said. "It'll be all right."

She might have heard the chugging of his heart if it hadn't been for the noise of her own.

"If you'll visit me," he said. "And bring things."

"Tuesdays and Fridays are the days, I believe. And what sort of things would you like?" she asked.

"Jujubes," he said. "The orange ones."

"Jujubes. And anything else. Oh, I'll come, Arthur! I'll never miss!"

Until they were looking at each other so close they were reflected in each other's eyes.

"Have you got that thing?" she asked. "That marble?"

Her leg was hurting her, her knees, from kneeling all that while on the lino.

"I got one," he said. "I lost Waldo's on the way."

"I have mine," she said, "somewhere."

Because in the course of years, and really it had all been a piece of nonsense, something pagan she dared say, she would never of let on to the minister, she had put it away, and forgot where, and not really regretted till now. When Arthur was bringing out his.

They might have paired.

But there was no need, she saw. In her wrinkling misery for a moment she was pretty certain she saw their two faces becoming one, at the centre of that glass eye, which Arthur sat holding in his hand.

Nonsense really. It was the blur which made it. For when she had wiped her eyes on his shoulder, there was the same steady unblinking marble, or boy's toy.

"You'll have that at least," she said brightly, "to take along with you."

"Yes," he said, with faint conviction.

Putting it back for safety in his pocket.

When Sergeant Foyle came in, there was that Mrs. Poulter kneeling beside Arthur Brown. The sergeant had noticed her in her day, but had stopped giving her thought. Now she had her back to him, broad in the beam, the veins showing blue in the white skin behind her knees, just above where the stockings ended, one of them torn.

As for Arthur Brown, he was sitting and staring, at nothing in the room, you felt. Now and then he flinched at outside noises, like a nervous dog.

People said there had been something on at one time between Mrs. Poulter and Arthur Brown. From what he saw the sergeant believed it, though, again from what he saw, nothing of an indecent nature. There she was, wiping and coaxing that nut, as a woman will cuddle a baby, provided it is hers, after she has let it mess itself. The sergeant couldn't abide a slut. But this old, at any rate elderly, biddy, was clean. Clean as beeswax. And as she half turned, rising half sighing on a probably needle-riddled foot, taking the weight off her numb knees, he was reminded of a boyhood smell of cold, almost deserted churches, and old people rising transparent and hopeful, chafing the blood back into their flesh after the sacrament.

"You have come, Sergeant, I expect," she said, "for my friend Mr. Arthur Brown."

On her feet, she was somewhat older than he had expected. She spoke in a high, clear, not altogether natural voice. But perhaps she was upset by his catching her out in too private a position. The train of events would have rocked many women hysterical by now.

"Yes," he said. "Mr. Brown will be all right with me. We'll take good care of him," he said.

The situation had begun to make Sergeant Foyle feel curiously insubstantial. The other side of the geranium plants the leaden evening was hanging lower than before. Those dogs. They shook young Gary Kentwell, who had trod back into a blooming baked custard someone had left standing on the path. For a moment perhaps each of the men had tasted a sick taste. Only for a moment. The sergeant himself shot the brutes, through the window, pretty quick. Old, mangy, in every way pitiful animals, if it had not been for the expression on them. As for their acts. Sergeant Foyle came as near as nothing to spitting on Mrs. Poulter's floor.

"There, you see," she was saying to Arthur Brown, "everyone will be kind. Until I come. You *must* be kind to him," she told the sergeant, as if the old boy hadn't been there, and more than likely he wasn't. "Kindness is something he understands."

Sergeant Foyle was not going to pass judgment, except superficially, on either the living brother or the dead.

When the old woman hunted him back towards the scullery, and said, "This is a good man, Sergeant. You know it in your heart"—he had to reply, "It's not a matter of hearts, Mrs. Poulter. The issue is something to be decided by better heads than mine."

But the old woman had worked herself into a state of exaltation.

"This man would be my saint," she said, "if we could still believe in saints. Nowadays," she said, "we've only men to believe in. I believe in this man."

"Okay, Mrs. Poulter."

The sergeant was pretty embarrassed. He couldn't remember, ever, having to get himself out of a similar corner.

"Well," he said, "Arthur—young fuller—how about coming along for a ride in the sidecar?"

Arthur Brown got up. Filling the room, the body of this very vast old man had become the least part of him.

"Yes," he said, and turning to the woman. "You'll come on Tuesday, Mrs. Poulter, as you promised?"

Then Mrs. Poulter no longer cared.

"Oh yes, I'll come! I'll come, my pet! You needn't worry! I'll come, my love!"

Her head adrift above her cardigan was on fire with all the reflections of grief.

"And bring the jujubes?"

"Yes," she cried, "the orange ones!"

For Arthur the orange disc had not moved noticeably since he began his upward climb. It was the accompaniment which confused, by its increase in complexity: the groaning, and tinkling, and splintering of invisible icebergs.

But he realized he should be talking to his friend.

So he said: "By Tuesday I'll have plenty to tell. We'll walk about the grounds together. That's how time passes. In little attentions."

Somewhere it had to happen, and at this point Sergeant Foyle led out his charge into a more normal air. The sergeant glanced back once—well, to nod, it was the only sociable thing he could do, and the old girl was still standing in the doorway, arms crossed, holding herself together by handfuls, from under the armpits. The sergeant turned, and went on, to avoid looking any longer at her mouth.

Later in the afternoon, after she had patted her cheeks with Cyclax, like they told you, and drunk a cup of strong tea, and switched on the telly, though not the sound, the flicker of pictures which she didn't have to look at, Mrs. Poulter got control of herself. She did the things which needed doing. She threw a handful to the hens, she milked the cow, she stood the milk. Then she saw about Bill's tea.

When Bill came in, from looking at a boar out Schofields' way, she could hear him stamping off the mud. He was still spry except when he stopped to think about himself.

"What's the news, Mother?" he asked.

It was his usual question, and that evening she would have to think a bit. Though of course you could always tell about the grub in the cabbage, or the double-yolkers. By news Bill never meant news. News could make Bill lay around without his teeth, imagining an ulcer. He would turn pale at any suggestion of the knife.

"Eh?" he asked. "Don't tell me nothun *catastrophic's* happened?"

It was one of the words he had picked up and particularly favoured.

"No," she said. "Nothing I can think of."

It would all trickle out in time. For Bill's temporary good she felt it would not be a kindness to announce: Waldo Brown is dead or worse killed several days the dogs eating him which the sergeant or young Kentwell shot and Arthur off his head gone with the sergeant Arthur who never hurt a fly Waldo can only of died of spite like a boil must burst at last with pus and nothing can touch Arthur nothing can touch me not the part of us that matters not if they tear our fingernails off.

"Saw old Dun," said Bill. "Had to fetch the doctor to his missus."

"Oh?" she said.

"Threw a sort of fit." It made Bill laugh.

"Mrs. Dun, I believe," Mrs. Poulter said, "is not very strong."

When she put his tea in front of him, Bill sat a moment, elbows cocked, hands laid on the knife and fork, looking down at the contents of his plate. He had always been suspicious.

"That's a real nice loin chop," she said, to encourage. "The other one isn't so presentable. But perhaps it will eat better than it looks. I think it's something Mr. Finlayson threw in for luck."

Then she turned, to do the expected things, before re-entering her actual sphere of life.